ALSO BY CHARLIE HUSTON

The Mystic Arts of Erasing All Signs of Death

The Shotgun Rule

In the Henry Thompson Trilogy:

Caught Stealing

Six Bad Things

A Dangerous Man

In the Joe Pitt Casebooks:

Already Dead

No Dominion

Half the Blood of Brooklyn

Every Last Drop

My Dead Body

SLEEPLESS

BALLANTINE BOOKS ⚏ NEW YORK

SLEEPLESS

a novel

CHARLIE HUSTON

Copyright © 2010 by Charlie Huston

Published in the United States by Ballantine Books,
an imprint of The Random House Publishing Group,
a division of Random House, Inc., New York.

BALLANTINE and colophon are registered trademarks of Random House, Inc.

LIBRARY OF CONGRESS CATALOGING-IN-PUBLICATION DATA

Huston, Charlie.
Sleepless : a novel / Charlie Huston. — 1st ed.
p.   cm.
ISBN 978-0-345-50113-4 (hardcover : alk. paper)
1. Insomniacs—Fiction.   2. Epidemics—Fiction.   3. Pharmaceutical industry—
Corrupt practices—Fiction.   I. Title.
PS3608.U855S64 2010
813'.6—dc22   2009036889

Printed in the United States of America on acid-free paper

www.ballantinebooks.com

2 4 6 8 9 7 5 3 1

First Edition

Book design by Jo Anne Metsch

My Darling Clementine
a better world

SLEEPLESS

1

PARK WATCHED THE HOMELESS MAN WEAVE IN AND OUT OF the gridlocked midnight traffic on La Cienega, his eyes fixed on the bright orange AM/FM receiver dangling from the man's neck on a black nylon lanyard. The same shade orange the SL response teams wore when they cleared a house. He closed his eyes, remembering the time an SLRT showed up on his street at the brown and green house three doors down. The sound of the saw coming from the garage, the pitch rising when it hit bone.

Techno-accented static opened his eyes. The homeless man was next to his window, dancing from foot to foot, neck held at an unmistakable stiff angle, flashing a hand-lettered sign on a square of smudged whiteboard:

BLESSINGS!!!

Park looked at the man's neck.

The people in the cars around him had noticed it as well; several rolled up their windows despite the ban on air-conditioning.

Park opened his ashtray, scooped out a handful of change, and was offering it to the wild-eyed sleepless when the human bomb detonated several blocks away and the explosion thrummed the glass of his windshield, ruffling the hairs on his arms with a rush of air hotter than the night.

He flinched, the change falling from his hand, scattering on the asphalt, the tinkle of it hitting and rolling in every direction, lost in the echoes bouncing off the faces of the buildings lining the avenue, the alarms set off when windows were shattered and parked cars blown onto their sides.

By the time the coins had stopped rolling and the homeless man had gotten down on his hands and knees to scrabble for his scattered handout, Park was reaching under his seat for his weapon.

The Walther PPS was in a holster held to the bottom of the driver's seat by a large patch of Velcro. Clean, oiled, and loaded, with the chamber empty. He didn't need to check, having done so before he left the house. He took it from its holster and dropped it in the side pocket of his cargo pants. It was unlikely any of his customers would be this far west, but it would be typical of the universe to send one just now to see him with a sidearm clipped to his waist.

Climbing from the car, he closed and locked the door, secure in the knowledge that the traffic jam would not be breaking up before sunrise. He was working his way through the cars, all but a very few of them sealed tight now, their occupants rigid and sweating inside, when the street was plunged into sudden darkness.

He stopped, touched his weapon to be sure of it, and thought about Rose and the baby, asking the frozen world to keep them safe if he should die here. But the darkness didn't invite any new attacks. Or if it did, they were yet to come. More likely it was an unscheduled rolling blackout.

He edged between the cars, watching a man in a sweat-twisted suit pounding the horn of his newly scarred Audi, raising similar protests from the cars around his. Or perhaps they were intended to drown out the screams coming from the flaming crater at the intersection.

Those flames were the brightest illumination on the street now, almost all the drivers having turned off their engines and headlights to conserve gas. He could feel them on his face already, the flames, baking the skin tight. And he remembered the cabin in Big Sur where he took Rose after they first knew about the baby, but before the diagnosis.

There had been a fireplace. And they'd sat before it until nearly dawn, using what had been meant as a weekend's supply of wood on their first night.

His face had felt like this then.

He tried to recall the name of the cabin they had stayed in. Bluebird? Bluebell? Blue Ridge? Blue something for sure, but blue what?

Blue Moon.

The name painted just above the door had been Blue Moon. With a little star-accented teal crescent that Rose had rolled her eyes at.

Are we supposed to think we're in fucking Connecticut, for Christ's sake?

He'd said something in response, some joke about not cursing in front of the baby, but before he could remember what it was he'd said, his foot slipped in a great deal of someone's blood, drawing him back to the present, and the flames here before him.

The wiper blades on a Hummer H3, one of the few vehicles with intact glass this close to the blast, were beating furiously, cleaner fluid spraying, smearing blood, batting what looked like a gnarled bit of scalp and ear back and forth across the windshield, while the young woman inside wiped vomit from her chin and screamed into a Bluetooth headset.

Looking at a man on the edge of the crater, his entire jawbone carried away by a piece of flying debris, Park only wondered now at the instinct that had made him take his weapon from the car rather than his first-aid kit.

█   █   █

IT WASN'T THE first human bomb in Los Angeles. Just the first one north of Exposition and west of the I-5.

The sound of the detonation rolling across the L.A. basin and washing up against the hills had brought me out to my deck. One expects the occasional crack of gunfire coming from Hollywood on any given night, but the crump of high explosives in West Hollywood was a novelty. A sound inclined to make me ruminant, recalling, as it did, a pack of C-4 wired to the ignition of a VC colonel's black Citroën in Hanoi, as well as other moments of my youth.

Thus nostalgic, I came onto the deck in time to see a slab of the city, framed by Santa Monica, Venice, Western, and Sepulveda, wink into blackness. Looking immediately skyward, knowing from experience that my eyes would subtly adjust to the reduction in ground light, I watched the emergence of seldom seen constellations.

Under these usually veiled stars, the city burned.

Only a small bit of it, yes, but one of the more expensive bits. A circumstance that would no doubt have serious repercussions.

It's all well and good in the general course of things if Mad Swan Bloods and Eight Trey Gangster Crips want to plant claymore mines in Manchester Park, or for Avenues and Cyprus Park to start launching RPGs across Eagle Rock Boulevard, but suicide bombers less than a mile from the Beverly Center would not be tolerated.

Uncorking a second bottle of Clos des Papes 2005, I rested secure in the knowledge that the National Guard would be shock-trooping South Central and East L.A. at first light.

Nothing like a show of force to keep up the morale of the general citizenry in times of duress. The fact that the display would be utterly misdirected and only serve to brew greater discontent was beside the point. We had long passed the stage where the consequences of tactical armed response were weighed in advance. Anyone with the time and wherewithal to put a map on a wall and stick pins in it could see quite clearly what was happening.

I had such a map, and said wherewithal, and many pins.

If red pins are acts of violence committed by people traditionally profiled as potentially criminal perpetrated against those who have *not* been so profiled, and yellow pins are acts of violence perpetrated *between* peoples traditionally so profiled, and blue pins indicate acts of violence carried out by uniformed and/or badged members of the soldiering and law enforcement professions *upon* peoples so profiled, one can clearly see patterns of tightly clustered yellow pins, encircled by blue pins, concentrated to the far south, east, and north of the most prime Los Angeles real estate, which is, in turn, becoming pockmarked by random bursts of red pins.

It is, on such a map, the vastness of the territory devoted to yellow-on-yellow acts of violence and blue responses in relative proportion to the wee acreage dotted with red, that should give one pause.

It looked, upon little or no reflection, like the pustules of a disease spreading inexorably against the feeble resistance of a failed vaccine, carrying infection along the arteries of the city, advancing no matter how many times the medics raised the point of amputation up the ravaged limb.

That it was a *symptom* of a disease rather than the disease *itself* was an irony I never chuckled at. There being little or no humor to be found in the prospect of the end of the world.

But I did appreciate it. The irony, and the fact that the disease that was killing us ignored the classifications and borders that defined so clearly for so many who they should be killing and why.

The disease didn't care for distinctions of class, race, income, religion, sex, or age. The disease seemed only to care that your eyes remain open to witness it all. That what nightmares you had haunted only your waking hours. The disease considered us all equal and wished that we share the same fate. That we should bear witness as we chewed our own intestines, snapping at what gnawed from the inside.

It wished that we become sleepless.

I could sleep.

Choosing, that night, not to.

Choosing, instead, to pour another glass of overrated but still quite good Rhone into an admittedly inappropriate jelly jar, and to settle into an overdesigned Swedish sling chair to watch that small, expensive fragment of the city burn.

Herald, I knew, of worse.

7/7/10

TODAY BEENIE SAID something about Hydo knowing "the guy." What's encouraging about this is that I didn't ask. Hydo called for a delivery and I went over to the farm to make the drop (100 15-mg Dexedrine spansules). He asked if I wanted a Coke and I hung around long enough to scroll through my texts and map my next couple deliveries. Beenie was there, making a deal to sell some gold he'd farmed, but mostly just hanging out with the guys. Hydo passed around the dex to his guys and they all started speed rapping while they hacked up zombies and stuff. One of them (I think his name is Zhou, but I need to check my notes) started talking about his cousin going sleepless. The other guys all started telling their own sleepless stories. Beenie asked if I knew anyone. I said yes. They all talked some more, and the one guy (Zhou?) said he put an ad on Craigslist to trade a level 100 Necromantic Warlord for Dreamer to give his cousin, but the only response he got was from a scammer. That's when Beenie looked at Hydo and said, "Hydo, man, what about the guy?" Hydo was in the middle of an exchange in Chasm Tide. His front character was on his monitor in the Purple Grotto, getting ready to pass off the gold to a Darkling Heller as soon as one of the guys confirmed that the PayPal transfer had come through. But everyone stopped talking right after Beenie spoke. Just Hydo talking to the Darkling on his headset, telling him he'd throw in a Mace of Chaos for another twenty euro. He was acting like he hadn't heard what Beenie said. But he gave him a look. And Beenie started shutting down his MacBook and said he had to roll. I pocketed my phone and finished my Coke and said later.

Beenie was my first in with the farms. I met him at a party on Hillhurst. He knows a lot of people. They like him. If he says Hydo knows "the guy," it might be true.

In any case, I didn't say anything. I just walked out of the farm behind Beenie. We talked while he was unlocking his Trek and putting on his helmet and elbow and knee pads. He said he was looking for some opium. He has this thing for old Hollywood and read somewhere that Errol Flynn described smoking opium, "like having your soul massaged with mink gloves." Now he wants to try it. I told him I'd see what I could do. Then he pedaled north on Aviation, probably headed for Randy's Donuts.

I made a note to ask around about opium. Made another note to look over my list of Hydo's known associates.

Finished deliveries.

A suicide bomber on the way home.

I did what I could. Not much. I think I stopped a boy's bleeding long enough for him to get to the hospital. Who knows what happened to him there. Traffic got messed up for miles. Once the EMTs and paramedics showed up, I spent most of my time passing out water. A lady thanked me when I saw her fainting in her car and got her a bottle. A witness said the bomber was a woman, a New America Jesus insurgent. He said he knew she was a NAJi because she screamed "something about Satan" before she blew herself up. He also said she was staggering like she was drunk. NAJis don't drink. A Guard told me that looking at the size of the crater she left, she was probably staggering under the weight of the bomb. He said that kind of blast was what they got in Iraq from car bombs. I said something about how at least he wasn't there anymore, and he asked me if I was "fucking joking." Almost noon before I got home.

Francine had to leave Rose alone with the baby.

She was in the backyard with her laptop. There was gardening stuff lying around, but she was logged into her Chasm Tide account, playing her elemental mage, Cipher Blue, trying again to get through the Clockwork Labyrinth on her own.

The baby was on a blanket next to her, under an umbrella, crying.

As I came up, Blue was being dismembered by a skeleton made of brass gears, wire, and rusting springs. Beenie says no one gets through the Labyrinth on their own. You have to join a campaign, but Rose refuses to try it that way. Which isn't surprising.

She closed the laptop and grabbed a garden trowel and started stabbing the dry earth, digging at the roots of one of the weeds that's taken over the garden. I picked up the baby and asked how she had been and Rose told me she had just started crying again right before I came home. Said she hadn't cried for hours before. But I think she was just saying that. Then she started talking about her grandma's garden, the topiary, vegetables, citrus trees, strawberry patch, and the rosebushes she was named for. She said she wanted the baby to have a garden to grow up in, learn about how seeds turn into plants. She had a packet of marigold seeds she was going to plant. I held the baby while Rose talked, and she stopped crying a little. Rose stopped talking and looked at me and asked what was on my clothes and I had to go in and clean up and when I set the baby down she started crying again.

I called Francine while I was inside and she said she was sorry for leaving, but she needed to get her kids to school. She said Rose didn't sleep at all. She said the baby might have slept, but her eyes never closed. But she was quiet for a couple hours just after midnight. I told her I'd see her tonight and got in the shower. There was stuff under my nails that was hard to get out. Then Rose got into the shower with me and asked me to wash her back and I had to tell her she had her clothes on. She looked at me and looked at her clothes like she didn't get it. Then she got it and started crying and told me she was sorry. I held her. She cried and the baby cried.

I'll go see Hydo tonight.

Maybe he really does know the guy.

2

PARK KNEW THERE WAS TROUBLE AT THE GOLD FARM WHEN he saw the door hanging open.

That door was never left open.

To get in you had to stand in front of a camera, be identified by someone inside, and run your finger over a biometric print reader before they buzzed you in. Then you were in the cage, and the inner door of the cage wouldn't open until the outer door closed and locked. So if someone stood out of range of the wide-angle camera lens and held a gun on you while you were cleared, and then tried to come in with you, they'd just end up in the cage. And someone in the box could decide whether to shoot them or gas them or whatever seemed best in the situation.

But the door was hanging open.

And Park didn't have a gun.

A visit like this, he left the gun under the front seat of his Subaru.

He could go get it. But someone inside might need help. The time it took to get to the car and come back, someone inside could be beyond help in that time.

Not that Park was thinking it out or weighing his options. As soon as he saw the open door, his hand reflexively went to the spot on his belt where he'd worn his weapon back when he'd worn a uniform, and then he went in. He may as well have gone for the gun; everyone inside had ample time to spare.

The cage door was open. He looked up at the tiny window near the ceiling and saw no sign of someone crammed behind it in the box. He looked at the floor and saw a series of red smears. Thin strips decorated on one side by a geometric pattern. The edges of half a dozen right foot-prints, each fainter than the one before, coming from the inner door, leading into the cage, and fading from existence before they could slip outside.

Ignoring the fact that the trail led away, he took his key ring from his pocket, unclipped the Mini Maglite, and palmed it; an inch of the narrow handle jutted from the base of his fist, suitable for sharp blows to the temple, throat, or eyes. But through the door beyond the cage, inside the gold farm itself, the first thing he used it for was to shine a bright beam of light into Hydo's dead eyes, looking for what he knew he wouldn't find: an impression of the killer's face.

He could have looked in any of their eyes. They were all equally dead.

Hydo. The one whose name Park thought was Zhou. Keebler and Tad and Melrose Tom. There was no sign of Oxnard Tom, but he was pretty much part time at this point, or at least that's what Park had gathered.

Park stood over Hydo's corpse, thinking.

He needed very much to not be there.

Quickly, and with a minimum of disorder, he needed to erase himself from the place.

He looked at the floor.

The room was always kept dim, minimizing reflection on the monitors as the guys plied their trade, but now the only light came from the one remaining corkscrew of energy-efficient bulb that hadn't been broken and the one live monitor that had likewise been spared.

The light cast by the monitor flickered in various shades of green and blue: a forest at night, a dead body pulsing with an ectoplasmic glow in the foreground, a dismal zombie lurching about the edge of the trees. A haunted grove that one of the guys had been mining. Killing hordes of zombies, one at a time, harvesting their meager treasure, banking it all in an ever-growing account, waiting for a buyer.

He shined the beam from the Maglite over the floor, picked out a blood-free path, and stepped as close to the center of the room as possible. Standing there, he took his phone from his pocket and began to slowly turn in place, snapping a picture after every few degrees of rotation. Finished, he took a similar series of shots covering the floor and ceiling, all the time wishing he'd bought a phone with a better camera.

Done with his photo map, he knelt next to Hydo, found his BlackBerry, opened the contacts list, and deleted his own number and email before wiping the device and putting it back in the dead man's pocket.

He looked at the ladder bolted to the wall, leading up to the coffin-space box. There was no one in the box now. No telltale feet sticking out from the opening. No trail of blood running down the wall. Park had been around when Hydo had told one of his guys to change a disk up there in the recorder for the security camera.

His face would be on several of those disks, but it would just be a face. In any case, there were far too many to go through now. His fingerprint biometric would be logged on a hard drive somewhere, but it would only be tagged to a JPEG of his face. Hydo might keep a record of his customers' names, but he wouldn't keep his dealer's name anywhere but his own phone.

Or that's what Park hoped for.

Park looked at the room: well over a hundred thousand dollars in highly portable equipment, some of it riddled with bullets, but nothing obviously missing. That didn't have to mean anything. The true wealth of this place wasn't materially present. Product and payment both were stored elsewhere, hosted on massively secure overseas servers. Immediate connections ran to One Wilshire, a downtown telco hotel where fiber optics wormed up the exterior, in through windows, converging in the service core, all of it connecting to Pacific submarine cables. Pure bandwidth, hardwired to a durable Far East product: miles of underground bomb shelters converted to climate-controlled server farms. Powered by black market reactors, the most reliable ISPs on the planet. Bulwarks, keeping the ephemeral real, if not touchable.

But while the gold and other treasures the guys farmed and fought and campaigned for online were not in this room, nor the digital payments they received in exchange, still a robbery could have taken place.

A password coerced before the trigger was pulled.

Park counted seconds, setting himself a limit of sixty more before he must leave.

With seventeen seconds remaining, he saw it.

Right at the foot of the ladder, a small workstation. A widescreen XPS Notebook cabled to a travel drive, connected to nothing else. Not the hardwired LAN the other machines in the room shared, not a printer or any other peripheral. Just the power cord running from a surge strip screwed to the baseboard next to eight more just like it, and the travel drive.

Park stepped over Hydo's body, his toe smearing a comma of blood on the sealed cement floor. He stood at the station, looking at the drive, and the red biohazard sticker adhered to its top.

In the months since Beenie had hooked him up with Hydo, and he had become the regular dealer for the farm, he'd seen this station used only once. Sitting in one of the Red Bull–stained Zody chairs, counting white tablets of foxy from his baggie into a Ziploc, he'd nodded when Hydo received a call and told him he had to take it.

Keeping his head down, double counting the savage little pills of 5-methoxy-dijopropyltryptamine, he'd relaxed the muscles around his eyes, letting his peripheral vision widen as his self-defense instructor had taught him, and at the edge of his vision he'd seen Hydo unzip a backpack, take out a small flat box decorated with a single dot of red, and connect it to the sleeping Dell. An action followed by a Bluetooth conversation regarding items such as a Tyrant's Pointing Hand, a Shadow Amulet, Crusader Gauntlets, someone named Thrad Redav, and a large amount of gold.

Park looked at his watch, self-winding, dependent on no power other than his own movement.

He'd been in the room for over five minutes.

He disconnected the drive's USB plug, wrapped the short cable around its body, and tucked it into a cargo pocket.

Coming out of the room, he paused to take a picture of one of the partial footprints and then walked out into the final linger of evening sun, leaving the door open behind him, moving without hurry to the WRX parked behind a Dumpster nearly buried in its own trash at the open end of the alley that let onto Aviation.

It wouldn't do to be seen running from here.

Even now the police investigated murder.

He told himself that was the point of the pictures he'd taken, and the hard drive he'd stolen.

But there was this as well: Beenie had said Hydo knew "the guy."

And Rose hadn't slept in over four weeks now. And late that afternoon, before leaving again for work, he'd come into the nursery and found her standing over the crying baby's crib, index finger against the baby's lips, making loud, desperate hushing noises, her finger pushing down hard enough to whiten the baby's new skin.

His phone buzzed. A text. A summons:

dr33m3r rpt 3hrs/highland+fountain

Three hours. He thought about the distance, the traffic. He might be able to get something to eat first. If he drove on a few curbs.

First things. He opened the driver-side door, reached under his seat, and gently ripped the holstered Walther from its Velcro patch. Taking the gun and the travel drive, he popped the hatchback. Clearing aside some of the trunk clutter, he pulled up the cover that concealed the jack and other tools, dug his fingers behind the undersized spare, and peeled open the flap of rubber, exposing the interior of the permanently flat tire. The gun, the drive, and his watch went inside, a baggie of low-grade Ecstasy and a couple bottles of Valium and Demerol came out. The cover went back, clutter redistributed, and hatch closed. The pills he tucked under the passenger seat for easy access.

He paused, wondering if he should put something more substantial down there, something to satisfy whoever found it, but decided against it. No reason to throw away his best stock on something like this.

Not pearls before swine, perhaps. But he still had, at this late date, his father's Protestant values deeply ingrained. In this case, "Waste not." Period.

Leave right now and there would be time to grab something to eat.

But he sat, hand on the key in the ignition, knowing he needed to turn it and drive away but frozen for the moment as he tried to remember what day of the week it was, and what month.

◼   ◼   ◼

THE FLAMES WERE extinguished when I got up the next morning, a thick smudge of black smoke still hanging over La Cienega, putting me in mind of the history of the basin.

Cradling a saucer and a demitasse of espresso, I'd thought about the swamp it had all been reclaimed from and of the clouds of gases that must have hung over it. And the oil fields that followed, the greasy plumes of industrial reek. And the '70s heyday of smog, before the catalytic converter and unleaded gas.

Those bruised yellow skies had never quite returned, but not for lack of trying. Traffic was a waking nightmare, but it had less to do with overall density of vehicles than it did with streets closed for lack of maintenance or the wreckage from a fatal accident that was never cleared or traffic rerouted around an incoming column of Guards or burst water mains flooding or downed power lines snaking or some group desperately protesting the condition of the roads and highways.

All that aside, the price of gas had put enough hybrids on the road and knocked enough low-income types off their wheels that the air quality probably would have been at its best in years, if not for the occasional explosion and the constant pall of smoke drifting in from brush fires to the south, east, and north of the city.

When I thought about it, I often regretted buying the house in the Hills rather than the one I'd looked at in Santa Monica. Sooner or later the last stand would be made with our backs to the sea and our ankles in the surf. Not that I relished the thought of being there for that final scene. Far from the point of things, that would be.

I spent the bulk of the day tending to my garden and my collections. Rotating pots and planters in and out of sun, pouring water liberally here, misting there. A bit of mulch. Then inside, running a dust cloth over the tops of canvases and prints, an urn or two, the flickering screens of two video installations that faced each other in an otherwise empty hall, adjusting the setting on a humidifier for fear the air might become too dry in a room devoted to original pen and ink drawings. Finally, oilcloth, soft bristle steel brushes, and silicon lubricant, removing dust and easing friction in the moving parts of my many firearms. The most time-consuming of the tasks, and the one to which I applied the greatest effort. Not for love of the things, but out of appreciation for the fact that any one of them was significantly more likely to save my life than even my most luscious tomato plant or most vibrant Murakami acrylic.

Done with my chores by afternoon, I was able to settle into a deck chair and contemplate those tomatoes and what wine I might drink with a plate of them doused in balsamic vinegar. For a moment I considered the possibility that the tomato plant might be more vital to me than my arsenal. The further possibility that those weapons posed more danger to me than they deflected. It was not a new thought.

I pictured myself, menaced by foes, brandishing a tomato.

A phone rang in the house.

A business phone.

"Welcome to My Nightmare" as ring tone.

I allowed myself to finish my exercise in visualization, picturing a bowl filled with bullets floating in a vermilion sauce of unknown origin. It was unappetizing. No, things were as they should be with me. My values in place. Such as they were.

I went inside, letting the tinted green glass door sigh closed behind me, my ears registering the slightest change in pressure as it shut. The song continued to play, Alice Cooper telling me he thought I'd feel like I belong in his nightmare.

Right at home.

I stood at the Dadox cube table, my face reflected in the chrome surface, framed top and bottom by the eight phones laid out in neat rows of four. From this angle, looking down, the recessed ceiling lights highlighted perfectly the strip of thinning hair running back to front on top of my head.

I made a mental note to shift the table so to diminish this effect, knowing the change would set off a chain reaction of furniture moving as I tried to keep the room in balance.

The song continued to play.

I considered the flashing screen on the bright blue Sanyo Katana. I'd assigned the phone to this particular client not out of any attempt at broadly ironic racist humor but because the shade of blue on the casing matched so well the color I'd seen highlighting the lower scales of a dragon tattoo encircling the length of her left arm. Still, sometimes the shoe fits.

I answered the phone.

"You let me ring for a very long time."

I nudged the Dadox with my knee, just a few inches to the right, looking down to gauge the impact the change had on my revealed bald spot.

"Yes, I did."

"You had something pressing."

"That sounds like a statement."

"Excuse me?"

"It sounds to me as if you just made a statement of fact, declaring that I had something more pressing to do than answer the phone, as opposed to asking if I did."

The light still glared unacceptably off the shiny skin topping my dome. Moved one inch farther from this spot, the relocation of the table would demand not only rearrangement of the room, but the jettisoning of several pieces and the acquisition of several new ones. In my mind I could see the shock waves this would create, radiating through every room in the house.

"And did you?"

I considered her question, looked at my reflection, thought briefly about my own vanity, and shook my head.

"No, I had nothing more pressing. I was simply procrastinating."

"Don't, in future, when I call, keep me waiting, please."

The "please" was an afterthought on her part, dedicated to the skill and efficiency with which I did my work. A bone of courtesy thrown my way, perhaps, but I knew it took some effort on her part. And I appreciated that.

"I will, in future, endeavor to be promptly responsive, thank you."

"Come and see me."

I looked out the glass at the smoking world.

"Someone blew up La Cienega last night. The Guards have checkpoints everywhere."

"Did you set off the bomb?"

"No. According to the news, whoever set off the bomb did so as a final editorial comment regarding the universe."

"Then you have nothing to fear from checkpoints."

"I don't fear the checkpoints, I simply don't care to be stuck in the resulting traffic."

A pause. Perhaps a slight exhalation over the line, betraying the thinnest reed of annoyance.

"You kept me waiting for you to answer. Do not keep me waiting any longer. Please."

The word, on this occasion, meant to imply that it was for my own sake she was pleading. And most certainly, it was.

"I'll be there as soon as I may."

The line went dead.

Was it me, or had there been coarseness in the quality of her tone, slight nicks and burrs along the usually sharp edge, betraying overuse or lack of care?

Even after all the carriers had merged under pressure from the government to pool their resources and keep the wireless taps open, it wasn't always possible to tell what was in a person's voice over a cell and what was simply static, interference, white noise. But, assuming I'd heard true, her tone implied nothing quite so much as someone very tired.

I held the phone in my hand, looked about the room, and set it on the pearlescent white top of the broad oval Thor coffee table.

It looked quite good there. And I could easily picture the other phones arranged around it. The change would require only the slightest echoing modifications of the room. The Dadox could simply remain in place, as I'd no longer be required to look into its reflective surface.

I pinched the bridge of my nose, picked up the Katana, and retuned it to the silver cube among the other phones. The point was that I should be required to look at myself when these phones rang. That I be taxed to con-template myself honestly before answering, knowing that to answer the phone would likely obligate me to take the job. And looking at oneself honestly must, sadly, include the contemplation of one's thinning hair.

So I carefully moved the table back to where it had been before, and went down the hall to my office, somewhat at peace, wondering which guns I should take with me to best suit my current mood.

7/8/10

LUNCH. OR DINNER. Does it matter at this point? Second meal of the day, eaten well after sundown. Hot dogs from the cart in Culver. How do they get their grass-fed beef dogs down here from SF? I suspect they are using different beef, more likely something other than beef. I know not all the California herds were destroyed, but I still can't imagine the cost of raising them organic. Better not to think too much about it.
Looking in my phone after the first batch of deliveries, realized I've fallen behind logging them. Trying to get caught up, but it's hard to remember everything. Was the Chinese Shabu dragon delivered to the models throwing the suite party at the Chateaus? Or did it go to the airbrush artist at the custom bodywork shop on South La Brea? There might be something in my journal, but I don't have time to go through it.
Guess?
No. The fault is mine for not keeping more accurate records. Better to record only what I can definitely remember about the sales than to implicate someone in a crime they had no part in.
Was that course work? Justice in Practice and Theory? Professor Steinman. An A– from Steinman because "a young man should always be left room to improve."
That pissed off Rose.
"An A is a fucking A."
I tried to tell her it didn't matter to me. Not like the minus was going to drag down my GPA and hurt my prospects.
She said that wasn't the point.

"You earned it. It's not fair that you earned it and he ticked a fucking minus after it because he thought it would teach some cute fucking lesson. Fuck that. You should report that shit to the chair of your department."

Had I ever met a girl who cursed so much? It was college, so I must have, even at Stanford, but I'd never had a beer with one before. And something about the cursing of a Cal girl was particularly blunt. They weren't test curses, dropped to see how you'd react, or tried on for the first time after moving away from mother and father; they were the real thing, casual and heartfelt.

I don't even remember who won The Game now. I barely watched after I got a look at her in the stands. So unlikely that she would be at a football game in the first place or that she'd talk to someone who looked like I did. Lucky the guy who brought her was such an asshole. Derrick. Thanks for being an asshole, Derrick. Thanks for leaving her at the after-game party.

Parties.

The party on Vermont.

Where Beenie introduced me to Hydo.

All Hydo could talk about was girls. Girls and gaming. Speed jabber. That girl over there looked just like a girl he wanted to nail when he was playing World of Warcraft for the first time. When it was "like just for fun an' shit, not like a career." He talked about the character he had, his first character, a dwarf. Told me its name.

Zolor? Zoler? Zolar? Zorlar? Zolrar? Zorlir?

Xorlar.

"Like with an *X*. Anytime you slap an *X* on something, you make it cooler."

Xorlar.

That's it.

Funny how those things float to the top.

Rose told me, "The point isn't to try and think about anything, don't try to solve anything, just write. What's important will float to the top." Me sitting with a thick leather-bound journal in my hand, flipping all those blank pages. The first gift she ever gave me. She wanted me to fill it with something. With me. I don't know. I tried. But I didn't have anything to write. It sat on our bookshelf for how long? 2001. We met at The Game. Spent Christmas together in her cold room in Berkeley. I remember because we talked about 9/11 so much. She was so pissed at us, America. I understood the point she was making, but it still made me angry. And she gave me the book.

Christmas 2001–Summer 2010. Eight years on the shelf. Until she handed me a gift-wrapped package and said, "Happy birthday." Months from my birthday. Opened it, saw the journal. Thought she was being sweet or trying to make a point of some kind. Took a few minutes before I realized she was serious, telling me where she had bought it, how she had almost forgotten my birthday.

Did I play along? I don't think so. She doesn't want me to play along when she gets confused. She wants me to tell her. But she'd never been so unhooked before, so much in another place. So damn out of it. I got confused myself. I didn't play along, I just didn't know what was happening.

By the time I read the inscription and realized it was the same old journal, her mind had moved on to something else. The baby. How she had smiled that morning, before she started crying.

Eight years.

And now all I want to do is write in the thing. Get it down. Whatever it is. Get us down. Before she disappears from me.

Don't think about it, just write.

Xorlar.

3

PARK HADN'T PLANNED ON MAKING A LIVING THIS WAY. Which was odd, for him to be doing something he hadn't planned to do. But that was the way of the world now. And he accepted it. Or that's what he would have said, but it wasn't true at all.

Park did not accept that this was the way of the world. He knew the true world was hibernating, waiting to come out from its long winter nap. People were waiting to be themselves again. It wasn't that human nature was base and obscene and brutal, it was only fear and confusion and despair that made them look and act that way.

He felt that deeply.

Felt it even as the plainclothes pushed his face a little harder against the raw heat of his car hood.

"What the fuck is this?"

Park didn't answer the question. He knew from experience that answering the question would just lead to more grief.

Grief, something he had in ample supply.

So when the plainclothes shoved the Ziploc of Ecstasy in his face, he kept his mouth shut.

"This your prescription, asshole?"

"What about this?"

The partner shook two large brown plastic bottles, one in each hand, like maracas.

"What we have? Ritalin? Xanax? Got ADD issues? Anxiety attacks? Can't really tell with these unmarked bottles. Pharmacy forget to print the labels, asshole?"

The first plainclothes, the one wearing a black Harley-Davidson T and chrome wraparounds, kicked Park's feet a little wider apart.

"He's got an anxiety attack now, motherfucker. Got anxiety about how far he's gonna have it up his ass once they see him inside."

The partner tipped his Angels cap.

"Too true, too true, he's a looker. Sistahs are gonna eat him up."

Park shifted, trying to peel his face up before it blistered.

The plainclothes grabbed him by the hair and gave his head a shake.

"Fuck do you think you're doing? Did I or did I not say not to fucking move?"

He nodded at his partner.

"This guy, he thinks he can get up and walk away when he wants. Thinks he's at liberty to split."

The partner pulled his head out of the car, flipping through the plastic zipper wallet that contained Park's registration, insurance card, AAA, and extra fuses. All of it, except the fuses, essentially useless at this point.

DMV had frozen up when the state went broke; it was unlikely there was an insurance company left with the holdings to cover a claim on a dented bumper; and the phones at AAA had been playing the same recorded apology for nearly a year now: "We regret that membership services have been suspended indefinitely."

Suspended indefinitely.

Thinking about those words, Park had a sudden mental image of the world, its activity and life frozen, paused, suspended indefinitely, waiting while this overlay of the world reeled about, aping the original.

At some point this interlude would expire, and that true world would resume from where it left off, transition seamless, strange interruption erased.

The partner slapped his face with the zippered wallet of useless paper.

"He's at liberty, at liberty to get his face fucked up if he fucking moves again."

He tossed the wallet back in the car.

"Nothing else in here."

The plainclothes yanked on the cuffs that locked Park's hands behind his back.

" 'Kay, fuckstick, let's go to jail."

He pulled Park up, frog-walked him to the unmarked, and pushed his head low as he shoved him into the backseat.

"Try not to piss yourself."

He slammed the door, slid behind the wheel.

"And away we go."

The partner climbed in on the passenger side.

"Off to see the wizard."

The Crown Victoria pulled from the curb, leaving behind the small crowd of rubberneckers that had surrounded the scene right after the unmarked had screeched up to where Park was idling at Highland and Fountain and the two cops had jumped out, guns first. They must have hung about to watch the old-fashioned novelty of a drug bust. It may or may not have occurred to any of them that this was a suspiciously frivolous use of law enforcement resources in a time of pandemic, economic collapse, and general social upheaval, but if they did notice, no one chose to speak out.

What would they have said?

Unhand that man.

Go do your job somewhere.

Tell the Fed to go back on the gold standard.

Put more resources into alternative energy sources.

Begin talks with the NAJis.

Find a cure.

Nothing the cops were doing was going to make that big a difference, anyway, so why not stand around and watch the bust?

Still, it was odd.

Except to Park.

The plainclothes started a low machine gun mutter of curses and hit the grille lights and siren.

"Fucking civilians. Fucking bulletins on the fucking TV, radio, fucking

Internet, they still gotta get in their fucking cars and come out on the road. Tell them, straight up, the alert level is fucking black. Black! What is that, subtle? We got to change it to *alert level everyone fucking dies*? Mean, no one saw the news? No one knows the NAJi blew up forty-something people last night? What do they think, it's a rumor? Government plot to keep them safe at home? Motherfucker!"

He jerked the steering wheel to the left, using the heavy bumper of the Crown Vic to shove a wheezing Focus farther into the left turn lane, making room for himself, gunning to beat the light at Sunset.

"Got to be just about the only functioning street light in the city, and no one pays it any mind. Fucking assholes."

He jabbed an elbow at his partner.

"So what the fuck, Kleiner?"

Kleiner was spilling pills from one of the brown bottles into his palm.

"Valium."

"No fucking."

The plainclothes shot Park his eyes in the rearview.

"Who the fuck is buying Valium? That's bullshit. That's your bullshit stash, isn't it? Mean, no one wants Valium. Where's your fucking ups?"

Park braced his feet against the back of the front seats as the plainclothes slammed the brakes to make the sharp right onto Franklin.

"It's for a sleepless guy."

"For a sleepless? Don't give me that shit. Valium does shit for sleepless. All they take is ups."

He wrenched the wheel, cutting across southbound traffic on Western, carving his own path onto Los Feliz Boulevard, gunning up the hill, past the fire-gutted hulk of the American Film Institute, where Park and Rose had once been invited by a friend to watch *Some Like it Hot,* Rose's favorite movie.

They jumped a curb, rode at a cant, half on the sidewalk, and bumped back even, past another logjam of cars.

Kleiner braced his hands against the door and the roof.

"Jesus, Hounds."

Hounds killed the siren.

"What else we got? Dreamer?"

A new note in Hounds's voice as he said the word. Same note that might have come into the voice of a drunk playing a scratcher at a gas station, before the state leased the lottery, before the company that bought it went bust. A note of hope and disbelief in the bare second before he confirms that the number that looks like it might be worth a million is indeed his usual two-buck winner. Just like he knew it would turn out to be.

Kleiner dropped the caps back in the bottle.

"No, Demerol."

The sedan lurched as it was broadsided by a hybrid edging into traffic from North Vermont, and the plainclothes pointed at the driver.

"Motherfucker! Fucking shoot that motherfucker!"

Kleiner ignored the request, opening the baggie.

"Who has Dreamer? No one has real Dreamer. Just bootleg crap."

Hounds turned to look again at Park.

"And you, what's this bullshit about a sleepless taking Valium?"

Park looked between his knees.

"This guy in Koreatown. Says they help. He takes them ten at a time. Drinks a bottle of red wine. Says he almost naps."

Hounds chewed his lip.

"Ten at a time. Does it work?"

Park shrugged.

"He thinks it does. Never heard of it before. But they all have things they try. Know a lady, she chops up melatonin and snorts it. Twenty, thirty grams at a time."

"Yeah, but the Valium?"

Park shook his head.

"I doubt it."

"Fuck. Fuck."

Griffith Park loomed brown on their left.

Park looked at the fire-scorched hillside. Tents were starting to repopulate it now that the wreckage and dead bodies from the original refugee camp had been mostly cleared away and the smoldering ground fires extinguished.

Hounds slapped the dash.

"Hey, what about the Demerol? That help sleepless any?"

"Not that I ever heard of. I sell that to a regular old pill head. Guy used to be a roadie for Tom Petty."

Park watched a crowd of refugees gathering at a Red Cross truck. Most of them had been burned out of the canyons between the Ventura Freeway and the coast, flushed from the chaparral as far north as Mugu Lagoon.

Looking at the lost and unmoored, his mind drifted.

"The only thing I ever heard of really working other than Dreamer is maybe Pentosan. But the molecule is too big to penetrate the blood-brain barrier. So they have to install a shunt to administer it."

He remembered the doctor who had described the procedure to him and Rose.

Basically we drill a hole in your skull and drive a bolt through it.

Rose had declined. Rather, Rose had said, *No fucking way in hell.*

Park shook his head.

"Anyway, all the Pentosan really does is keep you alive. You're still sleepless, still in pain. Some sleepless have been given massive doses of Quinacrine and recovered. Briefly. Then they get worse than before. Palsies. Liver failure."

He shrugged again.

"Valium, stuff like that, mostly it's people grabbing at whatever makes them feel better for an hour or two."

Hounds was tapping the brakes, slowing as they approached the line of cars before the Los Angeles River checkpoint.

"How you know all that shit?"

Again Park shrugged.

"I sell drugs."

"Shit."

Hounds wiped sweat from his forehead.

"My fucking mother-in-law, she's with us. Sleepless for a couple months now. Bitch is getting bad. Fucking insufferable. Stumbling around all fucking hours. Talking shit all the time. Freaking out the kids. *Why's Grandma calling me Billy, Daddy?* Try explaining to a kid, *Well, honey, it's cuz Granny's thalamus is being eaten away by misfolded proteins and she's having waking dreams that are more like fucking nightmares and she doesn't know where the hell she is and she thinks you're her son who was actually a miscarriage she had in high school when she was fifteen.* I could give her ten Valium and a bottle of Zinfandel and she'd chill out; I'd fucking kiss you that worked."

Park didn't say anything.

Hounds held out his hand.

"Fuck it, give me the fucking things."

His partner passed him the bottle of Valium.

"Yeah, you should give it a try. Got nothing to lose."

Hounds pocketed the pills.

Park looked away, and Hounds caught it in the rearview.

"What the fuck? This a problem for you, asshole?"

Park didn't say anything, just watched the crowd around the Red Cross truck start to roil as people realized there weren't enough bags of rice to go around.

Hounds drove.

"Worst can happen to the old lady is she can die."

He rubbed the back of his neck.

"Fucking real worst thing is that she could live another six months. Jesus. *I* get it, I go sleepless, I'm eating the bullet. Soon as I know it's for real, I'm out. My wife's mom, she gave us the money to put the down on our first place. Found out her daughter was marrying a black guy, she started reading *The Autobiography of Malcolm X.* I mean, that was bullshit, but I appreciated the thought. Now? Watching that, watching someone rot in front of you? I thought I could get my wife to go along, I'd put the bullet in her brain. And swear to God, she'd fucking love me for it. Aw, this fucking shit, what now?"

A SWAT in full body armor, visored Kevlar helmet, a belt of 5.56-mm draped over his shoulder feeding the M249 Squad Auto in his arms, waved them to the side.

Hounds stuck his head out the window.

"What the fuck? We got a perp in here."

The SWAT walked over, shifting the machine gun's butt to his hip and pulling off his helmet.

"Easy, man, just trying to cut you through the line. Roll up here on the side."

He pointed at the empty traffic lane, bordered by spools of razor wire, kept clear for military and emergency traffic.

Hounds nodded.

"Thanks, G, my bad with the attitude. Just someone up the chain put something in my captain's ass and we spent the day tracking down some fucking dealer."

The SWAT set his helmet on the roof of the car, looked in the back at Park.

"Dreamer?"

Hounds grunted.

"Right, you'd think that, make us roll for this shit when there's real police work to do. Fucking recreationals is what he's selling."

The SWAT ran a hand over the top of his crew cut, a fine spray of sweat getting caught in the halogen glow of the generator-driven spots lighting the checkpoint.

"Any ups? I'm about to fall over here."

Kleiner showed the remaining bottle and Baggie.

"Demerol and X."

The SWAT stuck out his hand.

"Hit me with a couple tabs of X. Might keep me from shooting some of these fucking spics."

Kleiner poured some pills into the outstretched hand.

"What's the go-down?"

The SWAT shook two of the pills into his mouth and started to chew, tucking the others into a pouch on his tac belt.

"Avenues are burying one of their warlords. Guy started his Impala the other day and it blew up under him. Fucking Cyprus Park psychos. Anyway, funeral cortege is gonna roll at midnight tonight, and they want to run it right through Cyprus Park turf and over to Forest Lawn. Send some kind of I-don't-know-what-the-fuck message."

Hounds pointed east.

"Fuck that. Tell them no fucking way. Blockade the street."

The SWAT nodded.

"Where you out of?"

Hounds took off his sunglasses.

"West Bureau, Hollywood Community. Something to say?"

The SWAT held up a hand.

"Nothing to say, police is police. But we got a treaty on with Avenues right now. They're doing neighborhood enforcement east of San Fernando. All it really means is we can hit their turf without worrying too much about taking fire. But we come down on them about how they bury their dead? Next thing you know, cop can't come out from behind the wire without a sniper taking potshots, getting shrapneled by a garbage can IED."

Hounds put his shades back on.

"Yeah, I get it. Keep some of the scumbags on our side while we deal with the worse scumbags."

The SWAT picked up his helmet.

"Hey, that's a nice way of looking at it, but a little optimistic from where I am."

He put on his helmet and pointed at the pedestrian bridge that crossed Los Feliz Boulevard where it jumped over the bone-dry bed of the Los Angeles River.

"See that?"

They could see it.

Hanging from the bridge, pinned in the light from one of the check-point halogens, a corpse, arms bound behind its back, skin blackened by fire, dangling by a chain that snaked down to what was left of its neck.

"That's a sixteen-year-old cousin of the Cyprus Park warlord. Avenues hung him up there this morning. Checkpoint commander, he said leave it up. Said he ain't gonna fucking antagonize Avenues as long as this is his post. Says he gives a fuck, just wants to stop watching his officers die. So you tell me."

He buckled the chin strap of his helmet.

"Who's dealing with whose scumbags over here? Cuz I don't fucking know."

"What do those fucking fashion plates have to do with it?"

Hounds pointed at a small group of men and women dressed in fitted black short-sleeve fatigues and Dragon Skin armor, Masada assault rifles at the ready, clustered around two armored Saab 9-7X SUVs with swoop-ing white door stickers that matched the patches on their shoulders.

The SWAT spit.

"Thousand Storks? They got fuck all to do with it. Waiting here to escort some assholes from city hall on a tour of Glassell Park. Local councilwoman wants to show how the situation has been *normalized*. Fucking showboaters will end up all over the evening news, speeding around, jumping out of their vehicles, securing perimeters and shit. Everyone will think they really deserve those huge security contracts. Tape won't show the three gunships they got hovering overhead giving cover. Know why they won't shoot that? Because a hovering helicopter isn't good TV. Fuck this shit."

The SWAT snapped his visor down and waved to the side of the road.

"Pull on in here, I'll move the wire."

Hounds rolled slowly forward as the SWAT carefully pulled aside one of the corkscrews of wire, giving the cop a nod as they accelerated toward the checkpoint.

"That fucking guy and this duty he's on, I got one thing to say about that guy."

He nodded to himself.

"Better him than me, man. Better him than me."

Park was looking out the right side window, down at the I-5.

Some stretches were still entirely open. This one, directly under a checkpoint, was sealed by barricades of abandoned cars a quarter mile to the north and the south. From what Park heard, the middle sections of the barricades would be rigged with charges to blow the cars out of the way if a military or law enforcement column needed to pass. Through most of the length of the 5, from the Mexican to the Canadian borders, a lane was supposed to be kept open for military traffic, but there were long unpoliced stretches of the interstate where road gangs set tariffs, using the lane to cruise north and south, pulling motorists over and siphoning their gas. Down here that kind of thing wasn't much of a worry. There was the more basic worry regarding the many choke points where abandoned cars had accumulated like plaque in an artery.

Like the plaques left behind on a sleepless brain, blocking its normal function, leading it to Baroque variations on its usual course of business.

Park thought about all these accretions of debris, within the body and without, driving it to more bizarre extremes. The Crown Vic rolled to a stop at the checkpoint, and he looked up at the hanged man twisting slightly to and fro in a hot shaft of air rising from the generators.

The cops in the front seat showed ID and badges to the cops manning the checkpoint, showed the ID they'd taken off Park, and were waved along with specific instructions about how to approach Silverlake Station.

Coming off the overpass, the bed of the Los Angeles River behind them, they passed the Los Feliz Golf Course, only slightly more brown now than it had been before severe water rationing became mandatory.

The boulevard here was all but empty. The bars and restaurants that had been outposts of East Side gentrification were gated, boarded up, or burned out. A few sleepless walking aimlessly, scratching their heads, rubbing their eyes, talking to themselves. Some Griffith Park refugees had managed to cross the I-5 and the river below the checkpoint and were scavenging in the abandoned storefronts. Not that there was much left. But once the boulevard dipped under the railroad just past Seneca, the blocks started to repopulate.

Heavily armed vatos, favoring AR15s and Tec 9s, were on every street corner. Sandbags lined the edges of rooftops, gun barrels peeking out from behind. Taco trucks and tamale carts were at the curbs, vendors sporting holstered sidearms. Kids played in the street, running in and out of the night traffic, young mothers calling to them in Chicano Spanish. Older men sat at tables on the sidewalks, playing cards or dominoes.

Hounds pulled his Glock from its holster and tucked it between his thighs.

"I find out who fingered us for this fucking detail, I'm gonna get his home address, come back here, and pay one of these vatos twenty bucks to go burn his house down with him and his family inside. I mean, look at this shit. Like another fucking country. What the fuck."

Kleiner stuck one of Park's Demerols between his lips.

"Be like this in the Fairfax pretty soon. The Jews, they're starting to put up sawhorses at the ends of their blocks. Yarmulkes and Uzis. Gonna change the name to Little Israel any day now."

They drove past a dropped 1980 Chevy Stepside, a man perched on the fender, leather holsters crossed over his chest Pancho Villa style, mad dogging them.

Hounds gritted his teeth.

"Give me the eye. Find your ass west of the Five, break your ass down you look at me like that. Fucking savages over here. Goddamn jungle. Show me now, show me the guy who thinks building a border fence would have been a bad idea, and let me make that asshole run naked through this shit."

Down San Fernando, just before Treadwell, they came to the concrete anti-car bomb barriers that closed the street around Silverlake Station. Freshly spray-painted across one of the barriers, over the tangle of tags, a new graffito:

ϛㄥƐƐdㄥϛϛ=PLOT=KILL ALL PIGS

The retrofitted minigun on a Stryker infantry fighting vehicle turned and trained its cluster of barrels on the Crown Vic, an amplified voice blaring.

"Welcome to Silverlake Station. Get out of the fucking car with your hands in view and get your fucking face on the pavement."

Hounds killed the engine.

"Fucking jungle."

DRIVING DOWN SKID Row had always been a prospect not unlike visiting the set of a George Romero movie. But with the advent of the sleepless prion, that effect had started to envelop the entire city. The sidewalks, malls, movie theaters, tourist attractions, beaches, and restaurants becoming populated with stiff-necked, shuffling sleepless.

Zombie jokes were common. Gallows humor being about all the situation made room for.

Movies themselves had not stopped shooting. Certainly production had been scaled back, and more than one studio had gone under or, more accurately, been consumed whole by somewhat heartier competitors, but even as energy costs spiked, even as all cities, most suburbs, and many rural areas, experienced outbreaks of organized violence, even as the standing army was deployed with obvious permanence to the oil fields in Alaska, Iraq, Iran, Venezuela, and Brazil, even as the draft was reinstated and the gears of the economy audibly snapped their teeth and ground to a squealing halt, even as the drought extended and crops withered, even as the ice caps melted and coastal waters rose, people still liked a good picture.

The fact of millions of sleepless wandering about trying to fill the dark hours meant an expansion of one market, even as it contracted in other areas.

Sleepless provided other new opportunities as well.

I'd been told by a client about an independent horror movie he was helping to finance. A zombie picture. The zombies played almost exclusively by sleepless extras.

A new standard in zombie verisimilitude.

Or so he said.

I said nothing, sometimes finding that even I can be rendered speechless. A not unpleasant sensation, except for those times when it is engendered by the rising of my gorge.

In any case, the traffic jam I found myself caught in was not caused by the shooting of this breakthrough in cinema, but it was indeed the result of a film crew somewhere in the waning afternoon light, ahead of me on Santa Monica.

SOP in traffic jams, and therefore SOP whenever one got in one's car, was to roll down the windows and turn off the engine. It was no longer a simple matter of common sense, it was also now enforceable by law. Sitting in deadlocked traffic with your engine running, powering your stereo, AC, seatback TV, game console, and recharging your various portable devices, was both unpatriotic and illegal.

Not being a patriot, giving not a damn about getting a ticket, and having more than enough wealth to fill the tank of my resolutely gas-guzzling STS-V, I blasted the air conditioner, listened to a bootleg MP3 of an original recording of Giuseppe di Stefano performing *Faust* at the Met in

1949, and ran my Toughbook off the AC outlet. I did, out of courtesy, keep the windows up, not wanting the people sweltering around me to grow resentful, but I suspect the low grumble of the V-8 gave me away. Certainly I registered a few nasty looks shot at me through the tinted glass, but those would have concerned me only if the glass, indeed the whole car, were not bulletproof. Had I been so inclined, I could have rammed my way straight through the mass of traffic and come out the other end with little more to worry about than scratched paint and a few dents, but I was surfing the Net, reading up on di Stefano's biography, so I endured.

Ten percent of the world's population could not sleep.

They were dying, yes, but it took the average sleepless as much as a year to die after becoming symptomatic. Once the oddly stiff neck, pinprick pupils, and sweat manifested, insomnia shortly followed, gradually worsening, until it was absolute. Months were endured by the sufferers, months of constant wakefulness, plunging in and out of REM-state dreams without ever falling asleep, alert, always, to the terrible wrack of their bodies. There was no cure, death was inevitable, and while one's self might gradually slip away, one's awareness of the pain and physical chaos never ceased.

The most sensible thing was to dose on massive quantities of speed.

By the time the sleepless entered the later stages and sleep became an utter impossibility, there was little the average amphetamine could do to the human body that it was not already doing to itself. But it could lend some artificial burst of vigor, it could also sharpen and focus the mind and sometimes stave off the disorienting slippage into dream and memory. Condemned to disquietude and fueled by bennies, one-tenth of the world's population not only wanted to go to the movies at midnight, they also wanted to surf the Internet.

At first glance it would appear a losing proposition to market to this demographic, seeing as they were set to expire. And that would have been true if the disease were not spreading.

It hadn't, after all, always been ten percent that were infected. It had, of course, started quite small. Indeed, in its infancy, the sleepless prion had been little more than a boutique disease. A fringe illness known as fatal familial insomnia. The name tells you all you need to know about its quaint beginnings.

Familial.

For virtually all of the 245-odd years of its recorded history, FFI had restricted itself to less than a handful of genetic lines. How and why it widened its scope so terribly and suddenly was, you'll understand, a subject greatly debated.

To be more precise, the sleepless prion was not the same as the FFI prion. For better or worse, FFI offered a much quicker, and therefore, many would say, more merciful death.

SLP was something else.

SLP.

Sleepless.

Or, to the kids, SL33PL3SS.

A slang variation playing off the chemical designation used in the patent for the only known treatment for the symptoms of SLP.

Commercial name: Dreamer.

Chemical designate: DR33M3R.

A wholly fortuitous alphanumeric, speaking in terms of marketing, that is. So serendipitous, so instantly obvious to even the most slack-jawed account exec, that one could almost be made suspicious.

If one were of a suspicious mind.

I am suspicious of very little, having, in my sixty years, been assured time and again that people are an utter waste and capable of anything when contemplating their own fortune and well-being. With such a worldview, there is little need for suspicion. Easier to simply assume the bastards are screwing everyone else, out for their own good.

Indeed, I was living proof of my own thesis, sitting there in my final generation Cadillac, listening to Gounod, my brow chilled by the cold air coming from the vents, reaping the benefits of a diseased population's need for distraction as manifested in the continued availability of broadband wireless service in the L.A. basin.

Humanity endures.

Excelsior.

I was so at peace with the world and myself that when the shockingly sinewy vegan in the Mercedes 300 plastered with biodiesel stickers got out of her car and started rapping on my window, screaming at me that I was "killing the planet and the children," I almost didn't roll down that window and point at her face the Beretta Tomcat I'd pulled from my ankle holster.

The Tomcat is a stunningly slight weapon, its 2.4-inch barrel virtually useless beyond the length of one's arm. In appearance, when wielded, it is often mistaken for a toy or tool of some kind. The nubbin of barrel poking from the fist doesn't appear to be a serious threat at all.

But it feels serious when crammed under your chin. And it sounds serious when the hammer is thumbed back. And in case she was in any doubt, I made certain she knew that both I and the gun were quite serious.

"You are going to die in front of dozens of witnesses, and none of them will do a thing to help you or avenge you. Because they know exactly what you know: The world is ending. The difference being, they have surrendered and are willing to watch it pass away as long as they can do it in relative comfort. You, on the other hand, are squandering what few resources of personal will and energy you have left by trying to stop an avalanche. Give up. Things are as bad as you fear they are. People are as self-serving as you fear they are. The universe does not care. And neither do you. Not really. Go find a warm body you can huddle against for animal comfort. Go get in your car and don't look at me again. I'm getting bored of talking now. Go away before I get bored of not pulling the trigger and not watching your brains fountain out the top of your head."

She made a noise deep in her throat, and then she walked away, eyes fixed at a level just above the roofs of the cars, in a gait that could be taken for sleepless but was merely despair.

And I touched a button, a button the engineers at GM, before going bankrupt, had considerately designed so that I did not need to hold it down while the window rolled up, and was sealed again in the perfect cool dimness of what the brochure had described as the car's cockpit, pressing the thumblike barrel of the Tomcat into the hollow below my jaw.

But even with the perfect lyric accompaniment, this was not the moment.

So, as the traffic began, mystically, to flow, all of it parting around the stalled Mercedes containing the sobbing woman, I slipped the gun back into its moleskin holster, and was carried smoothly on the pitted road, past the location shoot (an artfully reproduced scene of a traffic accident), wondering at the noise she had made, how in perfect dissonance with di Stefano's diminuendo on the high C in "Salut! Demeure" it had been:

I greet you, home chaste and pure,
I greet you, home chaste and pure,
Where is manifested the presence
Of a soul, innocent and divine!
I greet you, home chaste and pure.

■　■　■

PARK WAS HAVING trouble breathing.

It wasn't just the fact of the bag over his head, it was the fact that he was far from the first prisoner to have worn it. Stiff with old sweat, crusted at the open end with dry vomit, the black canvas sack stifled more than just air.

And his knees hurt.

He'd already learned not to try to lower his buttocks to his ankles for relief. Having done so once and received a truncheon blow across his shoulder blades.

And he'd lost feeling in his fingers.

That was a concern, but a far greater concern was that he'd started not to feel the zip-strip where it dug into his wrists. Losing circulation to the fingers was one thing, having it cut off from his hands entirely was more disquieting.

The man to his right moaned something in Spanish.

Boots crossed the tile room, echoing, and a nightstick bounced off a skull.

"Shut the fuck up!"

Park felt the man tumble against him and struggled to somehow catch him, leaning his body far backward, trying to support the man's weight against his torso. The muscles in his thighs, already trembling, gave out, and they both fell to the floor.

"Up! Get the fuck up!"

Someone grabbed a fistful of his hair through the bag and hauled him back up to his knees.

"Stay up! Up, asshole!"

A lazy fist caught him across the ear.

"Fucking shoot your ass now."

A loud buzz shocked the room, vibrating the rank air, a bolt slammed back into its socket, and a door opened, letting in a draft of fresher air that Park could just feel on his upper arms.

Sneakers squeaked on the tiles. Some papers rustled.

"Adam, three, three, zero, hotel, dash, four, dash, four, zero."

His arms were jerked as someone tried to get a look at the plastic bracelet fastened around his wrist.

"Yeah, that's this asshole."

The truncheon dug into his ribs.

"Up, asshole."

He tried to unfold his legs and rise but only succeeded in falling over again.

"Fucking."

The shaft of the truncheon crossed his throat, and he was dragged choking to his feet, stumbling, almost falling again, and caught under the arms.

"I got him."

"Yeah, well, fucking enjoy. And try not to leave too many marks."

Blind and lurching, led out into a quiet hallway where the air, only a couple of degrees cooler, felt like a spring breeze. Tripping over his own numb feet, saved again and again from falling, and then leaned against a wall.

"Can you hold yourself up for a second?"

He nodded but didn't know if it could be seen through the hood.

His voice cracked like his dry lips.

"I think so."

The hands left him, and he kept his feet.

Keys were jingled, one fitted to a lock, and another door opened.

"In here."

The hands took him again, not carrying him as much as guiding him this time, feeling coming back into his legs and feet.

"Sit."

A chair.

"Lean forward."

He leaned, found a table, and rested his head on it, his eyes sliding shut, almost instantly asleep. And brought back in seconds as the zip-strip was clipped from his wrists and blood rushed into his hands, filling them with needles.

The sack was yanked from his head, and he coughed on the sudden oxygen, blinking his eyes against hard fluorescents.

"Here."

A wiry man with a tonsure of gray hair, eyes hidden by green-tinted aviator sunglasses, placed a water bottle in front of him.

Park nodded. He tried to pick up the bottle but couldn't get his hands to close around it.

The man twisted the cap from the bottle and held it to Park's lips, slowly tilting it upward as Park swallowed.

"Enough?"

Park coughed, and the man lowered the bottle and set it back on the table. He took Park's hands in his own and started rubbing them.

"When were you picked up?"

Park looked for his watch, forgetting for the moment that he had stashed it before the bust.

"I don't know. Last night? What time is it?"

The needles in his hands were turning to pins, and he found he could flex them on his own.

The man let go and took a cell from a plastic clip on the belt of his navy blue Dickies.

"Little after midnight."

"I should call my wife."

The man put the phone back on his belt.

"Later."

From the corner of the table he picked up a wrinkled and stained manila envelope, names and numbers scrawled across it in long rows, each crossed out in turn, except for one: HAAS, PARKER, T./A330H-4-40

The man untwisted a frayed brown thread from a round tab, opened the envelope, looked inside, and then dumped the contents onto the table.

"What the hell is this?"

Park looked at the baggies of brown, seedy ditch weed.

"Not mine."

The man looked at the uncrossed name on the outside of the envelope.

"Says it is."

"It's not."

The man nodded.

"Lot of trouble to be in for a couple ounces of Mexican brown."

Park made fists; just the tips of his fingers tingled now. He looked at the door.

"Can we talk?"

The man folded his arms across the Dodgers jersey he wore open over a white tank.

"That's why we're here."

Park flicked one of the bags with his index finger.

"That's what they planted on me."

The man pointed at the bag.

"Because this isn't what I expected to find on you."

Park nodded.

"And it's not what I had on me."

"Hounds and Kleiner took what you had on you?"

"Yes."

"And planted this?"

"Yes."

The man folded his arms a little tighter.

"And what did the arresting officers take off you?"

Park looked at the man's cellphone.

"I should really call my wife. She'll worry."

The man shook his head.

"Later. Tell me what they took off you."

Park drank from the water bottle, draining what was left.

"Demerol. Valium. X."

The man nodded and unfolded his arms and picked up one of the baggies.

"Because this will get you nowhere."

Park touched the ear that had been punched while the black sack was over his head.

"I know. And it's not what I had. It's not what I've been doing."

The man waved a hand.

"I know what you've been doing."

Park shrugged.

"Well, then?"

The man stared at him, shook his head, and sat in the chair opposite.

"I want to hear it."

Park looked at the door again.

"We can talk?"

The man took off his sunglasses, revealing bagged eyes, bloodshot, sunk in deeply wrinkled sockets.

"We can talk."

Park pointed at the sack on the floor.

"Then can you tell me who the hell is running things here, Captain?"

The man with the worried eyes shrugged.

"We are."

Park didn't want the duty at first.

It wasn't what he'd joined for. He'd joined to help. He'd joined to do service. When asked by his friends what the hell he was going to do, he told them he was going to protect and to serve.

None of them laughed, knowing that Parker Thomas Haas did not joke about such things. He had, in fact, no sense of humor at all when it came to matters of justice and ethics.

Morality he found amusing, in the obscure way that only a man with a Ph.D. in philosophy could find such things amusing, but justice and ethics were inflexible measures, applicable to all, and not to be joked about.

Not by him, in any case.

And so he'd wanted to stay in uniform.

Long before he had finished at the academy, he had resolved for himself that justice within the courts did not often live up to the standards it should and must. Long, hot afternoons spent between classes in the downtown courthouses, watching the wheels of justice squeal and creak, had settled that case.

But street justice was another matter.

It could be applied directly. In the face of injustice, a man with a badge on the street could actually do something. What happened after the point of interdiction could be a mystery, but in the moment of arrest, leniency, summons, unexpected tolerance, no-BS takedown, comfort, lecture, or application of force, a cop on the beat could enact true justice.

A matter of setting a standard and applying it always, without exception, to everyone.

Including oneself.

For Park, that was as easy as breathing.

But hard as hell for anyone working with him.

Which was one of the arguments Captain Bartolome had used on him.

"No one likes you."

Standing in his office, in front of the autographed picture of himself as a boy with a smiling Vin Scully, Bartolome had shrugged.

"Not saying it to make you feel bad, it's just true."

Park had looked at the LAPD ball cap in his own hands.

"It doesn't make me feel bad."

"I didn't think it did. Another reason I think you'd be good for this. Helps not to care if people don't like you."

Park ran a hand up the back of his neck, felt the sharp horizontal hairline that his barber had carved at the bottom of his buzz cut.

"It's not that I don't care in general, Captain. Depends on why they don't like me."

Bartolome stuck the tip of his tongue behind his lower lip, then pulled it back, sucking his teeth.

"So it's just you don't care that they don't like you because you're a pain in the ass to work with? Other reasons people don't like you might bother you, that it?"

Park stopped playing with his hair.

"I don't care if they don't want to work with me, because I know I'm right."

The captain from narcotics raised both eyebrows.

"Jesus, Haas. No wonder they don't like you."

Park brushed something from the leg of his blues.

"May I go now?"

Bartolome pointed at the door.

"Can you leave my office now? Yes."

Park started to rise.

Bartolome pointed at the window.

"Can you go back out on the streets? No."

Park, half out of the hard plastic chair, stalled and looked at his superior. "Sir?"

Bartolome looked at his desk, frowned at the headline on the *L.A. Times* sports section spread there:

MLB ENDS SEASON

Play Not to Resume Until SLP Pandemic Has Been Contained

He looked at the officer across the desk.

"There will be no more solo acts, Haas. Everyone rides with a partner. Department can't afford the gas to put enough vehicles on the street. Until we see some more stimulus cash miraculously filling the motor pool with electrics and hybrids, all patrol cars roll with two, three, four officers."

He rubbed his eyes.

"And no one, absolutely no one, wants to ride with you anymore."

Park straightened.

"They never have."

"Uh-huh, but things weren't this bad before. Things weren't as dangerous as they're getting out there. The department wants maximum morale in the face of this shit. Maximum morale means we don't have to worry about the kind of desertions they got when Katrina hit. Cops losing faith in the system and just disappearing."

He stopped rubbing his eyes and looked Park up and down.

"Maximum morale also means that officers have each other's backs. We don't want guys cutting slack out there because they figure they'd be better off if the pain in the ass riding shotgun maybe took one in a gang incident."

Park thought about the time about a year before, riding with Del Rico. How they'd rolled on a two-eleven. Del had said the stockroom at the back of the liquor store was clear. But it wasn't. Turned out the perp wasn't strapped; what the Korean owner of the store had taken for a gun was a length of pipe. But it had been a gun call, and Del had let Park walk into a supposedly cleared room where a perp was hiding behind some boxes with a pipe that could easily have been a piece. Park walked with a couple bruises on his ribs. The perp took a series of baton spears to his genitals.

Del was always cool to Park's face, but he'd heard him making cracks with the guys. Talking about how he couldn't wait till his tour with *the monk* was over.

Park didn't think Del Rico knew the perp was back there. But he was a good cop. And he'd said the room was clear. Would he have been more thorough if he hadn't been thinking about when he'd be done riding with Park?

"You follow me, Haas?"

Park looked up at the captain.

"I could do bike patrols."

Bartolome rubbed the smooth brown top of his head.

"Bike cops are doubling up, too."

"Motorcycles. I can do traffic."

"You ever ride a hog?"

"No."

Bartolome pointed at a picture on the wall. A younger version of himself, traffic leathers, white and blue helmet, astride a Harley.

"Field training for the hogs, that takes weeks and costs the department. Tell you right now, the budget the way it is, the only retraining going on is for SWAT and the antiterrorism academy."

Park looked at the picture of Bartolome in his bucket-head rig.

SWATs were in love with their guns and the rush of blowing a door down and charging in. Why they were there, who had done what and to whom, didn't matter in the least to a SWAT. They just wanted a clean shot.

The antiterrorism academy was a one-way ticket to a desk. Paperwork. Intelligence review. Coordinating task forces with the CIA, FBI, Homeland Security, Customs and Border Protection.

He looked away from the picture.

"I don't think I'd be suited to either of those duties, sir."

"You aren't being offered either of those duties."

Bartolome weighed two invisible objects, one in either hand.

"You're being offered this one thing."

He showed the heft and gravity of what it was Park was being offered.

"Or you can accept online training for dispatch."

He displayed the relative lightness of a job relaying radio calls.

Park remembered his father asking him what he thought he could achieve as a police officer that he could not achieve in the family business. The family business having been government service and politics.

He shook his head.

"I simply don't think I'm suited to the duty, sir."

Bartolome nodded.

"Why?"

"From a practical perspective, I'm white. And I don't do street. I mean, I know the jargon, but it never sounds natural. And I've never done drugs myself, not even in college. I don't know where to begin a fake."

The captain smiled.

"Haas, what the hell? What are you thinking? Are you thinking I'm gonna send you down to Wilmington? Have you dealing meth to the longshoremen working the night shift at the port? Try and mix you in with the vatos down there? Think I'm gonna have you sling rock to the homies in South Central?"

Park found himself thinking about his father again.

"You said 'undercover,' sir. You said 'selling drugs.' "

Bartolome looked at his desk. He cleared away the sports page that had delivered the news that the bullshit going down outside wasn't going to be relieved any longer this summer by the distraction of a few ball games, and found a sheaf of pages that he'd printed on the back sides of old incident reports and call sheets. As per new department regulations that all paper be double printed before recycling.

"Haas."

He flipped through the pages, turning them over and back, finding the side he wanted.

"Most cops, being a cop is one of two things to them. One, being a cop is a job. Pay's not bad. Advancement is available to anyone with some initiative. Benefits are outstanding. No one these days gets the kind of medical police get. Good pension. Lots of perks. And, used to be, plenty of assignments where you don't have to even wear a gun, let alone worry about pulling it. A high school diploma, couple years at a JC, that or do your bit in the service, and you can get in the academy. It's a regular guy job. Average cop, his attitude has more in common with a welder than it does, say, a Treasury agent. Second thing is, for some, being a cop means the badge and the baton and the gun. Guys never gonna say it out loud, not sober, but they just plain like telling people what to do. Go to their house for a barbeque, see them talk to their wife and kids same way they talk to some guy they just busted for assault with intent. Guys come in badge-heavy and stay that way."

He peeled back the corner of one of the sheets of paper in his hand and looked at the one below it.

"Where do you fit in that lineup?"

Park was still thinking about his father, remembering the last time they met, at his mother's funeral. A month later he had chosen not to go east for his father's. The old man had said all he wanted to say to Park at his wife's graveside, though it wasn't until he got the call from his sister, telling him in stoic Pennsylvania tones that their father had done it with his favorite Weatherby 20-gauge, that he understood what had been meant by the words, *No need for you to come home again.* Standing over his mother's coffin, he'd assumed those words were the final dismissal that their entire relationship had been slowly building to. Hanging up after his sister's call, he knew they'd actually been T. Stegland Haas's last attempt at sheltering his son from the world's pain.

No need to come back. No need to stand at another parent's graveside. Go about your business. This is over. You are excused.

He rubbed the face of his watch with his thumb.

"I don't know where I fit in there, sir."

Barlolome nodded.

"Let's take a look. Trust-fund family. Deerfield Academy. Whatever the hell that is. Columbia BA. Stanford Ph.D. Doesn't sound like someone in need of solid job prospects."

He folded back another sheet of paper.

"And, well, you're not shy about use of force, but you've got no complaints of merit in here. Good collection of busts, but nothing that smells like you enjoy snapping the bracelets on. Doesn't read like a guy gets stiff from pushing people around."

He rolled the paper into a tube and pointed it at Park.

"What this is, this is the account of an educated young white man with a genuine desire to do the right thing and serve his community."

Park was twisting his wrist back and forth, letting the movement propel the self-winding mechanism inside the watch.

It had been his father's, a 1970 Omega Seamaster, a gift from his wife, given in turn to Park the same day he was excused from future funerals. His father taking it from his own wrist, handing it to him with these words, *It's a good watch. When they start dropping the bombs in a couple years, it won't be knocked out by an electromagnetic pulse. Even in the apocalypse, someone should know the correct time, Parker.*

He twisted his wrist a little more quickly.

"Is that an accusation, sir?"

Bartolome let the papers unroll in his hand, showed them to Park.

"No. It's just what I need. An educated young white who can talk to other educated young whites. The kind of people who not only have enough money to buy drugs but enough to be able to afford to be discriminating about who they buy them from. People who don't want to circle MacArthur park in their Mercedes. People who want to call a discreet phone number, place an order, and have it delivered. Like sushi. People like that, Officer Haas."

He leaned close.

"Those are the only kind of people who can afford to buy Dreamer."

Park stopped twisting his wrist.

"Sir."

Bartolome put the roll of papers on his desk.

"Have you seen anyone with it yet? Close up. Someone you know?"

Park touched the watch without looking at it.

"My mother. But I didn't see her. She died fast."

"Good."

Bartolome nodded twice.

"That's good. One of my brothers got it early. Before the test. When they still thought it was a virus. Quarantine. Nonstop tissue samples. Experimental treatment. On top of the fucking thing itself. His last week, that was when they allowed the first human Dreamer trials. His number got drawn, but he was in the placebo group. I saw a woman who got the real thing. She slept. She dreamed. Woke up, she smiled, talked to her family. She'd been screaming nonstop for five days before that. Covered in lesions. Those went away, too."

He looked at another picture on the wall: dress blues, the day he got his bars, between his two cop brothers, arms draped over one another's shoulders.

He looked away.

"Afronzo-New Day Pharm has finally agreed to a federally brokered deal to lease the patent on Dreamer internationally. A-ND will have to settle for profiting just a little less obscenely on this deal than they would have. Man, they can nationalize the banks, car manufacturers, utilities, and telecom, but as long as Big Pharm is still in the black those cocksuckers in Congress will scream 'free market' like someone nominated Marx for President."

He rubbed his nose and grunted.

"Anyway, no telling how long it will take for overseas production to ramp up, and even when it does, if it ever does, demand is going to stay way ahead of supply. But that's over the borders and across the seas, and I don't have the energy to give a shit. For the time being America has all there is and everyone wants it and we have to keep people from killing each other for it. To wit, FDA is going to take it off Schedule A and invent something called Schedule Z. Totally regulated. Distributed out of hospital pharmacies only. Administered directly by hospital personnel to admitted patients. One dose at a time. Rare exceptions will be possible for hospice and home care, limited scrips, signed by two doctors. Every box, every bottle has an RFID tag. Small batch produced, the pills in each batch will have three unique identifying features."

He put both hands on top of his head, fingers knitted.

"Everyone at least knows someone who has someone close who's had SLP. Pretty soon, everyone's gonna have someone they know *well.* Someone they love. Trade in Dreamer, if it hits the street, that'll cause a war. The stuff that's already out there, the counterfeits, that low-grade Southeast Asian knockoff junk; we'd like to cut it off, but that's not our mandate. We'll be working DR33M3R, the real stuff. A bottle here or there, a few dozen pills, that's gonna happen. But we can't have this stuff hitting the street in quantity. Busts of scale, that's what we'll be after."

Park crimped the bill of his cap.

"People have to know distribution is fair and equal and blind to money, class, and color. People can't start thinking it's only for the rich and the white."

Bartolome eyeballed him.

"Haas, to hell with what people *think.* Eighties crack? You know anything about how bad that was? You don't. You weren't here. It was bad. This, Dreamer, this is the highest-profit-margin dope in history. What I'm concerned about is a drug war. If someone figures out how to intercept the distribution chain or manufacture a quality clone, we'll go from the skirmishes out there straight to trench warfare in days. Some local cartel starts pulling down Dreamer money, they'll be outfitting their people with Russian and Chinese military ordnance. We'll need a flyover just to patrol Crenshaw."

Park nodded.

"What kind of resources are they committing?"

Bartolome blew out his cheeks.

"At the Fed? Got me. LAPD?"

He unlaced his fingers and pointed at himself and then at Park.

"No expense spared."

He put his hands back on top of his head.

"So, Officer Hass."

He rocked back in his chair.

"Does this sound like the kind of duty you're suited for?"

Park stood, fitted his cap onto his head, settled the weight of his weapon on his hip, and nodded.

"Yes, it does, sir."

Bartolome closed his eyes.

"Welcome to Seven Y, Narcotics Special Units. Go back to Van Nuys and clear your shit out of your locker. Anyone asks, you got transferred to Venice. That'll make them hate you even more."

Park stayed where he was.

Bartolome opened one eye.

"Yeah?"

Park scratched the side of his neck.

"One thing."

"Yeah?"

Park touched his badge.

"I'm not good at lying."

Bartolome rolled his eye.

"It'll come to you, Haas."

Parker nodded, turned to the door.

"Haas."

He stopped.

"Sir?"

"Hear your wife is pregnant."

"Yes, sir."

"A kid, that will make this kind of thing a lot harder."

Park didn't say anything.

Bartolome opened his other eye.

"You like that, don't you?"

Park didn't say anything.

4

CENTURY CITY WAS WHERE THEY KEPT THE LAWYERS.

Being lawyers, they were among the first to have themselves walled in when it became apparent that the pandemic wasn't going to simply kill the poor and be done with it. Century Park East and Century Park West were sealed at Santa Monica and West Olympic by twelve-foot-high concrete tank barriers. Constellation Boulevard was now a pedestrian mall running between CPE and CPW. The only way in or out was through the checkpoint gates at the north end of Avenue of the Stars.

The record labels, production companies, networks, talent agencies, and studio corporate offices that made CC home had long been seeking this kind of security from interlopers. No longer did they have to fear an unsolicited demo tape, head shot, or spec script. The gun towers were finally in place, and, rumor had it, a convoy of armored fighting vehicles was parked in one of the 20th Century Fox lot's many empty soundstages. Ready to whisk the inhabitants to safety should they come under siege.

I had a pass.

Of almost equal importance, I had a car that was suitably obscene and a wardrobe that matched. I'd been careful to choose both for the occasion.

Conspicuous consumption was the mode in these circles. Driving a Prius might still have scored status points in West Hollywood, but the power elites had taken to declaring their faith in the future and the sustainability of rampant consumerism by rededicating themselves to the better things in life.

African famine relief, environmentalism, election reform, alternative fuels, building homes for the poor, greenness of any shade, they all seemed to smack of ostentation, a self-glorifying austerity that betrayed a distinct lack of optimism.

If the rich could not be seen to believe that things were going to improve, then what hope for the masses?

I gave my name at the gate, let a black-uniformed, typically chiseled and severe Thousand Storks security contractor scan the RFID tag on my national ID card, pressed my thumb into a biometric reader, waited while they called to confirm my appointment, and took the parking ticket the contractor handed me, noting the sign that warned I'd be charged twenty-five dollars for every fifteen minutes, without validation.

I repeated a similar process at the security desk and elevator bank of Century Plaza Tower North.

In the old days the fortieth floor would not have been considered the penthouse level, but the top four floors of both buildings had been cleared of their regular tenants, replaced by multiservice command and observation posts. Southern California Theater of Operations Command was headquartered there, with liaison presences from the CIA, FBI, ATF, NSA, DEA, CDC, FEMA, CBP, LAPD, LACS, and, I'd heard rumored, representatives from the DGA, SAG, and WGA.

But that may have been one of those L.A. jokes.

The very top floors of both towers, the forty-fourth, had been evacuated entirely. It had been necessary to clear the floors so that additional load-bearing beams could be installed to support the weight of the batteries of Avengers and I-HAWKs that had been brought in and deposited on the roof by Chinook helicopters. That combination of antiaircraft weaponry meant to ensure that nothing from a traffic copter to a C-5 Galaxy could be crashed into the towers.

Hindsight paving the way, as usual, to a safer future.

Standing at a corner window of the north tower, looking up at the tip of an I-HAWK poking over the edge of the south tower, I couldn't help but reflect on the chaos that would ensue when one of those things launched, raining debris and shattered glass onto the rooftop tennis courts of 2000 Avenue of the Stars. Bankers and lawyers, maimed during their lunchtime matches, would sue the Pentagon into submission and put a lien on the GNP.

"Is something amusing you?"

I turned from the window, erasing the slight smile that had sketched my lips for a moment.

"Mutilated lawyers."

She looked up from the mechanism in front of her, considered, and squeezed a few drops of Birchwood Casey Gun Scrubber onto the tip of a cotton swab.

"Yes, I get that."

I came across the polished bamboo floor, gliding in my silk-stockinged feet, hands in my pockets, where they were required to be until I exited from her presence. Relieving me of my weapons not having been sufficient security as far as her various attendants and staff were concerned. Though it wasn't me personally they were so leery of. From what I understood, everyone admitted to her office was required to do the same.

An overly talkative greeter from her lobby staff, whom I had run into by chance having a drink at the Cameo in Santa Monica, shared with me over too many sake-tinis that visitors arriving pocketless were provided with an adjustable plastic belt equipped with two small cloth sacks lined in disposable tissue. He felt that a tasteful black blazer, with pockets, might make guests more comfortable, and intended to make such a suggestion to his employer's personal secretary the following morning.

After that encounter I never again saw the young man at the office. I don't expect it was the temerity he displayed in making such a suggestion that lost him his job but rather the lack of perception and awareness that it indicated. Not realizing that the point of such a belt was to disgrace visitors who didn't know enough to bring their own pockets was a demonstration that he was simply not one of her kind.

But no one was her kind.

No kith, no kin, no kind.

Unique and terrible. As exotic, and nearly as mythical, as the dragon tattooed on her arm.

I never forgot my pockets when I came to call. My hands rested inside faun summer-weight wool, the bottom of the left pocket seamed with a thin strip of nearly silent MicroPlast that I could push through should I want to get at the Boker Infinity ceramic drop-point blade tucked alongside my scrotum. A bit of custom tailoring I'd asked for after I'd first come to see her in her office. Mr. Lee had made these particular pockets for me before he was killed by a stray bullet fired by a Little Ethiopia gangster robbing the Jack in the Box near his shop.

For the record, I had nothing to do with Mr. Lee's untimely death soon after he made these and similarly styled slacks in black and navy. I would never dream of killing an excellent tailor, not even to keep a secret that could endanger my life.

However, in the interest of full disclosure, it was not by chance that I ran into the young greeter at Cameo. I had, in fact, overheard him mentioning to another greeter his plans for that evening and managed to find myself there as well. In truth, none of the intelligence I gleaned from him was of particular use, but he was shallowly charming, very fit, extremely pliable, and left the hotel room I arranged for us long before I stopped feigning sleep and rose to order breakfast.

So, not a total loss.

Chizu, lady of a thousand storks, watched as I approached her worktable. A rectangular slab of redwood, polished and smoothed by the oils in her hands. She knelt before it on the floor, one thin cushion under her knees, another between her narrow buttocks and the heels of her tiny feet.

She didn't look up.

"Is it always something dead or mutilated that amuses you?"

I stopped gliding, rose on my toes, lowered myself to my heels.

"No. Rarely. If ever. It was, I assure you, a rueful smile."

She made a slight hum and turned her attention to the gutted 1928 Rem-Blick in front of her, dabbing gun cleaner along the armature of one of the thirty keys of the vaguely insectoid typewheel typewriter.

"I need you to find something for me."

I allowed my gaze to elevate, letting it hopscotch over the dozens of cubbyholes that made up the long back wall of her office. The cubbies were filled with typewriters from every era, up until word processing software had dealt the machine its deathblow. Well, not quite, as evidenced by a Chinese Generation 3000, manufactured in 2005, displayed in an upper cubby. And truly, as things deteriorated, the manual typewriter was poised to make a comeback. But though all of these, from a wood-cased, gold paint–detailed 1873 Sholes & Glidden, to a marvelously streamlined East German Groma Kolibri, and up to the comical 1980s styling of the Generation 3000, were fully functioning, none were destined to endure greater use than the occasional gentle cleaning such as the Rem-Blick currently was undergoing. In an endless rotation she tended to the machines, oiling moving parts, replacing dry ribbons, carefully blowing away dust with a can of compressed air, and returning each to its lighted cubby on the display wall until its time came again.

The remaining walls were glass, two vast angles of it, honing her workplace to a point, aimed decisively west, at the ocean, and beyond to her native island home.

I stood with my back to that place whence she had been spawned, considered typewriters. And her request.

"Finding things is not generally a task for which I am best employed."

She picked up a small square of gauze.

"But one you are capable of executing."

"Capable, yes. But."

She ran the square of gauze along the underside of the V key, removing excess oil that had run there.

"But you would rather not?"

I twiddled my fingers, an invisible gesture of relative indifference.

"I'll admit that as I get older I am not particularly interested in work that is less than challenging. Recovering lost or stolen property does not tend to offer many opportunities for new experiences."

She dropped the soiled gauze in a steel tray that would more traditionally have been used for bloody surgical instruments.

"You will be paid at your accustomed rate."

I reserved comment, never having conceived the prospect of working for less than my accustomed rate. I had long passed the point where working for scale, no matter how much I loved the project, was a serious consideration.

I returned my gaze to the typewriters.

"There is something I've been wanting myself."

She looked up from her work.

"Yes?"

I nodded eastward.

"An artwork. Or, more accurately, a fragment of an artwork."

She set her swab aside, and white-gloved fingers indicated I should elaborate.

I closed my eyes.

"In September of 2007, at the Seventh Regiment Armory in New York City, a dozen professional motorcycle riders, led by Wink 1100, skidded about on a 72-by-128-foot plane of black-painted plywood. As they rode, bright orange paint layered under the black was revealed in fishtails and streaks."

I drew my toe across the glossy floor in a long arc.

"The work, in toto, was the creation of Aaron Young, who later supervised Mr. 1100 as he rode solo and embellished the piece with various flourishes, including a somewhat legible 'A.Y. '07' as signature."

I made a squiggle with my toe.

"Upon completion, the massive work was to have been cut into pieces of sizes varying from quite small bits suitable for wall hanging to billboard panels. There was, however, a fire that destroyed the vast majority of the piece's surface area, leaving just a few corners and edges to be recovered. Instantly recognized as being eminently collectible, these were snapped up by an assortment of real estate barons, investment bankers, rock stars, and third-generation old-money heirs. The most coveted sections being, no shock, those singed by the fire."

I opened my eyes.

"One of these sections has become available."

She pulled the customized four-finger glove from her left hand. The fifth finger on all her left gloves had been rendered superfluous at a time in the distant past when she had chosen to make a point of some kind by cutting off the pinkie on that hand.

She set the glove aside.

"It sounds hideous."

I nodded.

"Most definitely. In every possible way."

She pulled off her other glove, this one traditionally fingered.

"And the price is beyond you?"

I shook my head.

"Not at all. Which is not to suggest that it is in any way inexpensive. But no, it is not the work itself I need from you."

I turned and looked south, where we once could have expected to see, on an especially clear night, smoothly circling dots of light, tranquilized gnats, dense air traffic over LAX.

"I operate quite well on a local level, but secure cross-country shipping has become a chancy operation at best, and toxically expensive."

I faced her again.

"I am more than capable of bearing all the expenses, but having done so, I don't care to trust anything but the most reliable of transportation services."

Her left thumb folded across her palm and rubbed the nubbin of scar where her finger once was. A gesture that gave every appearance of unconsciousness, yet one I was certain originally had been adopted to unnerve. But in the realms of power and influence where she now moved, I doubted that very many were disconcerted by the prospect of self-mutilation. I imagined that the calculated detachment that informed the movement had been employed so long that it had evolved now to possess the spontaneity to which it had once only aspired.

An observation that might have gotten me killed had I given it voice. Chizu did not care to have her psychology plumbed. It implied the plumber's interest in the whys and wherefores of her dealings. An interest that could never be considered healthy. For the interested party.

She stopped rubbing the scar.

"You would like access to my infrastructure."

If I had been free to, I would have raised a hand in denial.

"I wish to place a shipping order. And to ask that you personally see that the order is carried out."

She rose, a grace that suggested a thread running from the ceiling to the very top of her head, pulling her gently to her bare feet.

"To have shipped a hideous painting?"

I faced the windows again, looking north this time, the inexhaustible glow of the wildfires above the rim of the Santa Monicas as evening fell.

"It's meant to be part of my apocalypse collection."

She came around the worktable, her hedgehog haircut no higher than my shoulder.

"In the face of this view, I see no need for such a collection."

I shrugged, helpless in the grip of one of my obsessions.

"I can't help but think that the creation of this piece was an undeniable sign that the end was looming. Even if it wasn't regarded."

She stood at the window, confronting her reflection.

"Does it have a name, this harbinger?"

I smiled at her reflection.

" 'Greeting Card.' "

Her lips twitched and drew into a smile that she allowed.

"Yes. I see the appeal."

I joined her at the window.

"I thought you might."

I looked down at her profile, admiring the smoothness of her complexion, how it showed in youthful contrast to her gray hair, telling the story of a long impassive life, the dearth of wrinkles speaking of displeasures concealed, laughter abated, furrowed brows smoothed, pursed lips straightened.

To eke a smile from that visage was a great pleasure.

So I bowed my head in thanks.

"And for you, Lady Chizu, what do you need found?"

The smile left, and she looked up at me.

"What is your opinion of these anachronisms?"

She glanced back at the wall of obsolete machines.

"My collection."

A thick wad of purple scar tissue behind my ear throbbed. There was shrapnel still under there, decades old, that sometimes reminded me of its presence when odd atmospheric changes were nigh.

I pursed my lips.

"Some are quite beautiful. Others not. I admire its completeness. The fact that no machine seems weighted with more value than any other. The fact that they are clearly organized with purpose. Whatever the guiding principle may be, it is not readily visible. Not age, country of manufacture, color, design specifications, size, condition. All these qualities are distributed randomly, but not necessarily evenly. There is undeniable balance. And order. I am not drawn to these things, but I understand the need for such a collection. And I admire it."

She looked out at the night.

"The typewriters around which the others are arranged, the singularities that define the collection, are those upon which suicide notes were written. And not another word, after."

I looked again at the devices and saw, in this new light, a subtle emphasis put on certain of them, a seeming willful distancing on the part of the surrounding machines, as if even the inanimate wished to avoid proximity to tragedy and madness.

"Ah."

I nodded.

"Yes."

I turned to her.

"I see."

And bowed my head again, in appreciation of her trust, sharing this detail with me.

Her mutilated hand lifted slightly from her side, dismissing my tribute.

"The provenance of these particular typewriters is unquestionable. Must be so. But they do not, of late, draw me as they have in the past. They seem dulled. And I wonder. An appetite such as I have had for these things."

A muscle in her forearm pulsed several times, causing the heart to beat beneath the dragon's breast.

"What will possibly fill it?"

She looked at me; eyes nearly black showed the same rim of fire as the mountains.

"A portable hard drive. It contains property of mine. It must be returned to me. And no memory of it remain."

I bowed a final time, accepting the contract.

Noticing as I did so, a tension revealed in the sternocleidomastoid and trapezius muscles of her neck, betraying an intense effort. An effort, I had no doubt, that was preventing an opposing tension, one that would produce the unmistakable stiff-neck posture that was the first outward sign of sleeplessness.

I turned away, not wishing to betray my discovery. And thus I betrayed to myself my own doubt that I could employ the blade concealed upon my person before she realized I had discerned her new weakness and let loose the dragon her tattoo proclaimed was just beneath her skin, waiting, not patiently.

5

7/9/10

CAPTAIN BARTOLOME HAD me arrested again. Old-timers named
Hounds and Kleiner. They took Ecstasy (30 tablets of Belgian Blue),
Demerol (15 commercial caps) and Valium (20 commercial) from my
stash and replaced them with what appeared to be no more than an
ounce of poor quality Mexican marijuana. Captain says the busts are still
the safest way for us to talk face-to-face. I say the arrest record tells too
much to anyone who takes a look. I keep getting picked up and kicked
loose. Doesn't matter that the booking is always at a different precinct
with different cops. Anyone who makes an effort looking in the file will
put it together. Either I'm a snitch or I'm undercover. Either way I'll be
against the wall. Bartolome says not to worry. He says no one but other
cops see the jacket. I say that's what I'm worried about. Hounds and
Kleiner. What would it take to buy those two? Or maybe not. Just
because they're pre-Rampart, that doesn't make them dirty. Or not any
dirtier than any narcs cherry-picking from a dealer's stash. But if not
them, then some other cop. Some other cop could be paid off to look in
my jacket. Bartolome says it won't happen. He says he won't push it too
far. I say it's already too far. Too long. I've been doing this too long.
Sitting and talking with him, I worried as much about the customers
blowing up my phone as I did about letting Rose know I was okay.
Bartolome says that dealers always make their customers wait. He says

it's like "part of their credo." But he's not out there. The people he wants me dealing to are not used to waiting. That was supposed to be the whole point of me doing this. He says my client list is getting too big, anyway. He says there is no point in keeping them for more than a few weeks. He says we're not trying to bust users, we're trying to find Dreamer. "If they don't connect to Dreamer, stop taking their texts." But I need the good referrals to get the new customers.

And some of them, they need what I get for them.

Srivar Dhar left five messages. He's in final stages, the suffering, and only Shabu keeps him from falling into waking REM states. Every time he hits a REM cycle, he hallucinates the Kargil War. He was an officer in the frontal assaults on Pakistani positions that were inaccessible to Bofors howitzers and airpower. Uphill at eighteen thousand feet, near zero Fahrenheit, in darkness. His house is built on a slope. In REMs he charges the slope, falls on his stomach, and starts to crawl, shivering and crying. He says he can feel the cold. Smoking Shabu keeps him fully awake. He's more aware of his body, the pain, but he says it's better than going back to Kargil.

Bartolome wants me to dump him.

I told him that Srivar introduced me to a whole community of western-educated wealthy Kashmiris. The kind who have connections to bootleg South Asian Dreamer. Dumping him before he dies would alienate all of them. He didn't say anything. But he didn't insist on getting rid of Srivar. Other than maybe a few bottles worth of loose pills, the bootlegs are the only Dreamer we've seen dealt in quantity. Busts of scale, the only kind he's interested in. Maybe the little ones are the only ones we'll get. Maybe the Dreamer distribution chain is just that tight. Maybe no one is dirty enough to try and steal from that supply. No one greedy enough to risk it. I said something like that to Bartolome once. He didn't laugh out loud, but only because he stopped himself. He says, "There's always someone dirty and greedy enough when there's that kind of money to be made. If they aren't dirty and greedy to start with, the money will make them that way." He can't imagine there aren't busts to be had. Big Dreamer busts. I hope he's wrong. But he's probably right. So I have to keep looking.

Something weird when I told him about the murders at the gold farm. He did that thing where he stares at me and knocks on the tabletop while he stares at me. I'm still not sure if it's an intimidation thing or if he's knocking on the table intead of my head. It's completely unlike anything my father would have done but carries some of the same exasperation. My father would have become utterly still. I'd have had to check his pulse to know he was alive. Then he would have asked something like, "Tell me, Parker, do you think that is wise?"

"I've submitted a Personal Qualifications Essay and begun prepping for the LAPD Academy tests."

Followed by the long stillness.

"Tell me, Parker, do you think that is wise?"

Anyway, when Captain Bartolome does the knocking thing, I get the same kind of feeling that I used to get when my father asked that question. A feeling like I want to either explain myself fully so that he'll understand, or knock him down and kick his teeth in. But Bartolome didn't ask if I thought something was "wise," he asked, "What the hell were you doing at the gold farm?"

He didn't want me there. Told me a couple weeks back to cut them off my client list.

Said they weren't "upscale" enough to connect to Dreamer. I'd been trying to explain to him that they were not only plenty upscale but that they were natural connectors for all social levels.

I didn't get it at first. At first Beenie was just a customer when I was building my cover dealing medical marijuana, but he was the one who got me to see the potential, and then he got me into the farms.

People don't leave home. Gas is too expensive to go anywhere you don't have to go. And people are getting more and more afraid to go outside, anyway. The servers that support most of the Internet have backup power for emergencies. Even when local Internet service is out or when you lose power, the Internet itself is still there. And so are the games. And these people, they're using the game environments not just for the usual adventures, they're using them socially. Families on opposite coasts can't afford to fly or drive to see one another, and who knows what the phone service might be like, but an online virtual world like Chasm Tide is there. And the more time people spend in-world, the more committed they are. The demand for in-world artifacts, gold, highly advanced characters, is huge. The real-market value on virtual money, possessions, and people keeps going up as the stock market continues to flounder. Now people are trading in Chasm Tide gold futures. Farmers who spend their time hacking up orcs and zombies and collecting their treasure until they have enough to push it onto the market are building almost equal value in real-world currency. Most of it in dollars. Euro and yuan are weaker against the dollar than Chasm gold is at this point.

Where you're from or what you're worth doesn't matter in Chasm. There's no class distinction in-world. The level 100 Eldritch Knight is the clerk at your local bodega. The level 2 Stone Druid is your boss. And they have a venue for interaction that wouldn't be there otherwise.

And they all come to gold farmers like Hydo and his guys for what they need.

And sleepless play. More than anyone else, sleepless play. Twenty-four hours a day they can go in-world and not be sick. Total insomnia becomes a virtue.

Rose plays. She always liked certain aspects of gaming. The parts that connected with her work. Like the graphics, the intricacies of world building. Her first real hit, the video she did for Gun Music, was all about the band falling into a game. But now she really plays. She says it feels like she's getting something done. When she can't focus enough to work. Which is pretty much all the time now.

Chasm Tide.

The ideal place to find connections to Dreamer.

But Captain Bartolome sat there and knocked on the tabletop and asked me, "What the hell were you doing at the gold farm?"

He told me to stay off it. Said, "Murder isn't your beat."

I nodded.

And I didn't tell him that Beenie had said Hydo Chang might know the guy.

If I'd had some sleep, I think I would have told him. With a clear head, I would have done what I always do, given a full and complete report. But I'm tired. I can sleep, but I'm not getting any sleep.

Is that ironic? I think it is. I mean, I know it is. I think. Rose could
tell me.

Rose.

After my paperwork was processed, Captain Bartolome cuffed me and
took me to his unmarked. Dawn again. They had me all night.

He drove me back across the checkpoint. A column of Guard vehicles
was forming up on the west side, getting ready to do a show-of-force
patrol. Part of the response to the suicide bombing. We drove past the
tanks and Humvees, a contingent of Thousand Storks, and neither of us
said anything. When we were past all of them, he pulled over and he
uncuffed me and drove me to my car.

It was still there. That was no surprise. No one steals cars anymore. But
no one had drained the tank. Bartolome waited while I got in, made sure
it started up, then stuck his head out his open window and told me
again, "It's not your beat. Stay off it."

I should have told him about the hard drive then. But he doesn't want to
follow the investigation where it wants to go. He only wants to follow it
toward those "busts of scale." I don't know if that's where the gold farm
murders lead. And it doesn't matter.

Yes, Dreamer is my beat, but Hydo and his guys were murdered on my
beat. And I don't have to explain why that's the way it is to Bartolome.
Or to anyone else. It just is.

I called Rose. She answered after half a ring. I told her I was fine. I told
her I'd been caught in traffic all night, that a blackout had taken down
the cell towers where I was and I couldn't call. She said she'd waited up
all night. And laughed at her joke. The way she laughs when she knows
she's the only one who thinks it's funny. I asked about the baby, but I
didn't need to. I could hear her crying in the background. Rose said
she'd just started, that she'd been quiet for hours. That she'd been
"sleeping like an angel."

That's how I knew she was lying. Rose never says things like "sleeping
like an angel." Rose says things like "She was out like a drunken sailor on
shore leave after fucking all night at the whorehouse." But she hasn't said
anything like that in forever. Not since the last time we were sure the
baby slept.

I told her I loved her and that I'd be home in a couple hours.
And then I drove to Srivar Dhar's and took him one of the Shabu
dragons in my stash. To keep him from going back to Kargil. A worse
place than this.

■   ■   ▮

PARK AND HIS family lived in a subprime short sale in Culver City. As
far as Park was concerned, there was initially little else to say about it. He
felt the taint of others' misfortune whenever he pulled into the driveway
next to the unwatered brown lawn that matched all the lawns on the
street.

He'd resisted buying, but Rose had been pregnant, and had wanted a
house, and had fallen in love with the place on first sight. Once he saw
Rose, with a swollen belly, smiling as she stood at a kitchen window and
looked out at a yard still canopied in trees, there was nothing left to do but
engage in some dispirited haggling with the seller. Both of them seeming
in a hurry to give in to the other's demands.

Now there was no separating the place from himself. The house where
his daughter was born, in their bed, on a covering of secondhand hospital
sheets. The house where his wife's illness first manifested, where she
slowly began to erode, losing layers of herself, being stripped slowly in
front of him to thin strata of fear, anger, and want.

Standing at the back of the car, he watched as two boys from up the
street took their skateboards over a ramp they'd made from bricks and a
sheet of plywood. Coming off the lip of the ramp, flipping the boards with
their feet, landing on hands and knees as often as on wheels. One of them
caught him watching and waved. Park waved back, then took his gun, his
father's watch, the travel drive, and his drugs from the car and went inside, where he could hear the baby howling.

The baby was on her back in the middle of the living room floor,
sprawled on a play mat, limbs flailing at the dangling ornaments and
chimes above her. Park let the screen door swing shut. The cooler morning air from the Pacific had already baked away, and the thin foreshadow

of a Santa Ana was snaking through the open windows and doors, shifting dust from corner to corner of the hardwood floors.

Park knelt next to the baby, called her name, cooed, and caught her eye. Just a few weeks before, her face would have opened into a wide smile at the sight of him, but that was when she was still sleeping, before the crying started. He called Rose's name, waited, called her again.

He knew it meant nothing, the lack of a response, but still he went through the house with dread.

And found her in the detached garage that they had converted into an office, seated at her workstation, eyes darting back and forth across three linked wide-screen monitors that showed the same looping frames from an old black-and-white cartoon, skeletons dancing on loose bones in a graveyard.

At first he thought she was lost in Chasm Tide again, but then he registered the two-dimensional craft of hand-drawn animation.

"Rose."

At the sound of her name she tilted her face slightly upward, eyes still on the screens.

"Hey, babe. Which one?"

Park came nearer.

"Which one?"

A finger lifted from a wireless mouse.

"Which one do you like better? I've been on this all fucking day, trying to get a loop that times at exactly three fucking seconds to run during that old school scratch Edison's Elephant has in the chorus of their new track. See, the song they're scratching is off a Putney Dandridge seventy-eight called 'The Skeleton in the Closet,' and I thought it'd be cool to use this clip from a Disney Silly Symphony. 'The Skeleton Dance,' yeah? No one will have a fucking clue what they're scratching; it will be like a subliminal clue. But there's no three seconds from the original that works as is. I've been clipping frames but still trying to keep that great cell animation fluidity. So these are the three best I've got. And I've been staring at them so fucking long, I don't know which one is best for the video. And where's my fucking kiss?"

Park bent and kissed her. Both their lips dry and cracked.

She pulled away.

"What the fuck, Park?"

She was staring at the gun he still had cradled in his hand.

"You know I don't want that fucking thing in the apartment. Leave it at the goddamn station, will you."

Park clipped the holstered weapon to his belt at the small of his back, out of sight.

"Rose."

She was staring at the screens again.

"Yeah, what? I'm trying to work, babe."

"The baby's crying."

"What?"

"The baby."

Her finger clicked the mouse, one of the screens froze, she moved a green slide at the bottom of the screen a fraction of a millimeter to the left and released the button, and the skeletons danced for her again.

She looked up at him.

"What the fuck are you talking about?"

Park touched the top of her hair, where they gray was coming in along the center part.

"The baby, Rose; she's crying. She's alone in the house, and she's crying."

When she changed, it was not so much like a veil was lifted but more like a briefly surfaced diver, perilously short on oxygen, was dragged below again after a moment's respite.

Park watched the memory of his wife submerge and her present self come bobbing to the surface.

"The baby. Christ. Fuck. How long? Fuck, Park, how long were you going to let me?"

She was out of her ergonomic editor's chair, leaving it spinning as she went to the door.

"Was she crying when you got home? I mean, is there a reason you didn't just pick her up, for fuck sake?"

"I have my gun."

She stopped at the door.

"Of course you do, I mean, of course you can't pick up your crying daughter because you have your gun in your hands."

"I don't like leaving it anywhere but in the safe. And I don't like holding her when I have it on me."

She turned.

"Then get fucking rid of it. Get rid of the fucking gun and the fucking job that goes with it and come home and be with your daughter before the fucking world blows the fuck up and you don't have her any fucking more, you fucking asshole!"

Park waited, and watched realization come over her, and wished he could do something to keep it at bay, at least stoke her anger further if he could not salve the regrets that always followed it.

She banged her forehead with her fists.

"Shit, shit, babe. I'm. I don't fucking. You know I don't. I just."

She pressed the heels of her hands into her eyes.

"I'm so fucking tired."

He came to her, pulled her hands down.

"I know. It's okay. I love you. It doesn't matter."

"It does, it does. It, everything is so hard anyway and I. Fuck."

He shook his head.

"Rose. It doesn't matter. I'm fine. Really."

Her head was turning, pulled to the sound of their crying daughter drifting across the small yard.

"I just. If we could have a little time, the two of us."

He nodded.

"Sure. I'll try and get a night. I'll just do it, get a night. Francine can be here with the baby. We can go stay somewhere for a night."

She was drifting out the door.

"Yeah. That would be. I'm gonna go check on her. She. I love you, babe."

"I love you."

She slipped out, Park standing at the door of the office, listening as she entered the house.

"Hey, kiddo, hey, sweetheart, Mom's here. I know, I know, you're right, yep, I left you alone, I know. I'm sorry, Mom's sorry. My bad. But you know what? Here I am. Yep, that's me. Right here. And I love you. I love you. I love you. Come here, come here, I got you, baby, I got you."

Before leaving the office he glanced at the monitors, seeing no difference at all in the way the skeletons danced.

He crossed the dry yard, back into the house.

In the bedroom where once he and Rose had slept together, before sleep had been taken from her entirely, Park stepped inside the closet, took a key from his pocket, inserted it into the lock of the Patriot Handgunner on the shelf above the clothes bar, punched a sequence into the keypad, turned the key, and opened the safe. Inside, a sheaf of birth certificates, passports, a marriage license, and various financial documents that may or may not have had any remaining value, also a .45 Para Warthog PXT that served as backup for the Walther, ammunition and extra clips for both weapons, an ivory broach that had been his mother's, four plastic-wrapped rolls of troy ounce Krugerrands, a four-gig flash drive that stored all his reports on his current assignment, and, in assorted baggies, vials, and bottles, his retail stash.

The drugs he'd taken from the car were in a faded olive drab canvas engineer's field bag that Rose had bought for him at an army-navy store on Telegraph when he'd moved to Berkeley to live with her after his Ph.D. was completed. He'd always complained about the number of pockets available in the average messenger bag or backpack, not nearly enough to organize his pens, pencils, student papers, grade books, cellphone, charger, laptop, extra battery, assorted disks, iPod, headphones, lunch, and miscellaneous. Now the pockets served to organize Ecstasy, ketamine, foxy methoxy, various shades of heroin, crack, crank, and powder cocaine, liquid LSD, squares of dark chocolate hash, gummy buds of medical marijuana, Dexedrine, BZP, Adderall, Ritalin, and two remaining Shabu dragons, carefully wrapped in origami-like complexities of tissue.

He needed to catalogue the stock. It had been more than two full twenty-four-hour cycles, nearly three, since he'd last done so. Much of what he'd sold and acquired was in his notes, and just as he'd been able to in college and at the academy, he relied on his exceptional memory and recall for details that he didn't have a chance to write down or record. But that memory was beginning to fragment.

No, not beginning to; it was well along in the process.

He needed to keep the record straight. When it came time to make arrests, issue indictments, call witnesses, do justice, he needed a clear record.

Names, dates, amounts. Crimes committed.

Captain Bartolome might not be concerned about anything but Dreamer, but Park didn't know how to approach his work with tunnel vision.

He needed to make a record. But he was too tired.

And the window of opportunity for sleep had swung past, as if he were fixed to a single point on the earth, waiting for the perfect alignment with the heavens that would allow him to ascend into orbit and, having missed that opening, was now forced to wait until it rotated back again.

He slid the engineer's bag onto the bottom shelf of the safe. Popped the clip from the Walther and placed it and the gun next to the Warthog. Snagged the flash drive by its lanyard and closed and locked the safe.

Gun hidden. From anyone who might use it. In desperation.

He buried that thought. There were ample options in the house if Rose ever decided she'd had enough. Locking away the guns eliminated only two of them.

Anyway, that was not the best way to protect her. Or the baby. The best way to protect them was to do what he was doing. That buried world, hidden, frozen beneath the madness outside, he had to dig, find it, and hack at the ice until it was free.

So he walked past the living room where Rose was feeding the baby from a bottle, her own milk having dried up after the first few days of sleeplessness, and did not stop, as he used to, to marvel at them. At the unlikelihood of them. Two people, entirely his, to love.

Back in the office, he switched off his wife's monitors, hiding the skeletons, though he knew they continued to dance invisibly; touched the power button on his own Gateway UC laptop, took the biohazard-stickered travel drive from his cargo pocket, and plugged in the USB cable.

And watched as Hydo's world appeared on his desktop.

A sickly luminous green mist spreading from the bottom of the screen, erasing Park's familiar wallpaper collage of baby pics, scattered with icons, that Rose had put together for him, leaving, as it crept upward, a hyper-real boneyard of rust.

An auto wrecker, somewhere in the Inland Empire, rendered by Hydo as a high dynamic range photograph. Digitally composited from various light exposures of the same image, HDR photography had been Hydo Chang's only passion beyond gaming, drugs, money, and pussy. What he'd referred to as his *higher calling.*

The wrecking yard on Park's screen, centered on twin rows of flattened cars stacked ten high under a sky tortured by streaks of fast-running cloud and the violent umbers of a doomsday southern California sunset, was photography as Van Gogh might have dreamed it. Thick lashings of color, layered so deep and in such relief, that it seemed you would feel them in ridges and dimples if you ran your fingertips over the screen.

Park's eye caught on a freeway sign glimpsed over the high barbed wire fence around the yard. No information regarding the next exit ahead, but a list of HDR forums and photo pools. Park ran his finger across the Gateway's touchpad and watched the cursor flicker from arrow to pointing hand and back. Now tuned to the detail, he started to see wrinkled license plates, alphanumerics exchanged for some of the usual names: Google, eBay, Firefox, Pornocopeia, YouTube, Facebook, Trash. And some not so usual: modblog, tindersnakes, felonyfights, shineyknifecut, riotclitshave.

Not just extra storage, a place to preserve and protect sensitive and valuable information away from the gold farm's Internet-linked LAN, the travel drive was a clone of Hydo's own personal machine. A mirror of the dead man's desktop mythology.

Park maneuvered the cursor over the screen, watching it douse icons on peeling bumper stickers, grease-smudged handbills on the side of an office shack, rocks, an airplane, a decapitated street lamp. All of them stamped with either a domain or a file, revealing it as the morphing hand passed over. Until it crossed a blackened grate of scaling iron set into a cube of graffitied concrete. The graffiti themselves were surprisingly dead to the cursor's touch, but the grate prompted the transformation into a hand without revealing what was beyond.

Park double clicked. A box appeared, requesting a password.

He chicken-pecked the keys with his forefingers: XORLAR

And a plain file blinked open, one that might be found on any accountant's computer, filled with Excel spreadsheets.

Labeled each with a name. Last, first, middle initial.

He flipped his finger down on the thin black line along the right edge of the touchpad, watched the thumbnails roll up the screen and stop. Then blinked at something subliminal and slowly dragged his finger up the same line, thumbnails rolling down now, eyes scanning left to right, and lifted his finger: AFRONZO, PARSIFAL, K., JR.

In 2007 the chances of having fatal familial insomnia were one in thirty million. In early 2008 those odds tilted fractionally against the players.

Until that point, virtually all cases of FFI had been restricted to about forty family lines, most of them in Italy. And then, quite suddenly, that was not so. A disease that was thought to be contained exclusively in a bit of genetic code, an inherited protein mutation in which aspartic acid was replaced by asparagine-178 and methionine was present at amino acid 129, inexplicably jumped ship.

The initial, and quite reasonable, theory espoused when these oddball cases emerged was that the sufferers must be unlucky distant relations to one of the FFI families. The fact that the number of new cases utterly defied the odds and rendered this theory all but laughable was circumspectly ignored.

And then there were more.

More people, diverse and dispersed, came stumbling stiff-necked, sweating, squinting from pinprick pupils, into the light. So many, and so widely distributed, that FFI was discarded entirely as a possible suspect in this mystery, and the true culprit was nabbed red-handed.

Mad cow disease.

Or, as it is more prosaically known, bovine spongiform encephalopathy.

As enabled by the global expansion of American fast food franchises and the rise of the hamburger.

Already well known as a prion disease with similarities to FFI, BSE was clearly the guilty party. Granted, this was some new mutation of BSE, one almost as communicable as it had been long feared BSE might someday prove to be, but most definitely BSE-related.

And how comforting it was to know what was killing people by stealing their sleep. To have a name to put to the face of misery. To know that these mutated BSE prions, simple proteins that had folded into shapes so baleful and malicious that they spread their geometry to any healthy proteins they came into proximity with, were caused by eating Quarter Pounders.

The fact that several of the infected were avowed vegetarians and vegans seemed to be no impediment to this theory, and the air soon smelled like barbeque. Hairy, shitty barbeque.

PETA and the SPCA lodged protests with the appropriate authorities, but public sentiment was against them. Which is not to say they were without allies. The team-up between animal rights activists and the Cattleman's Beef Board was one of the more amusing juxtapositions that heralded the rapid tilt of the world into a landscape that was less Dalí and more Hieronymus Bosch. As evidenced by the vision of vast herds of cattle being machine-gunned from above by helicopters, then coated in napalm and set ablaze. An inferno of beefs, not all of them dead. I summon for you the image of a wounded cow, running, in flames.

How shocking when it turned out that no BSE had been found in the dissected brains of the victims.

But the sheep and chicken ranchers made out well.

A fact that was pointed out by some of the more colorful cable commentators as they began to wax, inevitably, conspiratorial. Not that they were taken seriously. Not by anyone but the cattlemen, anyway. But truly, when the first indications of a deadly pandemic appear, how far does one have to search for a conspiracy?

It was clearly the work of The Terrorists.

Which ones was academic. A virtually simultaneous worldwide outbreak of a never before seen prion disease? Could there be any doubt of what we were dealing with? No, there could not; terrorists were at work. Pretty much all the countries of the world were in agreement and joined in pointing their fingers, or more lethal indicators, at one another.

And perhaps they were all right.

A new viral spongiform encephalopathy, exhibiting all the symptoms of fatal familial insomnia. Perhaps it *was* born in a lab. Twisted into existence by endless manipulations. Applied nucleation creating self-assembling systems, designed materials, refined, until a special grotesque was found, the shape of sleeplessness.

The shape of the sleeplessness prion, SLP, as it was dubbed, when isolated and revealed. That shape became a familiar thing. Part of the evening news graphic for every SLP-related story. Which meant pretty much every story. As what was not related to SLP?

An icon on protest signs. For. Against. Up. Down. Applied as needed. Defined as desired.

A T-shirt decal, endlessly riffed upon. Twisted and elongated for a Coca-Cola can. Blunted and squared for an MTV name check. Quadrupled in calligraphy over a burning *Hindenburg* in obtuse tribute to Led Zeppelin.

An endlessly repeated graffito. Black spray-over showing where the edges of a stencil had been. The absent portions of a negative image, applied to every surface. Recalling, somehow poignantly, the similarly sprayed aspect of Andre the Giant. Resonating, I guess, with the looming specter of his death, brought about, as it was, by a mysteriously mutating condition.

The tattooed insignia of an especially virulent strain of ultranationalistic fascism that seemed to manifest globally in much the same way as the disease itself. Spontaneously and without reason.

A spray-painted word on the front doors of homes, informing SL response teams that there was work to be done inside, decapitating the dead so that slides of their brains could be added to the CDC registry, the bodies added to the pyres.

The lone sigil of a thousand suicide notes.

A replacement, in the lexicon of Armageddon, for the number of the beast.

So much meaning and poetry in one squiggle of tissue.

Until, finally, it appeared in a slightly but significantly modified form: broken in two, pierced, in a brief corporate animation, by the chemical shape of DR33M3R.

One can imagine it, the shape of the SL prion, reflected in the eyes of the sales staff, breaking open like a piñata, dollar signs spilling out and heaping on the ground beneath it.

Those dollars were almost not scooped up. When word got out that there was a cure for SLP, an immunization, a salve that would bring the dead back to life, the labs where the drug was being perfected, the office where the packaging was being focus-grouped, the factories that were being geared for production, were all stormed.

Bloodshed was minimized. The military and police having had nearly a year of experience by then with quelling the madness of crowds. The traditional fire hoses, Tasers, tear gas, beanbag guns, and riot batons augmented with DARPA favorites such as microwave emitters, nausea-inducing lights, and focused-volume sound projectors that literally rattled metal fillings out of teeth.

The labs and offices and factories withstood the onslaught. And the story clarified. There was no cure, no panacea. Only relief. For the suffering millions upon millions, some relief.

A chance to dream. No more than that. A chemical plug to fit shorted sockets of the brain, a patch to allow the sleepless to sleep and to dream. An ease to suffering, but death just as assured at the end. With no other relief at hand, nothing short of a bullet, arms were outstretched, palms cupped. Dreams of sleep.

Dreams of Dreamer.

A chemical needle to knit the raveled sleeve of care.

Only, not enough.

Not enough Dreamer to go around. Not enough to bring rest to every mother, father, brother, sister, daughter, son, uncle, aunt, cousin, friend. A taste for sleep, a craving for it the world over, and only one curb for the general appetite.

So yes, the dollars rained down. A year or two earlier and it would have been raining Euro and yuan. But the initial SLP hysteria had put paid to the European Union and the might of that combined economy. Once Italy had been quarantined as the suspected ground zero of the disease, it had taken less than a month for all the countries of the union to seal their borders. Trade and travel faltered, xenophobia and nationalism flourished, and pounds, lira, francs, deutschmarks, and various other quaint relics were soon being dug out from beneath rocks in the gardens and put back into circulation. As for China, the world had seen the relative quality of the dragon's infrastructure when the earth shook in 2008. Tens of millions of sleepless leaving the workforce, burdening the health-care system, combined with the effective end of economic globalization and the contraction of markets clamoring for inexpensive goods, hexed the Chinese Miracle. The engine of their economy shuddered, lurched, and crashed to the ground, soon to be followed by the thrown-together factories of manufacturing cities like Shenzhen, as the inhabitants returned to the countryside, fleeing the plague, leaving the buildings and roads to deteriorate and begin crumbling in scant months. When the great droughts struck and wiped out the rice crops, it was an almost unnecessary grace note to the collapse.

The Yankee dollar ruled again.

The combined weight of the subprime fiasco, collapsed investment and commercial banking, credit freeze, and the GDP-sucking military adventures in Iraq, Afghanistan, and Iran had certainly wounded the beast, but once the United States declared de facto bankruptcy by refusing to pay its international creditors, it roared back to life.

The roads and bridges were crumbling, the waterways drying and clogging, the forests burning, the last-ditch conversion to national health was a Byzantine horror for the millions and millions forced into its clutches, power failed with great regularity, gasoline was nigh unto a luxury item, and one could not always be certain that the local supermarket would have received a toilet paper delivery this week, but the standard of living had been so vastly higher in the United States than in most of the rest of the world that there was still quite a distance left to fall before hitting the ground.

Global food shortages that might have struck deeper in the United States with the slaughter of the beefs were offset when the grain that had fed the bulk of the herds was redirected to human consumption. Corn, long bioengineered to pest and drought resistance, was the new American staple, as it was the world over; we just had more of it.

Free from the illusion that its debts could ever be paid, America was rich again. Yes, it did draw inward, a spine-backed turtle bristling with ICBMs, expeditionary forces establishing kill zones around the oil fields in Iraq, Venezuela, and Brazil, but still, in one way or another, it was the source of a dream.

Dreamer, a pillar of the new new economy.

There were mutterings.

It seemed odd that something so specific as DR33M3R should be so far along in development when the SL prion struck. After all, why should anyone have anticipated the need for an artificial hormone that could induce, in even the most damaged brain, one crippled by growths of amyloid plaques and peppered with star-shaped astrocytes, the long rolling delta waves that cradle bursts of REM sleep?

Congressional hearings were a must. Closed congressional hearings. And from what one heard, they seemed to answer all questions. Or, in any case, all questions that were asked. Whatever those may have been. In any case, when the doors opened, the patent holders on Dreamer came out smiling.

And why not? The world might have been ending, but Afronzo-New Day Pharm had what everyone wanted while the credits rolled. You could see it in the smile on Parsifal K. Afronzo Sr.'s face, as he read his prepared statement: A new day was clearly dawning.

And Park, in the month during which the chances of being infected with SLP had grown to one in ten, with the name Afronzo, Parsifal, K., Jr., on the screen of his computer, thought about what Beenie had said, that Hydo knew "the guy." He opened the file, a spreadsheet unfolding, cells filled with long number sets that struck a distant chord without imparting any meaning. But he listened to that chord and wondered if he heard a cracking in the ice around the world. Uncertain to say if it was the sound of a fracture announcing a thaw or another layer freezing over.

6

CASTING MY EYES TOWARD LAX FROM CENTURY TOWER NORTH
the evening before had been, as it turned out, prophetic. While a call from
the National Guard for close air support for an operation east of the I-5
required a redistribution of resources, still the dawn found me a Thousand Storks International airship, cruising at an altitude that would hope-
fully make us an outside chance for any Crenshaw denizens wishing to
amuse themselves by taking potshots as we crossed their airspace on approach. Not that the risk was excessive. Yes, a certain amount of military-
grade ordnance was making its way into the community, but only a
handful of Stingers or other surface-to-air missiles had been confirmed as
fired thus far. And only one target struck.

Changing our heading above South Vermont, I could see, over the
shoulder of the door gunner and her M60D, the rearmed compound of
the Crenshaw Christian Center, a sign painted across the parking lot pro-
claiming it to be still THE HOME OF THE FAITH DOME, despite the fact that
over half of said dome had been gutted by fire when the ATF task force
raided it.

Well, like hope, faith, I've been told, springs eternal. So why not its
dome?

Then we were dropping over the sprawling shantytown that had come
to occupy the long-term parking lots surrounding the airport. Refugees
fleeing insurgent-gang warfare in Inglewood.

Coming in low over the firetrap maze, the helicopter pilot's voice, French-accented, came across the headset radio.

"I flew a Bell for *Médecins sans Frontières* in 2007. In Darfur. Before the final genocide."

Leaving it to the gunner and myself to decipher why he felt the need to interject this bit of biography into the silence.

On the ground, my headset off and having taken a moment to ruffle my hair back into some kind of shape, I slipped on my vintage Dunhill 6011s and leaned into the cockpit.

"I'll be at least two hours."

The pilot continued flipping switches, completing his shutdown.

"On thirty minutes' notice, we have clearance to take off."

My eyebrows, I confess, rose behind the oversize lenses of my sunglasses.

"Thirty minutes?"

He jerked his thumb at the sky.

"Not as it was. The traffic. Thirty minutes' notice, you can fly."

He pointed in the direction of the U.S. Department of Defense–commandeered southern airstrip of LAX.

"Unless the fucking Army closes airspace. Then."

He turned his thumb to the ground.

"Then we all crawl."

"Even Thousand Storks?"

He shrugged.

"Thousand Storks carries the guns, but Pentagon pays the bills. All birds, when they say, we become dodo. Or."

He made his fingers like missiles, aimed at the sky.

"Shoot first. No warning."

He tilted his head east.

"That Air India flight, they say it gets hit by a gangbanger. Lucky shot with a Soviet-era Strela. Yes?"

I nodded.

He shook his head.

"Merde. Fucking bullshit."

He spit out the window toward the olive drab tents.

"Gung-ho. Trigger-happy. Yes?"

I nodded, fully understanding the trigger-happy gung-honess of American troops on high-stress posts.

"Yes."

He pointed at his watch.

"Thirty minutes' notice. Call on approach. I'll be ready to fly."

He made a button-pushing gesture with his thumb, and I handed him my Penck KDDI, a phone I carried when working because its metal finish recalled exactly the sheen of certain grades of weaponized steel. And thus helped to keep me focused. While looking quite stylish as well.

The pilot flipped it open, keyed in a number, and, after a moment, *"Le Boudin"* was sung by a full regiment in a utility pouch on the shoulder of his flak vest. He took his own Siemens M75 from the pouch, tapped a red hieroglyph, and returned it to its pouch, while offering me the Penck.

"You have my number. Sooner is best. After the human bomb, airspace has been down twice since then. If it shuts down again, I will call you. To make your own way home. If you wish. Or wait here. For how long, I cannot say."

My own way back, indeed.

Fifteen miles to Century City. Six miles to the relative safety to be found north of Venice Boulevard. I had little doubt of my ability to traverse these distances intact, but to do so in something close to utter assurance would require perhaps twenty-four hours. My compulsions would insist on frequent lay-lows. I could picture myself, rolled in mud and weeds, belly-crawling culverts and gutters, surveying intersections for long hours until convinced that the probabilities of a sniper waiting for me to break cover were suitably low enough to allow me to scamper across.

No, once I allowed myself to enter that mode of thought, that pattern of behaviors, I could operate only by entrenching myself there. Were I to strip to the most basic of my instincts for organization and harmony, those dealing with my own survival and the elimination of any obstacle that might interfere with that end, I would soon find that the carefully

arranged trinkets and fetishes deployed in defense about my civilized veneer had been blown asunder, scattered, both willy and nilly. Long to be
reassembled. If ever.

And some many people, who might otherwise not have to do so quite
as soon, would certainly die.

I smiled at the pilot.

"I will make haste."

Hefting my Tumi shoulder bag, walking away from the helicopter, the
Thousand Storks logo on its side gleaming pearlescent in the lights of an
inbound A380 from Hong Kong, I found myself oddly uplifted. Was it,
perhaps, the fact that the pilot had chosen to call his phone from mine, so
that we now had each other's numbers, that lightened my mood? After all,
he could quite as easily have *told* me his.

A French helicopter pilot. Dashing in the broken-nosed manner of a
Marseilles flic. One who flew humanitarian missions in Darfur. One who
was clearly very good at what he did. Lady Chizu's mercenaries being
nothing if not the best. And one who, judging by his ring tone, was a former legionnaire. The imagination could be excused if it ran a bit wild with
all of that.

A black Acura with the Thousand Storks logo discreetly stickered in the
lower right corner of the rear window was waiting nearby, keys in the ignition. I swung the door open and tossed my bag onto the passenger seat,
whistling to myself, *"Le Marseillaise,"* putting myself in mind of libera-
tion, before going to recover Lady Chizu's desire.

7/9/10

ROSE DOESN'T WANT me to go. When I came back into the house she
was in the nursery with the baby. The baby was in the crib with her sleep
machine making wave noises. She wasn't asleep, but she wasn't crying.
Her eyes looked glazed, like she wasn't seeing anything. She made little
noises, like someone talking in her sleep. Rose says this is how she sleeps
now, the baby. She says it's not that the baby has stopped sleeping, it's
that she sleeps with her eyes open now. She says the baby isn't sick. The
baby is colicky so she cries all the time and the crying exhausts her and

she falls asleep with her eyes open. She says this is the way the baby is responding to all the stress in the house.

Rose says the baby isn't sick.

But she won't let me have her tested for the SL prion.

She says the risks of the test are too high. Besides, she says, the baby isn't sick.

I watched her eyes in the crib. But I can't tell if she's sleeping. She doesn't look like she's sleeping. She looks like Rose when Rose loses herself in a REM state but is still awake.

She was sitting on the floor with her back against the wall, laptop propped on her legs, going at the Labyrinth again, taking Cipher Blue down a new route, marking the way with little glowing bulbs of water that floated inches above the floor.

When the baby was born, before Rose stopped sleeping and the baby started crying, when we knew about the diagnosis but it hadn't gotten bad, Rose used to fall asleep in the nursery all the time. The sleep machine would put her out faster than it did the baby. She'd curl on the floor, one hand reaching up, fingers through the slats of the crib, one of the baby's hands holding her pinkie.

Rose is so tiny, she could have curled up in the crib herself. I used to tease her about it. Told her that I had two babies.

Standing there and looking at them both, I wanted to scoop Rose off the floor and tuck them into the crib together, the baby nestled inside Rose's curl, like she was for months.

The grinding jaws of a steam-driven wyvern the color of pitted brass snapped through Blue's neck. A shadow Blue flew out of the dead body. A translucent digital soul. It would fly to the bottomless pit at the heart of the world, where the character would be reborn. And Rose could take her again to the Labyrinth for another attempt. Alone.

Rose closed the computer and her eyes.

She sighed and opened her eyes and saw me.

"How am I going to be able to look after you?" she asked.

I shook my head and told her I didn't know, and she kind of sighed like she always does when she thinks I'm not getting something.

"No, I mean, really, how am I gonna look the fuck after you?"

I told her she didn't have to look after me, that I was okay.

She was staring at the ceiling.

"You're such a, God, I hate the word, but you're such an innocent. I mean, how am I supposed to walk away from that?"

I didn't say anything, starting to understand.

She shook her head, wondering at something.

"I've known you how long? Already I can see it. You're destined to walk into traffic while reading a book. Or to get stabbed by a drunk asshole in a bar when you try to defend some tramp's honor. Or do something even stupider like join the Marines and go get killed for oil because you think it's the right thing to do."

I said her name. But she kept talking.

"And how am I supposed to keep you from doing something like that if you're up there and I'm down here? I mean, where did you come from?"

I said her name again and she looked at me this time and I said to her, "Rose Garden Hiller. It's 2010. We're married and we live in Culver City. You are a video editor and I am a police officer. We have a baby."

She blinked, and the swimmer dove away from me.

She said she knew all that. She said, "I was just remembering."

And she told me she didn't want me to leave until Francine came back. Until evening. And I told her I would stay. All day. That I would stay and help with the baby and she could relax. She closed her eyes and opened them. "Parker," she said, "I want to take the ferry into the city tonight and go to that free concert in the Panhandle."

I didn't tell her we didn't live in Berkeley anymore and that there were no more free concerts in Golden Gate Park. I just told her yes, and that it sounded like fun, and kissed her.

Beenie said Hydo knew "the guy." Afronzo Junior was a client.

I am a police officer. I must not jump to conclusions.

I must investigate.

THE WIKIPEDIA ENTRY for Parsifal K. Afronzo Junior was lengthy and showed signs of being constantly updated and edited by members of the Afronzo family publicity apparatus. The entry emphasized his charitable foundation, KidGames, his sponsorship of several professional video gamers, his fascination with massively multiplayer games, the drive and innovation that he had brought to that area, and the nightclub he'd opened within the borders of the Midnight Carnival, gutting and rebuilding the old Morrison Hotel to create a replica of his Chasm Tide castle, Denizone. Meanwhile, paragraphs regarding charges brought against him for identity theft, Internet fraud, online bullying, virtual pornography, and assorted civil complaints associated with hacking in vast legal gray areas of the Net were heavily flagged as needing proper source citation.

A brief sentence explained the evolution of his taken name. How his love of classic techno and rap had spawned the screen identity P-KAJR, behind which he'd anonymously become one of the most notorious trolls of the Web. Assuming the persona of a thirteen-year-old polymath, he'd become legendary for baiting the most even-tempered of bloggers into raging email flameouts, rife with misspellings, often concluding with impotent physical threats. Emails that would soon be posted on high-traffic sites devoted to the given blogger's area of expertise. When his identity was revealed, by his own design, he announced via podcast that he was assuming the phonetic of his screen identity as his legal name. Cager was born.

There was more, of course. Analysis of his disassociation from the family business dovetailed with standard biographical boilerplate about how the Afronzos had come through Ellis Island, name intact, found their way improbably to Carolina coal country, remained there, name still intact, becoming, after years of sweat and toil, a bootstrap American success story that blossomed when Cager's grandfather took out patents on a number of drills and saws that eventually proved especially useful in African gold mines. Cager's father, P.K.A. Senior, had taken the modest Afronzo family fortune and acquired a variety of assets related to the production of industrial solvents used to lubricate the hardware in those same mines before making a lateral move that involved purchasing a small chain of Eastern European vitamin and wellness stores, motivated primarily by the fact that they held the patent on an herbal sleep aid of tremendous popularity throughout the Balkan states that he, an insomniac himself, had found tremendously effective while traveling in that part of the world on a pleasure junket with Israeli government officials he was hoping would subsidize the construction of a new solvent plant in the industrial zone of northern Haifa. The deal was completed, but Afronzo International exports of drilling solvents to various Mediterranean oil-producing states were never as profitable as hoped. An unhappy fact that was offset when, after three years of bureaucracy in action, the herbal sleep remedy received FDA approval for over-the-counter sale in the United States, and almost immediately became the top-selling cure for insomnia.

It was the enormous profits from this windfall that allowed Afronzo to launch a hostile takeover attempt against the much larger New Day Pharmaceuticals, an attempt that was doomed from the outset but destined to cost NDP vast treasure, an inevitability that forced the NDP board into a merger, ceding control, and top billing, to the charismatic and populist Afronzo Senior. Affable and folksy, his soft Carolina country accent provided him with an impressive Americana aura, more than offsetting his difficult-to-pronounce name. A cult-of-personality business figure before the advent of SLP; Dreamer had put him on an equal media footing with Gates, Trump, Murdoch, and Redstone.

The last Wikiparagraph relating to Cager's family ended with a blue-tinted mention of Dreamer, linking to what was, at the time, the fourth longest Wikipedia entry, trailing Christianity, Islam, and, at the top, SL Prion.

The entry proper on Afronzo Junior went a bit further, mentioning a well documented public spat between father and son (link to a cellphone-quality YouTube video of the two men screaming obscenities at each other backstage of a humanitarian awards dinner at which Senior was the guest of honor), excerpting a magazine profile wherein Junior had opened up about the distance between the two ("It sucks not liking your dad. But sometimes people just don't like each other. Me and my dad, we don't like each other. I can live with that. It seems like it's most everybody else who has a problem with it."), and summing with the theory (again flagged as requiring a proper source and footnote) that Junior's personal wealth was, in fact, not his at all. That whatever resources that became his when he came of age had been rapidly sucked away by the massive multivenue club he'd had built, assorted legal defenses and settlements, and a whole-sale investment in funds that had been bulwarked all but entirely by shares in several Icelandic banks.

This snapshot of the wealthy scion of an international pharmaceuticals conglomerate was all Park had time to learn of the man. Looked up and printed in a small break during another day spent wrangling the baby and his wife. Immersing himself in the constantly replenishing swirl of tasks that engulfed a household with both a baby and someone fatally ill. Ex-hausted before he began the first load of laundry, not certain he could keep his feet through the day, he was repeatedly shocked to look up and see another hour had passed.

During that short break in the office, he looked at the pages he'd printed and thought about Dreamer and the bodies at the gold farm.

Captain Bartolome had told him to stay off it. Captain Bartolome had told him that murder wasn't his beat. For a code of behavior to mean anything, Park knew you had to adhere to it. By accepting the job of police officer, he had accepted the terms upon which that job had been offered. And he followed orders. To do otherwise was to betray a trust.

So he did not lie to himself as he opened his laptop, plugging the flash drive with his reports into a USB slot; he did not tell himself that what he was doing was excusable. Scrolling through months of his records until he found a notation and phone number he was looking for, he did not say to himself, *No, murder is not my beat, but Dreamer is. And I am investigating a possible Dreamer connection.* There was no need to lie to himself about what he was doing. He was ignoring orders and doing what he thought was best. So he placed a call, asked a few questions, bartered a deal, hung up, sent a text, and waited. When his phone chimed a moment later, he flicked to his inbox and read the reply to his message.

from bnie:
omfg so kool
when/where?

It was hours before Francine would arrive. He pictured the traffic at that time, estimated how long it would take to get to West Hollywood and make the swap, special k for opium, texted back.

midnight
denizone

1

LOOKING AT THE BODIES, IT WAS EASY ENOUGH TO SEE WHAT had happened. Someone who was familiar to the dead men had been admitted. He, and, this being a crime that involved multiple bodies, none of them wearing a wedding ring, the murderer was most assuredly a *he*, entered, carrying an easily concealable automatic weapon that fired standard NATO 5.56 × 45 ammunition. At least one of the cartridge casings on the floor showed the telltale scratches left when an already poor weapon is converted to full automatic. Forced to venture a guess, I'd have said he used one of Olympic Arms's nearly infinite variations on the AR-15. An LTF with the stock removed seemed about right.

Whatever easily procurable piece of mass-produced, consumer-grade ironmongery he had concealed upon his person, once inside he engaged in conversation. Had a soda. A Mountain Dew. His conversation was with a young Korean American who may have been a fan of the Black Panther comic book character or may simply have had a taste for very expensive designer T-shirts with superhero motifs. Regardless, the conversation between the two turned argumentative, sufficiently hostile that the other young, pasty Asian men in the room made a conscious effort to turn their backs and focus on their computer monitors. Which was the pose they were all essentially frozen in when the man who had entered so genially lost his shit and pulled his weapon from his backpack or messenger bag and sprayed the room. Putting several rounds in the Korean American's face while shooting the others in the back.

Or something similar.

In any case, they were all dead. Someone with a personal issue, and poor anger control, had done the deed. Murder is an acquaintance event; best always to assume the motive is personal. Or money. Or both. This looked, with very little effort invested, like a *both* scenario. Personal issue, involving money.

Oh, the humanity.

The only mystery I was concerned with was the absence of the travel drive that I was told would be sitting at a corner workstation. The most obvious scenario was that the same man who had executed his acquaintances had taken the drive. The fact that Lady Chizu wanted the object was as much indication of its value as one needed, but the fact that someone else might be willing to kill for it was fair evidence that the value was a *known* quantity. Something of a complication, but not at all outside the terms of my contract. Regardless, there was far too much valuable gear on hand for simple robbery to have been at the root of the evil deed. No, it appeared someone had come here with a clear purpose, to get the drive, had been denied possession of the drive, and had opened fire and taken the drive.

What I knew of the drive myself was slight:

It was wanted by Lady Chizu.

It was a Western Digital travel drive decorated with a red biohazard sticker.

It would be at the corner workstation by the ladder.

If, by some chance, it was not made available to me at my first request, I was to take it.

And I was to exact a mortal price from anyone who interfered with Lady Chizu's wishes on this matter.

Clearly I needed to find whoever had taken the drive, retrieve it, and do my client's bidding.

I began this process by climbing the ladder and poking my head in the cubbyhole it led to. I ignored the Benelli 12-gauge M4 that had been left there for the obvious purpose of being shoved through the mouse hole cut in the bottom of the three-inch-thick Plexiglas screen at the other end of the cubbyhole. I was already carrying what I considered a perfect balance of firearms and other lethal bits of steel, alloy, and ceramic upon my person. A tactical automatic shotgun would have thrown it all out of balance. Besides, the weapon wasn't nearly as compelling as the Mace four-channel DVR sitting next to it.

Surveillance technology had reached a point where it was rarely more difficult to master and operate than your average HDTV/digital cable box/Tivo/surround sound/universal remote setup. True, craning my neck to the side to get a clear view of the readout while I tapped various buttons wasn't terribly comfortable, but it still took me only a few moments to determine that the 500-gig hard drive had not been erased. Someone had thoughtfully left a spindle of disks on top of the recorder, so I slipped one inside the Mace's integral CD burner and set it to record the most recent two hours of activity. Assuming the motion-sensitive cameras outside had not been installed and calibrated by an idiot, they would not have been activated by the horde of rats in the alley, and one disk should provide me with two hours of high-quality time-lapse video, including the mass murder.

I took a few pictures of the room while the disk burned, used the forked tip of my Atwood Bug Out Blade to dig a spent round from the thick four-by-four leg of a homemade worktable, and was studying the blood spray on a Chasm Tide poster that covered half of the rear wall, when both the deadbolt and the knob on the outer door were blown out in rapid succession, leaving behind two neat, soup-can-size holes. I had just time enough to regret not closing the door of the inner security cage before the outer door was kicked open to allow three large men in khaki pants and black short sleeves to crouch and scuttle into the room, one sweeping the barrel of a Remington 870 across the space, two of them with their cheeks pressed tight against the stocks of their shouldered Tavor TAR-21s, proceeded by lasered red dots that skittered over the walls.

I immediately went slack-jawed, twisted my neck to an awkward angle, allowed a bit of drool to escape my mouth, and screamed: "Ratfuck! Ratfuck!"

This drew their attention, the laser dots racing to draw a bead on the middle of my chest. But every bit as professional as they appeared to be coming through the door, they didn't spasm and smear me over the wall. Instead, smoothly and without verbal communication, the two TARs took flanking positions as wide as the room would allow, pinning me in their theoretical cross fire and leaving a wide safe-angle down which the Remington could approach me. Which he did, after first switching on the halogen lamp slung under the barrel of his weapon. I felt certain, with the door now disabled, that his chambered round would be buckshot. It hardly mattered; at this range the compressed copper dust of a door-breaching cartridge would punch one of those soup can holes in the middle of my face.

So I continued to drool, adding a slight twitch.

"Ratfuck!"

The halogen swept me up and down, freezing on my stiffened neck.

"Sleepless."

A voice from one of the TARs.

"What is he doing here?"

The man with the Remington came closer.

"What are you doing here?"

I spun my eyes, clacked my teeth, let spittle fly from my lips.

"Ratfuuuuuuuuck!"

The circle of halogen lowered from my neck, angled to the side, away from my body.

"He's gone."

"Get him out of the way."

The twin dots arced away from me, out and up, clean and safe, firing lines staying clear of their partner.

The halogen cut rapidly up the wall.

"Sorry, old man."

The butt of his shotgun swung upward at the side of my head.

I lurched to the side, drooling a little more, the light synthetic stock missing me by an inch, putting its owner off balance, allowing time for a couple things to happen.

First, giving one of the TARs time to start to berate the Remington.

"Get your shit together . . ."

The second thing it allowed time for cut off whatever else might have been said, as I took advantage of my attacker's lack of balance and also took away his shotgun.

Of course there was more to it than that. He wasn't a child with a lollypop; I didn't simply pluck it from his hands. What I did was deliver a tightly coordinated series of blows, slapping the barrel of the shotgun to the side, kicking him in the stomach, chopping him in the throat, removing the shotgun from his limp hands, and using the base of the stock to crush his nose. This caused the halogen to race around the room while also putting the disarmed man and me in complicated proximity, the combination and suddenness of all this creating a fair amount of confusion for the two TARs.

Which is why their employer, whoever it may have been, might be expected to forgive them for not getting off a shot at me before I had emptied the remaining five rounds from the Remington 870 MCS, now in my hands, at their heads.

They were buckshot cartridges, double-aught, a bit of overkill in my book. I used two on one, three on the other, alternating between them until the weapon was empty. Then I dropped it, falling to the side, diving for cover under the worktable, drawing my Les Baer .45 Custom from the horizontal shoulder holster under my jacket and waiting there, patiently, holding aim on the doorway by the light of a computer monitor that had flared to life when a mouse had been jostled in the middle of the action incident.

I might have held that aim for an hour just to be certain there were only the three, but the man whose shotgun I had taken groaned, reminding me that I had best conclude my business.

I got out from under the worktable, checked the two dead bodies for ID, and found none. Nor any watches or jewelry, though one had a telltale band of white skin around his otherwise distinctly olive wrist, and the other a similar band around his left thumb, as well as piercings in both earlobes.

The third man groaned again. And then the Mace chimed. I went up the ladder and retrieved the newly burned CD and slipped it into my sport coat pocket. I hadn't yet inspected the material for stains or rips. I couldn't stand the thought that I might have damaged Mr. Lee's handi-work. His garments were, literally, irreplaceable. Putting that inspection off until later, I touched some buttons on the Mace, confirming twice that yes, I did want to erase all contents of the hard drive, and went back down the ladder.

There was now a considerable amount of confusing physical evidence in the room. And no time to tend to it efficiently.

For a moment this created an unpleasant frisson. The idea of leaving the room without bringing to it some order, without grooming it to tell a story that did not include me, was almost unbearable.

I touched my phone. I held it in one hand and the Les Baer with the matching finish in the other. I thought about a gardenia bush on my deck at home, how, three years ago, after a week of unprecedented rainfall, it had blossomed, flowering in utterly spontaneous perfection, no bloom out of place or proportion to the others, a jewel of nature.

My breathing continued to race.

The man on the floor groaned again.

I asked him, gasping, who he and his partners were, by whom em-ployed, and to what purpose. He groaned again, the tone of it telling me that he was not sensible enough to understand what I was asking.

I shot him. Once. Thought carefully. And shot him again. And my breathing began to even out. Not that killing the man brought any peace in and of itself. But the new symmetry in the room, the assortment and sprawl of all the dead bodies, was drawn into new balance by those two bullets, and I could move again.

Down to the end of the alley where I had parked the Acura between two Dumpsters and shoved some of the heaped garbage onto its roof, giv-ing it a cosmetic air of abandonment. From the passenger seat I retrieved my Tumi, drawing from it a shaped Octol charge. Intended to punch holes in armor plating while blasting molten alloy through the hole, it was a de-vice less than ideal for my purposes. But with a slight modification it would do. Taking the five-gallon gas can that the Thousand Storks motor pool always bungeed securely in the trunks of their vehicles, I went back to the gold farm and placed the charge at the mouth of the open inner door, with the can of gas just in front of it. Thus modified, the Octol would not create order in the room full of dead people, but it would make them all strangely equal to one another.

Driving away, I found an unlocked black Range Rover just before the street, facing out, ready for a speedy but never-to-be getaway. There was nothing of interest. Three black nylon athletic bags filled with the odds and ends of a tactical operation. Spare clips, black gaff tape, an assortment of plastic buckles and straps, a small tool kit, and various components for converting the TARs to 9 mm. That kind of thing.

I wasn't surprised by the lack of identifiers. Men like the professionals I'd killed couldn't be expected to leave their wallets behind in their car. Granted, yes, they could be expected to be suspiciously armed with weapons favored by the Israeli military and to wear the five-pocket, guyabera-style jackets favored by the Shabak secret service, but they were still very good at what they did. So I ignored the plates I knew would be dead ends, copied the VIN from the tag on the dash, for form's sake, dropped another Octol charge in the Range Rover, and drove away.

Just down the street I heard the whomp of the gasoline-modified charge going off, followed shortly by the sharper bang of the explosive in the SUV. The flames would reduce the gold farm and at least a few of the surrounding abandoned buildings to ash long before any emergency services could respond. Not that it was likely they would.

Back at LAX I realized that I had neglected to call the pilot in advance of my arrival. The thirty minutes needed before we could be cleared to take off had to be passed in some manner. As it turned out, he had no objection to my suggestion as to how we could spend the interval. And the door gunner was perceptive enough to take a hint and wander off to smoke a cigarette or three.

There was little enough time for conversation, but it turned out that he was indeed a legionnaire. A faded regimental tattoo on his shoulder giving evidence. He noticed my own age-spotted Special Forces tattoo and made a joke about soldiers and what really happens in foxholes, though neither of us laughed. The back of a helicopter is hardly conducive to romance, but it was far from the most uncomfortable place I've made love. And after the most pressing business was taken care of, there were still a few minutes left. So we held hands, his thumb returning again and again to rub a callus on the inside of my right index finger, just where it fits the trigger.

Soon after, we were airborne, headed north, the first step on my campaign to erase all evidence and record of the object I had been sent for now complete. There would, no doubt, be more to do once I looked at the security DVD and saw who it was who had come to call ahead of me.

Poor soul.

8

Working from a sheet of phone numbers Captain Bartolome had given him, he had become a regular customer with three delivery services that he found were consistently somewhat reliable and seemed to employ couriers who were a step above the typical stoner on a mountain bike who showed up two to three hours later than he said he would. Couriers who had cars and who looked more like USC film students than they did Venice Beach burnouts. Couriers who could hold a coherent conversation while a transaction was completed. Couriers who mostly talked about the job as a way to make fast cash to pay down a student loan or to finance a new laptop.

When Park had suggested to one of these couriers that he was looking for some part-time work before his wife had their first baby, the kid had scratched his belly under his Abercrombie & Fitch T-shirt and told him guys were always flaking out and that the service always needed new couriers. So the next time Park called, instead of leaving his code number and hanging up and waiting for a callback, he left a message.

"This is Park Haas, number six-two-three-nine. I talked to Rohan; he said you might be hiring. I'm interested."

Which did lead to a callback, but instead of being asked where he was and how long he would be there and being told how long it would take for a courier to arrive, he spent fifteen minutes talking with a young woman about reliability and time management and being asked if he'd gone to college and what his major had been and, finally, if he was a *police or other law enforcement officer.*

And Park lied. Which, as Captain Bartolome had promised, he'd already found himself getting better at. Though never without some twinge of regret, the voice of his father in the back of his mind: *Lying, Parker, is a great weakness in a man. I advise you to never allow it in yourself. Or you will become exposed.*

The danger of being exposed, physically or otherwise, having always been at the forefront of his father's considerations.

Following the man's example, Park had spent the majority of his life trying to restrict any such exposure. The elements of his existence had been few. Few possessions. Few relationships. A streamlined life, one best able to make passage without catching on any dangerous shoals. Beyond his parents, his sister, her rigid husband and two cold children, and an always reducing number of childhood friends, he had no emotional exposure of any measure when he left Philadelphia and headed west to study philosophy, acting upon a desire to better understand the nature of things, if not people.

Rose had changed that.

Slamming hard into his side, she had created an irreparable breach, a wound so deep and immediate that he'd nearly collapsed at the impact. Had almost fled, bleeding, to find some quiet place where he could either heal or die. But she hadn't let him. Instead, ungently, she had battered him, split him, spilled his life about, played among the bits, and convinced him that such a thing could be fun.

By the time Park was in a Starbucks on Melrose, watching through the window as a parade of sleepless and other night owls shopped the midnight hours away, listening as the young woman who belonged to the voice on the phone described exactly how he would pick up *product,* how he would be accountable for shortages, how much he would be paid per delivery, and asked him to show her his current driver's license, vehicle registration, and insurance, by that time Park was exposed on all fronts.

Made deeply vulnerable by the wound Rose had opened in him and the things he had come to understand that philosophy had never illuminated, Park was barely present in the coffee chain. Most of him back at the house, in the nursery, where his wife and child, still sharing a single body, were putting together a crib, while he took his first lesson in selling drugs.

Presentable, educated, white, behind the wheel of a decent car, and, most valuable of all in a dealer, both prompt and reliable, Park was very quickly specializing in deliveries to the service's top-end clients. Rather than being detailed to a specific geographic locale to maximize the number of deliveries he could make in one day, Park received a larger per-delivery commission and a fuel stipend and found himself often eyeballed by private security, buzzed through locked gates, ushered into exclusive clubs, ranging from what was left of Malibu, between the rising waters and sloughing hillsides, to Beverly Hills, Bel Air, Hancock Park, the Holly-wood Hills, certain blocks of West Hollywood, the Los Feliz homes of bright young reality TV stars, and the changing rooms of Rodeo Drive boutiques.

Then he became a buyer again. Making a move that his employers took for granted, he purchased three kilos of Canadian crippleweed. Agreeing not to pursue any of their clients, but not promising to turn down business that *came* to him, he left the service and began almost instantly to re-ceive texts from those clients.

As SLP spread, increasingly aggressive chemical responses were caught in its draft and pulled along. The not surprising desire shared by many to bubble-wrap their awareness and muffle any intrusions regarding what was happening in the world at large was compounded by the desire of many others to match the pace and awareness of the sleepless. The popu-lation was becoming rapidly segregated by personal taste: uppers, down-ers, or stridently clean.

With over thirty million sleepless in the United States, spanning all ages, economic classes, ethnicities, religions, or any other readily know-able demographic, the twenty-four-hour marketplace was in high gear. Needing not only to be staffed but fueled as well.

Staked to an evidence room nest egg of some of the rarer exotics, Park was able to enhance his already rock-solid reputation as a reliable source of the basics with equally glowing word of mouth as a finder of impossible things. A reputation that engendered, as it turned out, only one major problem: an unwillingness on the part of many of his clients to share his number.

No one wants to lose their good thing.

But no matter. Unable to do less than bring every ounce of his father's work ethic to bear on any effort, Park found that his market share grew.

Having spent most of his life around people with great deals of money, he knew more than he cared to about distractions such as box office receipts, celebrity infidelities, luxury cars, flux in the stock market, designer brands, real estate prices, workout routines, and the ever-increasing popularity of radical elective plastic surgery. He found, unexpectedly, that this chatter, the same kind that could be expected between retailers and customers everywhere, began to segue into the intimacies one would have expected to hear passing in a hair salon, or a doctor's exam room, or a therapist's office.

Observant and still, saying little, but that little always relevant and as likely to be an apt layman's reference to Descartes, Lao Tzu, Sontag, or Aquinas as it was to be taken from a recent episode of a given client's half-hour, single-camera sitcom, Park's customers found him to be a comforting presence. None suspecting that the keenness of his insights was largely based on the depth of his concentration, his desire to record everything that he saw and heard in his book of evidence.

So it was with the special aura of both a reliable source and a good listener that he had been invited to the party where Beenie had introduced him to Hydo. Where he'd had a conversation that led him to first suspect that the world's descent into madness was neither random nor the natural consequence of humanity's excesses, that there was a hand behind the wheel steering us into deepening misery. That someone, massive and unseen, was drawing profit from the piles of suffering dead. And that they must pay a price for their greed. If only he could find them.

7/9/10

ALMOST MIDNIGHT.

I was thinking about how Beenie told me about the Craigslist personals.
The new category that appeared in late '08. Sleepless-related.
Mostly about treatment.

> Has anyone tried? Someone told me. Is it true that? Twelve hour yoga to
> replace sleep. SLP acupuncture. SLP is mental not physical! SLP is an
> environmental allergy, stop using chemical, go organic!

Sales classifieds that I printed:

> Selling one king size bed—Hardly used. $100.00 or swap for a tank of
> gas.

> 4sale, thousands of comic books—These were my husbands. I'm not
> sure what they are worth, but we don't have room for them and I'm
> afraid they are a fire hazard and our area keeps losing services from
> the DWP and the fire department can't get pump trucks up our ac-
> cess road. I just want to get rid of them. Bring a truck and as much
> bottled water as you can carry and you can have them all.

> All my worldly possessions—The things I have spent a lifetime acquir-
> ing. Everything from my baby blanket to the house I paid off just last
> year. Fifty-two years worth of material objects. My letters and busi-
> ness papers. My 2007 BMW 6 series. My 56 inch plasma screen. My
> sectional. A collection of 12 numbered Hockney prints, framed. My
> Talor Made graphite clubs. My three Armani suits, 44 long jacket,
> 42/34 pants. My All-Clad pots and pans. My grandmother's wedding
> shoes. A really nice mountain bike that I never use. My letterman
> jacket, lettered in both football and track. My first tooth and a lock of
> my baby hair. A glass jar with a fistful of sand from a beach in France
> from my honeymoon. My divorce papers. A penny squashed flat after
> I put it on a train track. I have no family. I'm giving it all away. But only

to someone willing to move into my house and live here with these things and use them. These are my things. These are what I'm leaving. I want them to stay together. Call me and tell me why you should have my things.

Personals:

SLPM 4 SLPF—up late. LOL! Keep me company?

SLPM 4 ANYONE—I'm a virgin, you're experienced and gentle. Hold me.

SLP 4 ???—Alone in my apartment, the front door unlocked. I give you the address and tell you that I'll be in bed with my eyes closed and headphones on. I can't see you or hear you. How will you send me someplace better? Serious responders only, please. I don't have time to waste on anyone without the nerve. And, no, this is not a call for help.

SLP 4 DR33M3R—I'll do anything u want.

Thousands of listings.

I looked around. I tried to find out something that Rose and I hadn't already learned about SLP. I looked at a forum for family members of sleepless, but I could never post. Mostly I looked at the Dreamer listings. All the people looking to buy or trade for it. I placed a couple ads. The only responses I got that went further than one email were from obvious scammers:

I HAVE RECEIVED YOUR EMAIL AND WILL BE HAPPY TO ACCEPT YOUR OFFER!!! I AM TRAVELING ABROAD AND CANNOT MEET WITH YOU IN PERSON!!! SEND ME YOUR BANK ROUTING AND AC-COUNT NUMBERS AND I WILL ARRANGE A TRANSFER IN THE OF-FERED AMOUNT!!! A COURIER WILL DELIVER THE ITEMS!!!

People were often directed to Dreamer and SLP forums where they could get more information. Mostly identity theft scams. A few were legitimate but primarily concerned with counseling, online group therapy. Religious sites, preaching acceptance, conversion, hope, and, most of all, resistance to the temptation of suicide.

Rumors permeated almost all those sites. An insistence that Dreamer was out there, a large supply of it that other sleepless were tapping into. Captain Bartolome said it was "to be expected bullshit." Of course the sleepless were sharing rumors about a secret supply of Dreamer; what else would you expect? It would have been far stranger if there were no rumors. He said, "Look for the money." The money, he didn't need to say, would lead to busts of scale.

But there should be something. Sleepless spend so much time online, there should be something about black market Dreamer. CL is a natural place for dealers to look for customers. But I couldn't find anything.

At the party Hydo had said something about Dreamer that stuck in my head. Passing a bottle of Jack Daniels around a table, he'd said Dreamer was "on a special wavelength." He said part of that was literal. He was stoned, but it caught my attention, and I asked Beenie for an introduction. Hydo got more stoned, explained what he meant. Talking about how the RFID tags on the cases and bottles mean there are actual traceable radio signals that tell you where the Dreamer is. "The whole history of each bottle is in the air," is what he said. Which I already knew, but hadn't thought of that way. Not that it really helped.

Why isn't there an audible signal? A visible signal?

There's always a slang at work in drug deals. On CL people talk about 420 and going skiing and taking a vacation, when what they want is pot, cocaine, or LSD, but that was the kind of stuff you could get from an LAPD training pamphlet. I'd been able to pick up most of the cues I needed for my assignment by listening carefully and parsing what I heard. It was like philosophy. You don't glean anything useful with a surface reading of Nietzsche; you have to spend some time thinking about an idea like "God is dead" for it to be anything but a knee-jerk catchphrase.

But no trace of Dreamer slang or lingo can be picked up. Nothing that could hit the cops' radar and start them asking around the way they would if a new tag started showing up on top of old graffiti.

Dreamer has to be out there. Bartolome said the demand was too great and "the money's too high" for there not to be black market Dreamer. Real DR33M3R.

But if it is there, it is also somehow invisible. Not just down low, but without a trace. And that requires organization: a consciously designed distribution system for the only drug that law enforcement has any real interest in controlling.

Real Dreamer. Actual DR33M3R, in large and reliable quantities. Pills straight from the factories, stolen in the supply chain. Their absence should be known. The individual pills are traceable through the batch and production sequence codes stamped into them. Bottles and boxes, crates and pallets, all have their own RFID tags. Wherever a large amount of Dreamer may have slipped out of the system, someone must be aware of the shortage. Several people must be aware.

Afronzo-New Day DR33M3R being sold on a large scale. Several people within the production and distribution chain have to be involved in this trade in DR33M3R. Someone, somewhere, inside or outside of A-ND designed the system, recruited those involved and is reaping the bulk of the reward.

Hydo said, "On a special wavelength." Beenie said he thought Hydo knew "the guy."

I get that far, and it slips apart. Because Hydo is dead. Anything he knew about the "special wavelength" is gone.

Why am I writing this? It looks like paranoia.

Sleep deprivation.

I fell asleep on my way downtown. At least I think I must have. I don't remember driving here. I remember driving from Bel Air to a bungalow in West Hollywood (754 King). The girl who answered the door was in perfect "Like a Virgin" Madonna drag. Not dressed for a party or anything, just that's what she wears. That's what her mom told me. She said her daughter and her daughter's friends are all into the same stuff she thought sucked when she was their age. She said she was a punk in the eighties, hated Madonna. She said it doesn't really matter, because her daughter thinks Madonna is just this crazy "old lady that believes in magic and adopts African babies and needs to start acting more her age cuz it's kind of gross when she dresses up in underwear." She said her daughter just likes the old music and loves the clothes. She asked if I had kids, and I told her yes. She said, "Wait and see, whatever you thought sucked when you were a teenager, that'll be what's cool." Then she asked how old my kid is and I told her that I have a baby, and she stopped talking about it.

Her yard is all poppies. She raises them. When the blooms fall off, she slits the bulbs with a razor over and over, letting the sap ooze out and dry in layers. Then she scrapes it off and collects it. Homegrown opium. I traded her ketamine (10 milliliters, liquid) for a ball of opium roughly the size of a marble (weight indeterminate). Then I left as two boys arrived, one dressed in "Thriller" red and black leather, the other in "Purple Rain." At least that's what I think happened. I don't remember getting into the car or driving here. It's possible I dreamed the two boys.

I fell asleep behind the wheel.

I could have died. I would have left Rose and the baby alone.

I need to sleep. But I don't know when that will be. I have to meet Beenie. I need to find out what is going on. Something is going on. The world didn't just spin off its axis by itself. It didn't happen all by itself. Not now. Not just in time for Rose to get pregnant. Not just in time for my baby. The world didn't decide to end just in time for my baby to be born.

I need to sleep. But I can't now. So I need to stay awake.

I took two 5-milligram dexamphetamine sulfate tablets. My tongue is dry and my stomach feels tight. I'm grinding my teeth. I don't feel stupid like I did the few times I smoked pot with Rose before I joined the force. I never liked pot, but Rose liked the idea of smoking it together. I never told her how unpleasant it was for me. This feels different. I still feel tired, but not sleepy.

I shouldn't be writing this down. Except that it would be a lie not to.

It's midnight. Time to go inside and find Beenie.

First I'll call Rose and tell her I love her. I'll tell her to put the phone next to the baby's ear so she can hear me tell her I love her. So she can hear me when I tell her that I don't care how she dresses when she grows up. Or who she thinks is cool. Or if she goes out with boys who dress like Michael

Jackson and Prince. I'll tell her she can be and do whatever she wants when she grows up. Just that she has to grow up. She has to grow up.

I'm going to stop writing now. I don't think I'm making much sense.

But I know I'm right. I know the world is like this for a reason. I know that someone did something to sicken the world.

And it's not too late. It's not too late. It's not too late. I say that it is not too late.

9

THE MOST STRIKING THING ABOUT THE TWO YOUNG MEN ON
the security recording was the tremendous amounts of stress under which
they were both obviously laboring. In the first of them, this stress was
clearly etched in the the jittery suddenness of his movements, in the habit
of constantly raking a comb across his head, defining and redefining the
side part in his assiduously composed geek haircut. Finally, and most decisively, his stress was revealed in the way he yanked his Olympic from his
retro leather book satchel and sprayed the room without giving any warning that he intended to do so.

It was, for the record, a K3B-M4. So I got the make but not the model.

I got most of the rest of it right. The escalation of the argument with
the Korean American, the tactfully turned backs of the workers. And then
my re-creation went awry. He did not search the premises. He did not
even glance at the travel drive that I could clearly see sitting exactly where
I'd been told it would be. He came, he killed, and he left. Leaving the drive.

I watched as the cameras went into delay mode, recording in shorter
and shorter bursts at longer and longer intervals, allowing hours to pass
in minutes, slight stutters in the lighting caused as one of the monitors
continued to flicker. And then the cameras revived, movement bringing
them back to life, and a second young man under duress entered the
room.

He surveyed the crime scene with some thoroughness, taking several photos, recording the positions of bodies, the placement of entry wounds and blood sprays. Then pausing for a final assessment, he noticed the drive, made a brief mental calculation of some kind, took the travel drive, and left. Giving the impression that the theft of the drive was ·not at all premeditated.

As for his obvious anxiety and stress, they were revealed not in any particular tick of behavior but rather in the contrast between the efficiency with which he went about his business, and the blind distraction apparent in his failure to erase himself from the security hard drive from which I had recorded the DVD I was watching.

I watched it again. I watched it several times over.

His frame was lanky but fit. The haircut wasn't one. It was what had been very short hair neglected over several months. The clothes were practical and inexpensive. Off-brand khaki cargo pants, a plain black T-shirt. Only his shoes were of any particular interest. A pair of black Tsubo Korphs, legendarily durable, comfortable, and ugly. Excellent for anyone who spends a great deal of time on his feet. Nurses and hospital orderlies often favor the white ones. In terms of palette and basic silhouette, he could quite easily have been taken for one of the mercenaries I had killed in the room several hours after he had gone carefully through the procedures I was watching him execute.

But he was not one of them. He was, in fact, a cop. Young, not terribly experienced at detective work, but game and apt. He'd obviously done his homework and listened up in class. He went about his business with care, but with concern for the time it was taking, frequently looking at the anachronism on his wrist. I watched and came to another conclusion.

The camera image could be magnified enough for me to see that he was deleting something from the Korean American's BlackBerry. That, combined with his time sensitivity, the impulsive theft of the drive, and his stress level, seemed to make a simple case. Dirty cop. Covering up traces of whatever dirty business he had been engaged in there.

This diagnosis was contraindicated by a few details: the time he took to survey the crime scene, take pictures, and check the pulses of the dead. Dirty? Well, certainly he had something to hide. More than likely it was some form of dirtiness. Always best to assume the worst about a stranger until you know otherwise.

The killer, for instance, had killed out of juvenile rage. There might be money involved, nothing would be more natural, but when it boiled down to the moment of the deed, he simply lost his self-control and, because he had one handy, pulled his gun and opened fire. It was on his face. Not beforehand, not even while he was shooting. But afterward, with smoke still oozing from the barrel of his weapon, the absolute shock on his face. The look that said explicitly, *Did I just do that?* I hardly needed to see his lips move: *Oh, shit.* Or to observe the nervous giggle that escaped from them. He'd never planned to go in there and kill those people. He'd just walked into a room where he knew he was going to have an argument with someone and took a high-powered assault rifle with him. For no real reason. Just because he thought he might need it. For what, he would have found it impossible to say.

The other young man, the one with the well-maintained ancient watch, the practical shoes, and the precise methodology, he'd never have lost control in that manner. Had he wanted to kill those people, he'd have gone in with a plan and carried it out with great efficiency. And possibly still have walked out having forgotten to take care of the cameras.

I was, I will admit it, intrigued.

Not that my curiosity was a matter of concern. I would have had to track him down whether or not I was keen to know just how and why he'd come to be there.

He had Lady Chizu's drive.

Inevitably, I must find him. And take it. And do all that she had asked of me.

Sitting in my Cadillac, spending another late evening in traffic, some hours after the dear French pilot had touched down on the Thousand Storks pad in Century City and reminded me that I had his number, as if I had forgotten, I found a section of the recording where the cop's face was turned almost directly to one of the cameras. I froze it, grabbed the frame, saved it as "Young Faust," connected via Bluetooth to the Canon Pixma in the glove box, and printed several copies. Then I left-clicked the touchpad button on my Toughbook and skipped back on the recording, watching Young Faust depart backward, and the killer enter similarly, and, would that it were so easy, watched the dead jump joyously to life, expelling bullets from their bodies in sheer relief that it had all been a bad dream. Or so I chose to reimagine the scene.

I froze the picture and considered the killer. I would need no assistance from business associates who owed me favors to identify this face and give it a name. I owned a TV, after all.

Parsifal K. Afronzo Jr. Cager to his friends. Freshly minted mass murderer.

The policeman, dirty to whatever degree, would likely be seeking him, or vice versa. So then must I.

10

PARK DIDN'T KNOW MUCH ABOUT MUSIC. HIS IPOD WAS FILLED with playlists that Rose made and loaded for him. Music she thought *he should listen to.* Or things she just thought he might enjoy. He listened to all of them, trying always to listen to them in the manner she suggested.

Listen to this on the ride to class, she'd said the first time she made him a list. She did this after buying him the iPod as a birthday present and seeing that it hadn't left the box in the two weeks since he'd unwrapped it. She thought that once he saw how much fun the little gadget could be, he'd start filling it himself, seeking out new music to expand his world. But he didn't.

What he enjoyed was listening to what she chose for him. He'd never have told her what she came to suspect anyway, that he consciously avoided loading new music onto the player so that she would feel compelled to keep doing it herself. Over the years it gradually filled with music that came to be a part of the day-to-day communication between a woman who didn't know how to edit a thought or emotion that crossed her mind and a man who barely understood that there might be a need to communicate anything that wasn't absolutely essential to the immediate situation.

Playlist titles:

The ride to the water
Walking on Telegraph
Mowing the lawn
Missing Rose
We're having a baby
Cheese sandwich for lunch
Keep your head down
What I'll do to you tonight
Don't forget the toilet paper
It's not that big a deal, I'm not really mad at you, just frustrated with my
    fucking work
The baby kicked me this morning
Don't worry so much
She has your eyes
Come home safe
Awake without you

When she asked at the end of a day how he'd felt about a new list, what songs he liked best, he never knew the song titles or the names of the artists. The songs were the messages from her; it never occurred to him to care what they were called or who was playing them. He'd say he liked, *That one in the middle, with the happy beat, but it was kind of sad, about the kid falling down on the playing field and everyone looking at him and he just lies there.* Or he'd hum the melody as he remembered it. Or, when she insisted, sing a lyric that had stuck in his head.

That's what he was thinking about as he walked down the line of people waiting to get inside Denizone. Every time the doors, designed to look like the much-battered gates of an under-siege castle, opened to admit another tan and fit young thing, Park heard a bit of a song he'd once sung for Rose. The chorus only, sung to her in a high whisper, with a tempo more appropriate to a waltz than to a rock song: *This heart's on fire, this heart's on fire, this heart's on fire, this heart's on fire.*

It froze him for a moment, just before the velvet rope, the doorman, in the blockbuster-fantasy distressed leather and chain mail of a mythical kingdom, nodding at him.

" 'Sup, Park?"

The door swung closed, cutting off the song, and Park came back, letting go of the memory, the night he'd sung it for her.

"Priest."

He offered his hand, and Priest took it, palming an offered vial of powdered Ecstasy.

He held it up between forefinger and thumb.

"Same stuff as before?"

Park shook his head.

"Better."

Priest pocketed the vial and unhooked the rope.

"Big party tonight. Tournament in the basement. Top gladiators."

Park waited while the Priest's counterpart, a young man of similar girth, wearing an equally detailed costume, put a bracelet of brown microsuede around his wrist, fastening it with a pincer that snapped a thin copper rivet into place.

"I'm just meeting a customer."

Priest waved a macelike baton at the door, tripping an electric eye.

"Hope they're in there already. We're at capacity."

The huge door swung open.

"We'll find each other."

Priest offered his fist.

"Have a good one."

Park gave him a bump, a gesture that never felt genuine to him, but one he'd learned to execute without a grimace.

"Always."

He passed into an entryway of textured concrete contoured to look like living stone, the mouth of a tunnel hewed into the side of a mountain, the walls pulsing with projected images from Chasm Tide. Desert landscapes of the Wilting Lands, the Aerie's Village, a pontoon city he'd never seen, it looked scavenged from the remains of a great twentieth-century seaport, and the Lair of Brralwarr, the great dragon worm rampaging on an overmatched band of adventurers.

These would be live player views from gamers currently in-world, snagged and sampled and projected here, stirred and flashing by, perspectives randomly distorted, colors filtered, resolution mixed and pixelated.

A giant ax blade cut down the wall, and he flinched, recognizing a trap from the Clockwork Labyrinth. He stopped, staring, wondering if he might catch a glimpse of Cipher Blue. It was always possible, watching someone else's game, that you could see, in the distance or close at hand, the avatar of someone you knew, friend or enemy.

But she wasn't there. And then the scene was gone, replaced by the Precipice Bacchanal, a ceaseless orgy of virtual flesh that endured with ever increasing frenzy in the circular city of Gyre, hemming the edge of the Chasm itself.

A new song was playing. One he didn't know, one that vibrated through the floor and walls, beating at the doors at the opposite end of the hall, past the coat check and the cashier.

Heaped on the cashier's table, trinkets of jewelry, packets and tubes of intoxicants, a stack of gift cards from high-end merchants, a few rare coins, a pair of ostrich cowboy boots, a samurai sword, a bowl full of car keys, each with a pink slip rubber-banded to it, several thick wads of cash money, and, on the floor, a fifteen-gallon gas can.

The cashier, a man who had discarded the robe that was meant to make him look like a cleric, wearing instead two-sizes-loose factory-distressed black jeans of recycled cotton held up by wide blue suspenders that draped thin bare shoulders, looked up at Park and pointed a fat plastic pistol.

Park held out his wrist, and the cashier aimed the RFID interrogator at it and pulled the trigger. There was a beep as the device read the signal the tiny silver chip on the bracelet broadcast in response to the interrogator's prompt. The clerk looked at the code that appeared on an LCD screen on the plastic gun.

"Comp."

Park offered his hand anyway, slipping the clerk a tiny Ziploc packed tight with gummy buds. He'd learned in the past months that even when he was comped into clubs it always paid to tip the staff. It engendered goodwill. Something a dealer could never have too much of. As it often led to early warnings of trouble. Rival dealers. Unhappy customers. Law.

The Ziploc disappeared into a pocket, and the clerk knocked lightly on his table in acknowledgment while tapping his toe on a floor switch that triggered the inner doors, exposing Park to a blast of bass that went through his chest and slammed against the beat of his heart.

Inside, a scene reminiscent of the Precipice Bacchanal. More clothes in place, less blatant penetration, and no elves, but the same mass spasms of desperation and fear manifesting as revelry. The place reeked of sweat, ganja, cigarette smoke, infused vodkas, and cherry lip gloss. The flashing screen grabs from the hall were here: panoramas projected on the ceiling, crisscrossed by shadows cast by several catwalks that were populated by the most astonishingly beautiful of the club's clientele, culled from the crowd by unemployed assistant casting directors who traded their expertise for drink tickets. The dancers themselves took their chances on the catwalks, after signing releases against any and all bodily harm, for the pure glory of having been selected, their physical perfection singled out and highlighted.

Park didn't work Denizone. He didn't work any of the clubs regularly. Came to them only at the request of regular customers who needed special deliveries. In the early days, before it had become apparent how rapidly SLP was spreading, he had been circumspect in these places. Doing his business in the bathrooms and back hallways, in the alleys where the clubbers slipped out to smoke in the night air. But soon enough everyone was lighting up inside, antismoking laws not carrying quite the same bite any longer, likewise the dangers of indulging the habit, and as the smokers moved inside and multiplied, so too did the drug deals. A subtle handoff was still appreciated as a point of style but was barely a legal necessity. To say nothing of using.

Staying on the cabaret level above the dance floor, moving toward the bar, Park walked past booths where lines of coke were being snorted from the black enameled tabletops, where a girl with a cupped palm full of little blue capsules doled them out to her circle of friends, where a couple snapped amyl poppers under each other's noses, where any number of people took hits off pipes, joints, or blunts, and where a man slumped half off his banquette, rubber tourniquet still around his upper arm, hypo loose in his fingers, a drop of fresh blood welling amid a hash of purplish tracks in the hollow of his elbow. Park almost stopped to check the man's pulse but saw him open and close his lizard eyes, a slight smile coming to his lips as he licked them, and so moved on.

These places were not for Park. Rose, on the one occasion when she made the mistake of dragging him to the Exotic Erotic Halloween Ball, thinking that he might lose his self-consciousness in the cheesy exuberance, realized almost instantly that she had made an awful mistake. It wasn't that Park was a prude. Not by any measure. He was not offended or made uncomfortable by the expanses of flesh, the free displays of human sexuality in all its variations, the men dressed as naughty nuns, the women dressed as Nazi angels; it was simply that the whole affair made him terribly sad. The general air of insecurity and affectation made it too easy for him to imagine these once-a-year fabulous creatures as the cubicle dwellers most of them were in everyday life. Overly sensitive to the jittery signals regarding sex, longing, and rejection that were being bounced around the hall, he soon felt as if his nerve endings were being scrubbed with fine sandpaper. Seeing the look of extreme discomfort on his face, through the zombie pancake she had painted him with, she made the excuse that she wasn't feeling well and asked if he minded if they left. He did not mind.

Riding BART under the bay, he watched their pale reflections in the dark glass, whited out in beats of safety lights as they swept down the tunnel. Dressed as an especially tawdry Raggedy Ann, Rose put her head on his shoulder.

He was thinking that he was a fool, that it was absurd to imagine that he knew what those people's lives were like, that his inability to relax and enjoy himself had nothing to do with self-confidence and everything to do with immaturity and insecurity. Only a weak child would be afraid at a party. Stand in the corner. Not talk to anyone. Project his fears onto the people who were enjoying themselves. He added another entry to his personal accounting of his weaknesses. And swore to be better.

But crossing Denizone, turning sideways, plastering himself to the waste-high chains meant to keep people from tumbling onto the dance floor, finding an eddy in the crowd in which he felt for a moment almost alone, he could only look at them all and wonder which had kids at home, unattended, while their parents reveled.

Lost for a moment, he almost didn't feel his phone vibrating, the tiny sensation lost in the whomping bass notes. When he answered, he could hear only the slightest tinny chatter. Clicking a button on the side of the phone, boosting the volume to max, and sticking a finger in his other ear, he shouted.

"Beenie?"

A barely audible scream.

"Yeah, man. What's up?"

Overwhelmed by the combination of the noise, the crowd, fatigue, and the speed he'd taken, Park found honesty coming out of his mouth.

"Not much. Just standing here judging people I don't know."

He heard Beenie's gulping laugh.

"Yeah, kinda hard not to in here, isn't it?"

Park raised himself on his toes and scanned the crowd.

"Where are you?"

"I'm in the main dance hall. You?"

"Same."

"Do you see, look up at the catwalks, do you see the girl dressed like classic Mortal Kombat Sonya?

Park looked up at the catwalks, and in a stutter of strobes found the girl, shaggy blond hair, big dangling earrings, green headband and matching spandex jazzercise gear, dancing, mixing crunk with choreographed kicks and punches straight from the old video game.

"Yeah, I see her."

"Well I'm pretty much right under her, trying to decide if it's worth going up there and risking getting my spine ripped out for a shot at living a junior high sex fantasy."

Park started moving.

"I'm west of you, circling around the tables."

"Good call, man. You don't want to be on the floor right now. Not unless you had your shots and got a lifetime supply of condoms and dental dams with you. Swear to God, man, I have never seen it get so freaky in here."

Park took a look at the dance floor, a single heaving mass, no way to tell who was meant to be dancing with whom, people clinging to one another, hoping not to get dragged down alone.

He stopped moving, looked up at the catwalks, found the Sonya.

"I'm about ten yards southeast of your dream girl. Can't see you."

"Draw a line from her to the back wall, where they're flashing that tavern fight."

"Okay."

"Look straight down from there."

"Okay."

"See the sconce that's been knocked crooked?"

"Yeah."

"I'm just to the, wait, I see you. Don't move."

Park didn't move, and a moment later Beenie was in front of him, buzzed head dripping sweat, narrow almond-shaped eyes bloodshot and dark-bagged, wearing his usual biking shorts and powder blue Manchester City FC jersey.

Beenie slid his phone closed and tucked it into the pouch on one of the shoulder straps of his tightly cinched backpack, leaning close to shout in Park's ear.

"Good to see you, bro."

Their hands met, the little ball of opium passing.

Beenie wrapped an arm around Park's shoulders and gave him a light squeeze.

"Thanks for hitting me back so fast on this shit. That's above and beyond, man. What do I owe you?"

Park looked around, found an archway that led to one of the alternative spaces in the club, and pointed. Beenie nodded and followed him around a knot of bodies, through the arch, into the reduced volume of a room shaped like the interior of a conch shell, center reached after a swirl of corridor, walls ringed with cushions and pillows, a haze of incense added to the cigarette and pot smoke, all of it fluoresced by a lighting system that was cycling slowly through various cool shades of green and blue. Clubbers reclined on the pillows or swayed to a slow trance beat.

Park moved them away from the arch, found an acoustic pocket where he could speak.

"You said something the other day."

Beenie shook his head.

"Okay."

"You said Hydo maybe knew the guy."

Beenie winced.

"Yeah, I guess, but I don't know if I knew what I was talking about."

Park stared at him.

He liked Beenie. Liked him better than was smart. Knowing that Beenie was someone he'd have to bust eventually, Park shouldn't have liked him at all. Not because Beenie was a criminal, which he barely was, but because no one wants to put the cuffs on someone he almost thinks of as a friend. Most undercover cops are vastly skilled at compartmentalization. It is a talent as valued as lying. They seal off their real feelings and create imitation emotions. Easily torn down when it's time to show the badge, drag someone downtown, and sit across from him in an interrogation cell and tell him how fucked he is now.

That is what they tell themselves, anyway. Talking up how deep they can get, how far into their cover. Bragging about the secrets their *friends* on the other side of that cover have revealed to them. Not the criminal stuff, but the real dirt.

Park had heard them when he was in uniform. Undercovers playing shuffleboard at the Cozy Inn, off duty, sharing secrets about assholes who had cried on their shoulders as they told about the time they tried it with another guy, lost their temper and hit their kid, screwed their brother's wife, wished their old man would hurry up and die, had their mother put in a home so they could sell her house and use the money for gambling debts, turned the wheel of a car to hit a stray dog to see what would happen. They laughed about it, talked about how they'd use the information to break the assholes when they made their busts.

Coming away from the bar with a beer and a seltzer, Park had watched how they slammed their Jack and Cokes, shots of Cuervo, double Dewars on the rocks, and had recognized the fierce talk and drinking of troubled men. Returning to the corner table where he and Rose were going over lists of baby names, he'd been grateful that he didn't have to concern himself with such deceptions. With his badge on his chest, his job was not easy, but it was straightforward.

Without a badge, his default setting of cool and distant actually attracted rather than held off his customers. Most illegal drugs are used socially or for self-medication. Social users find it hard to get a word in edgewise with other social users. Conversely, the isolationists are entirely alone. Without trying to, Park projected his natural aura of trustworthiness. And his customers responded, sharing more than their shames and petty crimes, exposing themselves in ways that the undercovers at the Cozy would not have recognized as valuable. But they were treasures for Park, those tales: secret dreams of an artist's life abandoned for money, the detailed story of an epiphany that changed a lifetime of faith, a revelation about receiving a healthy kidney from a deeply estranged sister, and the recitation of a poem that had won an award when the writer was thirteen.

That these intimacies were painful to Park, being based on a lie, his lie, was not unusual at all. Any intimacy was painful to him. Another exposure. Another rough flange that could be sheared away from him. Another potential loss in this world.

Sitting in customers' living rooms, listening to them as they spoke about the intensity of their love for a particular painting by Botero and how seeing it for the first time had changed how they saw their own body, watching as they went to a shelf to find the book where the painting was reproduced, Park would silently beg, *Don't share this with me. I am not who you think I am. I will betray this trust.* But even with his business completed, he would not get up and walk away, so addicted had he become to these barbed disclosures.

So he knew that Beenie was Korean by birth, had been adopted by a white American couple who could not have children of their own, that he'd been raised in Oklahoma, where assimilation was not the easiest thing for an Asian, that he took up bike riding because it put distance between himself and the other kids, that his parents had loved him but had never been able to adjust to his innate alienness as they had assumed they would, that he didn't blame them at all for that fact, that loving them hadn't made it any harder for him to leave home the moment he got the chance, that he chose to take on enormous debt in order to attend UCLA rather than stay at home and let his parents pick up the tab for OU, that he'd felt almost as estranged being a Sooner in Los Angeles as he had felt being a Korean in Liberty, that he'd met a girl and fallen in love and that she'd helped him get over it, that he'd married the girl while still in school, that she'd been pregnant twice and miscarried both times, that the reason for the miscarriages was related to the lupus she suffered from, that she died after they had been married only five years, that Beenie had quit his job as an in-demand art director for video games, that he'd sold both his cars, lived now on a day cruiser berthed at Marina Del Rey, and devoted himself to cycling. That he started every day with a joint to help create a cloud around what he had lost, that as the day progressed he thickened and thinned this cloud with various concoctions and combinations of pot and coke and heroin and pills and alcohol, that periodically throughout the day he slipped an Area-51 laptop from his bag and entered Chasm Tide, where he played a character named Liberty, a wandering Cliff Monk who he used to accumulate gold and artifacts that he dealt to other players and to farmers like Hydo, and that he rode hundreds of miles a day without ever creating distance between himself and what was at his heels, evading it for at best a few hours a night, when exhaustion and the chemicals in his body dragged him into the dreamless sleep he craved more than anything, other than to see his wife again.

Because Park knew all this, he was able to say what he had to, leaning close to Beenie so no one else in a room of strangers could hear.

"My wife has it."

Beenie flinched again.

"Oh. Shit."

He looked at the swirled walls of the room, ended up looking at his feet.

"The baby?"

Park knew this would be the next question. He thought he'd be ready to hear it, but he was wrong. He tried to find an answer that would allow for the maximum window of hope. But there was really only one thing that could be said.

"We don't know."

Beenie was shaking his head now, shaking it as he looked up at the low ceiling, the span of a night sky painted there, the constellations of Chasm Tide, unreal astronomies.

"This world, man. It tries to break us."

He looked at Park.

"It's not a place to be brittle."

Park thought of his father putting the barrels of his favorite shotgun beneath his chin. He didn't move, his eyes on Beenie's.

Beenie put a hand on top of his own head and pressed down.

"I need to get high now."

"Beenie."

Beenie didn't move.

Park put his hand on top of Beenie's.

"The guy you mentioned, is it the guy who owns this place?"

Beenie's mouth was twisting, his eyes moving from side to side like a man who felt something coming up behind him.

"Yeah, he's the guy I meant."

"And do you know him? You've done something with him? Business? He's a gamer. You've sold to him?"

"We've done some things."

"I want to meet him."

Beenie pulled his hand from under Park's.

"Honestly, Park, I got to tell you, if you want something from this guy, I am probably not the one to handle the introduction. He's not too cool with me these days. We should look for an alternative."

Park kept his hand on top of Beenie's head.

"I don't have time for an alternative."

Beenie took hold of Park's wrist and squeezed.

"Yeah. I know. Just let me get high really quick, and we'll see what we can do."

He let go of Park, ducked away from the larger man's hand, and headed toward the bathrooms, one of the generation that believed in doing their drugs out of sight.

11

PARK WATCHED THE UNDULATED BLADE OF A FLAMBERGE pierce the side of the Northerner and rip upward, unzipping the huge barbarian's rib cage in a spray of blood. He watched it again and again as the highlight replayed on the screens of the main gaming salon on the basement level below the thumping dance floor.

The bass reverberated from the ceiling, frequently lost in the screams, applause, and cheers from the crowd that had packed in to watch the gladiators.

A banner over the bar announced that this was a North American Video Gaming Federation Regional War Hole Tournament. The winner of the regional would face off against three other gladiators in a national championship, and the winner of that event would then be sent to the Global Champs in Dubai. Standing at the back of the long room Beenie explained it to Park, as the reptilian wielder of the flamberge flexed on-screen at the command of a prototypically slouching, rail-thin Asian gamer sitting in one of the two articulated black mesh chairs on a raised dais at the middle of the room.

There seemed little reason for having the gamers on the platform. All eyes were riveted on the main screen, a massive composite made of four fifty-two-inch Sony LCD displays, or on one of the dozens of smaller screens jutting from the walls and ceiling. For all practical purposes, the gamers could be at home, comfortably ensconced in the custom-pressed ass grooves of their sofa cushions. Or so Park thought until he saw the press of fans forming as the gamer rose, casually dropped his heavily customized controller on the chair, flipped up the collar of the shiny nylon logo-covered jacket draped over his shoulder like a cape, and descended the three steps into the mob, plucking from their hands the scraps of paper, War Hole T-shirts, NAGVF caps, glossy eight-by-tens, and assorted other mementos offered to be autographed.

Beenie was shaking his head.

"I never much got into the hack-n-slash scene myself, but that dude there, Comicaze Y, he just laid some wicked shit on that barbarian."

Park rubbed his eyes. They felt grainy, almost pebbled, like they were sprouting sties. He couldn't stop grinding his teeth; his jaw muscles had started to cramp. He knew it was the speed, but knowing the cause of the symptoms gave him no relief. He knew only one of two things would make him feel any better: sleep or more speed. He wanted to be home, held by Rose, the baby safe between them

He opened his mouth wide, stretching his jaw, snapped his teeth together.

"I don't like games where people just kill each other."

Beenie took a sip of his screwdriver.

"Like I said, it's not my thing either, but I've played a couple rounds. It's like golf. You may not like it, but you try it once or twice and you know how hard it is. After that, every time you see those guys on tour, all you can think is that they must be witches with the things they make the ball do. Comicaze Y, the other guys at the top, they're like that. Voodoo with the controller."

Park understood that there were people who tired of the endless puzzles and problem-solving scenarios of Chasm Tide, the social dynamics that needed to be mastered if a player was going to integrate into a raiding party or quest. Advancement in the game required long hours spent picking at tangles of logic and personality, as well as hacking and slashing. He himself had no particular interest in the game. If it wasn't for Rose, he'd never have built a character of his own, let alone logged several hours adventuring and exploring the terrain. He lacked the ability to suspend disbelief to the extent required to make the experience immersive, but he admired the skill and workmanship that went into the building of the thing, the attention to detail. And he respected the values inherent in the system of levels that characters progressed through as they became more powerful. Certainly those levels could be bought with blood or gold, but the rewards for ingenuity and teamwork were far larger. Multiple levels could be jumped in a single bound if the right riddle was answered or puzzle assembled. He liked the idea of a world where mental acuity and the ability to play well with others were valued more highly than bloodlust or greed.

War Hole was a Chasm Tide spin-off for players who felt otherwise. Of whom there were many. War Hole rewarded their virtual brutality abundantly, but asked that something be risked. Whereas death in Chasm Tide led to an inconvenient reincarnation in the heart of the Chasm, gamers in War Hole could advance to the highest levels of proficiency only by permanently risking the lives of their warriors. Avatars killed in tournaments such as these did not emerge to fight again; they were lost. All record of them obliterated from the War Hole servers, locally stored copies locked from reloads.

Observing a squat, bald forty-year-old, silently sobbing as he drank the repeated shots of tequila poured for him by his sullen handlers, Park guessed that he was one of the erased. A defeated fighter who had seen the fruit of hundreds of hours of gaming cut down and dispersed into the unknown.

He ground his teeth.

"This is depressing."

Beenie sipped his drink.

"What isn't?"

An announcer's voice came over the PA, informing the fans that there would be a thirty-minute break before the final match, thanking various sponsors, listing drink specials, and tipping his hat to the evening's host.

"Cager!"

Several pin spots swarmed, raced around the room, convened on a bastion of banquettes and divans, settling on a reedy young man in black Levis that rode high at the cuffs to show a few inches of sagging mismatched red and blue socks, and a vintage sleeveless black Tubeway Army

T-shirt. Hunched over the silverfish glow of a smartphone screen, he took a black comb from his back pocket and used it to recut the side part in his immovably greased towhead blond hair. He tucked the comb away, vaguely acknowledged the crowd with a flip of fingers, and returned attention to his phone, thumbs dancing over a slide-down qwerty keyboard.

A brief cheer rose from the crowd, the spots went back to swimming the walls, and everyone moved toward the bar or the bathrooms. The screens cross-faded, tournament highlights replaced by pictures and snippets of video, taken and messaged by camera phone and smart device, the work of this evening's club patrons. Dance floor action, a couple shooting themselves having sex in a bathroom stall, a boy puking, several people doing assorted drugs, flashed anatomy, and a brawl in the valet line.

Park stared at the young man.

Child of great fortune, infamous wastrel and libertine, source of endless gossip-blog fodder. Suspected plague profiteer. He looked like nothing so much as any number of wallflower students Park had known at Stanford. Acolytes in fields of obscure digital study; he'd not socialized with them but recognized in their eyes the same desperate fever that had possessed the Ph.D. candidates in the philosophy department.

He finished the bottle of water he'd been sipping at, his tense stomach resisting, and set it on a cocktail table crowded with empty glasses stuffed with cigarette butts.

"I want to meet him."

Beenie finished his drink, set the glass aside, rolled his head from shoulder to shoulder, and bounced on the balls of his feet.

"Let's go see the prince."

The low tables and couches in the VIP section were littered with gadgets; minivideo recorders, gaming handhelds, ultraportable DVD players, a small stack of phones that someone appeared to have been using for an improvised game of Jenga, thumb drives, a fistful of memory cards, and all the attendant detritus of instillation disks, twist-tied USB cables, styrofoam and cardboard packing materials, rebate cards, and low-quality AA and AAA batteries.

Parsifal K. Afronzo Jr., perched on the edge of a slate leather ottoman, was apparently oblivious to this clutter or to the entourage scattered in his orbit. They sucked from bottles of raspberry vodka frozen in blocks of ice while unwrapping and almost immediately tiring of the electronic swag that had been piled there in tribute by the event's sponsors. Messaging their friends in the other rooms of the club to determine if they were missing anything good, they honed their nonchalance, as aspiring paparazzi caught them in the background of their Cager cell shots.

Trailing Beenie, Park took note of a crew-cut duo of alert young women wearing skintight head-to-toe ensembles of various nonreflective black tactical materials. A style that extended to the assault rifles slung on their backs and the pistols strapped to their thighs. That they had been costumed for roles as cannon fodder in a B-grade action picture didn't seem to interfere with their expertise. Spotting Park and Beenie approaching the VIP ropes on a direct line, one of them moved to intercept while the other shifted subtly to put herself in a position to offer cover fire or throw her body in front of her client.

The bodyguard who had stepped to the rope directed them toward a line of shoe gazers lining a nearby wall.

"Please take a spot at the back of the line. If Cager does any signing this evening, it will done on the line only."

Beenie raised a hand.

"Cager."

The bodyguard placed a hand on the butt of her sidearm.

"Please do not address Cager, sir."

"Cage, it's Beenie."

"Please move away from the rope, sir."

Beenie lifted himself on tiptoe, trying to see over her shoulder.

"Dude, it's Beenie; just wanted to discuss what we talked about that last time."

The bodyguard came down a step and jutted her face into Beenie's.

"Hey, asshole, you don't understand polite English? I said leave Cager the fuck alone and fuck off to the back of the line. Better, just fuck off out of the club before I Taser your ass and drag you out to the street."

"It's all right, Imelda."

She drew back.

"Sir?"

Cager's fingers paused, and he pointed.

"It's all right. Just go stand by Magda and keep looking hot and danger-ous."

She flared perfect nostrils.

"Sir?"

He tapped a message to elsewhere.

"Pose. You come over here, it throws the tableau out of balance. The bouncers can take care of this kind of thing. Unless it's something serious, I want you and Magda to maintain the composition up here. If we have a situation like when we were in Tijuana and those guys tried to kidnap me, you can break their knees and Magda can shoot them in the hands like you did there. Otherwise, I really want to uphold the integrity of the image."

Imelda gave half a nod.

"Yes, sir."

"And please call me 'boss' from now on."

"Yes, boss."

"Thank you."

She moved back to her position, her partner countering, giving them-selves maximum coverage of the perimeter.

Cager's typing had subsided into a single action, repeatedly stabbing one key.

"Beenie."

"Hey, Cager."

"Beenie, have you got my Aspiration Codex?"

Beenie looked at Park, gave him an I-told-you roll of the eyes, and shook his head.

"No, man, I don't."

Cager jabbed the single button violently three times, then held it down.

"Then why are you here bothering me? Why did I just keep Imelda from Tasering you? I want to break into the Apex Foundation, and I can't begin without the codex."

"Yeah, I know, man. And I thought I'd have one by now, but I got held up because a deal I was trying to make is still in escrow. As soon as it clears, as soon as I hear from Hydo that *that* deal is sealed, I'll be able to make a move and get your Codex."

"Fuck!"

Cager raised his arm and threw the phone at the floor. The screen went instantly dead, tiny numbered and lettered keys flew, and a ripple of silence circulated through his hangers-on.

"Loganred. I've been bidding on that Hammer of Ultimate Wrath for a week. That lurker pulls a speed bid and wins the auction in the last possible nanosecond. What is the point of bidding if you use software to place your bids for you? I can't even understand a mentality like that. Loganred. Does that feel like victory to him?"

On the banquette, a boy wearing a black frock coat over red jeans tucked into black motorcycle boots flipped up the smoked clip-on lenses from over his rectangular glasses.

"You don't need a Wrath Hammer, Cage. I got mine."

Cager picked up the wreckage of his phone and used a clipped thumbnail to pry open the SIM card door on the back.

"Yes, Adrian, I know. The whole point of getting my own hammer is so I don't need you and your hammer in the war party anymore."

He slid a chit of gilded blue plastic from the slot.

"That's why I'm so upset. Because now I have to be subjected to your derivative steampunk *style* for another night."

He turned his head toward the boy, the comb coming from its pocket, gliding across his head in sharp strokes.

"Do you know that everyone is laughing at you, Adrian? That clockwork lapel pin and that ascot, they are pretentious. Just, why can't you wear jeans and a T-shirt? You're not cool. It's okay not to be cool. Just stop trying so hard. You're embarrassing yourself."

Adrian flicked the dark lenses back into place over his eyes, but not before tears were clearly seen there.

"Fine, you don't need my hammer. Fine, man."

He stood up.

"Just go into the Tesseract Fold without me and see what happens."

Cager shrugged.

"Take it personally if you want. That's not how it was meant. I'm just trying to help."

He pointed at a little shaft of knobbed plastic that Adrian was holding.

"You can keep that night-vision scope you've been fondling. And you can stay."

Adrian fiddled with a dial on the side of the scope.

"Thanks, Cager. I didn't mean to be a dick or anything."

Cager shook his head.

"Sit down, Adrian. Even if you wanted to act like a dick, you couldn't. You're nice. For what that's worth. And I don't have my own hammer yet. So I need you in the picture until then."

Adrian dipped his head.

"Okay, man, you'll see. You're gonna need me in the Tesseract."

Cager had turned away, reaching inside a creased and cracked leather shoulder bag that rested between his feet.

"Hydo doesn't have a Codex, Beenie. If he did, I would have bought it from him. I always buy from Hydo first. He's reliable. I buy from Hydo. Then I buy from other people. Then I come to you. As a last resort. And you don't have my Codex."

Beenie played with the Velcro straps on the back of his biking gloves.

"I know Hydo doesn't have one. But he's brokering a package deal on a bunch of artifacts I bundled for one of his customers. Once that comes through, I'll have what I need to do the deal on the codex."

Cager took a phone, identical to the Nokia he had just smashed, from the bag and studied it.

"When did you talk to Hydo?"

"Uh, yesterday?"

Beenie looked at Park.

"Is that when I saw you there?"

Cager's eyes twitched from the phone to Park and back.

"You know Hydo?"

Park nodded.

"We do business."

Cager thumbed opened the SIM door on his new phone and slid in the card from the old phone.

"Can you get a Codex for me?"

Beenie coughed.

"That's not his deal. He does the other kind of business."

The tiny card door snapped shut.

Cager brought out the comb, raked the part, wiped it on his thigh, and put it in his pocket.

"Shabu?"

Looking at Cager's green eyes, Park had a moment when he was certain that he must be sleepless. It wasn't simply that the pupils were pinned tight, it was the sense of a vision that was perceiving a different wavelength of light. The look he saw in Rose's eyes when she began conversing with the past or with entire realities that had never existed. Then, just as quickly, Park realized his mistake. Cager wasn't sleepless; he just wasn't seeing the same world that most people saw. It was a look he recognized from childhood, from occasions when his family was required by the rules of protocol that governed his father's career to interact with the inhumanly wealthy.

He nodded.

"Yes. Shabu."

Cager's eyes took on a new focus as Park and his profession were fitted into his area of experience.

"Do you have it with you?"

"Yes."

Cager nodded.

"Imelda."

The bodyguard came to slight attention.

"Yes, boss?"

"Do you have any news for me?"

She unnecessarily touched the knob of a Bluetooth earbud.

"No, boss."

Cager looked Park down and back up.

"Okay."

He rose, slinging the bag over his shoulder, lifting the section of velvet rope closest to him.

"Come on."

Park ducked his head and stepped under the rope, Beenie following.

"Where?"

Cager waved his phone at the tournament room.

"Away from this."

He turned from them and touched a rivet on a strip of rusted iron trimming the scarlet wainscoting, and a secret panel swung open.

Adrian and several of the other followers rose to take their places in Cager's wake. He help up a hand.

"Guys, there won't be any rock stars to meet or have sex with, and I'm not going to be giving anything away. You may as well stay here and watch the hack-n-slash."

He pointed.

"You stay here too Beenie. I don't need any more middlemen."

Park shook his head.

"He's not a middleman."

"Then we don't need him to do business."

"I want him to come."

Cager popped open the keyboard on his new phone and started flicking buttons.

"Why?"

Park, tired and hitting the wrong side of the speed, was reminded of his years at Deerfield, the ruthlessness with which class warfare had been in practice there. Not of the purple himself, he had been close enough in terms of background, family wealth, connections, and physical appearance, that he'd been free to circulate with any given clique. And he found after his freshman year that the place where he felt most at ease was at the bottom of the food chain, with the scholarship and legacy students. Once there he found ample opportunities over the next three years to use his gifts when facing down bullies who had marked his friends as easy targets.

It took Rose, laughing hysterically at the thought that he'd never put it together, to point out that there *might* be some connection between that experience and his love of police work.

Thrown back to the school yard, he lost some of the dealer's natural subservience in the face of a rich client and slipped character.

"Because he's my friend."

Cager tilted his head to the side.

"He's your *friend*?"

"Yes."

Cager looked up from the phone.

"And what is that supposed to make me think about *you*?"

Park shook his head.

"I don't care what you think about me."

Cager smiled.

"Come on. You and your friend go first. That will give Imelda and Magda a better shot at you if you try to abuse my person."

Park looked down the passageway revealed by the open panel.

"So if there's no rock stars or freaky sex, why are we going?"

Cager used the comb again, pressed the tines to his chin, whitening the skin in stripes.

"To look at something beautiful."

The passageway had the feel of a disused maintenance access. Their feet clanked over steel grates laid on rusting train rails. A thin sluice of viscous reddish-brown liquid ran underneath, light came from a row of caged industrial lamps hanging from exposed conduit, all but two of them broken, dim, or flickering; the concrete walls seemed to sweat bile.

Park touched a wall and found it bone-dry and warm, could feel the delicate stipple of artfully layered paints.

Cager nodded.

"I told the designer that I wanted a secret passageway and that it should feel like you were being taken someplace to be tortured."

He pointed at a rust-mottled institutional door ahead, shifting light showing through a cracked panel of chicken-wire glass.

"This was going to be the insider's insider celebrity VIP lounge. Secret door, secret passage, establishing an expectation of decadence. Inside it was all luxury, of course. CCTV feeds from the dance floor and bathrooms, private bar and DJ, a majordomo you could send to fetch anyone you saw on the screens and wanted to bring behind the green curtain to see how the wizards of the world live. Ultimately it was just the same silly show that makes the rich and famous feel special. Or less bored for a few minutes. And I wasn't interested in catering to that crowd for very long."

He stepped past Park and Beenie and put a hand on the door.

"Money makes people stupid. They don't have to work as hard as people who don't have money. That's why the smart people who do have money mostly use it for one thing."

Park thought about his father.

"They use it to make sure the people without it don't get any more."

Cager tilted his head.

"You're not stupid. What's your name?"

"Park."

Cager adjusted the hang of his shoulder bag.

"You know what I think, Park?"

"No."

"I think that pretty soon we're going to find out which is more powerful, knowledge or money. I think the worse things get, the more distance there's going to be between the smart poor people and the stupid rich people. And that the smart poor people are going to figure out how to live, and the stupid rich people are going to probably do something very dumb. Like pushing a bunch of red buttons and blowing everything up. That's what I think."

He combed his hair.

"What do you think?"

Park felt the chill of the frozen world, but the scenario being described was not one he could believe in. His baby did not allow such visions. There was no place for his baby in a world like the one this wealthy alien was describing, so how could it ever come to be?

He pointed at the door.

"I think we better make a deal before money stops having any value."

Cager took a prison movie key from his bag.

"Not stupid. But you lack imagination. Or maybe just the will to use it."

He put the key in the lock and gave it a grinding 360-degree turn.

"This may be wasted on you."

He gave the door a push, and it swung open.

"But you'll dream about it whether you want to or not."

He stepped inside, combing again, a series of tiny adjustments to the lay of his hair, imperceptible.

Park and Beenie followed, stepping into the hidden round chamber that had once been the pleasure dome for Cager's most exclusive clientele. Now, instead of coke-addled starlets and inbred eurotrash demiroyals, the room was populated by a hushed collection of aesthetes and aficionados, a highly select inner circle.

Almost exclusively male, perhaps one as old as forty, most of the others topping out at thirty, status, such as it was, outwardly displayed in the obscurity of the movies, bands, literary quotes, or bits of machine language code displayed on their T-shirts. Eyeglasses, of which there were many pairs, tending toward either retro-huge plastics or slight and unframed geometrics. Hair at similar extremes of long and unkempt or military-grade buzz. Jeans only, black preferred, khakis allowed if obviously ironic. Chuck Taylors, black, red, or white, high or low, the footwear of choice. None managing the austerity of Cager's geek perfection. Their tablets, smartphones, net books, cloud links, heavily modded and customized. Hardware signaling not only to one another directly and over the club's ubiquitous WiFi but also beaming otherwise unspoken detailed information about their owner's beliefs and loyalties within this particular conclave.

As in the tournament room they had just left, attention was focused on a series of screens. Mounted on the wall and running 180 degrees of the room's circumference, they were set at intervals that minimized light spill or peripheral distraction from screen to screen. Blow-up photographs of processor chips and detailed screen shots of 1980s golden era 8-bit video games hung from the ceiling and covered bare sections of wall, hiding the speakers while simultaneously baffling and focusing the surround sound on the middle of the room.

At that center were a cluster of five black and red Erro Aarnio Ball Chairs. Occupants engulfed by the globes, only their legs dangling or jutting free from the openings directed at the screens.

The screens themselves flashed and swooped, perspectives zooming and receding, plucking particulars from a series of popping and dropping menus, settling on a map, pulling close until it unfolded into a richly detailed scene of a central square in a city made entirely of iron. Forge, the City of Smiths. One of the entry points for Chasm Tide. A destination for parties looking either to arm themselves heavily or to have fabricated tools of special trade.

The five central screens showed varied characters' points of view. Just off the shoulder, from behind the character's eyes, well overhead, depending on player preference. The remaining screens displayed a collection of wider master shots of the action. The five avatars themselves: dark, light, human, non, scaled, armored, burly, lithe, bristling with blades, carrying only a staff, hooded and cloaked, fur-bikinied. The archetypes of the fantasy role-playing tradition. They materialized with a whoosh and a hum, resolving from an artful blurring of space, and stood there, inert amid the fuming wonders of Forge.

The audience, seated at cabaret tables or on a banquette that arced along the curve of wall opposing the screens, shifted, some making entries on their devices, one or two whispering into headsets.

Park heard an acne-scarred boy in an Atari-logo T-shirt speaking softly into a digital voice recorder.

"They're going classic. Knight, mage, thief, barbarian, elf. Can't tell if it's meant as camp or homage."

Cager's entrance caused a slight stir, attention shifting from the screens. Nods were tossed his way, returned in the form of a general wave of the comb before he turned his back to the audience and inspected the screens himself.

He scratched the side of his neck with the tines of the comb.

"They know their crowd."

He looked at Park, nodded him aside to a small bar.

Helmed by a very young girl in Harajuku anime-schoolgirl geisha chic, the service area was sunk several feet below the floor, putting the glossy surface of the bar, collaged with pornographic Disney-inspired animation cels, knee level to approaching customers. Cager knelt and nodded at the bartender. She dipped her head and began filling a small green bamboo pitcher with cold sake. Park squatted on his haunches, waiting as she placed the pitcher and two small, tightly tongue-and-grooved cypress *masu* boxes before them.

Cager poured both boxes full, picked one up, handed it to Park, took the other for himself, and lifted it.

"Kanpai!"

Park lifted his own.

"Kanpai."

They drank.

Cager drained and refilled his box.

"I went to Japan for the first time when I was nine. For a year with my dad. Business. I found it alienating until I discovered the *otaku*. In terms of geek immersion, they were years ahead of me in every way. Of course, they had a natural advantage. All the most interesting technology was being developed for their market. My edge was that, compared to them, I was socially advanced. They trusted me very quickly and gave me access to their kung fu. Not pure code, which I've never had a gift for, but they helped me unlock game levels I didn't know existed. Secret moves. When I came back here, I'd had six months on PlayStation and it hadn't even been released in the States. It became a pilgrimage for me. Culturally I never penetrated deep. Too opaque. I'm low-affect myself. Not many outbursts like that one you saw with the phone. And I generally have a hard time reading other people's moods. The Japanese in Japan are very hard for me. With *otaku* it doesn't matter. No one cares what you're feeling. My dad never grasped the fascination. He's smart enough, but too old. He was over fifty when he had me. A gap like that, we can scream at each other and still not be heard."

He combed his hair.

"That's where I tried Shabu. To stay up. Keep playing."

He put his box down and waited.

Park put his own nearly full box aside and opened the flap on his engineer's bag. From a cylindrical pouch he tugged a cardboard toilet paper tube capped at either end with rubber-banded squares of cellophane. He undid one of the ends and drew from the tube a small package of crisply folded beige tissue. Untucking one corner of the paper, he peeled it aside, opening the package like a blossom, revealing the milky white coiled dragon nestled inside.

Cager nodded.

"Yes. That's it."

He reached for the dragon, Park pulled on the piece of paper it rested on, sliding it away.

Cager looked at him.

"Yes?"

Park placed the tip of his index finger on the barbed tail of the dragon.

"Twenty-five-gram dragon. Pure and real Shabu. Cash only. Up front."

" 'Cash only.' That seems a little shortsighted."

Park shrugged.

"I'm a dealer. It's a cash business. No one has come up with a barter model that makes sense."

"They will."

"Until then, the dragon is fifteen thousand U.S."

Cager nodded and placed a fingertip on the corner of the paper opposite Park's.

"Cash, then."

He started to draw the dragon toward himself.

Park considered the moment.

When Bartolome had offered him undercover and he had accepted the assignment, he'd done as much research as he could on the topic without actually resorting to talking with other cops. No one was supposed to know about the investigation into Dreamer. So Park could ask no one what risks his new job might carry beyond the obvious. Not that he would have asked, anyway. Even his most serviceable relationships within the department were strained. His well-known inflexibility marked him for little more than scoffing dismissal from any undercovers he might cross paths with.

Flexibility was one of their primary job requirements. Average undercovers, most of them working cases that touched at the very least tangentially on the drug trade, had forgotten how to see the world in any colors but muddy gray. The briefest spell spent dealing with the economies of narcotics quickly erased all traditional valuations of right and wrong, good and evil, or, in the end, legal and illegal. The few undercovers Park had dealt with personally had distilled police work to an essence of *us and them*. Making busts wasn't a matter of doing the right thing, of enforcing the law or doing your job, it was more akin to sticking it to the other side before they could stick it to yours.

Going undercover himself, Park had had little interest in learning from that perspective. Instead he'd gone to the books. Reading a handful of classic firsthand accounts. *Both Sides of the Fence, Judas Kiss, Serpico, Under and Alone.* He enhanced this reading with selections from the psych shelves, titles dealing with the pathology of lying, Stockholm syndrome, the limits of identity. And topped off with the copy of *An Actor Prepares* that Rose found on her own shelf, a leftover from her undergrad years.

Making his first deal, a purchase of a small amount of what Rose declared to be *utterly hazardous stinky buds* once she had persuaded him that he should let her smell the fruits of his labor just to be certain that he hadn't been taken, he juggled the various teachings he'd plucked from those tomes. His jargon in place, hair as mussed as its length allowed, newly purchased vintage jeans and Bob Marley T-shirt donned, he'd found himself undone and frozen by the banality of the transaction. Far from feeling that his identity was at risk, he'd felt more as though he'd called for a Pink Dot delivery. His nonchalantly crumpled and balled twenties were a subtlety of character completely lost on the City College student who knocked on his door, asked politely if he was Park, came inside, and delivered a concise and practiced rundown on his current selection of wares, their various potencies, and the scale of pricing. Park barely managed to negotiate the buy without convincing himself that he'd been made and pulling the Warthog he'd put in his ankle holster. That was when the kid asked if he knew who had won the Clippers game. Later, unloading the .45 and locking it in the safe with a deep sense of embarrassment that he'd put it on in the first place, he'd realized that the silent, gaping stare that the out-of-context question had drawn as his initial response had been the most authentic bit of behavior he'd mustered during the entire affair. In those silent moments he'd looked more genuinely stoned than in any of the practiced tics and phrases he'd tried to employ. The fact that he'd known not only that the Clippers had lost but also the final score and the performances of the star players, and that he had sputtered all these details in one rapid burst after his endless pause, had only added, he assumed, to the overall impression of someone who hardly needed to be smoking another bong load.

So he stumbled into his character, the one that came quite naturally, built off his quiet and observant nature, his loathing of and incompetence at executing any and all lies. He was, when all was said and done, just acting like himself.

Yes, he had mastered the language of the trade. Yes, he had come to recognize the twists and kinks of human nature brought to the surface by habitual drug use and/or addiction. And yes, he had come to know what was expected from a dealer in terms of both professionalism and disregard for the weaknesses of his customers. But he learned all those intricacies as Park. Employing no techniques for building a sham persona to scrim his true intentions, becoming, instead, genuinely masterful in the skills required of a dealer.

When he was introduced as *Park the dealer,* there was absolute truth in the description. Just as, simultaneously, he might have been as accurately described *Park the cop.*

Being inherently Park in both rolls carried minimum requirements. One of those was that when engaged in either job he expected certain rules and standards to be lived up to. And one of the most, if not *the* most, central of those to his job as a dealer was the one that any and all dealers adhered to as religion: *Cash, up fucking front.*

As cop it behooved him to remove his finger and allow Cager to take possession of the dragon. It would help build a case, and put him further inside Cager's good graces. The only cop worry being that to give up the dragon without cash in hand might be out of character for a dealer and arouse some slight suspicion.

Park the dealer had no quandary. For him it was simply a matter of how business was conducted in a professional manner with a new buyer.

The moment considered, he did his job.

"Cash, up fucking front. Please."

Covering the dragon with the cup of his hand.

Cager flicked the exposed edge of the dragon's wrapping.

Behind him, a restiveness was taking hold of the room. The audience, anticipation fully whetted, was starting to twitch, attention focusing less on the static scene still holding on the screens and more on the far smaller screens they all had in their possession. The gamers in the ball chairs were still invisible other than their legs, but those legs had begun to shift, cross and uncross; one pair was drawing into their chair slowly, as if the occupant were being slurped inside and swallowed. The characters on the screens remained frozen, unresponsive to the occasional avatar that had approached and attempted to engage them for whatever unknown purposes of commerce, information gathering, combat, or sex.

Cager took in the energy of the room and turned his attention to the bartender.

"Tadj, pass some drinks, please."

She dipped her head, placed several ceramic *choko* cups and a 1.8-liter bottle of sake on a tray, and rose, balancing the tray and herself on eight-inch platform Mary Janes as she scaled a stepladder out of the bar well.

Cager waited until she was kneeling well out of earshot in front of one of the members of the audience, holding the tray of cups in one hand, the huge bottle in her other hand, pouring one of the *choko* full to the point where only surface tension kept the sake from spilling over.

"She's an artist."

Park did not disagree.

Cager continued to watch as the boy she'd poured for lifted the cup, his touch disrupting the liquid, perhaps an ounce dribbling onto the tray.

"It's the presentation. If she looked like a gymnast, the way she controls the tray and bottle wouldn't be as impressive. But her delicacy, it disguises just how strong she has to be to do that."

The girl rose, moved a few steps, knelt in front of another fan boy, and poured again. The attention of all the young men had transferred from the screens, their impatience, their toys, and was now focused wholly on Tadj.

Cager shifted.

"Her medium is their imagination. She has a persona, the clothes, the attitude, the skill with the sake bottle, her grace; it makes them think she's something she's not. They think she's anime-schoolgirl bar chick. What she is really is a fairly conservative premed student at UCLA. But she can shape how she's perceived. Make her physical presentation into art."

Cager pointed at the hidden gamers in their chairs.

"Them, they're doing something similar, but on an entirely different level of complexity. We all manipulate how we present in everyday life, yes?"

He paused, and Park had a flash of that self-consciousness from his first deal. Thinking for a moment that Cager had seen through him and was making a point of letting Park know that he *knew* before summoning Imelda and Magda to deal with him. Which they could do with some ease, seeing as he didn't have the .45 or any other weapon on his body. But the moment passed. There was, after all, nothing to be seen through. There was only Park. He wasn't the bartender, carefully grooming herself, playing a role to maximize gratuities. He was himself. Always.

He nodded.

"Yes."

Cager nodded back.

"We present for work, for our friends, for women, for people we don't even know anymore. We present an image of ourselves that we think would impress some teacher who told us we'd never amount to anything back in sixth grade. Humans, we're presenters. We compose what we want people to see, and hope that they read it as we wrote it. Everyone does it. What makes Tadj special is that she gets her show across so clearly. But them, they're in another medium."

He was looking at the gamers again.

"They're creating perceptions out of whole cloth. They don't work on the canvas of themselves; they work from pure imagination. There's a palette they have to paint from: the races and character classes and all the elements that the game limits you to, but the variations, once you start manipulating them, are near infinite. And players around the world are constantly adding to the palette, building new artifacts, designing clothes, founding communities, breeding new races, starting fresh guilds. These artists, they use those materials to create second skins, and employ them to tell stories."

He was looking at the screens, at a landscape stretching without physical limits.

"They're creating myths and legends, founding empires."

He focused his gaze on Park.

"They're slaying dragons."

He turned.

"Bandoleros!"

One by one, heads peeked out from the mouths of the ball chairs, only the gamer who had been swallowed whole staying hidden. Park stared at them, and they stared at things unseen, eyes focused deep in the spaces between matter, necks at stiff angles, pupils narrowed to pins, seeing otherwise.

Park winced.

"They're sleepless."

Cager shook his head at something wonderful.

"Utterly lateral. They do things in there, twist the whole Chasm, make moves that shouldn't be possible. Because they're relentless. And seeing something we aren't. They've been someplace we have not and have special knowledge because of it. Like when I went to Japan."

He touched Park's hand with the end of the comb.

"But they need focus. To be able to create."

He opened the flap of his bag.

"I don't have fifteen thousand dollars."

He reached into the bag with one hand, waving at the air with the other.

"The club, it breathes money. What comes in, it gets taken apart to keep the place alive; what's left over goes back out. I can't interrupt that flow. If I do, I'll choke off what's going on down here. The heart of the place. I won't do that."

He fumbled with something in the bag, something large and heavy shifting. Pointing now at the audience, where Tadj was pouring the last of the sake.

"These guys, they've paid to see something special. They've paid to see the artists create. They're here to see an epic written before their eyes. What they pay, it goes to the costs of keeping this room up and running; that includes paying the crew for their artistry. Any profit I make off recordings of their quest, that goes back into the room as well. It all zeros out."

He shaped his hair.

"They have to perform tonight. And they need the Shabu to make it happen."

His other hand came out of the bag.

"This is what I have to offer you, Park."

He placed his closed fist on the bar, fingers wrapped around a small cylinder of some kind.

Park watched the fingers uncoil, blinked, and lifted his hand from the dragon, releasing it to Cager, who smiled, picked it up with great care, rose, and walked to the sleepless players of the game.

"*Bandoleros!* We ride tonight!"

Park didn't watch them as they broke up the dragon, placed slivers in glass pipes, ignited the pure Chinese crystal meth, and sucked down the perfumed smoke. His eyes remained fixed on the small white bottle on the bar, reading the label again and again to be sure, before picking it up carefully wrapped in the tissue that had cushioned the dragon, Dreamer in his grasp.

12

FATAL FAMILIAL INSOMNIA AND THE SLEEPLESS PRION ARE strikingly distinct from each other. The most essential of their many differences is that whereas FFI is a genetic disorder inherited by mischance of birth, SLP is communicable through a number of agencies.

Nearly immortal, if that can be said of something that is not entirely alive to begin with, the malformed protein that joins with healthy proteins and influences them to twist as malignantly as it has *can* be inherited. But it can also be communicated in exchanges of fluids, accidentally consumed when present in tainted meat, or, in fearsome concentrations, inhaled.

It can also be loaded into a syringe and injected.

If one should be inclined to do so.

The second most essential difference between the two is that the insomnia brought about by FFI does not manifest until the prion's work is well under way, forming amyloid protein plaques, literally eating holes in the brain, leaving star-shaped astrocytes.

With SLP, insomnia does not follow months or even years of other symptoms, as it does with FFI, but is almost always the first definitive indication that one has been infected. One could easily clear physical space around oneself with some alacrity by mentioning that one had been sleeping poorly of late.

The lack of sleep, the absence of rest for the body or the mind, is the *final* twist of FFI's dagger. By that time it has already eaten vast holes in the brain, leaving a cratered landscape, one of the side effects being the loss of sleep. Once insomnia does set in for sufferers of FFI, the end comes quite swiftly, if no less grotesquely. Twitching and covered in sores, sweating puss, nearly all homeostatic functions of the body malfunctioning at some level, FFI's victims lose the ability to communicate, may or may not lose their sense of self, but never become senseless. And as the body rots around them, the breakdowns become so complete that traditional pain relief no longer has any application. Chemical receptors no longer accept soothing shapes that might dull the agony.

It is, with no irony intended, a hell of a way to die.

SLP is somewhat worse.

Primarily this is due to the fact that it takes longer to do its work. When SLP lodges in a healthy body and begins the process of conformational influence that mutates the proteins around it, it attacks the thalamus *directly*. The seat of sleep, the thalamus is also a switching station for communications and telemetry within the brain, a key target where a terrorist of the mind with only one bomb at his disposal might choose to blow himself up. In doing so, said terrorist would be particularly successful in the ultimate goal of his trade. For there is nothing quite so terror-inducing as the loss of sleep. It creates phantoms and doubts, causes one to question one's own abilities and judgment, and, over time, dismantles, from within, the body.

SLP could not be more effective if it entered the body wearing a balaclava and a vest packed with C-4. Detonated, it spreads, instead of shrapnel, copies of itself. The copies chain, reproduce, and the thalamus forgets how to sleep. Signals are sent, telling the body and varied territories of the brain what to do and when, but they are hopelessly scrambled. And there is no rest.

Once the bomb has gone off, the infrastructure of the body begins to degrade as a result of sleep deprivation. But the greater portion of the brain is untouched. Nights of restless sleep turn into hours of wakefulness staring at the ceiling, punctuated by the occasional sudden plunge into deep sleep, jarred back to the surface by dreams of stinging vividness. Segue to pacing marathons, pitiless channel flipping in the wee hours, aimless drives to no destination. And when no denial can possibly remain for comfort, end in absolute insomnia, shuffling out to join the wakeful millions, burning the midnight oil.

What was left of it.

I watched them, in the light cast from the glass face of the Staples Center, as they shifted and wandered through the Midnight Carnival.

Despite the hunger for entertainment and distraction, professional sports were not being played. Not on their previous scale.

At a certain point, leagues and owners had realized that uninfected fans had become gun-shy about enclosing themselves in massive venues with tens of thousands, a significant number of whom were statistically predetermined to be carrying SLP. Add to that fear the quite natural disinclination to be in such a place should there be one of the ever-increasing blackouts, and one found some remarkable bargains available at online ticket exchanges. The teams played on, TV revenue still being a big enough carrot that could draw the beast toward the unreachable end of the stick.

Things didn't fold entirely until a NAJi blew himself up inside Wrigley Field. It wasn't home run balls falling on Waveland Avenue that afternoon.

It didn't take more than a week for the leagues to suspend operations. The assumption being that once things were in hand the seasons that had been halted in progress would resume. Some months at most. Well into the second full lost season, there were no indications that the arenas and stadiums would be reopening any time soon.

Oddly, or ironically, perhaps, in South America and throughout Asia the football stadiums were still packed. Soccer was at last becoming the breakout U.S. spectator sport that television executives had long despaired it would never become. One heard that even Great Britain, almost immediately quarantined when SLP was thought to be mad cow disease, still packed the pitches for matches, and increasingly violent riots. Both of which found their way to the Web as pirate video, drawing fans to the teams and the hooligans of the more vicious clubs.

Without its regular tenants, and considering that the convention trade had also run a bit dry, the Staples Center was falling into disuse just as the

Midnight Carnival evolved. It began as an open-air market, part of an infrastructure that had accreted around the new borders of Skid Row as it burst from its traditional limits above Seventh and east of Main, consuming office blocks as they were emptied by bankruptcy, absorbing Little Tokyo along with the Wholesale and Fashion Districts. The ranks of the homeless swelled as every week brought a new firestorm, landslide, or pogrom to rid a particular neighborhood of whoever happened to be deemed undesirable in that locale. Clearly a population as dense as the one sprawling now from Alameda to the Harbor Freeway, from the Santa Monica to East Third, just blocks from L.A. Water and Power and the municipal and U.S. district courts, was a commercial opportunity. All of it loomed over by the squalettes on the roof and upper floors of the unfinished L.A. Live tower.

Taco truck drivers, dumpster-diving salvage experts, industrious home vegetable gardeners with ample yards, buskers, medicos whose licenses had been rendered useless for years after they crossed the border to El Norte, breeders of cats and dogs who knew from hard experience that qualms about where the meat comes from are the only thing soothed by true hunger, dealers in the looted contents of abandoned Inland Empire McMansions, oil drum barbeque chefs, experts in shiatsu massage, mechanics with a knack for cars that predated a preponderance of silicon chips, biodiesel siphon bandits with unfiltered bootleg fryer oil, pickpockets and whores, those with a gift for distilling caustic spirits from corn husks and potato peels, and the assorted enforcers and homegrown security who watched over them all, keeping the peace, or shattering it, depending on who was or was not paying.

Naturally, the city let it fester. And equally naturally, once it was settled with a degree of permanence that could not be defeated with anything short of bulldozers (an option championed by a city council member who was soon after dumped, partially eviscerated, from the open door of a speeding car at the emergency entrance of King Harbor Hospital), the city set out to regulate and tax the new outbreak of free trade. In terms of logistics this had resulted in a fence, a price for admission to the market, and a large deployment of former parking enforcement officers who, in the face of obsolescence, had been pressed into duty as ticket takers. They were supported in dire extremes by a small contingent of SWATs who emerged from their command trailer from time to time to fire shots into the air, quelling the more than occasional riots that threatened to break out each time the city upped the cost of a ticket. Industrious visitors circled the fence until they found one of the many rents that were opened daily in the chain link, always more holes than the harried crew of repairmen were capable of or, for their own well-being, cared to be seen sealing.

The Anschultz Entertainment Group saw their own opportunity and seized it, creating a kind of indoor annex to the market within the Staples. The goods and services were slightly more high-end; there was ample seating, plumbing; the ventilation system functioned, if not the AC; security was more present and less likely to shake one down; and it had the reassuring familiarity of a mall. There also tended to be a number of spontaneous parties breaking out of luxury suites that had been rented by slummers, or erupting in the aisles when the DJ who commanded the PA system played an especially groove-worthy track.

Initially only pockets of both markets served beyond midnight, but as more and more sleepless were drawn to the candle flames, wood-burning grills, and improvised bars built on cinder block and scrapped Formica countertops, more and more shopkeepers began to extend their hours. It was a matter of only a few months before the market's late-night trade was catering specifically to the sleepless demographic, a segment of the population that as often as not had little or no foreseeable need to keep its savings intact or to cling to personal possessions of value.

The Midnight Carnival was a name of unknown origin. And for any cheer it might suggest one could more realistically draw to memory the fetid smell of summer midways, the gap-toothed carneys, and the inevitable greasy stickiness unpleasantly covering one's hands at the end of the day.

Honestly, I have no idea why I loved the place.

Vinnie the Fish worked from the back of a permanently immobilized late-model El Camino. The tailgate, dismounted and resting on waist-high stacks of milk crates ballasted with chunks of broken concrete, served as his work surface and service area. Standing behind this improvised counter, he'd reach into one of the dozen or so coolers that filled the open bed of the El Camino and pull out calico bass, California sheeps-head, bonito, the occasional horn shark, yellowtail, or moray, and gut, scale, debone, or fillet the fish to order.

A wobbly Webber grill was home to three cast iron frying pans that he'd occasionally squirt with olive oil, tossing in fistfuls of mussels, smelt, and rock shrimp. A damp rag wrapped around his hand, he'd toss the mollusks, crustaceans, and fish, sprinkling them with salt and pepper, waiting for the mussels to open, the skin of the smelt to crisp, and the shrimps to pinken before dumping them onto thick folds of newspaper, datelines from two years gone by, garnished with half a lemon, a dollop of his wife's homemade tartar sauce, and a white plastic spork.

I sat on an upside-down bucket at the counter, watching as he passed one of these packages to the potbellied Cambodian he paid in fresh fish to sit on the roof of the El Camino with a sawed-off Louisville Slugger across his knees and the butt of a Smith & Wesson AirLite .41 Magnum sticking from his belt. The guard was only a few years younger than myself, bald, with a scar that should have been mortal running from ear to ear. He squeezed lemon over his meal and sporked it to his mouth, bite by bite, his eyes never ceasing to roam over the customers and the jostling crowd in the immediate area.

Vinnie dipped a meat hook into one of the coolers, brought out a two-foot kelp bass, and held it before a stout Salvadoran *abuela* attended by a whippetlike teenager with MS-13 tattoos on his neck and face who eyed the Cambodian much as his grandmother eyed the dead fish. She ran her fingers down its flank then held them to her nose and gave a sniff, instantly shaking her head and complaining in loud Spanish about the price Vinnie had chalked on a piece of broken slate in front of the counter.

Vinnie's only reaction was to drop the fish back in its cooler, lift one of the pans from the grill, give the contents a toss, and nod at the next customer, a young Chinese housewife who immediately requested the immaculate bass, setting off a wail of protest from the granny claiming prior ownership. The gangster grandson made a move toward the housewife, and the Cambodian slipped off the roof of the El Camino, half-finished dinner in one hand, stubbed baseball bat in the other. The boy struck a pose, chin out, arms akimbo, but his grandmother hooked him by the elbow, hissing in his ear, dragging him from the path of the bowlegged Cambodian, both of them disappearing into the crowd, trailed by the hood's string of threats and promises of retribution for the disrespect shown his grandmother.

He had good reason to love his grandmother, as she'd undoubtedly just saved him from a severe maiming. Watching the Cambodian carefully set his meal atop the roof before boosting himself back onto his watchtower, I was sure she had seen as clearly as I the easy menace of a death squad veteran. Though she would have remembered the look from National Republican Alliance soldiers; it was much the same in the face of a former Khmer Rouge.

Vinnie completed the sale of the disputed fish to the Chinese housewife, gave the pan a final toss, emptied it into a wad of paper, and passed my dinner to me, steam rising, oil and fluid from the mussels already seeping through the bottom.

I tossed one of the smelts in my mouth, the skin popping, soft flesh all but melting, tiny bones crunching.

A perfect moment. But for the murderer atop the car.

Two of us in such close proximity was a grave imbalance of things. But such was the world now. It was not rare to find two sets of hands covered in so much blood dining at the same establishment. And it would become less rare with every passing day. Our numbers would grow. That was the shape of things.

Sad world.

Vinnie took advantage of a pause in the line of customers and pulled a can of Tecate from one of the coolers, popping it open as he came around the counter and lowered himself onto another of the buckets.

"Mara Salvatrucha cocksuckers. That kid, he brought his grandmother here to try and start shit. One of their *jefes* was by last week. They're trying to lay claim to the fish trade. They already take a piece of every job down on the ports. All those empty shipping containers that piled up in '08, '09, MS-13 is running protection on the Inland Empire drought refugees FEMA has been stuffing into those things. Those are the lucky ones. Newcomers are being housed in the cars that never got off the docks when the dealers went belly up. Anyway, they run the ports, they think they should have a piece of anything that comes out of the Pacific. This punk, tattoos on his eyelids, like red monster eyes on his eyelids. His thing is, he tells you what he wants, what he's gonna take from you, then he goes eye to eye with you, but he closes his eyes. Supposed to freak you out, those monster eyes, plus the idea that he's so tough he can close his eyes in front of you and not worry about what you're gonna do. Vireak there was over at the port-o-potties. And don't think it was some damn coincidence that the asshole came around to baksheesh me while Vireak was taking a crap. So he tells me there's a new tax on fish. They're gonna be needing one pound out of every three I bring into the carnival. One-third of what my uncle Paulo and my cousins catch on my boat. A third of what I buy from the guys who ride their catches over from the piers every sundown. Guys who still hang their lines over the rail and put their catches in wicker creels and ride it here on bicycles. Not just from Venice and Santa Monica; I got a guy who rides up from Huntington. One-third. So he tells me that's the new tax, and then he puts his face close to mine, and he closes his eyes. And stands there waiting for me to fold."

I sucked a mussel from its shell, bit into it.

Vinnie took a long drink of beer and wiped his mouth with the back of a thick forearm stained with a faded blue network of nautical tattoos.

"So what I did was—"

He smiled, showing big square teeth the color of old scrimshaw.

"I went back to work. Asshole is standing there, ten, twenty seconds, half a minute maybe. People who'd been watching this go down, they're starting to giggle. I'm fileting some yellowtail for the sushi guy down the way, asshole is standing there with his eyes closed. And he's not alone. Got his posse with him. Three more assholes with face tattoos, standing there, they don't know what to do. Looking at each other. *What do we do? I don't know.* What they know is, none of them wants to be the one to tap *jefe* on the shoulder, have him open his eyes and see I've just thrown him a steaming pile of disrespect. No one wants to be looking at him when he realizes just how much face he's lost. So they all stand around, the crowd is laughing now, and then the asshole opens his eyes."

Vinnie spit between the scuffed toes of his chef's clogs.

"He wanted to make a move pretty bad. But I had the filet knife in my hand, the meat hook right there where I could get to it. Him and his boys were packing God knows what, but none of them had fisted up. He knew he made a move, he was gonna get opened up asshole to gullet whether his boys capped me or not. So we did the Salvadoran/Italian-American standoff thing for a few seconds. Then Vireak came back from the crapper."

He chugged the rest of his beer, crushed the can, tossed it back into the cooler he'd taken it from, and belched.

"And that was pretty much that. They shoved some old ladies around, stole a few oranges from the produce cart over there, swore I'd be eating my own cock within the week, and fucked off."

He took a box of Ukrainian knockoff Salems from a pocket of his black-and-white checked pants and lit one with a disposable Chiapas Jaguares lighter.

"That asshole today was the first any of them have come back. Promise you, the play was supposed to be that he brought his grandma because she always starts some kind of argument with the baker or the butcher over prices. He was gonna step in, shank me, and get the fuck out. No one told him that even if he stuck me he was gonna end up dealing with Vireak. No one told him shit because I guarantee you that he's someone's asshole baby cousin and no one is looking out for his ass. They figure maybe he gets lucky and puts the knife in me and I take a dirt nap. Whether or not he gets wasted they don't give a shit. Main thing is, they want me to know it's not over. But they wanted at least for him to get his blade out and cut me a little. Something. Didn't count on grandma being more savvy than all their asses combined. That old broad, she knew what the score was. Got her *niño* out of here. Good for her. Not that the world couldn't have afforded one less asshole around, but good for her getting him out."

He took a long drag and sent a plume of smoke up into the night.

"Good for her."

I poked through the empty mussel shells, trying to find one I might not have already eaten, looking for a last shrimp or smelt hidden at the bottom, but alas, it was not to be. I balled the now sopping paper around the shells and tossed it into another of the white plastic buckets.

"Delicious, Vinnie."

He flicked ash from his cigarette with a thumb callused and scarred by a thousand fishhooks.

"You let me, I'll make you something for real. One of those bass, I'll score it, pour some olive oil over it, rub in some sea salt and some pepper, shove a couple lemons inside, and drop the whole thing on the grill just like that. Get some red potatoes from the potato lady, wrap 'em in foil, drop 'em in the coals. Some arugula from the lettuce lady. When the bass is done, skin is crispy, the eyes are starting to pop out, I'll put the fish over the greens, toss the potatoes with some oil and salt and pepper and some dill, put 'em on the side, give you a lemon. Eat it just like that. Grilled bass alla salad. Shit, I'll even give you a real fork. You say the word, you can have that whenever you want."

I held up my hands.

"It sounds more than delightful."

I gestured at my rumpled slacks and jacket.

"But I'd have to come properly attired for such a feast. Evening clothes. Nothing less would do."

He smiled.

"You do that; you put on your tux and come down here. I'll find a tablecloth. Somewhere in here, someone is selling linens. I'll get a tablecloth and a napkin you can tuck in your collar. Real class."

I took a handkerchief from my pocket and wiped my greasy fingers and lips.

"Something to look forward to."

He dropped his cigarette butt and let it hiss out in a puddle of melted ice that had drained from the coolers.

"Yeah, something to look forward to. Who couldn't use something like that?"

I carefully folded my handkerchief away.

"Vincent, there was something I did want to have a word with you about."

He reached over the counter, took one of the empty frying pans from the grill, and banged it on the side of the El Camino. In response, the passenger door creaked open and a chubby brown teenager in a bloody white apron and checked pants climbed out, rubbing his eyes.

Vinnie rose and replaced the pan on the grill.

"Gonna take a walk, Ciccio."

The boy nodded, yawning.

Vinnie pointed at the coolers.

"Push the eel before it goes bad."

The boy scratched at a head covered in curly red hair.

"*Sí*, Zio Vincenzo. Anguilla. *Sí*."

I rose, dusting my backside, and followed Vinnie away from his fish stand, winding through the aisles of the carnival, away from the food stalls and carts that clustered near the gates where they could be easily accessed by visitors who did not care to take in the esoterica that lay deeper within.

If those outer layers of the carnival bore the character of a frontier marketplace, long on commerce and short on law enforcement, the interior felt much like a war-zone souk, bristling with opportunities to lose oneself, figuratively, literally, mortally. It was entirely of your choosing how far you cared to penetrate.

As the desires catered to became more perverse, the density of the sleepless increased. Existing on the far verge of human experience, there were tastes only they could reasonably be expected to acquire. The appeal, for instance, of being injected with mass volumes of amphetamine and then sealed in a sensory deprivation tank escaped even myself. But it was a service with popularity attested to by a long and twisting line of the haggard.

The concentration of sleepless in the darker zones of the carnival had led to rumor and superstition. A belief among the ignorant that one could contract SLP in this area simply by breathing the air. As if the sleepless were shedding and exhaling the SL prion in thick clouds. Not so. Of course one could be infected if one inhaled a sufficient quantity of SLP, but the sleepless did not walk about in a miasma of the illness.

Now, if there had been an incinerator on the site cremating sleepless remains, that would have been a definite threat. Prions, notoriously resilient, remain active even when burned. Prion ash is every bit as infectious as a wad of it residing, for the sake of argument, in a hamburger. Early in the course of the pandemic, before it was even known as such, CDC guidelines had called for the burning of SLP corpses.

SL response teams in orange vests would appear at hospitals, and increasingly at homes, unpacking electric saws. The bodies of the sleepless dead were decapitated so that tissue from the brains could be catalogued. Anomalies were sought, anything that might give promise of a cure. No one wanted to throw away the brain that might hold the key. But once the heads were packed in dry ice and sealed in a bucket, the bodies had to be dealt with.

Infection rates around crematoriums and landfill incinerators were well above national and global averages. Eventually the incongruity was noticed. Sleepless were no longer burned. They were limed and buried in concrete-lined mass graves. Deep.

Some countries were still burning. If one cared to track such things via the many thousands of SLP-related blogs, one gathered that the hinterlands of civilization had not gotten the word. In wide swaths of Africa and Asia, corpse pyres burned nonstop, the new dead piled on by the lowest castes. The longer the fires burned, the larger they grew, their plumes of smoke and infection creating more fuel. I'd been told by a Navy airman I'd met in casual circumstances that his carrier strike group fighter wing had flown escort for tankers dropping flame retardant on those blazes. The natives restarted their fires in short order, and the strategy shifted. Before his group had been recalled to waters closer to home, the airman had flown multiple missions firing Maverick missiles at towering piles of burning human bodies. The logic behind this new strategy, if one can use the word "logic" in this scenario, was not only to decimate the burn site but to terrorize the populace out of the practice of corpse burning. The fact that the attacks rained SLP ash and mist upon the locals seemed to be considered an acceptable level of collateral damage.

I never saw the airman again, naturally, but I have occasionally thought about him. He woke in the middle of the night, crying. He had reason. And I held him until the sun brought some light into the room and he said he had to go. His CSG was setting sail again, for where he was not certain. But the *George Washington* was soon offshore of Venezuela, and I am certain he became embroiled in that bit of twenty-first-century gunboat diplomacy. Finding new raw materials for his nightmares.

No, contagion was not an issue, no matter how deeply or extensively one chose to plumb the Midnight Carnival. Which is not to say that there wasn't an ample supply of unpleasant deaths available to the unwary. Along with perversity in their desires, many sleepless also brought with them an absolute disregard for their own well-being. So it was that Vinnie and I maintained a prudent watchfulness as we strolled.

A thick-bodied boy in a faded Los Angeles Raiders hoodie shuffled past, offering a whispered chant.

"Dreamer. Dreamer. Dreamer."

It would be bootleg, of course. A compound of heroin and ketamine most likely. Called double horse, it was the most popular home brew version of the real drug. So potent, it could knock even a late-stages sleepless to his knees and offer a brief period of sensation that I'd been told felt much like severe food poisoning without the diarrhea and vomiting. That this should be desirable was all one really needed to know about the ravages of SLP.

At a table filled with hand-painted miniatures of stock nonplayer characters and creatures from Chasm Tide, Vinnie paused to look over the selection.

"The kid back there, Ciccio, he loves the game."

I stood at an angle to him, keeping an eye on the aisle at his back.

"A nephew?"

He shook his head, inspecting the detail on an ogre.

"Grandson of one of my uncle's war buddies. His mom is Italian. His scumbag dad who split on the kid and his mom, he's American. We were able to get some paperwork done, make something happen. Got him out of the Mid-European Quarantine Zone. Traveling with that accent, kid must have caught shit everywhere. You know, they still haven't unsealed the Italian border. Known for how long that SLP and FFI aren't the same thing, but the UN still won't open the damn border."

He put the ogre down and picked up a Chasm Wraith.

"Once he was out of the MEQZ, he went into the pipeline. A guy who used to handle mostly Bulgarian girls for the skin trade when you had to reach overseas for that kind of thing, got him across for us. Dealing with INS once he was here, that was an exercise in bullshit that I never want to repeat. Finally, I asked some guy in an office downtown what the hell it would cost, theoretically, to get the kid out of processing, with or without papers."

I nodded.

"And what was the theoretical cost?"

"Ten theoretical grand. U.S. Cash money. Asshole. I could have done double that if he'd asked. Cheapskate corruption."

He held a Kraken between thumb and forefinger.

"How much?"

The proprietor looked up from the elf he was painting, squinted.

"Fifty."

From the neck of his fish gut–stained butcher's smock Vinnie pulled a plastic card on a chain. The miniatures painter took an RFID interrogator from below his table, aimed it at the card, and pulled the trigger, reading the details from the chip embedded in the card as they scrolled on the small screen at the butt of the interrogator.

"Fishmonger?"

Vinnie nodded.

"I got eels, fresh as daisies, give you ten pounds."

The man set the plastic gun down.

"I'll pick them up before morning."

They shook hands. And we walked away, Vinnie dropping the card all carnival-licensed vendors were meant to carry back inside his smock.

"The kid's mom, her we couldn't do shit about. *Child* of an American, sure. Full-blooded Italian *wife* of an American, no. Kid plays that game every chance he gets. His mom is in there. They meet up. Talk. Walk around. Whatever. I don't really get it, but it's what they do."

He looked at the Kraken, shrugged, put it in his pocket.

"So before I start up again with another story, you want to tell me what's on your mind?"

I reached inside my jacket and took out one of the pictures I had printed from the gold farm security DVD.

"He's a police officer, Vincent. Undercover. I assume narcotics."

He took a passing glance at the picture and stuffed it into a pocket, coming out with his Salems and his lighter.

"Quality's not great."

"No, it is not."

He lit a cigarette.

"It's been a long time for me. Finished my twenty years a long time ago."

"I know, Vincent."

He blew some smoke as we passed a tent that promised the spectacle of sleepless fighting barehanded, no quarter asked or given.

"Not too many of my people left on the force."

"Yes."

He held up a hand.

"Not that I won't try. I'm just saying that this may be my last trip to that well. And I can't say for sure than I'll find any water this time."

"Whatever you can do would be appreciated."

"I'll see what I see."

I patted his arm.

"And if there is anything I could do for you?"

He stopped walking.

"Well, I hate to ask."

"Please."

He shook his head.

"Just those MS-13 cocksuckers. Nothing I can't handle in the long run. But I'd rather not be looking over my shoulder."

I nodded.

"Tattoos of red monster eyes on his eyelids, you said?"

"Yeah. Him."

I smiled.

"Well, then, he should be easy enough to find."

He put out his hand.

"Thanks, Jasper, that's a load off."

"My pleasure, Vincent."

And we parted ways.

It was, in fact, easy enough to find the young Salvadoran gangster with the tattooed eyelids. And, as advertised, he did, when I presumed to confront him, close his eyes as a form of attempted intimidation.

An unfortunate choice of tactics on his part.

His posse, when I had finished with him, wisely stood down. Safe to say they saw no reason to avenge him, so certain it was that some other of them would have to assume his mantle of leadership.

No matter. *Jefe* or not, Vinnie's antagonist would no longer be showing his monster eyes to intended victims. He'd not be closing his eyes at all. Not until such time as he might be able to find a plastic surgeon willing to perhaps take flaps of skin from his buttocks out of which to form new eyelids.

1 3

7/10/10

IT'S JUST BEFORE dawn on July 10, 2010, 5:17 a.m. I am in possession
of what appears to be a factory-manufactured bottle of Afronzo-New
Day Pharm DR33M3R. The bottle's seal appears to be intact. The
identifying hologram on the label is clear; the borders of the three
primary elements, a small cloud, the letter z, and a stick-figure sheep, are
sharp. No indication that it is a counterfeit. The bottle is numbered
#ff688-6-2648-9. If authentic, the bottle was manufactured in
Farmington, IL, part of batch 688, from the sixth pod in that batch,
twenty-sixth case in that pod, forty-eighth bottle in that case, with a use
code of 9.

The 9 indicates the batch, pod, case, and bottle were meant for
distribution by the National Heath and Wellness Administration. Public
hospitals, federally insured patients. The radio frequency ID interrogator
I removed from the gallery shows that the active RFID chip under the
label is present and functioning. The chip is broadcasting the same
manufacture and batch information. If it is undamaged, it should also
detail when the contents of the bottle were manufactured, when the pod
was loaded and left the factory, its precise intended destination, and
whether it was ever received at that destination. But I do not have the
reference manual to decipher anything beyond point of origin, etc. I've
dusted the bottle for latent fingerprints and have removed several

smudged prints, two clear partial impressions of both a right index and a right ring finger, and one very clear full impression of a right middle finger. The bottle was removed from a bag in my presence, and since then has been touched only by the person who gave it to me at that time. I believe that the smudges were already present on the bottle before it was removed from the bag. I believe that both clear partials and the clear full belong to the person who gave me the bottle of what I believe will prove to be factory-manufactured DR33M3R. For the record, that person was Afronzo Jr., Parsifal K. He didn't even blink. He took the bottle from his bag and offered it to me like it was something he does every night. Like his bag is full of Dreamer that he has to use to make drug deals because his daddy cut off his allowance. Dreamer. He used it to get what he wanted, like that is all it's good for.

Stay focused.

Working in the bathroom, I lifted the prints and applied them to slides from my evidence kit. I placed the bottle of DR33M3R and the slides, in separate evidence bags, in the safe. Rose wanted to know what I was doing in the bathroom for so long. She wasn't suspicious, she just knows the stress from the job gives me stomach and digestion problems. "Irregularity isn't a joke, Park." She gave me some tea once, but I spent the whole next day in the bathroom and never took it again. I think when I went in there after I got home she was just excited to think I might be using the toilet. "There is nothing more mysterious than a marriage." That's what my father told me when I called him and my mother to say I'd gotten married. Nothing in my marriage to Rose has proved him wrong. When I finally took her east two years later to meet them, he was strange with her. Not strange like he was with everyone else, not his standard detachment, something else. I don't think he liked her, but I think he may have been impressed by her. Her directness. "Good to meet you, Ambassador Haas." He'd shook his head. "Please don't feel you need to use my title. Mr. Haas will suffice." And she'd nodded back. "I think, sir, that we'll both be more comfortable if I stick with Ambassador Haas." And she was right. I think he'd have been more comfortable if my sister and I had called him Ambassador Haas instead of Father. He'd have preferred that from everyone but my mother. To her

he was always Peachy. A reference to something that happened long
before I was born. She called him Peachy everywhere except at what she
referred to as "occasions." Ambassador Haas to everyone else, Peachy to
my mother. Is it any wonder he killed himself after she died?
Stay focused.
In exchange for what I believe to be FDA Schedule Z DR33M3R, I gave
to Afronzo, Parsifal K., twenty-five grams of Shabu-quality Chinese
crystal methamphetamine, which I then witnessed him distribute to five
unidentified individuals. He was right about them in Chasm Tide. The
sleepless did amazing things. They must have been heavy gamers to
begin with, but their approach was almost pure chaos. There was no
indication that they were working together, they immediately split up;
the barbarian stormed Forge, cutting down anyone in his path, and
another, on an entirely different errand, healed anyone and everyone,
including those the barbarian had wounded. It was all like that, every
move at cross-purposes, using up their power unnecessarily, but by the
time they reassembled, they had the weapons, tools, and keys they'd
come for, and through some perfect calculation of costs and benefits, the
overall power of the group had increased. It wasn't random. They see
holes in the game. Rules that can be slipped between. Moves that I've
seen Rose attempt with Cipher Blue, they executed cleanly, proving that
they are possible. Rose was playing when I got home. Francine was still
here. She had the baby, was sitting in the rocking chair in the nursery
with the baby on a pillow in her lap. The baby looked asleep. Really
asleep. She only looks that way when Francine holds her and rocks her. I
wanted to pick her up, but I knew if I did she would wake up. Francine
said she'd been quiet for almost two hours. She said her eyes had been
closed for over forty minutes. She looked asleep. Rose was in our
bedroom, in bed with her laptop on her knees, trying the Labyrinth
again. I went straight to the safe to lock up the guns and my stash. She
didn't look up, just asked me how "classes" had been. I told her I needed
to go to the bathroom. I didn't want to lie and say anything about the
classes that I haven't taught in over three years, and I didn't have time to
sit next to her and bring her back to here. When I came out of the
bathroom and locked the bottle and slides in the safe and she asked why

I'd been in there for so long, she seemed normal. Normal for how normal is now. Not the old normal. Not the old Rose. But she's still Rose. Still concerned that I'm not getting enough fiber. She had put the laptop aside and was stretching her back on the floor. Her muscles are knotted into golf balls up and down her spine. Francine does kinesiology as well as being a doula. That was one of the reasons she was Rose's favorite when we were finding someone to help us with the home birth. She's massaged Rose's back a few times. The first time, I heard the cracking from the office and ran out because I thought someone was breaking things. She gave Rose some exercises to do. So Rose was on her back when I got out of the bathroom, knees up and pointed to one side, arms out, head facing the other way. "Did you shit?" I saw the look on her face. And I lied. "Yeah, I did." She looked so happy for a moment. Nothing more mysterious.

Stay focused.

The art gallery. After the sleepless had launched their quest and were under way, Cager whispered in my ear. "Come make some money." He took me to the gallery to sell to his friends. I wanted to stay and watch the sleepless in Chasm, but I'm a dealer, so I needed to go and make some money, or he might have started thinking that I might be a cop. Rose remembered that I'm a cop. She asked me again to quit and stay at home. She asked me to take her and the baby out of the city. She said she wanted to see the ocean. She closed her eyes and said we should go to Half Moon Bay and watch the sunset and drink a bottle of wine and make love on the beach.

She sighed and opened her eyes and saw me.

"How am I going to be able to look after you?" she asked.

I shook my head and told her I didn't know, and she kind of sighed like she always does when she thinks I'm not getting something.

"No, I mean, really, how am I gonna look the fuck after you?"

I told her she didn't have to look after me, that I was okay.

She was staring at the ceiling.

"You're such a, God I hate the word, but you're such an innocent. I mean, how am I supposed to walk away from that?"

I wanted to tell her, I wanted to say what she wanted to hear, and I wanted to hear what she would say next, but she would have been mad if she knew what I did. So instead I told her her name, I told her who I was, I told her about the baby, and she looked at me and struggled with it all and told me she knew all that. "Sometimes," she said, "it's just easier not to try and keep it straight." And she put her head on the floor. "God, I wish I could sleep." I thought about the DR33M3R in the safe. And came out here to the car with my journal and laptop and Hydo's travel drive. There's more to learn in there. But I don't have time to search. Stay focused.

Francine is leaving. I need to help with the baby.

Stay focused.

▮ ▮ ▮

THE GALLERY WAS beyond the southeastern edge of Skid Row, in one of the abandoned warehouses of the Los Angeles wholesale produce market. It was not, fortunately, in one of the warehouses decommissioned while still full of fruits and vegetables that had been half-rotted by the time they were received, and thoroughly rotted by the time it was realized that the cost of moving whatever was salvageable to market would far outstrip any profits. Those warehouses were some distance away; still, the massive tonnage of what was, by now, high-quality compost permeated the air with a sweetness that was nearly overwhelming. I saw more than one black-swathed artiste with previous experience of the space sniffing at a sachet of potpourri. Most made do by dipping cocktail napkins into their plastic cups of wine, using them to cover their noses.

Making no effort to camouflage the smell, I found that it became increasingly difficult to concentrate on the present moment. As is often the case with intense and singular odors, this one evoked a powerful nostalgia. Our sense of smell registers in the reptile bits of the brain at the top of the spine. Who hasn't been thrown back to some unpleasantness or delight by a sudden whiff of an old lover's cologne or the unexpected combination of burned toast and mint dish soap? In the gallery, I was recalling deep loam and mulch, limitless greenery and rains, rot that ate your uniform from your back, undergrowth matted in sweet jungle muck soil.

In mind of my formative years.

In such a state it was essential that I concentrate. I was, after all, armed and in the presence of a large number of people. The smell and the tide of memory could have easily washed away my controls and defenses, leaving behind the exposed carcass of my true self.

I will confess that I allowed that self a moment's freedom. It duly took stock of the strategic situation, selected targets, and calculated how many innocent dead might be manufactured before some of the more able personal security contractors attached to the gallery's wealthier patrons took action and maneuvered me into an inevitable cross fire at the far corner of the warehouse near the bathrooms. But before I could mount the three steps that led to a lectern from which select pieces in the show would soon be auctioned, and which afforded superior firing lines, I focused my concentration on a square of tagboard and its hand-lettered description of the work of art above it.

It would not do to be run to ground in such a place, riddled with bullets by hired guns. That it was an art gallery was insufficient. The smell aside, the DJ was playing irritating French chamber pop. I would not die to that sound track.

My painstakingly assembled life had meaning. The litter of bodies that lined the path I had walked these many years were not incidental or random. There was a reason for so much death.

I would know the moment. Vague about so much else, I knew with utter certainty that I would see and recognize the moment of my death, the shape and purpose of my life revealed in my passing.

I could bear to wait some more.

So I looked at the art.

Mounted on an eighteen-by-eighteen-inch square of what appeared to be salvaged parquet flooring, framed in Deco chrome, long black enamel accents at the corners, the piece was a kind of collage. In the lower right corner was a list of enemies vanquished, quests completed, treasures found, mountains scaled, riddles answered. In the lower left, a clumsy but earnest pencil portrait on blue-lined graph paper of a one-eyed pirate, long hair held back by a bandanna, dangling chains and trinkets revealed by an open-neck shirt. Above both of these elements was a handheld gaming or Internet device. It was difficult to identify a make or model as the case of the gadget had been removed, leaving a green resin board etched in thin lines of gold and silver, miniature numbered and lettered keys, several chips, a disk of bright silicon, a cluster of colored wires, and a screen with a five-inch diagonal. Across this screen a high-resolution version of what I took to be the pirate pictured below swashed and buckled. On the high seas, at land, with cutlass, dagger, or bare wits, he gave proof that the list of derring-do below were not the bluffs of an armchair buccaneer. Dead center of the three items was a dull silver thumb drive. Nondescript, a Memorex 2G. Fragments of yellowed computer punch cards, the inner works of broken clocks, and cloudy paste stones, Salvation Army junk jewelry, decorated the spaces between the key elements.

The tagboard below the piece explained that I was looking at Kelvin Ripu, a level 87 Raider Prince, Last Commodore of the Orcan Fleet, Possessor of the Trident Perilous, Rider of Winds, Lord of Waves. It explained further that Kelvin was the creation of "gamer/artist" Kevin Puri, a twenty-seven-year-old call-center team manager in Mumbai. Kevin had been "crafting" Kelvin for five years. The piece was composed of Kevin Puri's handwritten and signed account of Kelvin's greatest accomplishments within Chasm Tide, his own drawing of the character, digitally preserved highlights of Kelvin in action, and the character itself, password, account number, the entire long string of 1s and 0s that it was knitted from, preserved in the thumb drive. All other traces of Kelvin Ripu, I was assured by the description, had been erased from the Chasm Tide mainframes and Kevin Puri's own desktop and backup hard drive.

The art object itself had been conceived and assembled by Shadrach, best known for the street and performance art he executed within Chasm Tide.

Kelvin was being offered for sale at 25,000 U.S. dollars. A little red sticker on the wall let me know that someone had already met that price.

A young man projecting a passable counterfeit of the negligent aura of an obscure rock star or fiercely independent film director stood at the center of a small crowd, commenting on the market for the works on display.

"Are they collectible? Yes. But they're more than that. They're also fully playable. As is, they are static works of art. Lavished with attention by the gamer/artists. The accomplishments, the artifacts they carry, the look of the characters, are the fulfillment of dreams. Inspired by a setting in Chasm Tide, or a mounting surface, or a frame, or some found object that he wishes to incorporate, Shadrach seeks out the characters that can be ultimately completed by inclusion in one of his pieces. But once *you* own them, these works of art change in nature. The owner of a character's account is the animating soul. The life. If you so choose, you can break the glass, pay to reactivate the account, and evolve the work. These pieces are finished as they hang on the wall, but you decide if they are alive."

He touched the corner of a heavy Baroque frame, the gilding peeling off in long curls, a sorceress of some kind pinned behind the glass.

"They are collectible. Changeable. In-game, you can breed them if you like. They are unique."

"They're fake."

This interjection came from another young man, one whose quite genuine aura of wealth, privilege, and fame easily outshone the lecturer and exposed highlights of envy and resentment.

The lecturer put his hands in the pockets of the narrow-lapeled, three-button black sharkskin jacket he wore over a blue and white argyle V-neck sweater vest.

"These are thoroughly authenticated Shadrach originals. These are first-sale items, fresh from Shad's studio. Each one has an RFID chip on the mounting, worked into the aesthetics of the piece, actively broadcasting a catalogue number, date of completion, and title."

The famous youth, now illuminated by the staccato flashes of the event's official photographer, and lesser blips of light from the cells and digicams of the growing crowd of onlookers, turned his attention to the sorceress on the wall, presenting his profile to the lenses.

"I'm not suggesting that Shadrach, when he wasn't wandering around Chasm painting his tag on castle walls or working on the logos for his new T-shirt line, didn't have his assistant place an ad on a few message boards offering to buy high-level characters for cash. Or that he didn't have some other assistants go out and hit a few dozen estate sales and come back with crates of stuff they could break up and glue-gun back together into these. What I'm saying is that they're fake art. They are not art at all."

There was a general mutter of titillation, over which the heathen youth raised his voice.

"These are piecemeal imitations of real art created by real artists. These are random characters. Some of them are interesting, but they are mostly just high-level hack-n-slashers loaded with uberartifacts that the players likely bought black market. People sold them to Shadrach because they don't play the game anymore or they have better characters and they're bored of these ones or because they're hard up for the money. The real art, the *real* characters are being created by gamers who have a vision when they *enter* Chasm. They start with the blank canvas, and they fill it, working toward a specific skill set, level, a list of deeds that adds up to something. They spend hundreds of hours, months, crafting a character until it's done. Artists like Tierra Boswell, Manute, Carolyn Liu, they're painting with the game, making beautiful things. These on the wall, these are just toys no one plays with anymore."

The mutter threatened to boil over into hubbub.

The lecturer raised his hand.

"Process is process. Michelangelo didn't paint the Sistine Chapel on his own; he had dozens of assistants helping him. Warhol? He used an assembly line. Is anyone going to dispute that he was creating art? Shadrach's process does involve commerce, and it does include the invaluable help of his apprentices. And certainly other artists are working in this medium. Rodin wasn't the only sculptor to work in bronze, was he? That doesn't change the uniqueness of his vision."

A cell rang, the opening synthesizer drone from "Down in the Park," and the famous young man took a Nokia e77 from his messenger bag.

"If it doesn't bother you people that Shadrach buys half these characters directly from the gold farms, by all means buy them and hang them on your walls. Your character will show in the quality of the character art you display. Excuse me, I have a call I have to take."

He put the phone to his ear, turned his back, and walked away, the gravity of his fame drawing not only his own entourage but also the photographer and the majority of the lecturer's audience.

I followed him myself, drifting at the periphery of the orbiting mass, shuffling my feet somewhat aimlessly, the shameless gawking about me allowing me to similarly crane my neck and gather an eyeful. It lasted only minutes, just until it became clear that he was done making a slight spectacle of himself for the evening, and that he would not be inviting everyone back to his place for cocaine and caviar. As the crowd realized the show was over, they captured a last few sullen pictures of him sequestered in the corner, talking into his phone, a pair of female bodyguards facing outward to keep intruders on his privacy at bay.

I was forced to meander away with the rest of the herd, nodding occasionally to give the impression that I might be engaged in the detailed recaps they were sharing with one another, reliving what had just happened in front of all their eyes, making it more real for themselves, showing one another the pictures they had all just taken to emphasize the absolute solidity of their brush with fame and art scandal. Returning to my perusal of the walls, I was able to use the glass face of a piece mounted on onyx tile to continue my observation surreptitiously.

I saw the conclusion of the young man's phone conversation, his apparent irritation at how it concluded, the equally irritated fashion in which he waved away all members of his entourage, the manner in which they floundered when set adrift, and the impulsiveness with which he grabbed a solitary figure near the door as he made his exit.

I'd already noted this figure. Alone but not aloof, he'd never joined the crowd when the unevenly matched debate had been engaged. Instead, he'd wandered to the desk near the lectern, the location where the gallerist conducted business, confirming sales and arranging deliveries. He'd passed in front of her desk, and, not coincidentally, I think, there was a sudden absence of one of the two RFID interrogators that had been left there to establish the absolute authenticity of Shadrach's work.

Plucking a catalogue from the hand of a thin, young, black-miniskirted woman in architect's glasses, I walked out onto the former warehouse's loading dock, face stuck between the glossy pages, reading an introduction that largely echoed what the lecturer had pronounced inside.

From that vantage I glanced above the edge of the page and watched as the famous young man took his companion by the arm and escorted him to a pig-nosed Subaru WRX and talked to him for a moment, his attractive bodyguards nearby, scanning rooflines for snipers. At the conclusion of his monologue he received some form of assent from the loner and made a beeline to an unsubtly armored Maserati Quattroporte that was soon squealing from the parking lot with one of the bodyguards at the wheel, the other in the backseat where she could throw her body across her employer's lap if called upon to do so.

By then I was opening the door of my Cadillac, having started the engine remotely, thus activating both the AC and the stereo. Inside, I waited while the companion of Parsifal K. Afronzo Jr. made a phone call, and then I followed him out the parking lot exit and along a lengthy and circuitous route to Culver City.

So it was that the lurking I'd engaged in after I had finished with Vinnie's antagonist was rewarded. The few hours I'd spent outside Denizone waiting for young Afronzo to appear, on the off chance that I might find the police officer somewhere near at hand, had borne surprising fruit. I'd not expected to stumble onto such luck, finding the young policeman at Afronzo's side. An association that confirmed the police officer was every bit as dirty as I'd suspected.

Their conversation outside the gallery, I assumed, concerned the travel drive. Which, I further assumed, was the source of Afronzo's dispute with the gold farmer. And, finally, I assumed that he'd simply been too shocked by his own actions to remember to take it with him. The dirty cop, likely a well-used family appendage, had been asked to recover the drive. His photography and other evidence gathering were intended to generate potential blackmail material should he ever find himself in dire straits with members of his own profession.

At the curb across from his home, I contemplated entering and obtaining the drive. Were it hidden, there was no reason to think I would be unable to force the secret of its location from him. Or any other secrets, for that matter. I only deferred this errand to another time because of the possibility that he had already passed the drive to Afronzo Jr. Pillaging the Culver City two-bedroom Craftsman of a dirty cop was a mission I could undertake spontaneously. Raiding the Afronzo compound could require days of planning with no guarantee of survival. If he had given the drive to his client, I would need his assistance recovering it. Better, for the moment, to gather more intelligence.

Several windows showed light. At the back of the house I found two that were open and uncovered, allowing the night air inside for the illusion of cool it might create.

Through the master bedroom window I watched a woman in bed, propped on a mound of pillows, as she clicked away at the laptop on her knees. The pace and rhythm of her keystrokes told me that she wasn't writing. She was either very rapidly clicking through web pages or gaming. The bit of lower lip she chewed at in concentration suggested gaming. The hollowness and intensity of her eyes, the stiffness in her neck, the twitch of a muscle in her upper thigh, and her careworn beauty, told me she was sleepless.

As I watched, the police officer came out of a walk-in closet, they passed a few words, and he disappeared into the bathroom, closing the door behind him.

Through the second window I saw a stout-limbed woman teetering on the edge of forty, her hair kept very short for reasons her no-nonsense features suggested were entirely practical. Her eyes were closed; she may or may not have been asleep. On her lap was a baby, fitful, twitching.

These scenes of home life telling me as much as I needed to know about why this particular cop chose to exchange his oath for money. And amply supplying me with the means and weapons with which to attack and bend him, should the need arise, before I did away with him entirely.

14

drmr-nw inf-rqst sit-snst

Park sent the text as the sun was rising, shortly before Francine roused herself to go take care of her own children and the baby began crying again. He received a response less than an hour later as he was trying to persuade his always restless daughter to both open wide and remain still for the moment it would take for him to get the nipple of a baby bottle into her mouth. The text he read as he wrangled her on his lap was succinct.

0730

He'd need to leave soon. Leave Rose alone with the baby again.

Until the last few weeks Park wouldn't have hesitated. Throughout her illness, from the sixth month of the pregnancy when Park had finally convinced her to have the test done if only so they could take it off the list of things to worry over, caring for the baby had always centered Rose. *She'll die without us,* she'd said to Park when she first held the small bloody thing against her chest. But she'd acted more as if the baby would die without *her.* Not that she excluded Park. Not that. She'd always told him that one of the things she most looked forward to about having a baby was seeing how it would take him *out of himself.*

You live too much in your head, Park. With a baby there's no thinking, you just do what needs to be done. It's gonna be great for you. You're gonna be a great fucking dad, she'd told him more than once. Often enough for him to have it memorized.

So it wasn't that she didn't want him involved. It was more that she refused to ask for help. Insisted on doing anything and everything that she possibly could. Not because she didn't trust Park but because it gave her focus.

The baby would die without them. And as long as she was consumed with that thought and the small daily concerns of keeping a baby alive, she did not think about her own dying. Inevitable. Imminent. Horrible. The baby drew her away from dying, into a realm where the future was not a looming wall but a limitless horizon. For many months taking care of her daughter was Rose's refuge, a source of great calm and concentration. During those months Park didn't simply feel comfortable leaving Rose with the baby, he felt relieved to be able to do so. With the baby in her arms, fear, an emotion he'd thought she might well be incapable of feeling, until the moment of diagnosis, left his wife's eyes.

Now the only time the fear appeared to subside was when she became awash in the past. The increasingly frequent hallucinations that seemed always to stretch back to the years before the baby, and therefore did not allow for her.

Finding his daughter abandoned on the living room floor had not been the worst of it. Park had come home a week earlier and discovered her in the bathtub, squirming and crying in three inches of cooling water in the bus tub they bathed her in. Rose, he found along the side of the house where they kept the bicycles and lawn mower, sneaking a cigarette. God knows where she had found the cigarette, at the bottom of a shoe box in the garage perhaps. She'd reduced her habit to the occasional smoke behind Park's back shortly after they had met and she'd realized just how much he loathed the damn things. When she stopped using birth control she'd given them up completely, without a second thought.

Caught by Park in the side yard, she'd dropped the butt and begun to whistle casually, looking at the sky as she ground it under her heel, making a joke of being busted by her cop husband, just as she had on a dozen occasions in the past. But it wasn't the past. The wet and screaming baby girl in Park's arms had at first confused her and then brought the fear back to her eyes. So horrified at what she had done that she ran into the house and hid in a closet, to be coaxed out only after Park had sat outside the door for an hour, singing the ABCs to their baby over and over again until she calmed, and Rose calmed as well.

More and more often she could be found drifting, either lost in the past or immersed in Chasm Tide. The baby forgotten.

When Park had accepted Bartolome's assignment, there had been no concerns about schedule; day or night, he did what he needed to do when it needed to be done. Two months later, as Park had just started establishing his own clientele, he had noticed the stiffness in his wife's neck, the sweats and sharp pupils, and the increasingly restless sleep that she said was due to the pregnancy weight and the onset of an early summer.

Everything is changing, babe. Your work. My work. A house. Baby on the way. Of course I'm not sleeping. And of course my fucking neck is stiff. Let's slap ten, twelve pounds on your stomach and add a bra size, see how your back feels. Don't make a big fucking deal out of nothing was what she'd said.

Five months into the assignment and she'd been diagnosed. Doctors raised the specter of a late miscarriage, should her health suddenly erode and her body not be capable of carrying the baby to term. Inducing the birth early was discussed, then put aside by Rose.

No fucking way.

Park found himself silently agreeing, and soon made several phone calls to find out if LAPD health insurance would cover the expenses of a midwife and a home birth. It would. And the remains of Park's trust fund, what the markets had not decimated in the daily roller coaster rides of '08, covered the expense of having Francine stay on as their night nurse, initially an extra pair of hands when the one week Park had been able to take off was over (*Taking a break, hitting Cabo for a week,* he'd told his clients), and then as watchdog, keeping an eye out for the moments when Rose's eyes lost clarity and she would walk suddenly from a room without explanation, seeming to edit Francine and the baby from her awareness so as to pass more easily into another place and time.

His business had naturally inclined toward night trade, but Francine's availability had made it necessary for Park to cut out all day deliveries, except to his oldest and best connected clients, those he relied upon for introductions and invitations to exclusive events where he could expand his base and his pursuit of Dreamer. But the last few weeks' duty and events had pulled him regularly away from home during the daylight hours when Francine took care of her own children and gathered a few extra hours of sleep before the long nights with Rose and the baby. Park couldn't always dictate where he would be at five in the morning, how far from home, how bad the twenty-four-hour traffic jams would be. He couldn't anticipate where the Guard might have shut down eight square blocks around a raid on a suspected NAJi cell.

And soon Rose would be entering what the doctors expected would be her final two months. A period referred to in the hospitals and among professional caregivers as *the suffering*.

He'd planned to change something. Without knowing what or how. Change things so that he could be there. But that was before the murders at the gold farm. Before he met Cager. Before he had evidence in his hand. There was too much to do now. Too much for just himself and Captain Bartolome. The investigation would have to be expanded as soon as possible. The full extent of this abuse of power had to be exposed.

Plague profiteers.

The side trade in DR33M3R would be the tip of the iceberg. If they were selling it into restricted markets, that meant the supply was being shorted in other markets. Price manipulation for all intents and purposes.

And what else? Could it be worse?

The ability to treat the symptoms of SLP so effectively, implied mastery of several aspects of the disease. Park had heard dozens of conspiracy theories thrown about as he drove from house to house dispensing his wears. He'd heard them on the airwaves, barked and pontificated, and he'd heard them in the houses themselves, jabbered or mumbled. Inevitably Afronzo-New Day was mentioned.

A basic precept of detective work: When a crime is committed, who stands to profit?

Assuming a crime had been committed, no one had profited like A-ND. No one in the history of the world had profited as they had.

The baby slapped the bottle away from her face yet again, and Park found himself trying to shove the soft rubber nipple between her tight lips.

"Just take the damn thing!"

He froze. Pulled the bottle from her face and put it on the kitchen table. He touched his forehead to hers.

"I'm sorry. I'm sorry. Daddy's a little. I don't know what. I'm tired is all. I'm sorry."

She slapped the top of his head and began crying. He picked up the bottle and popped it into her open mouth, and her lips closed around it and she started to suck, gasping between mouthfuls, her eyes rimmed red.

He looked at the clock.

He found Rose at the bathroom sink. She'd just finished brushing her teeth, spitting water tinged dark pink by the blood that oozed from her receding gums. She splashed water on her face, blotted it away with a towel, and looked at herself in the mirror, touching a hollowed cheek.

"Did she eat?"

Just outside the doorway, Park shifted, his reflection appearing in the glass.

"It took awhile, but she did."

Rose ran fingers tipped with chewed nails through her hair, pulling it back from her forehead, taking an elastic band from a collection of them looped around the doorknob, snapping it around an ever thinning ponytail.

"How much?"

"Four ounces."

She took a makeup bag from the edge of the sink and unzipped it.

"I can't hear her."

"She's in her playpen out in the office. I put some music on the computer; she's watching the visualizer. She quieted down a little. The monitor's on in the kitchen."

Rose uncapped a tube of brick red lipstick.

"Our psychedelic baby, tripping out on the light show. We should get some glow-in-the-dark stars for the ceiling of the nursery."

"We did."

She twirled the lipstick up and back down, recapped it without putting any on, and dropped it into the bag.

"Yeah. I forgot."

She put the bag back on the sink.

"Hey, husband."

"Wife."

She looked at him.

"I'm kinda tired of doing the whole makeup and trying to look pretty thing. You mind if I go natural the rest of the way?"

He stepped into the bathroom and slipped his arms around her waist.

"That's all I ever want."

She looked up at him.

"Park."

"Rose."

She closed her eyes.

"I'm so tired, Park. I want to sleep so bad. And I think. I may. I just."

She opened her mouth and muffled it against his chest and screamed.

Park held her, the vibrations from her scream cutting through him as surely as a blade.

She stopped, turned her face from his chest and gulped air.

"Okay, okay. I'm back. I'm okay. I'm okay."

She pushed away from him, wiping her eyes.

"I just want to stop sometimes. And I can't. And I think about. Being done. And it sounds. Not so bad."

She touched his chin.

"It's okay, I wouldn't. I just. Sometimes. If I could fall asleep. And skip the rest of what's going to happen. Sometimes. That's all. It's just a temptation is all. Because I'm tired."

He spoke.

"It's not too late to go to a hospital. They'd still accept you. You could get Dreamer."

She raised a hand.

"Park."

He opened his mouth, but she didn't let him speak.

"I won't. And then what, anyway? If I'm in the hospital and you're on the street. And then what? Francine can't always be here. So, what? Who takes care of her? God knows it's not that I'm opposed to taking the drugs. But I won't go to a hospital. I won't leave her alone. Not while there's no one, no one to take care of her."

He forced his words between hers.

"I'm here. I can take care of her."

She looked at him.

"Parker, I love you, but you're not here. You can't take care of her."

Park remained utterly still, afraid that if he moved in the least he would shatter, shocked that the beating of his heart had not already turned him to shards.

When Park requested a sit-down, he never specified where; they simply met at whatever spot was next on a list they'd made at the outset of the assignment. Once used, a safe location was crossed from the list, never revisited. The track that ran around the football field at Culver City High, where the Centaurs once played, was next on the list. Within walking distance, it was, literally, a little close to home, but Park was grateful for that proximity on this occasion. The meeting would take some time, explaining to Bartolome what he'd discovered and how, but at least he wouldn't have to worry about the hazards of traffic. He'd get home soon, just as he'd promised Rose he would.

He waited on the curve of track behind one of the field's end zones, trying not to fidget with the thumb drive hanging around his neck, one of the ten-gig drives Rose had used for work, onto which he had loaded a copy of his reports.

Driving around the neighborhood before they bought the house, he and Rose had talked about how loud it might be on game nights, both of them enjoying the idea of hearing the dull roar on Friday evenings. But by the time the season began and many parents pulled their children out of school, and particularly off the football squad (sports in which blood was regularly spilled did not seem like a wise choice of extracurricular activities in a time of plague), there weren't enough players to field a team. Not that they would have played more than one home game. It wasn't long after the school year began that most districts across the country began canceling *all* sports, dances, clubs, band practice, theatricals, or any other event that might require students to gather after school hours. Eventually the classes themselves would be canceled. For the time being a much-reduced curriculum was still offered to students whose parents signed waivers relieving the schools of all liability for any harm that might befall their children from morning to final afternoon bell. Classes taught by teachers who had signed similar waivers for the privilege. The numbers on both sides of the classroom greatly reduced, it was, nonetheless, a sad fact that teacher-to-student ratios had not improved overall.

Park rubbed his foot back and forth on the latex track surface, the sole of his shoe squeaking. He'd taken another Dexedrine spansule before leaving home. He hadn't felt he needed it to keep awake, having passed his window of sleep opportunity yet again, but his thoughts were unruly; he'd need to marshal them to make his case to Bartolome. Twenty-four hours of hard sleep was out of the realm of possibility, so the speed had been his best option. He'd taken the pill, recorded it in his journal, police report, and dealer inventory, and left Rose playing Chasm Tide in the office, with the baby cradled around her neck in a hammocklike carrier, both of them wide awake but neither of them crying.

He looked at his father's watch.

"Where'd you get that watch?"

Hearing the voice, Park almost bolted. Dealer's instinct fueled by the speed almost sent him sprinting down the length of the football field, aiming for the dry L.A. River runoff beyond the parking lot.

"I don't remember seeing that watch."

Before he could run, another instinct had overridden the first. Cop instinct, telling him that if he ran he'd end up with boots in his backside, if not bullets.

"I'd have remembered a watch as nice as that."

Parked thumbed the rotating bezel that his father had used to time course changes when sailing with only a compass and the sun or stars.

The man walking from the parking lot raised one of his arms and displayed a pair of handcuffs.

"I'll make you a trade, my bracelets for your watch."

He grabbed the back of Park's neck and squeezed, kicking his right foot out from under him, and Park went to his knees.

"Only I'm gonna want my bracelets back."

Park didn't move as the watch was removed from his wrist.

"I'm going to look for that in my property envelope."

The wrist that had worn the watch was pulled to the small of his back and forced upward, and the cuff went on.

"Yeah, you look in there, trust me, you'll find a fucking watch."

Hands patted him down, took his keys and phone, his wallet and the backup thumb drive, all that he'd carried with him out the front door, and he was yanked to his feet.

He looked at the man who'd come from underneath the bleachers as he shook the watch and held it to his ear.

"*That* watch better be the one I find when I look in my property envelope."

"Or what, asshole?"

"Or I'll come looking for you."

The man shoved Park toward the street beyond the west bleachers.

"Asshole, you come looking, you better pray you don't fucking find me."

He shoved Park again.

"And by the way, that's fucking threatening a public officer as far as I'm concerned, and I'm putting it in your jacket along with obstruction, no matter what the fuck kind of rat-fink asshole you are. Asshole."

Park said nothing more.

He'd asked for a sit-down with Bartolome. He'd gotten Hounds. He knew when he was being told to shut up.

■ ■ ■

I HAD DISPENSED with burglar alarms and other home security measures long ago. That was shortly after I had become an independent contractor and found myself at odds with a long-established firm that provided services similar to mine. A boutique operation, they'd had business cards. No name, just the discreet number of an old-fashioned answering service, and a motto: *Solutions for Extreme Circumstances.*

As you can imagine, having such a card offered to you by a crew-cut gentleman with obviously scarred knuckles, wearing a well-tailored suit, was very impressive. This operation had a wonderful sense of theater. They were also, I must admit, quite good. Their solutions were effective more often than not, and most definitely extreme. The specific reason they had become displeased with me personally had to do with what they perceived as my poaching of a client they had serviced for some years. *Poaching* was the word they used when they called to advise me that I should desist and renege on the contract I had already accepted. All fairly polite but rendered with the unmistakable subtext that I had best *get the fuck out of town on the next train.* Or something equally Old West.

I declined.

There were a minimum of ways they could menace me. I was young. Capable of excellence in my field. Confident in my ability to succeed in the marketplace against any form of competition. And I lived within a highly secured property. The rule of law was strong, and my business was largely conducted in civilized countries; I had little to fear while engaged in my professional affairs. Having established what I believed to be my terminal exposures, I set to defending them, and went about my working days.

They came at me at night. Within the unbreachable security of my home. Dulled by the sense of safety that the locks, pressure-sensitive plates, armored doors, unbreakable glass, air density detectors, CCTV cameras, and obligatory infrared beams had imparted, I did not know I was at risk until I awoke with a blade at my throat. I was saved only by the fact that these were the kind of men who felt that an affront could be redressed only to the offender's face. If they'd been of another sort, the kind who are genuinely happy to discover their victims asleep and to kill them in that state because of the many hazards and difficulties it eliminates, they would have survived. They were not of that sort.

I am.

So, finding myself alive when I should have been dead, I knew I had a slight momentary advantage. That advantage born of two facts: the first being that they clearly believed me to be helpless and at their mercy, the second being that I was clearly more ruthless than they.

No one expects that a naked man who was fast asleep only a moment ago will ignore the knife you have at his throat and attack you. What sane person would do such a thing? What sane person would do anything but beg for his life and pray for God's forgiveness of his sins?

It is not a trick question. I am, by any recognizable measure, quite sane. Baroquely obsessive, but not to the point of insanity.

Regardless, I attacked. From my supine position I brought my knee up and struck the back of the knife wielder's head. Simultaneously I slipped my hand between my body and his wrist, preventing him from cutting my neck deeply when my knee made contact and he lurched forward. Taking hold of his knife arm at the wrist and elbow, I pushed over to my right, rolling him off the edge of the bed while shielding myself with his body, discouraging his friends across the room from opening fire. That discretion would last only a moment. Landing atop my assailant on the floor, I maintained my grip and bent his arm at the elbow, forcing the knife into his throat just above the thick shield of the thyroid cartilage. I was deft enough that I could have thrown the knife at the others. Not so much out of any real hope that I could kill or disable either of them but rather to distract them for a precious moment while I took the dying man's sidearm from its shoulder holster. But there was no real need to attempt such a high-risk maneuver. Instead, I ran and hid in the closet.

Bullets struck the armored door. After a pause while the men in my bedroom did some quick mental geometry, more bullets ripped through the wall next to the door at a sharp angle and struck the armored plates that lined the interior walls of the closet. If the men had squirmed under the house and attempted to shoot upward through the floor of the closet or climbed to the roof and fired down through its ceiling, they would have met with equal success. The closet was an informal panic room. Not proof against gases or radiation, or stocked with batteries and bottled water, simply a secure hard point when under fire from small arms. But these men would not be wasting any more time probing for the closet's weaknesses. They would be placing a grenade just outside the door. A fact I confirmed when I entered the room through the main door behind them and shot them both in the back with a single short burst from an HK MP5 submachine gun. To a hindsight observer it may seem obvious that, once they knew I had retreated to an armored position, they should have taken care to defend their rear in case I had rearmed and emerged behind their line via an alternate egress. But in the heat of battle such mistakes are often made, and it never occurred to them to consider that the closet might have a concealed panel at the back, opening into a large linen closet in the guest bedroom next door. A linen closet stocked more amply with firearms than with sheets and pillowcases.

Still naked, I went through the house, determined that no others had participated in the intrusion, and went out the guest bathroom window. Screened by an overhang of pussy willow I'd had planted for this purpose, I was able to take the sentry by the pool unawares. I used a knife. The integral suppressor on the MP5SD was effective where there were walls to help baffle the noise, but in the open air even a round or two would have been heard by anyone at the front of the property. Still, I miscalculated. Coming up behind the man, I cut once across the back of his right knee; his leg went out and his body dropped, and I stabbed him once in the kidney and once in the side of the neck as he dropped lower still. The first two wounds were inflicted rapidly enough that they elicited nothing but a loud gasp, but the third, which should have pierced horizontally through his windpipe and ended any vocalizations, was off the mark and he managed a gurgled cry. Acting without appropriate forethought, I pushed him into the pool to silence him, forgetting that it was covered. Entangled in the blue plastic sheet, he thrashed loudly. Loud enough to draw whoever had been left in front of the house, but not so loud that I couldn't hear them coming. The dying man's struggles had pulled the cover away from the edge of the pool, so I dove in myself, gliding beneath his death throes and the growing red cloud that was spilling from the cover into the water.

Latched onto the ladder at the deep end, I used my knife to create a slit in the cover, which was still fairly taut at that side of the pool, and surfaced far enough to peek through and see two more men come into the backyard. Sensibly, they did nothing to help their coworker, focusing instead on the darker shadows among the foliage, searching for where I might be hidden. But they could not afford to be overly thorough. Though I had a generous full-acre plot, heavily landscaped in a tall and dripping southern style that suited the area where I lived, there were still neighbors. There was little doubt that they were at the limits of their time allowance for this operation, if not already beyond it. And they still needed to collect their dead and transport them for disposal.

Haste made them negligent.

And me, as well.

Letting go the ladder, kicking softly, I circled the edge of the pool just below the surface. Coming back into the shallow end, I waited another moment to be sure that the men were fully engaged trying to haul the dead man from the pool. Their hands were occupied, but I did not wish to make the same mistake they had made when they allowed me to wake. Rather than surfacing entirely, I bobbed only my head above the water-line. My weapon was capable of operating quite efficiently for a limited period while submerged, but I had no desire to subject my eardrums to the shock waves when I pulled the trigger. What I should have been more concerned about was the ammunition I had preloaded into the clips stored with the MP5.

There are those who will say that loading an SMG with hollow-point ammunition is overdoing it, but aside from the fact that the ammunition must be custom made and is somewhat expensive, there are no real draw-backs. It gives an all but absolute guarantee that one's target will be stopped instantly by a short burst. Expanding and staying inside the body, the bullets transfer all of their kinetic energy to the target. And the typical lack of an exit wound means less mess. Indeed, when I'd shot the two men in my bedroom I'd created virtually no splatter to be concerned over. Nonetheless, I would not, given any other option, use the combination ever again.

I was far more lucky than I deserved to be considering my oversight. The first eight rounds fired without incident. The water disrupted the tra-jectory of the bullets only minimally, and, at such close range, any loss in velocity was irrelevant. Six of the bullets struck their targets. The men were falling back away from the pool as the bullets forced their inertia upon them; my finger was lightening on the trigger, a scant four ounces of pressure less and the gun would cease to fire, but not before the ninth round hit the water that filled the barrel, the flawed hollow-point mushrooming under the pressure, turning the barrel and suppressor to shrapnel.

As I said, far more lucky than I deserved to be.

A five-inch shard found its way into my abdomen. I was able to remove it myself and stitch the wound closed, but only after I had triggered the timer that would ignite the phosphorous charges set at various key structural points around the house, gotten myself into the well-stocked Series III Land Rover in the garage, and driven five miles so as to be out of the immediate area when emergency vehicles began to arrive.

Doing all this while still nude.

In the end it was a week before I had reasserted control over my survival compulsions to the extent that I was able to comfortably seek medical care within my professional sphere. By then the wound had become horribly infected and I ended up losing several feet of intestine. Smaller shards had peppered my left hand and I permanently lost all feeling in the palm and along the inside of the thumb. Had I been firing the weapon while fully submerged, shouldering the stock as would have been proper, the barrel fragment that caused me a year of severe discomfort would have likely lodged in my brain.

It haunts me still, how close I came to a death that would have registered as little more than blackly humorous. If I dwell on it for any length it is enough to draw me into an instinctive posture of attack. A dangerous memory.

It took almost as long to repair the damage I'd done to my fledgling business concern as it did to heal fully. The competitors who had challenged me were no longer an issue, but they did get one of their wishes.

It was a tightly knit world I worked in; some egos, and a few wallets, needed to be flattered after such a display. I did as much, relocated to Los Angeles, and put out a fresh shingle. Perfectly happy to leave town in the end. But when I moved into my new home, I forewent any security measures. They had, I felt, made me more vulnerable than safe. Instilled a false sense of security. A few good locks and a fraudulent sticker declaring that my home was "protected by armed security" were enough for common housebreakers. As for my peers, I could think of no measures that could keep them from going about their business should it come to that again. Short of succumbing to my compulsion and retreating to the woods to live in a cave, there was no level of safety that could put me entirely at ease. Which was as it should be.

My home became a spiderweb of sorts. An elaborately arranged mosaic of architecture, landscaping, and possessions. Strictly organized, my familiarity with the placement and resonance of every element was literally sensuously intimate. I could, without exaggeration, feel when everything was right with my home, as well as when discordance intruded. It took little more than a raccoon crossing the deck and upsetting a planter in my herb garden for me to wake from a sound sleep.

So it was not by sheer surprise that I was taken when I returned home from Culver City very early that morning, but rather by overwhelming force.

15

THERE WAS NO BAG ON THE HEAD THIS TIME. INSTEAD HE waited to be booked at the front desk by a level III reserve officer showing clear early indications that she was sleepless.

A skinny black man in an orange jumpsuit, the slack in his ankle chains looped around the leg of a heavy wood bench bolted to the floor, eyeballed him and grunted loudly.

"I know you? Yeah, I know you. I know you? Yeah, I think I know you."

Turning away from the man, Park faced toward the reserve officer as she spoke on the phone with an IT intern, trying to determine why she'd lost access to the National Crime Information Center, and found himself trying not to focus on her red eyes, stiff neck, and profuse sweat but unable to do otherwise. Reminded by every minute that passed, Rose home alone with the baby. He shifted his gaze and watched Hounds scroll through the contacts list in his phone, deleting names, talking to himself.

"Dead. Who the fuck? Dead. Dead. Don't know and don't care. Dead. Dead. Dead."

The man on the other bench rattled his chain.

"I know you? Yeah, I must know you."

Park turned farther away from the man, tilting his head to look down at Hounds's phone.

Hounds looked up.

"Something you're curious about, asshole? A peek in my little black book, intrigues your ass? Back the fuck off, motherfucker."

Park shifted, still looking at Hounds.

"Where's Kleiner?"

Hounds snapped his phone shut.

" 'Where's Kleiner?' That what you asked? 'Where's Kleiner?' "

Park shrugged.

"Just wondering how you split up my watch if he's not here."

Hounds growled, a phlegmy rattle that warned of imminent police brutality.

The man on the other bench was leaning forward, trying to get a better look at Park.

"Know you? Sure. Maybe. I don't know."

Park scratched his head, covering that side of his face, and ignored the growl.

"Or do you just pocket it and Kleiner can go fuck himself?"

Hounds slapped him, a heavy open hand that knocked Park from the bench to the floor, drawing a hushing gesture from the reserve on the phone, and an admiring whistle from the con in the orange jumpsuit.

"No windup. Just bang. Damn."

Park got back on the bench.

Hounds opened his phone again.

" 'Where's Kleiner?' Tell you."

He showed Park the screen of his phone, an entry displayed: kleiner, cecil. He pushed a button; the entry blinked twice and disappeared.

"Kleiner's in the land of *motherfucker better not ever show his face around me if he knows what's good for him.*"

He closed the phone.

"In the land of *gone over the fence.* Partnered five years. Know what I know about Kleiner? Turns out I know what his farts smell like and fuck-all besides."

The reserve hung up her phone.

"What?"

Hounds looked at her.

"Said nothing. Said my fucking partner bugged out."

She shook her head.

"One of those."

Hounds pulled Park to his feet.

"One of those."

He pushed Park against the high front desk.

"Used to play, during Katrina when we heard about those cops walking out on the job, used to play *would he or wouldn't he?* Looking at other cops, talking about which ones we figured as the assholes who'd bolt when the shit dropped like that. Cops started making for the exits this last year, he talked about what he's gonna do he ever sees one of those fuckers. Now, what, gone. Waited to collect his last pay, and gone."

She pulled her earlobe.

"You got paid?"

Hounds held up a hand.

"The fuck. That's what? We got paid. It's staggered, yeah. Some precinct gets paid here, some other gets paid there. Alternating whenever the fuck they feel like it. First pay in nine weeks. Point is he chickenshitted and. Fuck this. Fuck. Just. This asshole, deal with him."

He watched as the reserve dropped Park's wallet and keys and the thumb drive into a property envelope. He gave her Park's name, and she punched it up on the now-connected computer.

"Why did you pick him up?"

Hounds was fiddling with Park's watch; he looked at her.

"Because I got a tip."

She sealed the envelope, looked at something on her computer monitor, tapped a button a few times, frowned, and rubbed her eyes.

"You picked him up before?"

Hounds buckled the watch on his wrist.

"Yeah. Another tip."

"And he got cut loose because?"

"Fuck do I know? What's it say?"

She tapped the screen.

"Says because you blew Miranda. Someone still cares about Miranda."

He looked at Park.

"Asshole, did we card you last time? Honestly, did we? I can't even fucking remember."

He flipped over the badge folder hanging from his neck and displayed a Miranda card with frayed edges.

"But check this out. Call me nostalgic."

He looked at the reserve officer.

"He's someone's snitch. What the fuck do I know what they want? They want it to look like a bust is what they want. What they put there for why the charge doesn't stick, fuck do I care."

She rubbed at a visibly knotted muscle in her neck.

"Looks bad on your record, not following procedure."

Hounds adjusted his sunglasses.

"Hey, part-timer, fuck you."

She stopped rubbing her neck.

"Excuse me?"

"Excuse you what the fuck. I care, my record? Fuck you. I care about I do my job. I'm, you know what, I'm past my fucking twenty, lady; think I give a shit what some fucker wanting to talk to this piece of shit does to my record with his whatever the fuck sleight of hand trying to cover his tracks? I don't. I don't give a fuck. Someone calls on the radio, says, 'Pick the fucker up,' I pick the fucker up."

The reserve rocked back in her chair and wiped sweat from under her chin.

"Hey, asshole."

Hounds smiled at Park.

"Here it comes, man, about to get my comeuppance."

The reserve settled her hand on the butt of her sidearm.

"Comeuppance this, asshole. I'm fucking dying. I haven't slept in like two weeks. I'm running my brain on Diet Coke and NoDoz and chocolate-covered coffee beans. I'm not so far along that my hormones have gone off the rails, so I'm also on the fucking rag. I got no kids, and my husband, a fucking cop who I thought I might understand better if I became a reserve, left me for a younger model three fucking years ago. Now, the job, it's the only thing I got in my life that I give a shit about. And at the end of next week my captain says he's gonna have to put me on unpaid leave because I'm losing it. So I'm gonna go home and die alone."

She leaned forward, hand still resting on her weapon.

"You think I give a fuck if I die in jail, or get popped myself, if before I go I can shoot some big shot fucking dickhead detective like my ex?"

She stared at Hounds.

Hounds took off his sunglasses and looked at the reserve.

"I'm sorry for your troubles."

Her lips thinned, she took her hand from her gun, and she wiped her eyes.

"Yeah, well, we all got something on our minds."

Hounds put his sunglasses back on.

"Yes, we do."

She leaned forward and rested her fingers on the keyboard.

"What charge?"

Hounds picked at the peeling decal on the front of the faded black XXL Metallica T-shirt stretched over his chest.

"Resisting. And threatening a public o."

She clacked a few keys.

"Code sixty-nine and seventy-one it is. You want to do a report?"

"Fuck no. He stays inside for more than a couple days I'll write something up. Pen an epic about him he stays inside."

She nodded.

"I get it. Okay. Bring him around."

Hounds grabbed Park by the elbow and led him over to a steel door.

"Time to go wait for your girlfriend, whoever the hell it is."

The skinny black man on the bench raised an eyebrow.

"Yeah, I know you. I know you? Yeah, I do."

Hounds kicked the bench.

"Asshole, you got something to say?"

The man shook his head.

"Thought I know the man is all."

Hounds took Park by the shoulder and spun him around.

"This asshole?"

"Yeah-hm, that asshole."

"You know him?"

The man dropped his head to the side and squinted.

"I know you?"

Standing there in the West Los Angeles Community Police Station on Butler Avenue, roughly five miles from his home, a station he'd patrolled out of for his first six months on the job, Park looked directly at the man and nodded.

"Yeah, you know me."

The man grinned.

"I thought as much, I did. What was it?"

Park looked at Hounds, looked back at the man.

"I ripped you off once."

The man's eyes got big.

"Bullshit?"

"No, no bullshit. I sold you some dope, went light on the weight."

The man shook his head.

"I bought dope from a white guy?"

He raised his shoulders high and dropped them, sighing.

"See, that right there a reason to stay off the shit. How high a man gotta be to buy off a white guy? Like it a mystery a white guy gonna rip you off?"

"Just business."

"Shit, just business to you. I don't get high, I'm like to go rob or kill someone. An now you in here for resisting, nice white dope dealer like you."

Park closed his eyes for a moment, thinking about a big red button he could push to stop all this, just pause everything around him and allow him to walk away from it, back home.

He opened his eyes.

"We all make mistakes."

The man opened his mouth wide, showing a junkie's rotted teeth, and laughed.

"Ain't that the truth. Ain't it, though. All make mistakes. And then some, I tell you. Yeah, I thought I know you. Wasn't where I thought it was from, but I thought so. All make mistakes. Yeah, we do."

Hounds kicked the bench again, shutting off the skinny black man's laughter.

"That's it, that's where you know him from?"

The man shrugged with his whole body again, his chains jingling.

"He's the expert. He say that was where it was, why I got a reason to disbelieve him?"

Hounds turned to the door.

"Should have known."

The reserve put her finger on a button.

"Did you think they were gonna know each other from when they were in the CIA together?"

She hit the button and a buzzer sounded.

Hounds pulled the door open.

"Just like to know why this asshole gets the treatment. He ain't a regular asshole is all I'm saying. Right, asshole?"

Park didn't say anything.

The skinny black man was laughing again.

"All make mistakes. Yeah-hm, we do. We do."

Holding the door open, Hounds jerked his chin at the man.

"What's laughing boy up for?"

The reserve drank from a can of Diet Coke, drained it.

"Killed his family. His grandma and two sisters he was living with."

She took another can from a desk drawer and opened it.

"They were all sleepless. All three. Killed them, he said, so they wouldn't have to do the suffering."

Hounds stared at the man, kicked the bench again, spoke soft.

"Hey."

The man reached down and fingered a link in his chain, didn't say anything.

Hounds cleared his throat.

"How'd that go down? How'd they take it?"

The man didn't look up.

Park scuffed the floor with his heel, looking at his father's watch on Hounds wrist.

"How do you think it went down? Leave him alone."

Hounds slammed him into the wall next to the door, got his fingers on his neck, and banged his head off the plaster twice.

"Fuck do you know about it? Fuck do you know? Shut the fuck up."

The reserve coughed.

Hounds let go of Park's neck.

Park looked at the man on the bench playing with the chain; the reserve rubbing the knot in her neck; Hounds opening and closing the hand he'd used to grab Park's throat.

"I have a wife. I'm not special. I know about it. I have a wife."

No one looked at anyone else.

Hounds lightly kicked the bench again, but the skinny man just played with his chain.

Hounds looked over at the reserve.

"Why's he out here instead of the cage?"

She spun on her chair.

"Keeping me company."

He moved Park through the open door into the lockbox.

"Let's go."

He waited for the door to swing closed and a second buzzer to sound and the door on the opposite side of the box to open.

Hounds nodded at the cop standing on the other side, unlocked the cuffs from Park's wrists.

"Your part-timer out there is losing it."

The cop pulled a zip-strip from his belt.

"Yeah she is. You want in, we got a pool going; when she's gonna off herself."

Hounds pocketed his cuffs.

"Fucking. You got someone?"

The cop paused.

"What?"

Hounds shook his head.

"No, you don't."

He bumped Park's shoulder with his fist.

"Asshole, he don't know."

The cop looked at them both.

"What the fuck?"

Park looked at Hounds, shrugged.

"I don't know who knows what."

Hounds shook his head.

"But you got a wife."

Park looked at him.

"I have a wife."

The cop started to zip Park's wrists.

"Fuck you guys."

Hounds held up a hand.

"Hang on a fuck."

He looked at the floor.

"Shit."

He unbuckled the watch, stuck it in Park's pocket, and looked at the cop.

"Don't touch the fucking watch."

Park looked at him.

"Sorry about Kleiner."

Hounds settled his sunglasses a little tighter over his eyes.

"The fuck out of here."

And turned and buzzed out the door.

The cop zipped Park's wrists and shoved him down a hall of cells. A din of imprisoned men crammed against the bars, held there by the pressure of the bodies at their backs.

The guard shoving him along, talking to himself.

"I need a watch to know what time it is? Please. It's five minutes before we're gonna stuff one too many in there. Gonna stuff one too many in there and the bars are just gonna pop off and we're gonna be fucked. Five minutes."

Silently, Park agreed.

▓   ▓   ▓

STANDING ON MY deck to enjoy the morning air, I was having my worldview reinforced by a phone call from Vinnie the Fish.

"You punch this guy in, you get Officer Haas, Parker, T. Assigned to Venice. Patrol car cop. My guy calls over there to ask someone he knows what they think of Haas, that guy never heard of him, can't find him on the station roster. So he's a cop. Four years on the job. Almost three of those he was in uniform. Then there's some kind of hanky-panky. There's a file, but it's a special assignments file, for someone else's eyes only. Your guy, someone fingered him for undercover somewhere. They transferred him to Venice so no one would know he was going SA, but it's a paper transfer is all, because someone doesn't want anyone to know he's going under."

I pinched the flowering tops from a basil plant.

"What does that suggest?"

"To me it suggests one of two. Number one is that he's gone undercover for IAD. They like new cops, guys who haven't had a chance to get too dirty yet. The fact my guy was able to find his SA file, even if he can't get a look, that doesn't speak well of the effort to hide your cop. And that smells very IAD. Get all sneaky, but do it in a half-assed way."

"And number two?"

"Number two is bagman."

I inhaled deeply, oils from the basil filling the air.

"Ah."

"Yeah, *ah*. Way the force is now, is it's kind of fragmented. Goes way beyond *this* division won't share with *that* one. There are units that are off the map. Gone dark. Fringe law enforcement. They operate without sanction, but also without rebuke. As long as bad guys are being removed from the board, there's a lot of looking the other way. Financing operations like that is tricky. Can't draw too much from the budget. Can't dedicate too many visible resources. So most of the money comes from the bad guys. Asshole A pays to have his operation protected and, just as important, to see that Asshole B is struck from the record. In this number two scenario, your guy is dirty from when he walks through the door, someone spots his potential, and he's recruited. They move him to the margins of the books, and he's your new invisible bagman. Drawing pay, carrying a badge, but all he does is call on assholes and take donations."

I thought about the conversation I'd witnessed a few hours before, outside the gallery.

"Yes, Vincent, that sounds quite plausible."

"Yeah, it's a sad, dirty world."

"My thoughts almost exactly."

"Of course there's another possibility."

"Yes?"

Vinnie coughed as if he might be embarrassed to bring something up.

"He could just be a cop doing his job."

I considered the possibility.

"Is that likely?"

"No."

I nodded.

"My feeling as well."

"Anything else?"

"No. This was extremely helpful."

"My pleasure. And thanks for taking care of things on my end."

"No trouble at all."

"Keep your head down, Jasper."

"And you as well, Vincent."

I closed my phone and dropped it in my pocket.

Above the San Gabriels the sun shone silver behind an unseasonable marine layer. Though, at that point, labeling any weather phenomenon as seasonable or otherwise was a fool's errand. It was not the intense early morning brightness of just a few years prior, but plenty hot. The cool I'd enjoyed a moment before was fading. I brushed my hand along the tops of the basil and the other herbs in my little container garden. Rosemary, lemon thyme, Mexican oregano, peppermint, bay, coriander, all of them releasing their oils.

I needed to get out of the previous day's clothes. I needed a shower. I needed a few hours' sleep. Refreshed, I would return to Officer Haas's home and pursue my business with him. I still harbored a slight hope that he was in possession of the drive. But imagined it more likely that it had been sold to Afronzo Jr. for monies that would fatten the coffers of whatever secret police squad Haas was a member of.

The blend of herbs was disrupted. A change in the breeze taking it from me. But there was no breeze. I began to turn, and, as I did, my attention was caught by the sight of an intense bead of light arcing up out of the Los Angeles basin.

Perched on an extreme southern foot of the Santa Monicas, just above West Hollywood, overlooking the entire basin from an advantageous elevation, Number One Electra Court was a natural location for SoCal

Theater of Operations Command to place an observation post. Yes, the high-rent owners within the dubiously named Mount Olympus development objected, but national security was invoked and little more could be said. Had anyone known the flying saucer–shaped house was also a forward firebase the objections might have endured. *I* knew that it was a forward firebase. As I am certain that anyone with any personal experience of artillery knew it was a forward firebase. Not only could such a position be used to call in pinpoint coordinates for bombardments from the 16"/50 Mark 7 guns of any Iowa-class battleship that might one day find itself anchored off Santa Monica, it was also the ideal spot from which to launch surface-to-surface rockets, or lob mortars onto the street below.

Just across Laurel Canyon, with my own spectacular view of the basin, I was shocked to see that the first shot fired did not come *from* Mount Olympus, but from *below*. It flashed across the sky, leaving a contrail. More than likely a Javelin, it could have come from anywhere within twenty-five hundred meters. Anywhere with a clear line of sight. Any number of parking lots along Fairfax would have worked. Whether by luck or by virtue of poor marksmanship, it didn't strike the house directly but impacted on the blast walls covered in soldiers' graffiti that had been staggered across the yard to defend from just such an attack.

Still, it served its purpose. Served it if I may be so bold as to suggest that Electra Court was not the actual target of the rocket. Assuming my own ego has not run away with me, the Javelin scored an absolute bull's-eye on my awareness. I watched it hit, watched it explode, a bare moment before it rolled thunder over the hills, felt the trailing waves of super-heated air, the reverse suck as the fireball rolled upward, smelled the burned plastic odor of modern warfare, and came back to myself.

The scent of herbs. How the air had shifted unexpectedly seconds before. What had caused that change? All too late considered.

Two teams of three. Well-trained units of mercenaries like the ones I had killed at the gold farm. One coming up from below the deck, one from within the house.

I said they did not take me by virtue of surprise. And if there had been only two attackers, indeed they would not have been successful, as that is the number I killed before I was subdued.

16

IN A WINDOWLESS ROOM, A COMBINATION OF FATIGUE POISONS, adrenaline dregs, and the waning influence of the spansule he'd taken before leaving his house, had twisted the hands from Park's internal clock. Counting slowly to himself, Mississippi by Mississippi, as if he were "it," Park waited, his face buried in his hands, until he could count high enough for someone to let him start seeking, peeking from time to time at his father's watch, his guesses about how much time had passed never correct.

The door opened.

"What were you doing there?"

He stopped counting and looked up at Captain Bartolome.

Bartolome looked at the AC vent mounted on the wall. He lifted one of the limp pieces of ribbon tied to the grille and let it drop.

"This thing been off since you came in?"

Park pulled the front of his sweat-soaked shirt from his chest.

"Yes."

Bartolome dragged a chair away from the table at which Park sat.

"You tell anyone?"

"No one has been in since they left me here."

Bartolome set a few sheets of copy paper on the table.

"That's not what I meant."

Park lifted his left hand and jerked it twice against the cuffs that latched him to a steel ring welded to the tabletop.

Bartolome dropped his keys on the table.

"You tell anyone?"

Park found the stubby cuff key and unlocked himself.

"What time is it?"

Bartolome scooped up his keys.

"Did you tell anyone?"

Park rubbed his wrist.

"Tell anyone what? That the AC doesn't work? I haven't seen anyone. Except Hounds. He thinks I'm a snitch."

"Haas."

Bartolome picked one of the sheets of copy paper and turned it over, revealing the reverse side; a photo print blurred by a printer running low on toner.

"Officer Haas, did you tell anyone?"

Park looked at the fuzzy image, a still from a video, taken in a dark room, blown up, himself sitting at a table, speaking with Cager.

Bartolome took off his sunglasses; his eyes had sunk yet farther into their sockets since Park had last seen them.

"Did you tell anyone?"

Park took the picture. The ink had soaked into the cheap paper and rippled the surface, distorting both their faces.

"I was going to tell you."

Bartolome used his hand to whisk sweat from his bald crown.

"Tell me what? That you've gone out of your fucking mind?"

"No."

Park rotated the picture so that it faced his captain.

Earlier, while he'd waited on the track, he'd arranged his case into a detailed outline. An order of fact and supporting evidence, bullet-pointed and footnoted with everything that had happened over the previous forty-eight hours and during the vast hours of observation he'd logged working Dreamer. He'd been prepared. He tried to recall that tightly rendered diagram of logic, cause and effect. But it was gone now, blown from the page by exhaustion and worry. Only the principal assumption remained legible in the mental scraps.

He placed his finger on the picture, pointing at Cager.

"It's him."

Bartolome took another poor photo print from his papers and showed Park a close-up of Cager.

"I know who it is. Everyone knows who he is. That's the point."

"No, it's not."

Park was remembering his father again. Remembering conversations where they seemed always to be speaking different languages. Or talking in code, each lacking the key that would unlock the secret of the other's meaning. Conversations about why he was taking a Ph.D. in philosophy instead of carrying on in political science. About taking the degree at Stanford rather than Harvard. About joining the police force. About having a child. His father had shifted the phone, a crinkle of newspaper, and then read a few headlines from the front page of the *Washington Post.* Sighed. *Having a child, Parker? Now? What possible sense does that make?* And Park had stopped trying to explain.

But now he needed to be understood.

He covered the picture of Cager with his hand.

"It's him. He's the one doing it."

Bartolome squinted at him.

"Can you pass a piss test?"

Sweat ran from Park's hairline, beaded in his eyebrows, stung his eyes, and made him blink.

"What?"

Bartolome stood up.

"Jesus, Haas. Of all the asshole rookie moves, hitting your stash. No one expects you to be a saint on a job like this, but you don't get high when you've requested a sit-down."

Park rubbed the sweat from his eyes.

"I didn't. I."

Bartomome was looking at the AC vent.

"Bullshit."

"Captain."

He walked to the vent.

"Goddamned thing."

Park watched as Bartolome took a butterfly knife from his pocket, twirled it open. He remembered how his father would shift an awkward conversation by suddenly embarking on some small task. After his mother's funeral, standing in a far corner of the room as close to the door as possible, he'd watched as his sister had asked their father what his plans were for the house. Watched his father rise in midconversation, go to the wall, and stick his finger into a divot that Park had put there nearly twenty years before while playing field hockey indoors. *That,* he'd said, *should have been tended to by now.* And he'd gone to the garden shed for a can of spackle and a putty knife.

Bartolome slide the blade of his knife into the slot on the back of one of the screws that held the vent grille in place.

Park remembered following his father from the room, breaking off into the kitchen, calling a car to come pick him up, and leaving a half hour later while Ambassador Haas was still in the library covering one of the few remaining signs that indicated his children had been raised in his home. The patch, his sister told him when they next spoke, had not been painted over. Their father had left it visible. *Apparently,* she mused, *he forgot to finish the job.*

Park watched the older man unscrewing the grille.

"He gave me Dreamer."

Bartolome kept his back turned.

"Captain."

He didn't look at Park.

"The real thing, Captain."

He pocketed the two bottom screws, began turning the one in the grille's top right corner.

Park rapped two points of his argument into the tabletop with his knuckles.

"Hologram. RFID."

Bartolome jabbed the knife point into the wall and left it sticking there as he used his fingertips to pry at the edges of the grille.

"Shut up."

Park rose.

"He used it to conduct a transaction."

"Shut the fuck up."

The grille swung loose, hanging from the remaining screw in the upper left corner, revealing a cluster of tiny microphones and cameras mounted around the rim of the duct.

Park walked over. He looked at the listening and observation devices. He looked at his captain. He remembered his father's final act of surrender in the face of a world that had grown wild beyond his ability to keep himself and his family safe. He pointed at the pictures still resting faceup on the table and raised his voice.

"Parsifal K. Afronzo Junior. He gave me Dreamer in exchange for Shabu."

Bartolome stuck a hand inside the duct and began ripping out the mikes and cameras. He dropped them on the floor, a bristle of wires and antennae, and stomped the pile twice with his Kevlar-soled boot.

He put on his sunglasses, yanked his knife from the wall, scooped the papers from the table, and pulled the door open.

"Come on."

Park looked at the pile of broken surveillance equipment and started to open his mouth again.

Bartolome came back into the room and grabbed his arm.

"You have a family, Haas. Keep your mouth shut and come on. Those were just the ones we could see."

He pulled Park down a hall of two-way mirrored glass peering in on interrogation rooms. Park saw a woman sitting alone, picking at a cake of scab on her neck. A small soot-smeared boy being screamed at by two uniformed officers. A man being beaten with a bloodstained telephone book. He pulled to a stop at the last room. Someone with a black bag over his head hung by his wrists from a U-bolt driven into the ceiling. An officer sat in a chair, smoking, occasionally setting the hanging body to swinging with prods from a PR-24 baton.

"Captain."

Bartolome shoved him down the hall.

"Shut up."

Bartolome slapped a button next to the door at the end of the hall and looked up at a camera in the corner where the wall and ceiling met.

"Coming out."

A squelch of feedback, then a crackled voice.

"With what?"

"With my fucking collar."

"Where's his cuffs?"

Bartolome kicked the door.

"In your fucking ass if you don't buzz me out."

The door buzzed, they walked out into a box, the door swung closed, another buzzer, and they opened the second door, onto a loading dock in the parking garage. A van beeped as it backed up to the dock. Park could see faces smashed against the heavy-gauge wire screens that covered the openings where the windows had been shattered.

Cops waited on the dock with batons, zip-cuffs, and riot helmets. Bartolome pushed through them. One of the cops flipped up her visor, the reserve who had processed Park.

"Where you going with him?"

Bartolome started down the steps, keeping Park in front of him.

"Out of your hair."

"Where? I got paperwork."

"What the hell do you care? I just opened a space in your cells."

The reserve waved at Park.

"Must be nice having a fairy godmother, asshole."

The back door of the van opened and the cops on the dock started pulling the prisoners out, swinging the batons as they emerged, beating them to the ground and putting on the zips.

Bartolome unlocked a silver Explorer, planted Park in the passenger seat, and slammed the door before circling the truck and putting himself behind the steering wheel.

"You incredible asshole."

He started the engine and pulled out of his space, up a ramp, swerving to miss another incoming van, and bounced out the exit onto the street.

Late afternoon, sun dropping out of the zenith of the sky, an angry red. Columns of smoke rose, pillars supporting a low brown roof.

Bartolome pulled around a burning pile of uncollected garbage onto Sawtelle and looked upward as a gunship hovering over the 405 opened fire on someone below.

"Been a long day."

Bullets hit a gas tank on the overpass, and a fireball burned the air.

Park touched where his father's watch.

"What did you mean, Captain, 'you have a family'?"

Bartolome gunned the Explorer into an alley running down the back side of Sawtelle.

"I meant you have something to lose."

A FIRST TASER had taken me to my knees in convulsions; a second Taser blacked me out. I had brief moments of awareness, a certainty that I had lost control of both my bladder and my bowels, pain as the razor being wielded to cut my clothes away nicked my chest, a blur of bodies in my living room, a wrench of nausea as I realized they were moving my furniture about, several mental blanks that could have been seconds or hours, stab of needle in my arm, and a fierce rush of intense lucidity that flooded through my bloodstream, directly to my heart and up to my brain.

Time had passed. The sky was again dimming. I was naked on my couch, hands behind my back, a taut line of wire running from my wrists to a noose around my neck, legs splayed, ankles tied to the legs of a low table, this position giving them easier access to my genitals while preventing me from instinctively closing my legs when they began to use the soldering iron.

I had been tortured twice before.

The first time, I'd been barely twenty years of age. I was discovered someplace I should not have been, out of uniform, committing warlike acts. Clearly in violation of the Geneva Conventions, I could have been tried for war crimes. But I was tortured instead, encouraged to make a confession that included crimes I had nothing to do with, and to repudiate my country. After three days I did as I was asked. Three months later, after I had been included as part of a covert prisoner exchange, I returned with a squad of Degar guerrillas to the camp where I had been held, and took part in my first and only revenge killings.

The second time I was tortured I was nearly forty. I had been accepting several freelance contracts from an agency of my government, and returned excellent results on all of them. Results so excellent, in fact, that it was strongly suspected that I must be in possession of intelligence that could only have been passed to me by members of the primary opposition. I was deemed both volatile and disposable by someone determined to clean the slate and to winnow from me the details of my supposed betrayal. As there had been no betrayal, there was nothing to winnow. After two weeks I began to lie. Simple lies at first, but growing ever more elaborate as each lie led to more questions, until they all unraveled. Thus, the torture continued. After another two weeks I ceased to lie. I ceased to talk. I ceased to scream or cry or beg for mercy. I silently repeated a mantra to myself that heartened me and bore me up: *They will kill me soon. They will kill me soon. They will kill me soon.*

But they did not.

Instead, apparently inspired by my silence, they stopped asking me questions. While continuing to torture me. Randomly, without discernible reason or purpose, I was subjected to a variety of abuses for an additional two weeks. I've come to suspect that once I became silent I had been judged a loss. Convinced that they had passed the point where I might still be capable of revealing anything of value, my captors were quite prepared to kill me. I believe some spirit of frugality took hold, and I was kept about the place as a training subject. In those final two weeks I was a kind of living cadaver upon which students of the trade could hone their skills.

That I was let go at the end of those two weeks did not, I am quite sure, have anything to do with my ability to perform this service. Rather, someone somewhere lost his job. Footing in the intelligence trade is notoriously slippery. A pioneer one day, it takes only a single misjudgment and the trail is lost, the fall to the bottom long, the ground, when it comes, littered with other once-adventurous climbers. Whoever had commanded my capture, retention, and course of interrogation had made a mess where he lived. Not in regard to me, however. That I was released was merely a sign of how singularly this person had let down the side. I intuited a general cleaning of house, all the pet projects of this persona non grata undone and swept from the scene.

They could have killed me still. But that would have implied a belief on someone's part, a belief that whoever was being cut loose from the firm had been on to something when they had me detained. So much more humiliating and nullifying to set me on my way. No harm, no foul. Though there was a use I could still be put to.

There was an interim, of course. Medical attention, which, as it was applied in my cell, I initially thought was a part of the torture. An effort to restore some of my health before beginning anew. But it wasn't. A man wearing the same surgical mask worn by anyone who came into my presence asked me questions in a flat voice with no accent. A voice that was the product of excellent training. And for another two weeks my worst hurts were ministered to. Several times I was given injections that put me to sleep. Each time I believed I would not wake up. Each time I did.

The last time I woke in my cell a slight-framed person stood at the foot of the bed. From a manila folder this person drew several eight-by-ten black-and-white photographs with a glossy finish. The photos were all of the same person. A man with a conservative haircut and suit. Nondescript. Two of the photos showed him entering a residence, the house number clearly visible. One of the photos showed him driving a car, turning onto a street where both that same house and a street sign were clearly visible. Another photo showed him walking in a busy downtown area of a large city, a well-known tourist attraction in that city clearly visible. That was the last photo. The lights went out, a needle pricked my arm, I went to sleep, and when I woke up I was home, in my own bed.

Not one to question a message so crisply enunciated, I called my travel agent that day, booked a flight to the city I had identified by the well-known tourist attraction, flew to that city, rented a car, drove to the street whose sign I had clearly seen, parked up a bit from the house I had also clearly seen, waited until the nondescript haircut and suit arrived and went inside, followed him in soon after, and killed everyone within.

No, this was not revenge. I did not doubt that this was the person who had ordered me held and tortured, but, as I was a mature man at this point, revenge was not on my mind. I was simply behaving in a prudent and professional manner. I had been told, as clearly as if the words had been spoken in my ear, that I should not take my release for granted, that payment was due. So I paid up.

And that was the last that was ever made of it. I have never worked since for my government; a mutual accord. Could, one day, there be an accounting? Could some drone of the services uncover a dusty file while in the process of digitalizing back data and, seeing an opportunity for advancement, approach his or her superiors with this nugget of ancient history, a loose end left perilously undone? Could a fellow practitioner arrive by stealth and tie off that dangling line? Yes, to all questions, yes. But the prospect did not keep me awake at night.

I was sent a message by whoever released me: *Kill this man for us, or else.* The particular savagery and bloody-mindedness I expressed in the fulfillment of that unspoken contract composed the text of my own reply message: *Leave me alone, or I'll do this to you.*

We heard one another, loud and clear.

In both cases of torture, the questions I had been asked bore little relation to any actions I had ever taken. Though I was most certainly guilty of any number of misdeeds for which I might have been held accountable, I was always quizzed on matters unrelated. And so it was again.

There were four people in the room with me. Well, six, but two of them were dead. One of those remaining four had collected some of my possessions. Papers, two external hard drives, two laptops and a tablet computer, five thumb drives, my slender bamboo-sided desktop tower, and anything else that might reasonably store information, including my DVR. Though I doubted they'd learn anything from the classic episodes of *Twilight Zone* and several cooking and gardening shows that I was addicted to.

Done with that, he'd unrolled a nylon tool caddy and sorted through various cables, fitting them to my phones and downloading assorted numbers and call logs before tossing the phones themselves into a knapsack. He'd be disappointed. The business phones were each assigned to a specific individual whose number I had memorized; they contained only one number each: their own. Call logs I erased after each call in or out from a particular phone. My personal phones were similarly barren of numbers. An advantage of a nearly photographic memory. I erased logs at day's end in general. The phone I'd had on me when they attacked would have the helicopter pilot's number, Vinnie's incoming call, and a few others. Nothing I was concerned with.

A second survivor was at the glass wall that looked out over the basin. He took frequent peeks through a pair of binoculars and spoke in occasional whispers into his headset. The glass was thick, impact- but not bullet-resistant; still the faint whines of sirens and crackle of gunfire penetrated. He primarily spoke modern Hebrew, with an Israeli accent, though I did catch a frequent, emphatic "fuck." The third, a man who could only be described as "battle-scarred and proud of it," asked me questions that, while they didn't confuse me, did confound me. The fourth had plugged in the soldering iron and placed it carefully on the Thor table while it heated.

The only obvious mistake they had made was in not wearing masks of any sort. Not that revealing their features marked them for an eventual vicious demise when I freed myself and set about to hunt them down one by one, rather that it revealed their intention to kill me no matter the outcome of their questioning. Tipping their hand a bit. For whatever it might be worth. Knowing I was going to die was hardly any comfort, but it did define the field of play, spurring me to actions I might otherwise not have taken.

The battle-scarred man referred to a number of laminated sheets of paper on a clipboard. I had seen something similar in the past. An interrogation script, it would have been prepared in advance, each question allowing for only a limited number of answers. Each of these allowable answers leading to the next question. All roads leading to one of two conclusions only: *You are the fucker we're after* or *You are not the fucker we're after*. It didn't matter that I could tell them outright that the answer in my case was the second option. They would only accept one of these two conclusions if it were arrived at after the script had been followed.

The first act began.

"Who are you working for?"

Well, obviously I was going to give no answer.

Yes, there was a grim possibility that this ritual of pain was the death my life had been shaping. And yes, there would be symmetry in the design if I were to end broken and drooling, gasping out all my secrets under ultimate duress. But there could be no completion of my long endeavor if I blurted the name of my employer at the first request. The mental image of Lady Chizu's bland disregard for that sort of weakness and lack of professionalism was enough to keep my lips sealed.

"What is the plan?"

Again, I had no answer. But here it was less a case of will and desire and more a case of being at an utter loss. It was possible he meant whatever plan I had to recover the drive from Haas, but his tone suggested something altogether more specific. In any case, I had nothing to say.

"Who are your accomplices?"

It took, you see, only three questions to realize that his script was not pertinent to me. It concerned suspicions he held *regarding* me but which had little or nothing to do with my true intentions.

"Are you working with the cop?"

A question that did little more than reinforce my growing feeling that I had been misapprehended.

"Where were you going to take Mr. Afronzo Junior?"

Here, a little light appeared at the end of the tunnel.

"What were your demands to be?"

Clarity, when it comes, is literally physical. Tension is released from muscles, shoulders unbunch, jaws unclench, brows unfurrow. The body lightens, becomes, for a moment, less earthbound. A delightful sensation. No wonder many people make of it a lifelong quest.

"Is your employer political or criminal?"

It was then that I might have begun to state my case. I could have told them that I understood that I had been observed in proximity to Mr. Afronzo Junior. That, yes, the behavior I exhibited was suspicious, and yes, I was surveilling someone. Yes, I understood that anyone in Mr. Afronzo Junior's buffer zone who engaged in certain proscribed activities, such as spying, would have their faces extensively photographed, their actions videoed, their utterances parabolically recorded, and the resulting archive submitted for review by teams of experts in tightly sealed rooms where secrets were doled out a syllable at a time to protect against leaks. Yes, frankly, I might have said, this situation is as much of my making as anyone's. I should have realized that the history attached to my features, mannerisms, and voice is precisely the kind that should set every red light on Afronzo security consoles to blazing, and taken greater care when I was observing the young man. Certainly I understood that of the vast range of threats I represented, the greatest was kidnap. And yes, the highest possible threat level should be applied to such as I, and action taken immediately. Nonetheless, I would have been forced to conclude, shooting a missile at a SoCal TOC observation post in order to distract me was perhaps an ill-advised overreaction. For, you see, I could have explained, you have the wrong man.

It was then, after those seven essential questions had been asked in an offhand manner, with no reply expected, that I could have launched that defense. I might even have gone so far as to have sketched the barest outline of my actual goals. But it would have been to cross-purposes. No, I had no intention of kidnapping Mr. Afronzo Junior, but I was seeking to take possession of a hard drive for which he had killed several men. Cut too close to *that* truth and the result would be the same. It was possible things would reach a point where I would speak the truth about my lack of interest in kidnapping the young man, but what lies I might concoct to cover my actual intentions escaped me for the moment, as I became distracted by the slight click the soldering iron emitted when it had reached the optimal temperature.

17

space where he had left the bottle of DR33M3R.

"It doesn't matter."

He ignored Bartolome's words, going through the remaining contents of the safe. His legal documents, the gold coins, his weapons and spare clips, even his stash, all still there. But the print slides, the thumb drive with his reports, and the DR33M3R itself were gone.

"It doesn't matter, Haas."

Park turned from the safe, walked out of the closet, and looked at his captain.

"Who?"

Bartolome stood at the bedroom window, watching something in the yard.

"DEA. FBI. Fuck, CIA. I don't know. Guys in Washington suits. It doesn't matter."

Park started to strip out of the shirt he'd worn all day.

"It's all that matters."

"They make it, Officer. They make it."

"That's the point."

Bartolome turned from the window.

"Yes, it is, but not how you're thinking about it."

Park was at the dresser, digging in his shirt drawer.

"It doesn't matter how I *think* about it. It's either what it *is* or it's *not* what it is."

"Jesus. Jesus, Park. Will you? Just look over here for a minute. Just. Officer, look at me for a fucking minute right fucking now."

Park looked at Bartolome. Beyond him, through the window screen, he could see Rose in the backyard, cross-legged on the dead lawn, picking dead weeds. Francine sat in the hammock strung between a palm tree and a ficus, the baby in her lap, singing a French lullaby.

Standing in the middle of the disordered living room when he came through the door, Rose had looked at him, looked around the room, said, *Some men were here for you,* and walked out of the room.

"There were men in my house. Men who are supposed to be working with us came here and stole evidence from my safe."

Bartolme sat on the edge of the bed.

"No wonder no one wanted to work with you. Haas. They didn't steal shit. Patriot II says they can take what they want when they want. And you didn't have anything, anyway."

"I had Dreamer that was given to me by an Afronzo."

Bartolome came off the bed.

"Yes! And what is that? Are you listening to me? They make it. They make the stuff, Haas. Of course he had Dreamer. He probably has it coming out of his ass. He probably shits it. And so what? You think what? That the Afronzos are illegally distributing Dreamer? Dealing their own invention on the black market? Why? So they can make more money?"

Park stood there with a clean T-shirt in his hand, saying nothing.

Bartolome nodded.

"Yeah, right? Motive, Haas. They have no motive at all to deal Dreamer off the market. All it would do is put at risk the most profitable revenue stream since oil. So he had a bottle on him and he traded it for Shabu? What does that get you in court against their lawyers? It gets you litigation for a hundred years."

He stepped closer to Park.

"No. It gets you riots. It gets you blood in the streets. It hits the gossip sites, *ET* and *Gawker,* and it gets you a bunch of people dead. Why? Because the kid is using extra bottles of his family product to score drugs?

What we drove through coming over here, crackdown because some militia or insurgent or flat-out gangbanger took a shot at that TOC outpost. That won't be shit. People will die by the thousands. For something that just doesn't matter."

Park twisted the shirt between his hands.

"What did they tell you?"

Bartolome crossed his arms.

"They came to me and showed me those pictures of you and Afronzo and asked me *What the fuck?* I told them I didn't know what the fuck. They said you had something they needed to recover and asked what they could expect from you in the way of cooperation. I told them they could expect you to be a hellacious pain in the ass."

He looked out the window again.

Both men stayed where they were.

Bartolome looked back at Park.

"So they said to get you someplace secure and to make sure you kept your mouth shut. About then, you messaged for a sit-down. I had to deal with the feds, so I sent Hounds."

"Why him?"

Barlolome waved a hand.

"Because he's old school. Because he hates Washington suits. Because I didn't think he could be bought by the feds to take you to the airport to be flown to Gitmo."

Park looked at the drawer full of black T-shirts he'd bought when Rose became ill. He'd thrown out all his old ones. Kept just the blacks. One less decision to be made every day. He stared at them as if one might have greater value than the others.

Then he closed the drawer and put on the shirt already in his hands.

"Now?"

Bartolome looked around the bedroom.

"Now you make the call. Dreamer is still your beat if you want it. Busts of scale. Real busts. Not this conspiracy bullshit. Or you deal with what you got here at home. My job, I've been doing it too long to do anything any other way. Someone tells me what I'm after, I find my guys, send them after it. Make busts. I make busts. You, your wife. You've been a cop a couple years. Time comes, you need to deal with what's *here,* no one will have anything to say about that. I won't have anything to say about that. Your call."

Park was looking at the bed. Would he see it differently if he slept? Was exhaustion making him paranoid? The modern world record for staying awake, before SLP, was held by Randy Gardner. Eleven days. When sleepless went their first eleven days, they called it pulling a Randy. Park knew he hadn't pulled a Randy, but he couldn't remember being up this long before. If he crawled into bed and switched off the light, what would happen? Would he sleep and find sense again when he woke? Or, once in the dark, would he find sleep had abandoned him as it had his wife?

He thought about Kleiner.

Bartolome was looking out the window again.

Park came to the window and looked out at his wife.

"My deal is to do my job."

Bartolome looked at him, took his sunglasses from his breast pocket, covered his eyes, and walked to the door.

"Get some sleep, Haas. It'll all make more sense when you get some sleep."

Park waited until he heard the captain's Explorer start in the driveway and pull away down the street. Then he walked out to the front of the house and unlocked the hatchback of the Subaru. He shoved the trash, first-aid, and roadside emergency kits out of the way, lifted the carpet flap, and exposed the spare. Reaching inside, he took out Hydo's travel drive and his own red-spine journal. He slammed the hatch closed, went back into the house, and ripped open the property envelope Bartolome had given him on the ride home; the thumb drive he'd copied his reports on spilled out.

He took his father's watch from his back pocket and buckled it around his wrist and checked the time.

He'd sleep later.

■　■　■

A FULL-THICKNESS, or third-degree, burn occurs when the epidermis is lost entirely, with partial damage to the fatty superficial fascia below. Such a burn is characterized by charring of the skin, black necrotic tissue, loss of sweat glands and sense of touch. Exposure to a temperature of roughly 160 degrees Fahrenheit for one second is enough to produce such a burn in an adult.

Lead-based solder requires a temperature between 482 and 572 degrees Fahrenheit. Lead-free solder requires 662 to 752 degrees. There was no way to say for certain which solder the iron was designed for, but it seemed certain that even at its lowest possible setting it was bound to leave a mark.

Something more than a slight touch was likely to bore through the epidermis, dermis, fascia, muscle, and allow the man wielding the tool to burn his initials into my bones if he cared to.

How fortunate that he had yet to touch me with the iron. Which is not to say that it didn't do its job admirably when held a centimeter from the skin. He'd not started with my genitals. Well trained, he left himself something to escalate to. He started instead with the pockets of tender skin behind my knees.

I focused, at first, on the dead animals in the room. The collection of three was the work of a Minnesota artist whose medium was "salvaged roadkill." One of the pieces was composed of two flayed and gutted squirrel carcasses posed as if dancing a jitterbug. One was a cow eye preserved in a jar of Formalin. And one was a very lifelike black cat with the spread wings of a blackbird attached to its shoulders.

Elements in my apocalypse collection, they had occasionally served me as barometers of human nature, measuring the extent to which certain people had been deadened to revulsion by their reactions at seeing them lined up on a shelf in the bookcase. None of the men in the room had given them more than a glance. But they were worthy of a second look. Excellent craft had gone into their making. The jitterbugging squirrels and the cow eye were gallery pieces, the winged cat was a special commission I had waited over a year to receive. I'd requested a large cat, and the artist had had to wait until an appropriate corpse became available. In the end she'd asked if I would accept a calico dyed black. I did. The dimensions were my primary concern; the authenticity of color was never an issue. Its girth anchored the entire bookcase; everything on the shelves referred back to it. The black-winged cat in its book-lined aerie.

It became impossible to continue along that line of thought, however. The smell of burning hair and seared skin had become punctuated by a whiff of rendered fat. My scream shocked me from my reverie, and I became aware again of the questions that were being asked.

"Is your employer political or criminal?"

The question had been asked many times, but, for some reason, it was only at that moment that the humor of it struck me, and as my scream diminished, I laughed.

There was a general pause in the room. The man inventorying my data and records looked up from the laptop he was currently trying to access without my password. The man at the windows took the binoculars from his eyes. The interrogator glanced away from his script. And the man with the soldering iron pulled it from my leg, holding it poised in the air like a quill that he would soon dip again into a well of ink.

They waited out my moment of hysteria, knowing that if they forged on I might well slip over an edge and become insensible for several hours. My composure returned in a matter of moments, but I continued to laugh for a full three minutes. Laughter, they say, is the best medicine. I have never accepted that bit of homespun, but I indulged myself nonetheless.

I used some of the time to flex my right leg what little bit my bonds would allow, reassuring myself that no permanent damage had yet been done to the ligaments and muscles in my knee. I used the rest of the few minutes to release whatever tensions the false laughter could shake loose. I needed a degree of relaxation from which to rebuild my concentration. Which is how I used the final moments I had to myself. Fixing, this time, on a canvas by Wu Shanzhuan, "Today No Water—Chapter 29."

Covering most of the wall opposite the floor-to-ceiling windows looking over the city, the reds of the painting glowed when a proper Los Angeles sunset lit the sky. Dense with schematic images of architecture, religion, anatomy, geometry, and plumbing, all intertwined with English and Chinese text. My eyes settled of their own will on the words "open box." I pictured lifting the lid from a shoe box. Peeling the tape from a cardboard carton. Prying the top from a crate. Easing open a clamshell jewelry case. I tried to reconstruct in detail the inner workings of a classic box escape no longer in vogue but very popular among stage magicians of the nineteenth century. Wishing, when the soldering iron was newly applied to my inner thigh, that it was only a box I was trapped in.

"Are your employers political or criminal?"

I did not laugh this time.

▌ ▐ ▌

7/10/10

CAN THAT BE right? Is it still the tenth? This morning was what? Yes, it's the tenth. This morning was when I sat in the car and wrote here before going to the high school. A little over twelve hours since I stashed the journal and travel drive in the spare before going.

Francine came out with the baby and told me Rose was in the bedroom trying to meditate. I took the baby from Francine, she started to cry. After Francine left I didn't want to go into the bedroom and disturb Rose. The meditation doesn't work as well as it used to, but sometimes she can still put herself into a slight trance. She says it's not like sleeping at all, but she gets perspective.

Perspective.

Captain Bartolome didn't say anything about the murders at the gold farm. He didn't say anything about Hydo's drive. The feds who came here didn't search the house after they found the safe. They only took my police reports, the DR33M3R, and the slides. If they had known about the drive and the file with Cager's name on it they would have looked for it also.

They don't know about the drive.

Captain Bartolome and the Washington suits don't know Cager did business with the gold farmers.

They only came for the DR33M3R and my reports. They took the fingerprints because they were right there in the safe.

My reports. I mention the murders.

The drive?

No, I didn't. I hid it from Bartolome. It's not in the reports. But the murders are. They won't care. Yes, they will. If they know that Cager did some kind of business with Hydo Chang, they will care. But they didn't know about the drive. So they don't know I was there.

But they will when they read the reports.

What then?

What do they want? They want to keep the Afronzos clean. And? What else? Anything? Why am I here? Why am I working Dreamer? If they don't want the Afronzos implicated in DR33M3R trade and they know Cager is using it for barter, why look for DR33M3R trade?

Perspective. They don't think like I do. They think like they do.

Father used to say something about being posted on foreign soil: "It's not their job, Parker, to accommodate our ways, it is our job to understand theirs. Once we understand how they think, we can begin to predict their behavior. Once our predictions become accurate, we can begin to manipulate their behavior. That is diplomacy."

Perspective.

They know there is something to be found. They know Cager is selling Dreamer. They know that it will cause trouble if he is found. But they have the police, me, investigating anyway.

Because?

Because they don't want anyone to know. Because they don't want anyone they can't control to find out. If it leaks, if their system leaks, they have to know first. People they control have to know first.

To find leaks. To find leaks that lead to Cager and the Afronzo family. To find the leaks before anyone else does so they can be patched.

I'm a plumber.

Rose. Are you reading this? You gave me this book. I write in it, and I think of you. Are you reading this?

I am a plumber.

They have me doing their dirty work for them. Rose. I thought. I don't know what. I thought there was a reason for the time I spent away from you and the baby. I thought this was something that was essential. If the world is going to be normal again, if we are all going to be sane again, if the baby is going to be safe, I thought this was something that had to be done. I thought that I had to be a police officer. When Captain Bartolome offered it to me, I thought that this was the job I needed to do. To make things better. I am such an innocent.

No, that's wrong; innocent is the last thing I am. You are wrong about that, Rose. But I am naïve. And proud. To think that I thought I was doing something to help save the world.

I am their plumber.

I am doing maintenance on the world they are making. I am a fool. Perspective.

Don't whine, Rose would say. Don't fucking whine. Do something about it.

She won't talk to me. Still. After Captain Bartolome left I went to the yard to try and talk to her. When I left in the morning I told her I would be back soon. And I wasn't. Francine said she found Rose rigid at the foot of the crib, watching the baby cry. Talking to herself, saying again and again, "This is my baby, this is my baby." She didn't want to take her out of the crib. She was afraid that she would forget where and when she was, forget the baby, and put her down somewhere dangerous. She spent all day at the crib, afraid to touch the crying baby, telling herself who she is, when it is, and who the baby is. She shouldn't talk to me.

Rose, you're right not to talk to me. I left you alone.

And I am going to leave you alone again.

I can't take care of the baby, you said.

But I have to try. They've used me to help them bury the old world. Our world. The baby's world. The one she deserves. The one we promised her. I can't let that happen. I can't protect her in the world they're trying to make. You could. I can't. I can't take care of her there. But I can take care of her in the world they want to kill. I have to live in that world. If I step into theirs, try to live by their rules, I'll lose her.

I can't lose you both.

I remember everything you said.

"How am I going to be able to look after you?" you asked.

I shook my head and told you that you didn't have to. And you kind of sighed like you always did when you thought I wasn't getting something.

"No, I mean, really, how am I gonna look the fuck after you?"

I told you that I was okay.

You were staring at the ceiling.

"You're such a, God I hate to use the word, but you're such an innocent. I mean, how am I supposed to walk away from that?"

Don't walk away from me, Rose.

I am not innocent.

But do not walk away from me.

18

BEENIE WASN'T ANSWERING HIS PHONE.

He hadn't gone with Park to the gallery. When Cager had made a point of not inviting him along, Park had been about to insist, but Beenie had shook his head. His long day was over. He had miles to ride to get back home. He was looking forward to smoking a little of the opium before the ride. Taking a bicycle in and out of the stalled and abandoned cars of L.A. was a surreal pleasure. He wanted to compound that enjoyment. And he was looking forward to sleep. He knew his sleep would not be truly dreamless, but with a little luck he wouldn't remember the dreams when he woke.

He'd told Park not to worry, he didn't want to go to the gallery. He didn't want to be driven home. He wanted to ride and to sleep. Outside Denizone, when Park had reached out to shake hands, Beenie had given him a one-arm embrace that was too brief for Park to return.

"If you're around the farm tomorrow, I'll maybe see you there, bro."

Park had wanted to tell him not to go to the farm. Stay away. But Cager was nearby, Twittering, texting, messaging, sending his thoughts into the night.

He planned to call Beenie early. Tell him he'd heard there was trouble at the farm. Keep clear. It could wait until then.

But then everything had gone wrong. Too much time had passed. And Beenie wasn't answering his phone. The Washington suits had photographs of Park and Cager at the club. They had to have photos of Cager and Beenie as well.

And Beenie wasn't answering his phone. Park pictured him with his wrists chained to ankle restraints, a bag over his head, in the air somewhere between Los Angeles and Guantanamo.

Driving southwest on Washington Boulevard, Park hit redial again, and again it flipped over to voice mail. He'd tried the call fifteen times. For half of the attempts he'd not been about to get service at all. The network was jammed.

Waiting in line at a new checkpoint just east of the PCH, Park looked back toward Hollywood. Above the north-south border of the Santa Monica Freeway, the sky was thick with gunship searchlights. Smoke rose, lit from below in flickering yellow, orange, and red. Without any elevation, it was difficult to pinpoint which areas had been blacked out, but it was clear from the quality of the ground light that entire neighborhoods were without power. Whether that was by design of SoCal TOC, caused by the usual unannounced easing of strain on the grid, or the result of an attack like the rocket Bartolome had told him about, was impossible to know.

What was clear, the only thing that was clear, was that a great deal of hell was breaking out. If he needed any further evidence, he could simply look at one of the lighted signs that loomed at intervals all over the city. The usual traffic advisories, long become a local joke, had been replaced by a single flashing message:

MARTIAL LAW HAS BEEN INVOKED IN THE FOLLOWING AREAS

LOS ANGELES COUNTY

SANTA MONICA

MALIBU

WEST HOLLYWOOD

And so on. The list was long. It ended with a scrolling notice that if you were reading the message, you should go immediately to someplace where you could no longer read it. Get the hell inside. Advice that most people seemed to be heeding. The traffic had not flowed so smoothly even before the outbreak of SLP.

Park had seen the LAPD directives for martial law. He knew the extraordinary police powers invoked through Patriot II. Knowing what the police were empowered to do, he assumed the military had a weapons-free policy that would allow them to shoot at the least provocation, without regard for consequences mortal or legal.

Long before it was his turn at the checkpoint, he had hung his badge from his neck and done a mental inventory of the car to assure himself that there were no drugs or weapons anywhere but in the spare tire. When he pulled forward to the barrier of abandoned cars resting on blown-out tires and bent rims, he realized that the greatest danger was not that he would be shot as a suspected looter, but that one of the terrified young Guards might flinch at the sound of distant gunfire and riddle his car with an entire M4 clip.

A very young black man with sergeant's bars and a drawl from well below the Mason-Dixon approached the car.

"Sir, turn off your vehicle, please, sir."

Keeping his left hand visible on the steering wheel, Park switched off the engine with his right and brought it immediately back into view of the Guards.

"Sir, your ID, please, sir."

Again leaving his left on the wheel, Park lifted the badge from his chest, ducked his head out of the lanyard, and offered it to the young man.

There was a pause while the sergeant raised a hand in the air, flashed several fingers at his squadmates in quick succession, like a catcher running through his signals, and stepped forward, reaching for something on his belt. Park almost ducked as the RFID interrogator was raised, a gesture that surely would have required a few rounds fired, but he recognized the device at the last moment and remained still as the Guard aimed it at the badge, pulled the trigger, read the results, and flashed another series of signals that resulted in most of the weapons in the immediate vicinity being aimed in other directions.

"Sir, Officer Haas, sir, I need to ask what your business is, sir."

Park dropped the badge back around his neck and replaced his hands on the wheel.

"I'm on assignment, Sergeant. Venice Beach."

"Sir, I have to ask if this assignment is urgent business, sir. If it is not, I have to request that you return to your home or domicile."

Park knew it wasn't by chance that this Deep South native had found his Guard unit dropped in California. Patriot II policy was to deploy the Guard away from their native states when suppressing civil unrest. The fewer the connections the soldiers had to the locals, the more easily they would pull the trigger when necessary.

Park looked at the other Guards. All as young as this one, nearly all black or brown, arrayed behind the barricade of cars that they knew would do little to stop any remotely decent firepower. Let alone provide cover from an RPG or, God forbid, a car bomb. Neither of the two Humvees parked behind the barricade had been up-armored, and only one was equipped with a heavy machine gun. The young woman behind the machine gun kept pushing her helmet up as it repeatedly tilted down over her eyes.

"Yes, Sergeant, my investigation is urgent."

The NCO pulled a logbook from one of the side pockets of his fatigues.

"Sir, I'll need an address, sir."

Park gave him a random sequence of numbers and the first Venice Beach street name he thought of.

The sergeant wrote it down, returned the logbook to his pocket, nodded at Park, and leaned against the car, dipping his face close to the open window.

"Sir, I don't suppose you've heard anything, sir."

Park shook his head.

"I was just about to ask you."

He looked over his shoulder at his command and smiled.

"He was gonna ask me what the fuck is going on. Believe that?"

A round of weary soldiers' laughter went through the squad.

He looked back at Park.

"They ain't told us shit. We get what y'all get from the radio. Some bad guys shot a rocket at some of our guys. We hit Little Persia. Little Russia.

Things didn't get kerfucked until we hit a Church of the New American Jesus in Hollywood and a couple flash-bangs started a fire and burned the fucking thing down. That was around thirteen hundred hours. We got rolled here by fourteen hundred. Haven't heard shit from the space ants since."

Park nodded.

"Wish I knew something I could tell you, Sergeant."

The sergeant flashed another sequence of fingers, and the Humvee with the gun mount backed up a few yards to clear a space in the middle of the barricade.

"Shit, we ain't worried."

He pointed at the hood of the Subaru, and Park started the engine.

The sergeant looked north, where all the trouble was.

"This is America, motherfuckers. We'll be just fine."

He waved a hand, and Park drove through the opening. West, away from the worst of it.

The few other cars on the boulevard were driven by those whose cares were great enough to take the risk, who were stupid enough not to see the danger as real, brave enough to face it with a desire to find some way to help, or the sleepless. No reason to fear anything, they wandered the sidewalks and drove the roads. Sudden bursts of speed, violent turns, or constant meandering between lanes tipped one off that the car ahead should be given a wide berth.

After turning south onto Oxford, Park found another checkpoint at the Admiralty Way entrance to Marina Del Rey. This one manned by an impromptu militia of boat owners and sail buffs who had failed to get their vessels out before the Navy sealed the marina to cut it off from use by smugglers bringing arms in to the NAJi.

Carrying sporting shotguns last used shooting skeet from the decks of their yachts, a few illegally modified assault rifles ostensibly necessary for repelling South Asian pirates but more often fired during drunken barbeques in international waters, two flare pistols, and one spear gun, they told Park to turn around and fuck off.

He showed them his badge.

They asked him who he was there to see.

He told them to get out of the way and stop interfering with police business before he put in a call to the Guard checkpoint on Washington and told them there was a well-armed insurgent group raiding the marina.

They let him pass, and he drove out Bali Way onto one of the relatively low-rent piers, parked, walked to the end of the fourth dock, found Beenie's day cruiser floating in its slip, and crept on board, his Walther PPS in his hands.

Coming down the steps from the deck into the cabin, the boat bobbing gently, he leaned back to duck under the hatch and found his left ankle grabbed from below, his leg pulled from underneath him. Twisting, he fell to the side, his hip, elbow, and shoulder cracking against the steps. The gun slipped partially from his grasp, and he fumbled his finger inside the guard while bringing it up.

Someone waved an arm from beneath the steps.

"What the fuck! What the fuck!"

Park froze, the weapon half-raised, and waited as Beenie emerged.

"What the fuck, Park? I could have killed you, man. Hail the vessel before you come aboard."

Park lowered his gun.

"I thought. Was anyone here?"

Beenie put down the steak knife he was holding.

"No, man. Who's going to be here? No one is going anywhere. No one except Guards and. Oh, Jesus."

Park followed Beenie's eyes down to the badge hanging from his neck.

"Oh, Jesus, Park."

Park got up slowly, stretching his arm and leg, rubbing his hip, determining that nothing was broken.

He holstered his gun.

Beenie dropped onto his bunk and put his face in his hands.

"Fuck, Park. I told you shit."

He looked up.

"I mean, fuck. We were friends."

Park looked around, found Beenie's day pack and held it out to him.

"We need to fill this with anything you can't live without."

* * *

When they drove away from the marina Beenie's favorite trail bike was in the back of Park's car along with his helmet, elbow and knee pads, riding clips, and halogen lamp, along with a solo tent and mummy bag strapped to the frame with loops of bungee cord. The day pack was in Beenie's lap. Inside were his laptop, several accessories, a jumble of thumb drives and cards, tangled chargers, an ounce of British Columbian weed, some clean socks, biking shorts and jerseys, his phone, a copy of *On the Road,* a set of silk long underwear, and a thick envelope filled with pictures of his wife and a letter he had never been able to read, written by her for him to open after she died.

Park had helped Beenie collect those things, opening drawers and digging under piles of dirty laundry as directed while Beenie changed into hiking pants with zip-off lower legs, an EMS Techwick shirt, and a boot-style pair of mountain biking shoes. He'd recognized the unopened light blue envelope with the frayed edges not because he'd ever seen it before, but because Beenie had described it to him one evening nearly a year before. On the anniversary of her death, uncharacteristically sober, he had told Park about it while they waited in line at Randy's Donuts. He'd told him that he kept trying to lose it. Carelessly flipping it to the back of a drawer, finding it after a few months and stuffing it into his pocket, leaving it there when he tossed the pants into a laundry pile, only to have it fall out before they went into a machine weeks later. On the boat, Park had found it poking from the bottom of a stack of cycling magazines, pulled it free, and, without asking, slid it in with the photos.

In the car, Beenie put the finishing touches on a joint and showed it to Park.

"Any objections?"

Park shook his head; Beenie lit the joint and took a hit.

"Were you going to bust me?"

Park concentrated on the car ahead of him. It zigged across two lanes as if to make a last-second right at Ocean Avenue and then zagged back to the middle, straddling the broken white line, blocking both westbound lanes.

Beenie blew smoke out the open window.

"If whatever's happening hadn't happened, were you going to bust me?"

Park shifted into fourth, swung the Subaru into a gap in the sparse eastbound traffic, and passed the car, stealing a glance at the stiff-necked driver, an old man wearing no shirt, howling like a dog along to a German death metal song that was cracking his speakers.

He pulled back into the westbound lanes.

"Yes. I would have busted you."

Beenie looked at the joint pinched between his fingers and frowned.

"But now?"

Park drove them over the small bridge that crossed the Grand Canal, the water on either side scummed with a thick pelt of algae broken by flotillas of plastic bottles.

"If I bust you, I think someone might kill you."

Beenie brought the joint to his lips, took it away without inhaling, and flicked it out the window.

"What's it about, Park?"

Park edged the car to the curb on Strongs Drive.

The Venice Beach encampment spilled up Washington from the shore. Tents, lean-tos, corrugated shanties, they stretched along the sand from the park at Horizon Avenue to just below Catamaran. A combination of the homeless who had long ago staked their claims to this stretch of oceanfront, canyon country fire evacuees, and refugees from Inglewood and Hawthorne. They had run until they hit the ocean. Those trying to flee farther north hit chain link and barbed wire on the southern edge of Santa Monica and found themselves turned about. No one bothered to go south. Assuming they could skirt the marina, the beach at the foot of the LAX runways was patrolled by Marines. If they somehow made it past either of those hazards, they would surely be machine-gunned by the private security agents at the El Segundo Chevron refinery.

There was still a great deal of tattered tie-dye and faded army surplus to be found in the encampment, but any vagabond spirit of the past was all but dead. Park had never thought of Venice as anything but a grimy sideshow distraction featuring destitute junkies and aging acid heads so thoroughly burned out that you could all but see the broken filaments behind their eyes. There was no romance in the legend of the place as far as he was concerned, but that didn't make its present less desperate.

He switched off the engine and ran his thumb along the teeth of his house key.

"It's about Dreamer."

Beenie dropped his head and shook it.

"Fuck."

He looked at Park.

"I introduced you to Cager."

Park watched a scramble of dusty boys and girls kicking a soccer ball in and out of the darkness between two unbroken street lamps.

"I know."

Beenie opened his door and climbed out.

"Fuck."

Park got out, went to the rear of the car, opened the hatch, and stood aside.

Beenie pulled out his bike.

"Hold this."

Park took the handlebars and held the forks off the ground as Beenie reattached the front wheel he'd removed to fit the bike in the back of the small five-door.

"Even so, man, Cager is an asshole, but I don't think he would kill me. I mean, you're a cop. You can ruin *my* life, but what can you do to *him?*"

Park leaned the bike against the car.

"Someone hit the gold farm yesterday morning."

"Hit it?"

Park looked at the kids again. An argument had broken out over the boundaries of the field.

"They killed Hydo and the guys. Shot them."

Beenie winced.

"Keebler?"

"And Melrose Tom and Tad, and I think his name was Zhou."

"With the scimitar earring?"

"Yeah, him."

Beenie nodded.

"Yeah, that's Zhou. Fuck. Fuck."

He started to cry, stopped himself, started again, punched the roof of the car, and stopped.

"Fuck. Those guys. They. That's just fucking stupid, killing those guys."

Park nodded.

Beenie wiped his eyes.

"Cager?"

Park looked away from the kids.

"What was he doing with Hydo, other than buying artifacts?"

Beenie sat on the bumper and started strapping his clips to his riding boots.

"Park, how the fuck do I know? I didn't even know you were a cop."

He put his feet down, the clips tapping against the asphalt.

"Hydo was like his house dealer for anything in-world."

He strapped on an elbow pad.

"Anything Cager wanted for Chasm, anything he wanted for one of his quests, Hydo got it for him. Only reason I was involved is because Hydo subcontracted some of it to me when Cager's requisition list was too long. I came through, and every now and then Cager would throw me some business."

Park reached in the back of the car, pulled out the other elbow pad and handed it to him.

"Why?"

Beenie strapped it on, grabbed the knee pads.

"Because he likes being in the middle. He likes the hustle. Like meeting you and making that Shabu deal on the fly. He could have that shit delivered whenever he wants, but he likes to play. He likes action."

He sat with a knee pad in either hand, clacking them together.

"Me and Hydo talked about it. The way you talk about someone famous when you meet them. Try to figure out what they're really about. That whole cult of celebrity thing and the way it gets inside your head, man. Like you don't even want to think about these people, but they're so relentlessly shoved in your face, you can't help it. Then you meet someone you only saw before on TV, and you really trip out."

Park was again rubbing his father's watch.

"What did you guys think?"

"Thing about Cager is, we thought, he's all about the game."

He looked up at Park.

"He talks about Chasm different than other people. Lots of players, they talk about it like it's real. Shit, I do sometimes. But he talks about it like it's more than real. Or more important than real. The way he games out here, how he plays people, that's him trying to live the game outside the game. Not like wear a sword or anything, but he loves barter. He loves to put together different teams to take on different tasks. He's got groups of friends for gaming, groups for dancing, groups for getting into trouble. Different teams for different quests. Like those sleepless he puts together in Chasm. And just like in the game, he likes each person in one of his groups to be a specialist. Look at you."

He bent to buckle on a pad.

Park put his hands in his pocket.

"What?"

Beenie buckled on the other pad.

"The way he swept you up, took you in. He wants to make you part of one of his teams."

He sat up.

"He knows you're smart. He took you to that gallery show. He probably wants to make you the dealer for his art team."

He stood up.

"He invite you to something tonight?"

Park was looking at the kids. They had circled up around two girls who were shoving each other back and forth.

"Yeah. He said to text him, he'd let me know where."

Beenie put on his day pack and tightened the straps.

"Welcome to the court of the Prince of Dreams."

Park looked at him.

"What?"

Beenie nodded.

"What he goes by in Chasm. Prince of Dreams. Nice, huh?"

The fight hadn't boiled over yet. Park stepped to the back of the car, exposed the spare, and pulled out the engineer's bag.

Beenie straddled the trail bike.

Park flipped open the bag.

"Hang on."

He took out a tube like the one he'd given Cager, put it back inside the spare, and offered the bag to Beenie.

"Here."

Beenie took the bag and looked inside. He looked at Park.

"If this is an evidence plant, it's the worst one ever."

Park looked north, at the glow of the canyon fires.

"You can use it. Barter. Sell."

Beenie closed the bag.

"Your bosses don't keep track of this stuff?"

"They don't care."

"And neither do you?"

Park was watching the girls. One had picked up a rock.

"I do care. I just don't need it to do my job anymore."

Beenie took a dangling bungee from the side of his day pack and strapped the engineer's bag to the frame of the bike.

"Thanks. Should be something in there to get me past the Santa Monica fence."

The other girl picked up a stick.

Park shifted on his feet.

"From there?"

Beenie scratched the back of his neck.

"People camped out up in Big Sur, I hear. I always liked it up there."

Park closed the hatchback.

"Yeah. It's nice. Long way."

Beenie pointed at the smoke and fires, the searchlights in the sky.

"May as well be riding somewhere else."

Park stepped away from the car.

"Come back when things settle down. I'll do my best to get you in the clear."

Beenie shook his head.

" 'When things settle down.' You're an interesting guy, Park."

"No. I'm not."

Beenie shrugged, stood up on his pedals.

"Take care of the family."

Park raised a hand.

"Travel safe."

He didn't watch Beenie ride away, turning instead toward the brewing fight, wading in, pulling the girls apart, stopping them before they could go too far.

I WAS REMEMBERING Texas.

This was odd, as I had endeavored for oh so many years never to remember Texas. Nonetheless, there it was, as if in front of me, the endless brown plain. Scrubby little Odessa. Youth recaptured.

Specifically, I was having visions of high school. The final month of my senior year, my eighteenth birthday, walking into the army recruiting office with my father and signing the papers, saluting the recruiting officer as I had been taught, turning heel-toe and saluting my father, holding it until he returned it. I was so happy that day.

I was even happier at Fort Bragg. I wouldn't be qualified to apply to the Special Forces Recruiting Detachment until after I had finished basic and done a tour, but I could see the soldiers on Smoke Bomb Hill, going after their green berets. Rarely are the dreams of childhood so close and so tangible. Even the drill sergeants couldn't ruin my mood at Bragg. Brutal and unfair, they were only slightly more abusive than the coaches on my high school football team.

None of it really prepared me for First Air Cavalry. Pure joy. Jumping in and out of Cobras. Patrols between Da Nang and Quang Ngai. Stringing jungle paths with claymore snares.

The message stamped on the business end of a claymore mine still strikes me with both its clarity and wisdom: FRONT TOWARD ENEMY.

Returning after my first tour, the two weeks spent in Odessa were the most difficult. Far more trying than Special Forces Assessment and Selection, more brutal than the six-month Special Forces Qualification course

MOS 18B SF Weapons Sergeant. That had been second nature. But trying to hang out with my buddies from the football team after a year in-country had been akin to torture.

Ah, torture.

That was why I was reminiscing so vividly.

Yes, those callow youths. Chasing tail. Trying to tear off a piece. Guzzling Lone Star. Asking me how many gooks I'd killed over there.

The most troubling aspect wasn't the tedium, it was the aching desire I felt almost every moment I was with those friends of mine to kill. It would have been quite easy. There was no lack of firearms. Virtually every day of my leave included some form of drunken blasting at small animals or the endless supply of empty beer cans we produced.

After five days of it I refused their invitations. Preferring to stay at home with my father, sitting on the patio of what had once been the family horse ranch, staring at the horizon beyond the small stone that marked the place where he had buried my mother. We spoke little enough to each other. I knew that he had been with Darby's Rangers and scaled the cliffs at Pointe du Hoc on D-Day. And he knew that I had seen action myself. What could we possibly say to each other?

Returning with my beret, assigned to the Fifth Army group at Nha Trang, I walked back into the jungle, only my excellent training and self-discipline keeping a bounce from my step.

Remembering the jungle made more sense than remembering Texas. If, during torture, you are going to attempt to cast your mind to another time and place, the best strategy is to choose a time and place where you were *happy*.

Though it is imprecise to say that I was *happy* in the jungle, more accurate that I was most *myself* there. Nowhere else, at no other time, has my nature been so nurtured and rewarded by an environment. By simply relaxing all restraints on my impulses, I thrived. No choking jungle vine flourished as did I.

Truly, I didn't wish to come home.

In fact, it's hard to say that I did come home. I most definitely did not return to Texas. Nor did I return to the name I had been given at birth. From the great distance I had traveled since then, it was hard to see what connection or relation I could possibly have with the rawboned, sun-burned youth grappling at the line of scrimmage on a playing field that was mostly dirt and rock.

Except perhaps a certain hunger for it to be over.

That boy's desire that he could magically turn eighteen right away and begin service. My own desire that the man with the soldering iron could suffer a sudden embolism and die.

Both of us forced to endure.

Coming to that conclusion seemed to exhaust the pool of memory, leaving me again in the present, doing my best not to look at the long parallel lines of seared dermis running up my inner right thigh. But that was a fool's errand. I looked. And I screamed. Shrieked, really. Pain always becomes less bearable and more horrifying when one can see the effect it is having on one's body. Container for the immortal, or mere meat, the body is what we have to work with. Having it ripped into, sliced, or burned in a manner that leaves no doubt as to the hideous nature of the scars that will mar that flesh if one is lucky enough to survive, brings out the craven.

It did so in me.

The battle-scarred man was in the middle of his script at that moment.

"Are you working with the cop?"

I cannot honestly say that I had reached my absolute threshold at that point. I feel, in retrospect, that I had endured worse before. It is therefore difficult to explain why I broke at that moment. Why I embraced the sudden soothing wave of relief that came over me when I succumbed to my collapse of will. I was prepared in that instant to answer any and all questions without any hidden agenda. Happy in the knowledge that the soldering iron would be put to the side once I began to speak.

Accepting the fact that this course led inevitably to my death, I spoke.

"No, I am not working with the cop."

Used to hearing only my panting and rasping breath or my cries of pain, the men all started slightly at the sound of my voice. The man with the soldering iron drew back and looked over his shoulder at the questioner. He, in turn, consulted his script, flipped forward a page, flipped back, and nodded. At which point the man with the soldering iron placed the tool directly against my left kneecap.

The script, apparently, did not allow for that answer. Caught unpre-pared, I didn't scream this time, but rather hissed, a sound very much like the one coming from my knee.

Then the lights went out.

And in the dark, with no one to see, I was free to be myself again. At last.

19

HIS TEXT TOLD me to come to the XF-11 house. I texted him that I
didn't know what he was talking about. I could almost hear the sigh in
his next text when he told me to Google it.

805 North Linden Drive. The house where Howard Hughes crashed
when test-flying a spy plane he'd designed for the Army.

Venice Beach to Beverly Hills. Before SLP broke out and things started
getting bad, it would have been the kind of a drive that people groan
about. In the last year these would have been some of the worst hours to
try to drive it. But the streets are as close to empty now as I have ever
seen them.

National Guard trucks. A motorcade escorted by Thousand Storks
contractors. LAPD and LACS cars. Marine airships flown up from San
Diego. I hit my first checkpoint at Rose Avenue on my way north.
Sheriff's deputies. Mostly trying to steer people away from Santa
Monica. Things are still under control there, I couldn't see any fires
anyway, so they don't want any more people coming in. The deputies
didn't care about my badge. LAPD has no jurisdiction in SM, but they
let me cross.

Rose Avenue. I tried to call. She didn't answer. The phone might be off.
She might have forgotten about it. Somewhere inside Chasm Tide, trying
to beat the Labyrinth. I'm asking myself, did she see when the feds

opened my safe? Did she see the bottle? Did she see that I had Dreamer? Did she know it was in the house and that I didn't give it to her?

It doesn't matter. She knows. She knows me. She wouldn't expect anything else. But I didn't even think of it. The bottle in my hand, I didn't even think about giving it to her.

Rose Avenue.

Stay with the story. Someone will care.

Rose will care. Won't you, Rose?

There were searchlights on top of the twin apartment towers between Hill and Ashland. They swept back and forth, up and down the beach and the surf line. Looking for refugees trying to float up from Venice. Are there machine guns up there as well? There can't be. We haven't gone that far. Not yet. Not that far yet.

Another checkpoint when Gateway went under the 10.

Waiting in a line of cars, I looked up and saw men and women in black uniforms without insignia, rappelling from the freeway, dangling on lines underneath, stringing wire and attaching small satchels. Rigging explosives to blow the Santa Monica Freeway just west of the 405.

After I passed through, not far from the 405, I glanced down a side street and saw a man running from a gang of sleepless skaters. Tweens, kicking their boards down the street after him, making a buzzing sound with their lips. A fake snoring sound sleepless kids make when they go after a "sleeper." I'd heard about the attacks, read the accounts on news sites, but never seen one. I turned around in the middle of the block, but by the time I got back to the side street they were all gone. Sleeper and sleepless. And I wasn't sure I'd seen them at all.

Another checkpoint at Wilshire and Westwood Boulevard. Most of Westwood Village and the UCLA campus have been sealed off. I could see the lights from Marshall Field, and a Thousand Storks helicopter landing there.

No checkpoint at Wilshire and Whittier, but the Beverly Hills Hilton was lit up and there was heavy private security. Limos and armored SUVs. Men in tuxedos, women in gowns. Part of the parking lot taken up by news vans, video trucks. An awards show? Bleachers on the sidewalk for fans of whatever the event was. They were full. From a distance it seemed that every seat was taken by sleepless.

Driving north on Whittier, I could hear shots fired in Hollywood. Everything west of La Cienega and north of Beverly appeared to be blacked out. Even the hills were dark. Not in Bel Air, but east of Coldwater Canyon.

The L.A. Country Club golf course was still green this side of Wilshire. Hidden from the traffic along the boulevard, they're still running the sprinklers. I could hear them, softer than the gunfire and more constant.

A big house with a crescent drive. I had to park a block away. The street was clogged with cars. Smart Cars mixed in with battered diesels adapted for bio, but mostly the kind of sports cars and SUVs that Rose likes to run her key over if she walks past one in the street.

She used to only talk about doing that. But a few moths ago she did it for real. I looked at her, and she shrugged. "If not now, when?"

She'd have worn her keys out at the XF-11 house.

Security at the foot of the drive. Bouncers I may have seen at Denizone, wearing plain black T-shirts and slacks for this job. They asked to see my invitation, and I showed them my phone, the email and attachment Cager had sent me displayed on the screen. There was no bracelet, but they offered me a gift bag that I declined.

Usually when I make deliveries to parties with gift bags, I take them. Rose and I would go through them at home and laugh. Then I would catalogue the contents and put the bags in the back of the closet. But every now and then I'd find a bottle of apricot-lemon body wash in the shower and know that Rose had been in the bags.

Is it all hypocrisy, the things I laughed at when Rose did them? Keying expensive cars? Stealing useless evidence that I only catalogued to avoid any suggestion that I took gifts from suspects?

Should I have been mad at her? At myself for allowing it?

Smoke spewed from somewhere behind the house. Not a fire. Artificial smoke, like at one of Rose's rock concerts. A show she might drag me to because she had free tickets that a band gave her when she worked on their video.

A huge cloud, from a big machine, or several of them. Projected on the smoke, a loop of video, a double-prop plane with an odd tail assembly. A stutter of stills in black and white, and then color and movement as it crashed into several houses, setting the last on fire. And repeating.

I went inside. He was out back. Through the smoke pouring from the machines, lying on the end of a diving board over an empty pool, his legs dangling. He was holding his phone in the air and waving his arm back and forth. He saw me and asked, "Do you have signal?"

I looked at my phone; it showed two bars. He pointed at my phone. Said, "It's because your phone is mostly a phone. It's telling, the features we pack our phones with. Mine is weighted heavily toward messaging. When it comes to small talk, I'm more comfortable in text. Chat upsets me in the personal mode. Text conversations of some depth expose a person's emotional states more clearly to me. But it's the gaming components of my phone that make it less reliable as a phone." He sat up and picked up his bag from the foot of the diving board and dropped the phone inside and said, "Let's move. Not having signal is like being a stateless person. I don't like it."

He put the bag over his shoulder and stood up and walked up the board. It bobbed slightly under him. He looked into the empty pool and said, "If I fell in and broke my neck it would make this house famous again. But not for very long."

He had something he wanted me to see, and we walked through the cloud of smoke toward the house. He pointed up at the projection and said it was a "Fahlala installation. His commentary on the end of the age of manned flight. Have you seen the Reapers yet? They deployed here this week. Flying robot death machines. Very hard to shoot down in *Armored Assault*. Not that I really play anymore."

His bodyguards came out of the bushes at the edge of the yard. He told them he wanted them "lurking in the darkness." Imelda said she knew that, but they couldn't do it if he was going inside. He looked at the crowd packing the inside of the house and pointed at it and said, "Make an entrance for us, please." Imelda went into the house ahead of us. She had a kind of crowd jujitsu, applying extra weight to someone's back and shifting whole knots of bodies at once. We followed, Magda behind us making sure no one tried to slipstream Cager's route.

A wall in the living room was covered in black velvet paintings, portraits of sleepless with their eyes made huge and weepy like the little girls and puppies and cats by Margaret Keane.

Rose had a Keane print on the back of the bathroom door in the big house she shared on Telegraph. I told her it made me feel sad and guilty. She said that's what made it good kitsch.

The paintings of the sleepless made me angry.

Cager was talking about Imelda and Magda. He wanted to know what I thought of their "look." I told him they looked effective. He said he thought the *Matrix* thing was "over" and he wanted something new. He was thinking about *Road Warrior,* but he was afraid it might be too early. He didn't elaborate on what it was too early for. But I knew what he meant.

I rarely want to hit people just for being who they are. But I wanted to hit him. Instead I told him the truth, I told him he was right, it was too early. I told him he should try *Blade Runner.* He liked that. I knew he would.

There weren't many people in the upstairs room that looked over the pool. Hardly any. The gallerist who had curated the work there stood near the door. Two teenagers in cloaks and buckskin leggings sat on the floor in the middle of the room. And a slight, sweaty man, clucking his tongue obsessively, muscles jumping on his pale bald scalp, skin hanging loose on his upper arms. Sleepless, he paced back and forth across the small room. He was talking to himself, I think, saying, "But it doesn't prove anything. It doesn't explain anything. It doesn't say anything."

The walls were paneled in brand-new plywood veneer. Framed photographs in chrome plate frames from Kmart or Target. The photos were all of glowing white abstract shapes, loops and curls, edges tinged cobalt, on a deep black background.

Cager nodded at the gallerist and pulled me to the middle of the room near the two teenagers. Both of them stared openly at him.

I started to say something. Trying to steer the conversation to where I needed it to go. But he wouldn't listen. He told me to be quiet and to "look at the future."

I looked at the photographs. They all looked the same.

Before I drove from Venice I chipped a claw from the Shabu dragon and let it dissolve in my mouth. It made my tongue numb and tasted like bleach and gardenias. A headache was starting at the base of my neck and climbing over my skull.

Cager asked me if I saw it.

I looked again, and I saw it. One of the photos was SLP. A huge negative image blowup of the prion. Looking again, I recognized others from the research I had done after Rose's diagnosis. Bovine spongiform encephalopathy. Kuru. Creutzfeldt-Jakobs disease. Chronic wasting disease.

The gallerist pointed at the photos, explaining, "Those are the classics, the past. BSE. CJD. CWD. Kuru. Scrapie. These are a series of SLP, the present. The artist has lost his entire immediate family. Mother, father, two brothers, wife, and three sons. All were very early SLP victims. Each of these are photographs of a single SL prion isolated from the brain tissue of his deceased family members. The photographs are end product, but process is the point. The artist is a designed materials specialist."

The gallerist pointed at the final series of photos. He told us, "Those are the future. Designed materials. The artist customizes proteins, refolding them, creating new prions. Using applied nucleation, better known as conformational influence, the same process by which prions cause healthy proteins to malform, he allows his self-assembling systems of prions to grow. And then kills them. But not before preserving a visual ghost."

The pacing sleepless halted and raised his voice, "Shuguang Zhang Zhang told us, 'We have had the Stone Age, the Bronze Age, and the plastic age. The future is the designed materials age.' "

The gallerist nodded toward the sleepless and smiled at us, "Mr. Afronzo, have you met Ian Berry?"

Cager shook his head and faced the sleepless man and stuck out his hand, "No, that's why I'm here."

A wave of twitches, Rose's doctor called them fasciculations, ran over the man's body. He stuck out his own hand, but it waved from side to side. Cager took it in both of his and held it steady. "Thank you," he said. "Thank you for showing me something new."

Either the man pulled his hand free or it jerked free of its own will, I couldn't tell which. Just like I couldn't tell if the expression on the man's face was true disgust or if it was the result of his musculature run out of control.

Cager turned to me and gestured at the man and smiled and said, "Haas, meet the artist." Ian Berry offered me his jerking hand, and I took it. His eyelids kept fluttering. He said to me, "Don't be afraid, it's just the suffering."

I pulled my hand back, but he didn't let go. He asked me, "How long has it been?" I shook my head. He asked me, "How long have you been sleepless?" I shook my head again. He let go of my hand and started pacing again and said, "There's nothing to be afraid of. It's just the suffering. It's just the future coming."

20

THERE WERE THREE TABLES IN MY LIVING ROOM. LEST THIS be thought cluttered, please keep in mind that the house was open floor plan, the kitchen, dining, and living areas all sweeping into one another. Keep also in mind that one of the tables was the very small chrome Dadox cube on which I kept my business phones. The large oval Thor coffee table was central to the room, planted diagonally in the middle of a luxuriously shaggy white alpaca rug. The third table was a rather cheap Sui, chosen because its light color offset the dark hardwood it stood on, and because its ten inches of height placed its surface just slightly over a foot below the top of the Mies van der Rohe daybed it complemented. That difference in height was perfect for Saturday afternoons when I would sprawl on the daybed while listening to live broadcasts from the Met. Without looking or stretching I could find my espresso, any pastry I might have allowed myself, or a bowl of in-season grapes. On the rare occasions I had dinner company we generally ate on the deck or removed our shoes and sat on the rug at the Thor table.

The men in the room with me at this time had not removed their shoes. Nor had they placed me on the floor and tied my ankles to the thick sculpted end pieces that flowed directly out of the base into the upper surface of the Thor. For that matter, they had not pilloried me on the Dadox cube, arching my back across it, wire running from my neck, lines stretched to my wrists and ankles, the tension of my own muscles keeping my limbs splayed. Instead, they had sat me on the daybed and tied my ankles to the legs of the Sui. Nothing wrong with this arrangement in principle, until the lights went out.

Curling, I hunched my shoulders so that as I rose I would minimize tension on the wire that ran from my neck to my wrists. The weight of my upper body coming forward was not enough to lift me from the daybed, but my ankles had been tied with my feet quite flat against the floor. Pressing down with the muscles in my upper legs, I lifted myself, lunged, and fell over the Sui table atop the man kneeling between my legs with the soldering iron.

For a moment the man was pinned between my body and the table. I heard a clunk that might have been the soldering iron, then a cracking of wood as our combined weight splintered the rather delicate piece and I tumbled, tucking my head, turning my shoulder, feeling the wire dig into my throat, the rope on my ankles snagging before slipping loose from the broken table legs.

Pain cannot be ignored. However, it can be endured. When necessary, a great deal of pain can be endured. Just ask any mother.

Naked on the floor, in a litter of kindling, third-degree burns on the backs of my knees and inner thighs, I had a moment of instability at the thought of a world that could twice see a man unclothed in such circumstances in the span of a single life. Pain returned me to a semblance of balance. Indeed, I experienced a tremendous amount of pain in silence while listening very carefully for the voice of the man who had been burning me. There was a shuffle of movement that quickly subsided, the other men in the room shifting their positions slightly from where they had been when the lights went out, followed by a single spoken syllable coming from that man on the floor as he made them aware of his own position so as not to end up in the line of fire.

"Here."

"Here," as it turned out, was just a foot or two away. I knew this already because one of the protrusions poking his shoulder wasn't a bit of broken table, was, in fact, one of my toes. But the word did serve a purpose, allowing me to develop a clear mental picture of just where his face was. So that when I lashed out with the heel of my other foot, I felt the very distinct sensation of a man's nose caving in.

He made another sound, long and loud, and I used it to cover the noise I made as I kicked both legs high into the air, brought them down, and rolled up to my feet, pulling the wire yet deeper into my flesh.

The initial shock of darkness was fading from my eyes. The canopy of stars that might have given some light during a typical blackout was screened by the smoke that was capping the basin after a day of fires. That left the fires themselves to illuminate the room. A handful of blazes, flickering, none closer than half a mile. There was little at all that could be seen. Shadows of various thickness.

I changed my ground, keeping close to the north wall to avoid the spot where the floor creaked, and scurried to the kitchen. There was similar shifting happening in the living and dining areas. The scream of the man whose face I'd ruined had passed, settling into a series of moans and grunts, punctuated by gurgles as the blood ran out of his sinuses into his throat and he hacked it up so as not to drown.

The other three would be attempting to seal the room. The one who had been standing watch at the windows would be very near that same position to cover the glass door. In fact, I could see a small hump of darkness against the slightly brighter darkness outside, not a regular part of the room's silhouette. The man who had been going through my possessions would be moving to block the hall that led back to the bedrooms and bathrooms. He had the greatest distance to traverse, the most obstacles to avoid. And he would, no doubt, make the most noise. The battle-scarred man would position himself at the entryway that opened from the front door into the living area. A short direct path that would put him closest to me.

I crouched behind the kitchen island; heard when the man crossing the room stepped into the wreckage of the table and cursed involuntarily; felt the surge in the room's tension as his coworkers mentally scolded him; and gently ran my fingers over the kitchen tools hanging on the side of the island until I was fully confident that I understood the orientation of the poultry shears on their hook. Lifting it free, I undid the clasp at the end of the grips with my pinkie. The spring bolt opened silently. I drew a long, slow breath and, with a minimum of arching, slipped the upward-curving lower blade between the wire and the small of my back. Nonetheless, the noose around my neck had been drawn beyond the point where it would allow any more arching at all. Tugged a final three centimeters, it sealed my larynx. The wire dropped into the bone notch at the base of the lower blade, I squeezed, there was a moment of resistance, and the wire snapped with a clear twang.

The reaction was immediate. The floor squeaked.

Yes, it may not seem very much, but it was a squeak that revealed a great deal of subtext. First, it told me that either the battle-scarred man or the man blocking off the back of the house was approaching me. Second, the fact that I'd heard no footsteps told me that whoever it was had removed his shoes. Third, it told me they were not inclined to simply open fire on me. This final point suggesting that there was more question and answer left to engage in should they recapture me.

Sufficiently motivated, I hurt myself. I inflicted this pain on myself by lying on my back, drawing my knees up, curling tightly, and slipping my bound hands under my bottom and down the length of my legs. Being naked would usually make this maneuver much easier than it would be clothed, but the friction on my burns more than compensated for the case. It was also impossible to execute without making a great amount of slithery noise. Noise that drew a response in the form of a quick patter of footfalls.

I still couldn't breathe. It was that fact that had caused the urgency with which I brought my hands from behind my back. I'd hoped the first thing I'd be doing with them was to dig the wire out of the rut it had worn in my neck. Instead, I joined them together at my chest in a prayerful gesture as I came to my knees.

When the man crossing the room came around the island, he came low, arms spread, a knife in his right fist, blade pointing down the length of his forearm, edge facing out. Ready to cut or stab, or catch an incoming blade. An advanced knife-fighting technique.

Intimately close, I could see the shadow of him quite well. I've no doubt he could see me even better. At sixty, one does not play games with the southern California sun, I'd not had a tan in decades. I was, I daresay, pale as a ghost. With such an excellent target at hand, he attacked, coming closer yet, leading with the blade, a slash that was meant to drive me flopping onto my back as I tried to avoid it. From that position I might scuttle farther away and into the arms of the man by the glass door. A pitiful defense, but reasonable, as the only other option was to fall forward at his feet, fair game for him to drop his knee into the back of my neck and pin me while his friends came to bind me.

I fell forward.

Things went awry for my attacker only when I separated my forearms and exposed the curved blades of the poultry shears I'd been hiding. The shears are made by Wüsthof. Stainless steel, the lower blade has a serrated edge. I'd allowed them to spring open a few centimeters as I brought them down on his right foot. When they sliced through his instep and out his sole, both tips bit into the hardwood floor that extended into the kitchen. Why a man would dress entirely in black but wear white athletic socks is beyond me.

I didn't stay to disable him further and search him for guns. I took it on faith that he'd not have attacked me without having first set his firearms aside. They didn't know if I might have retrieved a gun myself, but they certainly weren't going to risk supplying me with one. And there was no hurry as far as killing him. I knew where he was and where he would be for at least the next several moments.

I shifted ground again. We all did. Those of us free to do so.

The two men I'd not incapacitated would be changing to firing positions. Their initial advantage over me had been numbers, firepower, and well-being. Their need to capture me alive had negated that firepower. My survival compulsion was compensating for the damage that had been inflicted upon me. And the numbers were beginning to even out. Seeing as *my* advantages were my knowledge of the terrain and the desperate nature of my situation, they would be calculating the risks and rewards involved in taking a few shots when the opportunity presented itself, letting the chips fall as they would.

A tattoo of finger snaps went back and forth across the room as they established who would cover which fields of fire. Privy to this code, the injured men would flatten themselves on the floor to avoid stray bullets.

I was breathing again. I'd accomplished this feat with no small discomfort. After digging the wire noose from my neck and pulling it over my head, I indulged myself in air. Opening my mouth wide, minimizing the risk that I might gasp.

Crossing the room to my new hiding place, I'd avoided the alpaca rug. I wasn't concerned about bloodstains, it was well ruined already, but I was not so pale that I could blend with that whiteness, and in the dark it would have revealed me all too clearly. Indeed, at the edge of the rug I could see the black cube of a Shuttle computer I'd used to teach myself Linux. One of the bits of hardware they had taken from my office to be searched for data that might pertain to my suspicious behavior in Afronzo Junior's vicinity.

The wire noose had a tail of about a half meter. The wire, while of a thick gauge, was flexible. I opened the noose a slight bit, took aim, tossed it underhand, and heard it give the slightest of clicks as it dropped over the computer and nicked a corner.

No one opened fire, indicating either that they had not heard the sound or that it was too faint to allow for any accuracy. I made up for that faintness by yanking hard on the wire with a sweep of my arm that sent the Shuttle clattering onto the wood floor in the direction of the glass wall. A heartbeat's pause, followed by a series of three well-spaced shots that traced the path of the computer, another pause, and a fourth shot placed just ahead of where the computer came to rest, another pause, and a fifth shot placed just behind the point where the computer began its journey. That final point was the one I'd occupied a scant second before.

But I was no longer there.

I was pinned in the corner of the room farthest from the front door. The jumble of my computer equipment, and the man who had been lookout, were between myself and the glass door. And I would have to climb over the length of the daybed if I wanted to reach the hallway to the back of the house or front door.

Cornered, if that is not redundant.

The shots had come from the battle-scarred side of the room. In such tight quarters his flash suppressor had done little to hide his position. Irrelevant, as I'd not had a gun in my hand with which to return fire. And he'd shifted yet again, in any case. Still, it seemed clear he was covering the living area and at least half the dining area. The last shot he'd fired had punched a hole in the thick glass wall. I mentally drew a line from that point to where he'd been when he pulled the trigger. The remaining man would be covering the other half of the dining area and the kitchen. And he would be doing so from a point just beyond where that last round had struck the glass.

Of course, I couldn't be certain of any of this. I'd been tortured for hours. The wounds inflicted on me were still causing extreme pain. I'd been deprived of oxygen, and I'd lost blood. The room was dark and littered with objects and the remains of the Sui table. The two men I'd disabled were not by any means crippled and would likely be reentering the fray. My circumstances were dire and I was beyond desperate. My strategic evaluations had to be considered questionable, at best.

Thank God I had a winged cat taxidermy sculpture in my hands.

The artist who created the winged cat had been amused when I told her why I wanted one of some girth. She'd embraced the concept, along with the various custom features I'd requested. She told me she "enjoyed the James Bond irony." I didn't tell her that there was nothing ironic about the piece at all. To my sensibility, a dead cat with crow's wings stitched to its back and a rocket pistol concealed in its hollow carcass was a grim foreshadow of what humanity had in store for itself.

To be clear, what was inside the winged cat was not an actual rocket pistol. It was, in fact, a Lund and Company Variable Velocity Weapons System. The "rocket" nomenclature was popular among bloggers with a fascination for fanciful weapons technology but little understanding of actual weapons. A VVW was essentially a self-contained launch system for both lethal and nonlethal projectiles. Buttons on the side of the gun determined how much fuel would be released into the combustion chamber behind the projectile when the trigger was pulled. It did not at all fire rockets, which are self-propelled. Rather, a controlled explosion, localized within the weapon, created a preselected muzzle velocity that could be changed from round to round. Designed for use in combat environments where civilians and hostiles mixed and were difficult to differentiate between, only a handful of VVW prototypes were ever produced. When I'd heard that one had come on the market a year prior, I'd spent a foolish amount of money to own it. It came with only a handful of the specialized ammunition and two refills of the fuel. Unable to help myself, I'd test-fired half the rounds. Loaded with rubber bullets it was combat-effective *non*lethal as close as five meters. Loaded with full metal jacket it was *lethal* to as far as a thousand meters, though not at all accurate to even a tenth of that range. Multiple vents kept muzzle flash all but nonexistent and minimized sound. Because the amount of propellant was not dictated by the size of the round, a small bullet that loses little of its energy to air resistance could be fired at muzzle velocities generally reserved for high-caliber rifles. Set to *red,* the VVW can fire a .22-caliber armor-piercing round at one thousand meters per second. Comparable to a .300 Winchester Magnum round fired from an Accuracy International AWM sniper rifle.

I'd placed it inside the winged cat, loaded and primed, the red button depressed. When I slipped my hand into the belly of the cat and pulled the weapon free, I didn't bother to change the setting in favor of the orange, yellow, or green buttons. My mood quite suited red.

On my belly, in my corner, I aimed under the couch at an angle, using the sound of a man gargling his own blood as a guide. I pulled the trigger, there was a slight flicker under the couch, as if a cap pistol had been fired, a sound like two overstuffed feather pillows being plumped against each other, and an almost instantaneous human grunt, followed by another distinct sound, this one as if a large and very wet paintbrush had been vigorously shaken at a wall.

Despite the vents, the recoil was tremendous. It was just as well my wrists were still bound and I was forced to use a two-hand grip.

Fire was being returned from the battle-scarred man's side of the room, but with less consideration for decorum this time. I put a stop to this sloppy behavior before it could reach the point of general mayhem. There were ample muzzle flashes. I could see them clearly from the point I'd rolled to after firing my first shot. I took a bead on the ghost of one of the flashes, made a slight adjustment to the right, following the trail he was leaving as he moved and fired, moved and fired, and pulled the trigger again.

Less splatter this time, and an echo of broken crockery. The bullet must have pierced the body armor under his light jacket and struck the inner surface of a ceramic back plate, the bullet and plate both shattering on impact.

There was a respite of silence. Just a faint burble as the last bit of pressure in the battle-scarred man's circulatory system pumped a few milliliters of blood from the tiny wound that would be in his torso. He'd probably not lose much blood from such a small wound as the one the .22 would leave. But even if it hadn't fragmented when it hit the plate, the static shock from a bullet traveling at that velocity had no doubt killed him before he dropped.

On red, the VVW would fire only four rounds. Even if I had been tempted by dialing down to gain a few more shots, the symmetry of four men and four projectiles would have stopped me.

The silence wore on the man who had been lookout. He snapped a quick rhythm with his fingers, attempting to strategize. Before the man I'd stabbed in the foot could answer him, I did. The pillow sound again, splatter of paint, and the sharp tink of a crack appearing suddenly in a cold glass when something hot is poured inside. I could only hope that the bullet had expended most of its energy passing through its target and the glass and that it would drop harmlessly to some empty spot in the basin.

The last of them was still behind the kitchen island. One of his socks was no longer white. When I approached, he rose with his knife in one hand and the shears in the other. I ended any suspense by placing the last round in the middle of his chest.

I set the VVW on the island, picked up the bloody poultry shears from where they'd fallen, angled the blades between my wrists, and clipped the wires that bound them. Setting the shears aside, I walked down the hallway to the master bedroom and into the bathroom. In my first-aid cupboard I found gauze bandages, silver sulfadiazine, scissors, tape, an IV needle and hose, and two bags of saline fluid. Standing at the sink, I began using gauze pads to blot pus and blood from the insides and backs of my legs. The pain was intense, largely focused at the edges of the wounds where the burns were only second degree. The nerves at the hearts of the worst of the burns were entirely dead. Still, I'd need to salve and bandage them to stave off infection. And I'd need to rehydrate. And there was other business that needed taking care of.

Tending my hurts, I began plotting a route that would take me from my ruined house to the home of Officer Parker Haas.

21

PARK WASN'T SLEEPLESS. HE KNEW HE WASN'T SLEEPLESS. After Rose had been diagnosed, he'd been tested at once. Rose had been typically explicit. *If we both have it, I'm ending the pregnancy.*

Park's results had been negative. He wasn't sleepless. Whatever Ian Berry thought he saw in Park's eyes, it was just fatigue and stress and amphetamine.

But tests could return false negatives. And it had been almost a year since the test. If the test had been wrong, or if he had contracted SLP soon after the test, he could be symptomatic by now.

But he wasn't. He knew he wasn't sleepless. How could he be? If he was, who would take care of the baby? It was unthinkable. Therefore, he didn't think about it.

Faking as if he had received a vibrating call, he took the phone from his pocket, nodded at Cager, and walked from the room. Standing in the hall with the phone to his ear, he watched while Cager simultaneously bought several of Berry's photographs and talked Chasm Tide with the teenagers who had overcome their awe long enough to request autographs.

Automatically, he spoke into the dead phone.

"I don't know when I'll be home. I hope soon. At a gallery. A house, really. But they have art. You'd like some of it. I think you'd make fun of the people. Too much money, mostly. Yes, but trying to look like they don't have any money. Or the opposite. The funniest I've seen is a guy at the foot of the stairs right now. He has a comb-over, but it's a Mohawk comb-over. I can't really tell. It's like it's so long he can push it up in the middle. I can't. Because it's embarrassing. And I don't like taking pictures of people so I can make fun of them. It's different to just talk about them. Anyway, I'm not making fun, I'm just telling you who's the funniest person here. Business. A guy I have to see. It's about business. He may know something I need to know. Because. Because I think the world is getting too dangerous. Just too dangerous. Too dangerous for everything. For you. For the baby. I have to go. I love you."

He put the phone back in his pocket as Cager came out of the room, one of the photographs in his hands.

"Kuru. Do you know this one?"

Park was sweating; he could feel it running down the small of his back.

"A little."

Cager held up the photo.

"The first identified prion disease. Papua New Guinea, the Fore tribe. Supposedly they were cannibals. Kuru was thought to spread when they ate the infected brains of their enemies. It made them crazy. Of course, they didn't think it was a sickness. The Fore didn't need to be told what it was. It was a curse. They put the kuru on their enemies, and their enemies went mad and died."

He traced the shape of the kuru prion with his index finger.

"And I think sometimes, what if the scientists were wrong and the Fore were right? What if kuru was a curse? Maybe SLP is also a curse. Which leaves a big question."

He looked up from the photo.

"If mankind has been cursed with SLP, who did it? Who is the enemy that cursed us?"

He pointed a corner of the photo at the ceiling.

"It must be God. No other explanation."

He lowered the photo.

"Cursed by God. How can there be any escape from a curse like that?"

Park wiped sweat from the back of his neck.

"I don't believe in curses."

Cager opened his messenger bag and slipped the photo inside.

"If you spent a little time in Chasm, you would."

"That's not real."

Cager was parting his hair again. He stopped.

"It's real. What's happening in there, that's what counts. God is done with us out here. Reality is what we make now."

Park shook his wrist from side to side, winding his father's watch. He wanted a new watch, one that would tell him there was time left, enough of it to make things right again. A watch that would still be poised before midnight, allowing him the time he needed to repair his world.

He took the toilet paper tube from his side pocket and showed it to Cager.

"Same as before."

Cager had finished with his comb and was looking at his phone.

"No signal. Adrift."

Park was cradling the tube in his palm.

"Yes or no?"

Cager flicked the screen, and a long string of names rolled across it.

"I have the numbers for over fifty dealers in here. None of them are interesting at all. You seemed interesting. Smart. Emotionally opaque. I thought if I showed you amazing and beautiful things it would elicit an emotional reaction. But mostly you just act anxious. I think that's the emotion. Like you want to be somewhere else. That's boring for me. And I'm tempted to call another dealer and let you go where you like."

"I don't care, Cager."

He stopped scrolling, took out his comb, and raked the tines with a thumbnail.

Park displayed the tube.

"I don't care about your pronouncements. I don't care about your attitude. I don't care about your bodyguards. I don't care about your game. I care about if you can pay me. I'm a drug dealer. I'm not here to play straight man. I'm not here to give you all the cool lines. I'm here to sell you drugs and to sell your friends drugs and to go home. This is Shabu. Same stuff as last night. Same price. Do you want it, or should I sell it to one of these other lame people?"

Cager looked over his shoulder at nothing, smiled, and looked at Park.

"You are smart."

He reached into his bag. He brought out his hand. He opened it. And he began to shuffle through a thick stack of hundred-dollar bills.

"If you're really this focused in your business, you may be the first dealer to retire with a dime. Not that the money will be worth anything."

He held out a sheaf of bills.

"But if it's what you want, here's your fifteen thousand."

Park was looking at the money as if Cager had offered him a handful of kale.

"What?"

"I placed some bets on the War Hole tournament. Inside information, really. The gladiator Comicaze Y was facing in the Final lost his twin sister the day before the match. I know that's the kind of thing that bothers people."

He offered the money again.

Park took a half step back.

"I don't want that. I want the other thing. Like last night."

Cager brought the comb out.

"The other thing."

Cager was waving to Magda at the end of the hall.

"I don't have that. I have money. You want my money. Here it is."

Magda approached.

"Boss?"

"Do you have signal?"

She touched her Bluetooth, took a slab phone from a pouch on her gun belt, and looked at it.

"No signal."

"I'm becoming disconnected."

Cager pocketed the comb and held his hand out to Park.

"Your phone, please."

Park didn't move.

Cager folded the thick wad of money and stuffed it in his bag.

"If you want to work something out, give me your phone, please. I need signal. It will take me hours to reenter the flow of my communications if I'm away for too long."

Park took the phone from his pocket and handed it to him.

Cager looked at it, frowned, dialed, looked at it again.

"Where's your signal?"

He moved a few steps to his right.

"Is this where you were standing when you took that call?"

Park shook his head.

"I."

"No signal."

His thumb flicked across the navigation buttons just below the phone's screen.

"Your software is miserable."

He looked up.

"There's no call in your log."

Park held out the tube again.

"Just let's. Let's do this. And."

Cager drew his comb.

"Park."

He placed the teeth in the part and raked to the left.

"Are you well?"

Magda put a hand on the butt of her weapon and placed the palm of her other hand in the middle of Cager's chest.

"Step clear, boss."

Cager didn't step clear, he stepped closer, raking to the right.

"You seemed very animated when you were on the phone. Very engaged. I couldn't define the emotional state, but you were intent. Who were you talking to? I understand there was no one on the line, but who did you believe you were talking to? I'm curious."

Park was thinking about the conversations he'd been having with Rose more and more often. Talking about today, thinking she was as well, only to discover she was talking to him three years ago. He had that feeling now. He was having one conversation, Cager was having another. But he didn't know which was the real one.

"I was talking to my wife."

Cager held up the phone, displaying the call log that showed that the last incoming call was received hours before.

"No, you weren't. But that's who you thought you were talking to?"

Magda was sliding herself into the space between them.

"Back off, boss, he's not right."

Cager waved the comb at her.

"Be quiet, Magda. He's just sleepless. That's all."

He held the phone out.

"Yes, Park? Sleepless? And you need what I gave you before."

Park wanted his uniform. He wanted his badge plainly on his chest. His cap and his stick. He wanted his handcuffs. He wanted to make an arrest. To tell people it was all all right. *Just step back and make some room, everything is fine.* He wanted to show that he was here for a reason, to do a job. And he wanted to do the job. He wanted his surface to again match his interior. He wanted off.

He took the phone from Cager's hand.

"The other. Now. I."

Cager nodded.

"Yes. You don't have to explain."

He took his own phone from the bag again.

"But I wasn't lying. I don't have any with me. I know where it is, but you will have to get it yourself."

He was working buttons, accessing an application, scrolling down a list that flicked across the screen.

"Good. There's one nearby."

He held out his empty hand.

"The dragon. I have people waiting at the club."

Park handed him the tube. Cager handed it to Magda.

She took the cellophane cap from one end, pulled out the tissue wrap, and unfolded it. Cager watched as she unwrapped and then rewrapped the dragon and put it in yet another pocket on her vest.

He turned his phone toward Park and displayed a string of numbers.

"This will be an adventure for you, Park. A quest."

7/10/10

I UNDERSTAND.

He's playing a game. Like Beenie said, taking his fantasy and putting it over this world. Trying to change it to fit what he wants it to be.

He showed me a number and waited to see if that would be enough, if I could figure it out. I recognized the format: 34/04/26-118/25-31. The funny thing is, if the first number set had begun with 41 or 42, and the second with 69 or 70, I would have gotten it the first time I saw those sequences when I opened the Afronzo, Parsifal K. Jr. file on Hydo's hard drive. I would have recognized what it was, from sailing with my father. Looking at it on Cager's phone, it was familiar only from the file itself. He started to explain, and I understood before he could finish.

He thinks I'm sleepless. I'm not sleepless. Rose, I'm not sleepless. You don't have to worry about that. I'm not acting like myself, but I'm not sleepless. I acted sleepless for Cager. I acted like I couldn't remember the number. He took a pen from his bag and wrote it on my hand. "Don't wash your hands," he said.

He wanted to look at another room, one with more Chasm Tide characters, all created by sleepless. I couldn't see any more of that stuff. I don't have time anymore for anything else but what I have to do. I left and went to my car. I opened Google Earth on my laptop and zoomed on Los Angeles. Moving the cursor in sine waves, I tracked the numbers scrolling up and down at the bottom left of the screen. I found a match and zoomed in closer. Cager wasn't lying; it is nearby.

Before shutting down, I connected Hydo's hard drive and opened the secret Afronzo Junior file. Every cell in the spreadsheet has a sequence of two number sets. The first sets all start with 33 or 34, the second sets with 118. I scrolled through them and found the cell that contained the number Cager wrote on my hand. I held my open hand next to the screen and took a picture with my phone. Then I magnified the cell and took another picture. Then I put the laptop and hard drive away and took my Walther from the spare, along with the RFID interrogator I stole at the gallery of Chasm characters.

Walden Drive was just around the corner. The fence running behind the trees wasn't electrified. I'm sure the members wish it was, but the power bill would be too much even for them. I climbed the fence and crossed part of a fairway and ended up on the sixth green. The sprinklers were off. I've never played the north course of the Los Angeles Country Club, but I'm certain my father did.

He didn't care for golf particularly. He said, "Parker, there are some pursuits in life that one becomes proficient in for the sake of one's profession, and for no other reason." Golf was one of those pursuits. I think he appreciated the game itself; it was the gambling, cursing, and boozing that went along with it that he objected to.

I walked to the ninth green, to the strip of grass running between two large bunkers that protected the approach. I pointed the interrogator at one of the bunkers and pulled the trigger. It beeped and displayed a series of horizontal lines. I circled the bunker and pulled the trigger every two yards and got the same result. But the bunker was at least fifteen yards at its widest point. To be certain I hadn't missed anything, I walked to the middle, mentally quartered the trap, and pulled the trigger four times, one at a time, while aiming into each of the quarters. Nothing.

I started over with the second hazard, got one negative, walked two yards, pulled the trigger again, and the screen flashed a positive result: ff688-6-2623-56.

I had to narrow it down, so I circled the trap, pulling the trigger every few steps. And found that just one-third of the bunker gave me a positive. I found a rake at the edge of the hazard, dug the tines in deep, and began to rake the sand east to west. I didn't find anything, so I began raking north to south, crossing the marks I had already left. Occasionally I took a read with the interrogator to make sure I hadn't moved anything without realizing it, but it remained consistent.

Finally I had to spin the head of the rake and use the little leveling plane to shave the sand away. I sank it to about an inch's depth and pushed the sand into a pile and took a reading from the interrogator on the pile, then went back and did it again, working across the area where I got my first positive result. It took almost two hours. It was buried slightly less than a foot deep. Zipped into a plastic bag that had been double sealed with duct tape. I sat at the edge of the hazard and brushed damp sand from the bag and read the label on the bottle inside.

Afronzo-New Day
DR33M3R

There are hundreds of global coordinates in the Afronzo, Parsifal, K. Jr. file on Hydo's hard drive. Hundreds of bottles of Dreamer stashed from the Hollywood Hills down to Long Beach and from Santa Monica to Dodger Stadium.

Hydo said Dreamer was "in the air."

Getting caught with DR33M3R with intent to sell carries mandatory federal time.

Stashing the bottles minimizes the amount of time anyone has them in their possession. Risk reduction. Deals are made for the coordinates, not for the bottles themselves. It's safe. And like a game at the same time. Treasure hunting. Geo caching.

Busting anyone with this setup requires a snitch on the inside. Even then, you could only get a little. If Cager gave Hydo the franchise on selling the Dreamer, the arrests would stop with him and the guys at the farm, unless one of them talked.

And they were going to talk. Rose. They were killed because they were going to talk. Whoever was using me to make sure there were no leaks about this, they found out that Hydo was going to talk to someone or that he had threatened to talk to someone. Blackmail.

Or he might have been informing. He might have already been busted by the feds himself, may have started turning evidence. Whoever is protecting Cager, someone even higher up (national security?) could have arranged the attack on the gold farm. But they missed the drive. Or they didn't know about the drive. How could they know about everything else and not know about the drive?

Too much. It's too much for me. I'm not a detective. I never was. I'm a cop. I'm not supposed to be figuring out this kind of thing. I'm supposed to protect people. But something has happened. Afronzo-New Day has done something. People have been murdered.

No one will listen if I just try to tell them, no matter what evidence I have. I can only make them listen if they have no choice. If it's too big not to listen. I can only make them listen if I arrest Cager.

It will be too big then. Too much noise. They will have to listen to what I say. And someone will do something about it. Someone will stop what is happening to us. It's wrong. The world has gone wrong, Rose. Give me a little more time. I can do something to help. I can do something.

▮   ▮   ▮

OUTSIDE OF THE LAPD self-defense classes, Park had studied at a tiny studio in South Gate. A strip mall storefront below a doughnut shop where old Thai men from the neighborhood hung out to play the lotto and buy strips of scratch tickets. It had been recommended to him by an older officer who had taken a look at his light build and suggested that he might want to *heft up and get you to the Hurtin' Man.*

The Hurtin' Man had turned out to be a former Latin Kings chapter president who taught a form of martial arts that he described as *what we do on the inside when shit goes down.* The basic philosophy of the fighting style was concerned with ending any conflict in the swiftest possible manner. The Hurtin' Man exhorted his students to assess a given situation and place it into one of two categories: *Is this a runnin' scenario or a hurtin' scenario?* Indeed, a great deal of his training involved conditioning one to make that judgment as close to instantaneously as possible. So that action, whatever it might be, could be taken at once. This conditioning largely involved a stick that motivated pupils who found themselves frozen for the slightest moment. As far as actual methods of attack, the Hurtin' Man favored soft targets. Eyes, ears, nose, genitals, kidneys, throat, and solar plexus. All easily identified and struck in moments of extreme stress when adrenaline has a tendency to short-circuit training.

Once a situation was assessed, the course of action taken was never to be reversed unless there was literally no other choice. If one, for instance, ran oneself into a blind alley, one could turn and fight. If one, for another instance, found oneself suddenly outnumbered after beginning an attack on a single opponent, one could turn and run. Otherwise, one pressed the attack, always moving forward, always encroaching on the opponent's space and freedom of movement, always striking, until the opponent, or oneself, was disabled. Or one ran as fast as one could, as far as one could, and did not stop until it was physically impossible to run any farther, or one was caught.

Park had discovered many things about himself in the studio. Not the least of which was that he didn't mind being hit all that much. He didn't enjoy it, but he was more than willing to accept a few blows if it allowed him to deliver at least one blow more than he received. He also discovered that he didn't mind hitting other people. Again, he didn't enjoy it, but in the context of training or actual combat, it didn't bother him at all to find that he had hurt someone.

He was quite good at it, though his talent lay more in the purely martial side of the class than in the speed with which he made his decision to run or attack. Always, it seemed, there was a blip of hesitation before he took action. His attitude toward combat revealing his inner philosopher. Inquiry was not a light issue for Park, even when the answers had been reduced to *fight or flight*. Once decided, he would run until his lungs burst, or advance relentlessly on his opponent, but either course was often preceded by a sharp blow from the Hurtin' Man's stick.

Jumping down from the fence outside the golf course after he'd made the notes in his journal, he was only slightly surprised by the appearance of the men emerging from the shadows of the trees. It wasn't the fact of armed men waiting for him that was the slight surprise, but the fact that he'd never seen them before. Three tan men in khaki pants and what he took for dark guayabera shirts. He'd have expected Hounds.

Faced with three well-armed men who carried themselves with the same air of prowess as Cager's bodyguards, Park was able to choose his course of action before his feet had landed on the ground outside the fence. Action so suddenly committed to that he had cut between two of them and had a five-yard head start before they began pursuit.

None of which changed the fact that they were simply faster than he was. In fact, they caught up and overwhelmed him so quickly, he never had a chance to change his mode of action and begin an offensive. Instead he found himself rapidly disarmed, divested of all possessions upon his person, and tumbled into the backseat of an obligatorily black SUV, where he was comfortably ensconced in supple leather, offered a beverage, and driven, sans restraints, to the Afronzo family estate well inside the gates of Bel Air.

22

MY NATIONAL ID CARD WAS A MARVELOUSLY HACKED BIT OF the counterfeiter's art that took full advantage of the many loopholes that popped up when Patriot II dictated. We all walk about with cards broadcasting our personal data hither and yon. With the software that had come included in the mind-numbing cost of the card, I could, as often as I liked, log on to my cardholder's account, input my password, place my card on an RFID read/write/rewriter USBed to my computer, and have my card's RFID chip updated with all the latest travel clearances. Guaranteed to be current within five hours of any changes to local, state, and federal security. On any given day I would make a point of updating my clearance before leaving the house, thus ensuring that I might pass easily through the most stringent checkpoints and roadblocks. Even in a rapidly evolving security environment such as the one emerging outside, it saved me no end of trouble. Unfortunately, the card did not create an identity from scratch when it was updated; it simply altered one's clearance for sensitive and hazardous areas. Assuming that anyone was actively looking for the identity radioed from that tiny chip, it would appear on a number of data logs and registries every time it was scanned and cleared, leaving a trail of electronic bread crumbs to be followed wherever I should go.

In normal circumstances it would be an unthinkable breach of personal security to travel with that card after repulsing an attack. But it seemed that I had passed beyond the realm of normal circumstances, even for myself.

Having insinuated myself into a stream of events, I would have preferred to tack between obstacles until my goal was within range, only then snatching it from the current and veering unnoticed to a hidden tributary to observe until I was certain that I had left no trace. Clearly I had already failed. Speed was now more urgent than subtlety. Whatever cross-purposes the Afronzo family retainers might have to my own, they'd certainly be headed toward the same destination.

I'd bandaged my wounds, dressed, and taken from the dead a few items that I wished to add to the travel kit I always kept in my garage for an occasion such as this. I'd experienced them before. That I was being driven from my home so late in life seemed indisputable evidence that my life would soon be ending.

A conclusion that caused me some great confusion as it was difficult from my perspective in the moment to see how the shape of my life could resolve itself after being so thoroughly bent from the form I had crafted. It wasn't that I doubted a violent end was my due, but something about the nature of the assault I had endured had knocked a great many elements out of balance. Not the least of which was the hard-earned harmony I'd built into my home. It was, there are no other words, a mess. And I had no time to put it into any kind of order. Let alone deal with the bloodstains.

Aging, wounded to an extent I'd not been in many years, my painstakingly crafted home in shambles, the world rising on a tide of its own madness and a plague of unrest, I found it impossible to envision the grace notes that would allow the composition of my life to be completed upon my death. Yet it could not help but be imminent.

But the world, as it often has for me, provided some slight evidence that there was a pattern to events. Revealed in the ringing of a phone. Or, rather, in the tune this particular phone played when it was called. "Welcome to My Nightmare." A call that provided an improbably timed touchstone of purpose.

I did not keep Lady Chizu waiting any longer than the moments it took to find the phone in the knapsack where it had been stowed by my attackers.

"Yes?"

"I would like a progress report."

I looked at the bodies strewn about.

"There have been complications."

"Not insurmountable, I hope."

I stepped to the glass wall that overlooked the basin, gazing at the view that had convinced me years before to embrace the instability of hillside living in Los Angeles.

"Not at all."

"There is tension in your voice."

I looked down at my legs. I'd put on black slacks against any seepage through my bandages.

"Yes, I've been wounded."

There was a slight pause. I became aware of a rhythmic clicking that had accompanied our conversation to this point, as if Lady Chizu were repeatedly tapping the same key on one of her typewriters. The noise ceased in her own silence, started again as she spoke.

"Do you require assistance?"

I smiled at my reflection in the glass wall.

"No. Your wonderful sense of humor is an elixir in and of itself."

The tapping of the key hesitated, as if interrupted by silent amusement.

"Jasper."

I frowned now at my reflection, the sound of my name in her mouth troublesome.

"Lady Chizu."

"When may I expect my property to be returned?"

I made a mental calculation that took into account the best- and worst-case scenarios involved in crossing to Culver City, what obstacles might be thrown up against me by Officer Haas, how quickly he would capitulate when he realized the nature of the man he was dealing with, the possibility of further interference by Afronzo mercenaries, and additional travel to Century City.

"Some hours after dawn, I expect."

The key she was striking tapped three more times, and a chime rang as the carriage traversed to the end of its rail.

"I will delay my breakfast, then, in anticipation of you joining me."

The Century Plaza Towers were illuminated; I could see them, albeit dimly, through the smoke. I nodded, focusing my attention on what I took as the fortieth floor of the north tower, imagining Lady Chizu seated on her folded legs at her desk, assessing the function of one of the items in her collection, pondering what might have been communicated in the final note it had been used to write.

"I will bring a flower for the table."

A firm ratcheting as she returned the platen to its top position, ready to be struck again.

"Bring my property. Though the flower will be appreciated as well."

She hung up.

I pocketed the phone. Leaving behind the rest of my work phones. I didn't expect that I'd be doing business in the manner I had pursued it in the past. Should I need to contact any former clients, I had their numbers safely tucked in my head.

Standing one last moment at the glass, I realized that I'd reached a point of self-indulgence. There was nothing to be gained by staying any longer, nothing but increased risk. So I left.

In the garage I placed my travel kit in the trunk of the Cadillac. I no longer had the Land Rover I'd used years ago for a similar exodus, but the Cadillac was quite possibly more durable. The travel kit itself consisted of a Metolius Durathane mountaineering haul bag filled with various pieces of survival equipment, some of it lethal, most of it mundane, and a black canvas T. Anthony duffel filled with clean underwear, socks, a few of Mr. Lee's irreplaceable shirts, a spare laptop, phone, universal current adapter kit, an unopened deck of playing cards, a shaving case, two blank five-by-eight sketchbooks, a pencil box, a sweater with a hole worn under the right arm that I'd never mended because I was inexplicably attached to the garment and refused to remove it from the kit for fear I might have to run of a sudden and leave it behind, wool slacks in gray and navy, a black alligator belt, a crumple-resistant poly-blend black sport jacket made from, of all things, recycled plastic bottles, the front door key to the house I grew up in, and, a recent addition, the soldering iron that had been used on me. For which I expected I might have some need myself.

I opened the garage door, drove the Cadillac onto the driveway, and put it in park with the engine running while I climbed out and dug at the roots in a small bed of lamb's-tongue that bordered the walkway up to the entry. Before exiting the house I'd spent several minutes passing a degaussing wand over the computers and drives the men had piled in the living room. I didn't have time to ensure all data would be unrecoverable, but between my primary and secondary measures I felt I could afford a high level of confidence.

A few inches deep in the soil, I uncovered a plastic box and the capped end of a PVC pipe that ran toward the house. I twisted the cap from the pipe and freed the bare ends of two wires taped just inside its mouth. Black friction tape sealed the plastic box. I unwrapped it, opened the box, and took out a DELTADET 4 industrial detonator. I pressed the test button to be certain the batteries were charged, received a green light, clipped the two wires into a slot at the top of the detonator, flicked the arming switch, and pushed the red button that gave me a fifteen-second delay to leave the scene.

Leave I did, climbing through the open door of the Cadillac and accelerating away without buckling my seat belt, letting momentum close the door for me. There wasn't anything to be heard; the Thermate TH3 packs planted about the house would quickly incinerate my personal records, the accumulations of DNA I'd sloughed off in my bed and bathroom, and perhaps burn long enough to create difficulties in identifying the men I'd killed. But I doubted that last possibility. The charges were specifically sized and placed to erase as many of my traces as possible, but not to rage so thoroughly that the sprinkler system could not extinguish the blaze before the concrete, glass, and steel structure was burned through and the surrounding hills and homes put at risk. It was not sentiment. It was practicality. Enduring pursuit and notoriety being the inevitable rewards for starting wildfires in the Hollywood Hills. Should anyone investigate the smoke drifting from the sodden interior ruins of my home, they might be shocked to find the corpses, but that shock would be far outpaced by the relief that the fire was contained.

I drove down the narrow twisting streets, slowing to a crawl at one point while a party of drunken sleepless in fancy-dress ball gowns and tuxedos stumbled down the middle of the road for a quarter mile. They began to dance as they walked, puppeteers to the towering spider shadows that my high beams projected onto the walls of abandoned homes and the branches of dead trees.

Inching behind them, illuminating their capers, I felt my confusion again. A moment like this, a mystery play acted out just for my eyes, how could such a thing happen and my end not be at hand? Yet where was the beauty in my own life to offset the value of such a gift?

It was coming. The future.

It was already here.

23

PARK LISTENED TO ONE OF THE TEN WEALTHIEST MEN IN THE
world. A man who, if the world lasted long enough, would undoubtedly
become the single wealthiest. Past seventy, once-broad shoulders with a
wide chest now drifting toward portly, and apparently comfortable with
the fact; his iron-gray hair was thick as ever, and sharply parted at the side,
even at this hour. A man who, wealth aside, wore a thin cotton bathrobe,
that dangled threads from the cuffs, over a pair of equally worn red flan-
nel pajamas.

"I should be asleep, Officer Haas."

The man tugged at one of the hanging threads and pulled it loose.

"But then, shouldn't we all."

He wrapped the thread around the tip of his left index finger.

"Officer Haas. The name rang a bell when I first heard it. So I dug up
the most recent edition of *Who's Who*."

He pointed the now-purple tip of his finger at an open book resting on
the brass-riveted black leather arm of a Colonial chair under a tulip glass
reading lamp.

"Safe bet it will be the last edition. In any case, I was right about the
name. I'd heard it before. In fact, I met your father once."

He walked to the chair, unwrapping his finger, dropping the thread in
one of the pockets of his robe as he went, and picked up the book.

"That was when he was ambassador to the UAE. I was conducting business in Israel. We met as Americans abroad, at a diplomatic function in Saudi. He was a cordial man. I read his book."

He put a hand on the back of the black chair.

"Sitting in this chair. Read it straight through. I recall being alarmed by his predictions for the region. In retrospect, they seem optimistic."

He referred to the open page in the copy of *Who's Who*.

"*Opportunistic Militancy and the Inevitable Loss of the Middle East.* Published in 1988. Well ahead of the curve, your father. Must have been an interesting man to grow up around."

Park knew a response was expected, but he didn't have one. The complexities of growing up around his father not being a topic he was inclined to discuss with strangers under the best of circumstances.

Parsifal K. Afronzo Senior closed the copy of *Who's Who* with a slight thump.

"Am I right that he was passed over for the 9/11 commission?"

Other complexities aside, Park had been raised in an atmosphere of scrupulous politesse, and he was almost relieved to be asked a question he could answer.

"No. He was asked."

Afronzo Senior was at the bookshelves that covered the wall next to the wet bar.

"He declined?"

"Yes."

Afronzo slipped the copy of *Who's Who* onto the shelf.

"I'd think a man dedicated to public service would have jumped at that particular assignment."

Park remembered the conversation he'd had with his father regarding the commission.

"He said they only asked him because they knew he would say no. And he didn't want to disappoint them."

Afronzo's chuckle quickly turned to a cough.

"Excuse me. As much as I appreciated his book and enjoyed the brief conversation I had with him, I wouldn't have expected him to have much of a sense of humor."

Park shook his head.

"He didn't."

The rich man rubbed the back of his thick neck.

"When I was a boy, *my* father kept a copy of *Who's Who* on the back of the toilet for bathroom reading. He said that when he was the same age it had been corn husks in a outhouse. Back in the old country that was. Said if you crumpled them enough they weren't that rough at all. Said he kept the *Who's Who* in the can in case an emergency should arise."

He chuckled again.

"I don't expect that sort of humor would have sailed in your house."

Park shook his head again.

"No, sir, it would not."

Afronzo rested a hand on the bar.

"Though this is not a regular drinking hour for me, I don't believe I'll have a chance of getting back asleep if I don't have something."

He went around the bar.

"I'm having cognac. Would you care for one?"

Again Park shook his head.

"No thank you, sir."

Afronzo took a bottle of Pierre Ferrand Abel from under the bar and poured two fingers into a snifter.

"You are a very polite young man, Officer. A childhood in diplomacy seems to have served you."

"Serious crimes are being committed within your company, sir."

Afronzo placed the cork at the mouth of the bottle, settling it with a light slap of his palm.

"At the time I met your father, he told me that he thought the business I was conducting in Israel would likely put American citizens at risk. American workers I planned to hire and bring over. He told me that he opposed my proposal and had spoken out against it with his counterpart in our embassy in Israel. He was, as I said, very cordial, but also very direct."

He took a small sip of his drink.

"It seems his son inherited that directness along with his good manners."

He came from behind the bar and sat in the Colonial chair.

"Would you care to sit, Haas?"

"No, thank you, sir."

Afronzo looked at the young man still standing just inside the door of the guest cottage den, the same spot he'd been delivered to a few minutes before.

"I was told that you might be sleepless. That you might either be unaware of your condition or in denial. But looking at you, I don't believe that you are sleepless. I've seen a lot of them. Close up. From here, you just look very tired to me."

He gestured at a couch that matched his chair.

"You're just about out on your feet, Haas. Sit down."

Against his will, Park rubbed his eyes. He nodded. And he sat down.

"Thank you, sir."

"You're welcome. And by the way, I don't get called 'sir' much. Mostly I go by 'Senior' these days. If you don't mind."

Park knew there was a distinction between the wealthy and the rich. He had grown up with wealth. While there had been abundance and quality in his upbringing, security was always viewed as the greatest benefit of the wealth his father had inherited, carefully tended, and added to. Never a threat that the cupboard might someday be bare. New clothes every school year. No fear of the wolf. Also weekend trips to Boston, D.C., and New York for dinner, concerts, or theater. Tastes of his mother. And his father's sailboat, a 1969 Dufour Arpege 30. College funds for the children. Assurance of a secure old age should the fates not intervene. A life not so far removed from the general that they lost sight of just how great their blessings were and, as Park's father often pointed out, how great the responsibilities that came with that wealth.

The rich were another matter. The amount of money required to elevate someone to that level provided a great deal of insulation. In conversation with rich schoolmates, Park could sense in them a confusion as to why everyone didn't do the things they did, value what they valued, eat and consume what they ate and consumed. An implicit question they silently asked whenever subjects of want and need might come up: *Why doesn't everyone just live like this?* As though these things were a matter of choice. As these classmates aged and gained experience, they began to affect a posture of ironic self-awareness. They knew they were rich, they knew most everyone else wasn't, they knew it was unfair, but at least they cared that it was unfair, *not*. The final flourish was meant to indicate that of *course* they cared, but they cared in their own deeply personal way. Park thought that it indicated the opposite. The ability to make the joke only revealed the isolation in which they were sequestered by their money.

As usual, he aspired to make no judgments and made them nonethe-less.

But Afronzo Senior was something else again. Beyond rich, he had ascended to superrich. And scaled yet higher to become a market force. In the post-SLP economy, Afronzo-New Day, holders of the DR33M3R patent, sat at the table with oil, water, power, telecommunications, health care, and munitions. They were at the foot of the table, but demand for their product was limited only by the rate at which SLP infected and killed. Based on current trends, the overall *potential* market might shrink, but market *share* would swell. DR33M3R was a reliable grower. And Afronzo-New Day's voice at the table demanded attention.

As the personification and will of A-ND, Senior had become something *other*. More so than even his son, he was existing at another level of consciousness. Park suspected that it was difficult for him to focus within a one-to-one environment. The most alarming implication of that suspicion being the thought that whatever it was Park was digging into had drawn the man's personal attention. Attention that implied that some part of what Park believed about the world frozen under a surface of lies must be true. Attention that promised only a bad ending, as much as it did hope.

Park wished for only one thing in that moment: that his father would open the door of the cottage just behind the main house of the Afronzo estate, that he would walk in, wearing his brass-buttoned navy blue suit, assess the situation, and tell his son that he should leave the room and go play while the adults talked over some business.

He looked at the door. It did not open. He remembered his father speaking on the topic of diplomacy as practiced in countries where monarchies still reigned.

Speak truth to power. Always. Kings and potentates will be coddled, don't let it be by you. Speak truth to power and your voice will be heard. If it is disregarded, as is likely, still you will sleep better at night. And you will have done humanity some service. Which will comfort you when you are dismissed early from your post.

Park recalled that speech and the other memory it brought to mind: Rose and his father meeting for the first time.

Senior swished the cognac at the bottom of his glass.

"You look amused by something, Haas."

Park, straightened the odd smile that had come to his lips.

"Just something that occurred to me, sir."

"Asked if you'd call me Senior, please."

"I think we'll both be more comfortable if I call you sir."

Senior nodded.

"Then I suppose I best call you Officer."

Park nodded as well.

"Yes, that would suit the occasion."

"The occasion being?"

Park sat forward on the couch, his back straight, hands on his knees, not allowing himself to lean into the soft leather, to assume the conversational demeanor of the older man.

"The occasion being that I have been kidnapped by men that I believe are in your employ. Who I can only assume did so at your behest. And until I am given some indication otherwise, I assume I am being held by you against my will."

Senior waved his snifter toward the door.

"The door's unlocked. No one will get in your way if you leave."

He raised the snifter a little higher.

"If you do leave without our first having a talk, I'll have to pursue some inquiries about you and your business with my son, through official channels. That is not a threat, simply what I'll have to do. I'd just as soon have those questions answered here and now, face-to-face. And yes, that is to save my family and my business any awkwardness, as well as to save you any professional setbacks."

Park kept his seat.

Senior lowered his snifter.

"All right, then, let's talk. Safe to assume that when you mentioned 'serious crimes' you didn't mean my men picking you up and bringing you here. Yes?"

"That is correct."

Senior relaxed deeper into his chair and crossed his legs.

"Let's start there, then. What is it you suspect has been happening with my business?"

Park thought about his family and spoke.

"With or without your knowledge, an organized, high-level operation within Afronzo-New Day is diverting large shipments of DR33M3R and distributing them outside of the venues and restrictions of a Schedule Z drug. This large-scale black market enterprise has accessed inventory at the warehouses. This is not a matter of a few bottles or cases but entire pallets, pods, even shipping containers, leaving the legal supply chain. These shipments are being broken down and parceled for retailers to be sold a bottle at a time. Bottles are cached individually so that retailers are rarely in possession of enough Dreamer at any one time to be accused of intent to distribute. GPS coordinates of the caches are logged and sold to buyers. Many of these buyers are never physically in proximity to the retailers. I believe that transactions are often carried out online in social networking and gaming environments, primarily in Chasm Tide. I believe that it is likely that most of these transactions are completed through the barter of virtual goods that are translated into money and valuables in secondary transactions. Additionally, as the market is controlled by elements within A-ND, they have the wherewithal to break up the large shipments in secret after they have left your warehouses. Thus, the top end of distribution is shielded by its proximity to official Dreamer trade; the midsection, when shipments are broken down, are hidden by the financial and physical resources of the A-ND participants in the operation; the bottom end is hidden by the cache distribution, virtual space transactions, and infrequent use of traceable currencies. Seeing as the only potential users of the drug are sleepless, there is little risk that customers will reveal the existence of this black market. They are in desperate need of access to the drug, and most will die within a year of becoming fully symptomatic, the point at which Dreamer can be of use to them. It is an effectively invisible black market. But I have physical evidence of its existence, have personally witnessed a portion of it in action, and have grounds to arrest one of the architects and primary operators of the entire trade in black market DR33M3R."

Park's fingers had begun to dig into his knees.

"Furthermore, I believe, I believe."

Senior leaned slightly forward.

"Are you all right, Officer?"

Park shook his head violently once.

"Furthermore, I believe that the advent of the sleepless prion was somehow, intentionally or accidentally, a by-product of your company's initial development of Dreamer. I believe that your labs experimented with the fatal familial insomnia prion, seeking to find an application for your over-the-counter sleep aid. I believe, intentionally or by accident, that your labs created a new prion, a designed material, and that, intentionally or by accident, that prion escaped the clean zone of your labs and entered and infected the general population. I believe that prion is the prion that has come to be known as SLP. I believe that A-ND's ability to develop and bring to market a drug such as Dreamer was only possible because A-ND is the creator of SLP. I believe that A-ND, realizing that the market for their drug will eventually die out and that they will have no engine for the profits currently generated by Dreamer, have created a black market to circumvent limits placed on trade when Dreamer was designated Schedule Z. I believe. I believe."

Senior rose, walked to the bar, poured water from a cut-glass decanter into a matching glass, carried it to Park, and pressed it into his hand.

"I think you should take a moment to catch your breath, Officer. You've been carrying a heavy load. A load like that, you only realize how heavy it is when you set it down."

Staring at the dark wainscoted wall behind the bar, Park's mouth hung just slightly open, as if he were trying to weigh the implications of bad news that had just now been brought to him.

"My wife is dying."

Senior patted his shoulder and walked back to his chair.

"Yes, I know."

He sat.

"Mine died several years ago. My second wife. I was divorced from my first. Although she is dead as well. My *second* wife, it's odd to call her that, I only ever think of her as my *wife*. You have a baby."

Park spoke to the glass he held in his lap.

"A daughter."

"I'd been told about your wife, but the baby, is she?"

"I don't know. My wife doesn't want her tested."

"Yes, I can understand that. It was cancer that killed my wife. Lung cancer. We both smoked far beyond the point of reckless idiocy. To this day I refuse to have a lung X-ray. Afraid to know what may be waiting for me. Although at my age it hardly seems to matter. Something will finish me soon enough. Does your daughter sleep?"

Park took a sip of the water.

"She did, at first. But the last few weeks, it's hard to say."

"How's that?"

"She cries all the time. Or it seems that way. But I'm not home very much. And my wife, she. I'm not sure how clearly she remembers if the baby is sleeping when I'm not there. The woman who helps us, she says the baby sleeps, but it never looks like sleep when I see it. Her eyes are usually open. And it never lasts."

Senior looked at the ceiling.

"What I remember from having babies around, and I'll be the first to admit I wasn't at home often when I had babies, but what I remember is that they can be that way. Cry nonstop, go days without sleep, crying the whole time. Hours and hours of crying. Could be your daughter is just colicky."

Park didn't say anything.

Senior looked down from the ceiling.

"What's her name?"

Park ran a thumb up and down the facets on the side of his glass.

"Omaha."

"The hell you say."

"My wife said, 'No one will fuck with a girl named Omaha.' "

Senior smiled.

"She had a point there."

He dropped his smile.

"You should have her tested."

Park nodded, looked for somewhere to put down his water glass, placed it on a bookshelf behind his shoulder, and faced the other man.

"Your son sold me Dreamer on two separate occasions. I'm going to arrest him. Is he at home?"

Senior cocked his head to the side.

"You're going to arrest my son because he?"

"Charges of possession and sale of a restricted substance. But I have evidence that could lead to racketeering charges. Money laundering. Tax evasion. And charges relating to the murders of a man named Hydo Chang and several of his associates."

"You think my son killed someone."

"I believe that several young men found shot in gangland style were his Dreamer retailers and that they were killed over matters relating to the sale of Dreamer. I believe that it is likely Parsifal K. Afronzo Junior was involved in those killings."

Senior drew his brows together.

"Then it is my son who you suspect as the mastermind behind the Dreamer black market?"

"I think it is possible. Although I think you are a more likely suspect."

Senior pulled his brows apart.

"You are direct. You are direct. Well."

He placed his hand on the snifter he'd set down earlier.

"In the interest of directness, I'd like to say a few words that might shed considerable light on these suspicions of yours. If you don't mind?"

Park looked at the door. He was aware that a performance was taking place. He was aware that he was being manipulated. He knew that if he let it draw to its conclusion, he might never leave the cottage. He'd been trying to apply the principles he'd learned from the Hurtin' Man. That there was danger in the room was not at all in doubt, but whether that danger was best dealt with by attacking its source or by running from it was unclear. And probably beside the point. Park had little hope that either option would be successful. And it didn't matter. Because what Park was most aware of was the slippage of time. Dawn would be coming. He needed to be home.

But he also needed to stay to the end of the show so he could know what happened.

He lifted a hand from his knee and turned it palm up.

"I would like to hear anything you have to say that might clarify this matter."

Senior picked up the snifter, swirled the contents, and swallowed them. "Good. Good."

He kept hold of the empty glass.

"To start, you are correct; there is a black market trade in Dreamer. You are also correct that A-ND is involved in that trade. But frankly, that is the price of doing business today. Distribution, Officer, is not an easy matter. Beyond the fuel costs, security contractors to escort the shipments, cross-state inspections, Homeland Security checkpoints, and occasional corrupt officials, there are also the Teamsters. In order to bring our product to market in a timely and efficient manner, we often find we must circumvent criminal and bureaucratic roadblocks. Hell, our trucks sometimes have to deal with physical roadblocks. We have to *pay people off*. A lot of people. A great deal of *money*. Usually cash. Not only do we have to get this money from somewhere, but we have to hide it. What we're doing, the payments we're making, it doesn't matter that we're greasing people so we can get the Dreamer out where it will do some good; the payments, most of them, are far from legal. We're bribing officials at every level of government. We have no choice. It's mostly just a collection of fiefdoms at this point. City, state, federal, interdepartmental. Dealing with the road gangs is easier. And there's no telling who might get it in their head to blackmail us for more or, God forbid, look to prosecute us if they found traces of what we're doing. So we need invisible money. Dreamer itself is better than cash money. We *could* just toss a few cases off each truck whenever we hit a snag. But then what? Chaos is what. Dozens of free agents trying to sell off little stashes of Dreamer. It would be a mess. And the trail would lead directly to A-ND. Also, we saw that a Dreamer black market was inevitable. Too much demand and not enough supply. We saw that inevitability, matched it with our need for cash, and chose to create and control a black market ourselves. Shipments move through the supply chain to the local markets. Every time a container of Dreamer is randomly scanned, the RFID chips are right where the manifest says they should be. And that's because they are where they should be. We don't break them out until they reach the local level. Grease the folks handling inventory in the dispensaries, and that's that. We can pull what we need. We sell by the case and pallet to hospices that have raised money through donations from the families of their wealthier patients, medicinal marijuana outlets, and yes, to some very robust and well-structured open source drug operations servicing low-income neighborhoods that are not well policed these days. As you said, the Dreamer end user has no interest in endangering the supply chain. Some larger institutions get shorted, but I have to feel that's offset by the fact that this system actually gets Dreamer to many folks who wouldn't otherwise have access. We've had very few leaks in the months it's been running. As for Junior being the architect of all this, well, does my son strike you as an architect?"

Park thought about Cager.

"He strikes me as a very intelligent person."

Senior frowned into his empty glass.

"And he is, he is. Very intelligent. Off-the-scale intelligent if IQ tests matter a good goddamn. But unfocused. And not what you'd call a people person. Incapable of wrangling something on this scale. He couldn't bring his full abilities to bear on a problem like this because the human relations would make him too uncomfortable. That boy, I tell you, more natural ability, pure talent, than a father could hope to see in a son, and just, just, he cannot apply it to anything useful. Business, I understand it's not for everyone, and I could; he can paint. I mean, expressive, powerful images. So if it had been that, painting, I would have been all for it. An artist son? I would have been damn proud. But even art, he just."

Senior floated one hand through the air.

"Drifted from it. Lost focus, lost interest. All that energy. That ability. And the only thing he has ever stuck with are the damn games. That one damn game. He. He builds his life around that game now. So I, well, I'm his father, so I want to understand, be a part of what he loves, show him support, take him seriously. And I was, frankly, proud when he showed up and he'd, on his own, just through observation of the market, the implications of peak oil, credit collapse, infrastructure erosion, the outright impotence of the federal government, he saw that A-ND must have an outlet for off-market Dreamer. We were just getting it started, but that kid, smart as hell, he knew it was happening just because he could put it together. And he wanted a franchise. For himself."

He raised and dropped his shoulders.

"I have backed him in so many ventures. But he had a plan, a model that made a kind of sense. In this world. He showed me the numbers on sleepless players in Chasm Tide, showed me the online markets where in-game valuables were trading, the currency exchanges between virtual and real. That was an eye-opener. And I thought, well, maybe this is it, a business tied directly to his real passion, maybe this will be the thing that he locks into. So I supplied him with a couple pallets. Made sure the pricing was in line with the rest of the off-market trade. We don't gouge these people, Officer."

He leaned forward.

"That should be very clear. We set the price. And if we hear that one of our franchisers starts to spread the margin and pocket the difference, we take action. And I do not mean that in any metaphorical sense."

He leaned back.

"I'm in the pharmaceuticals trade, not the human misery trade."

He shook his head.

"Not the human misery trade."

He pointed vaguely east.

"Those people. In Washington. That homunculus in the White House. When I think about who our president could have been, who it should have been. Know the man who shot him had his NRA membership card on him? Bought his weapon at a gun show. Barely had to flash his driver's license. That day, I burned my own card. Hardly matters anymore. Person wants a gun, they can find a gun. Well, those people in Washington, they turned out to be about as useless as everybody knew they'd be when it really hit the fan. A plague of sleeplessness. Democrats and Republicans trying to deal with a plague of sleeplessness. If it wasn't for the tears, you'd laugh yourself to death. A plague of sleeplessness. Any wonder all the zealots are going even crazier than before? Like it should come after locusts and frogs and the deaths of the firstborn."

He touched the part in his hair.

"So it gets left to people like me, people with influence, with some infrastructure of their own, people with money, it gets left to us to, hell, to make sure something is, something is left. That's not right. That's not my job. No one elected me. But hell, it's got to be done. Someone has to do something. We can't just walk away from the table, throw up our hands, say, 'I'm out.' This is what's fallen to me, this is my duty, and I won't shirk it."

He turned the empty glass in his hands.

"Sorry. It's late. I'm tired. Sometimes the frustration just comes out. It's. It's hard to look at the world and. It's hard."

He set the glass on the little table next to his chair.

"We were talking about Junior. And his interpretation of business. Long story shorter, I should have paid more attention, trusted my gut, said no. He turned it into a game. That crazy distribution, the caches, making people, sleepless or their family members or friends, stumble around town with RFID scanners looking for hidden bottles of Dreamer. Like it was a damn Easter egg hunt. And of course he lost interest, anyway. Just let someone else run the whole thing for him. Supposed to turn the money around, put it back in, buy more Dreamer, put it on the market, take his margin and do whatever he wanted with it. Put it in that sad club. I don't know. But he didn't. None of that money came back, not to pay the advance I gave him to acquire the first pallets, not to buy more. It was a small loss in terms of A-ND, but it needed to be covered. I did it out of my own personal accounts. On principle. It was my mistake. I paid for it. And I confronted the boy, told him to return what hadn't been sold. Make good his debts. He offered me a spreadsheet of GPS coordinates. Told me he wasn't even getting paid for most of the Dreamer. He was trading it outright for goods to equip his gaming teams. Bartering for 'character art.' Other things I didn't understand. To my shame, I slapped him. Never did that before. Don't believe anything good comes of striking your flesh and blood. And, well, that was that. It didn't matter much what he was doing with the Dreamer once I covered the loss. His distribution method is slow, inefficient, and cruel, but you are correct, it's nearly invisible. I asked some people in law enforcement to keep an eye on the streets, told them that some Dreamer might have leaked from the system. They understood. Set something up so they'd know if rumors started spreading, make sure the general public didn't find out. Word got out that my son was dealing Dreamer, half the country would likely get burned down by the other half. We're just *that* close to the edge of what people can understand and endure without running mad in the streets. And. And that's about it. Pathetic is how it sounds. When I say it all aloud."

Park stared at the man.

"The murders."

Senior nodded.

"The murders."

He shrugged.

"I never met the people Junior was in business with. But they were doing the nuts and bolts for him. Maybe they stepped on another dealer's turf without realizing it. Started selling to sleepless south of the Santa Monica. We supply some very aggressive Dreamer franchises down there. Very protective of their clientele. And very traditional in terms of how they deal with competitors. *Gangland* sound like their style. Maybe it wasn't even about Dreamer. That gold farming, if the numbers Junior showed me are real, that's serious money. Could have been a competitor in that space. But Junior? Pulling the trigger? Or having those two ex-SEAL supermodels of his do it for him? No. He's a, a difficult boy, frivolous, but there's no killing in him. I may not be best friends with my son, but I know him that well. That well, at least."

They sat in silence for a moment.

Senior looked at the empty snifter again.

"I keep telling myself I may as well have another, but I hear my wife saying that one is enough."

Park was slumping slightly, his elbow coming to rest on his thigh.

"Sir. SLP."

Senior kept staring at the glass.

"No, you're wrong about that. I wish I could tell you we poisoned the well. That there was a reason for it. Greed. It could be undone. But there is no peace of mind to be had there."

He looked at Park.

"We did it, all right, people, I mean. We did it, but it wasn't about greed. It was about hunger. Are you certain you want to hear this?"

Park didn't move.

Senior closed his eyes.

"Not enough food. The people who were paying attention, they knew it was coming. No shock to a lot of us when the price of corn and beans and rice started to jump. Too many people. Not enough food. Poor distribution for what there is. The hungry getting hungrier. At its root, yes, it was market exploitation, seeking to take advantage of a massive demand, but it was also plain necessary."

Park had straightened.

"What was necessary, sir?"

Senior opened his eyes.

"Know anything about transgenic plants, Officer?"

Park shook his head.

Senior nodded.

"GMOs?"

Park shook his head again.

Senior looked once more at his glass.

"Well, you've eaten a load of them. Genetically modified organisms. Unless you're hooked up with an organic shared farming operation, you've eaten plenty of transgenic maize. Genetically altered corn. High-yield corn. More specific to this discussion, pest-resistant corn. Heard of a thing called a European corn borer? No, no reason why you should unless you're a farmer. Far back as 1938, in France, they were spraying corn with something called *Bacillus thuringiensis*. Bt. A naturally occurring biotoxin that kills beetles, flies, moths, butterflies, and the European corn borer. Problem with a spray is, it wears off the surface. If you could get the stuff inside the corn, then you'd be set. Corn borer eats corn with Bt in it and it ends up with holes in its digestive tract. Dies. Bt, it contains two classes of toxins: cytolysins, or Cyt toxins, and crystal delta-endotoxins, or

Cry toxins. Those are the ones that kill the corn borers. Smart people, they identified the genes encoding the Cry proteins."

Park licked dry lips.

Senior picked a new thread from his bathrobe.

"Yes, proteins; it's all about proteins. Cry9C is a pesticidal protein, a naturally occurring product of Bt. But it can be produced as a designed material. And introduced to the genetic code of regular old-fashioned corn. And it was. There were a few fusses about it, fears that people were reacting to the Cry9C, allergies, but nobody died, the fuss faded. And what people didn't realize was that it was far too late to go back anyhow. Hell, by 1999 thirty percent of all corn, globally I'm saying, was Bt-modified. Sure, there were concerns around the turn of the century; Cry9C corn was supposed to be limited to nonhuman consumption. But if you use it for feed, and humans eat the animals, well, proteins don't die. They don't wear out. They just are. By 2008 it was all moot. Between world hunger and ethanol, the market for corn was booming. In August '08 the FDA proposed eliminating all safety limits on Bt toxins in transgenic foods. And soon after it was so. Even if they hadn't, the horse was out of the barn. In 2001, down in Mexico, transgenic artificial DNA had been found in traditional cornfields. It was spreading, cross-pollinating. Anyhow, Cry9C wasn't the issue. It was Cry9E."

He was wrapping his finger with thread again.

"They tried to make a super bug killer. A protein that would kill off all corn pests. Superresilient corn. That was in 2000. It worked. Too well. Killed off just about any bug that crawled on the corn, pest or not. Well, even the lab boys knew that wouldn't fly in the ecosystem. But it was already out. Cry9E corn got mixed in with Cry9C, no one really knows how. And it got distributed. And it cross-pollinated. And there was what a white paper I read once called *Lateral Transfer of Antibiotic Resistance Marker Genes*."

Park had leaned forward, focusing on the other man's mouth. An insistent thrum, as if his hands were cupped over his ears, grew within his head.

Senior was pulling the thread tight, the tip of his finger becoming intensely purple.

"And that's it. Cry9E, a designed materials pesticidal protein. We ate it. Or we ate something that ate it. Or we breathed it when it was burned as ethanol. And what it was meant to do to the digestive system of an insect, it did to our brains. It spread through conformational influence and ate holes in our brains. Innocent as all hell, trying to feed and fuel the masses, some asshole in a lab somewhere created a species-killing prion. Without even knowing it."

He pulled the thread tighter.

"Took eight years from 2000 for it to spread, become recognizable as something clearly other than fatal familial insomnia or mad cow or CJD. And another two years for us to get here. One out of ten symptomatic."

Park stood.

"What's?"

He looked around the room.

"How do we? We have to."

He looked at Senior.

"We have to. Symptomatic?"

Senior rose.

"Ten percent symptomatic. Infection rates are way beyond that level. And it's still spreading."

Park took one step and froze.

"People are, no one has said anything. Who knows? People are eating corn. People are."

Senior took his empty glass to the bar.

"No one figured this out quickly. By the time anyone knew where SLP came from. It was. Hell. And what do you do? Tell people to stop eating corn? Tell them, 'We know it's all you have, all you can afford, and we know we can't afford to distribute alternatives to you, so just be quiet and starve, will you?' I saw a projection, one of these think tank types, a projection based on what would happen if someone could just kill off all the corn, spray it, something; this man's projection combined an assumed zero yield in corn with the impact of drought on rice and ended up with mass cannibalism in less than a decade. Socially accepted cannibalism."

He set his snifter on the bar.

"There's no one to *tell*. There's no one to *save*. There's no going *back*. A lot of people, most of us, are going to die. It's going to take some years, but that's the endgame. Society, what's out that front door, it's going to keep breaking down smaller and smaller. People are going to get more and more afraid. They're going to rely on what they know, what they can count on. It's too big already, too big to stop. People, people who know, people like me, we're just trying to tap the brakes, slow everything down, keep it as normal as possible, keep people as comfortable as possible. As long as possible."

He took the stopper from the bottle of cognac, then put it back.

"'The slower it happens, the better the chance it won't all just crash and burn. The less people know, the lower the chance they'll go crazy all at once and just tear everything down. And the projections on *that* scenario, you don't want to know about those. If the statistics I've seen are half-right, there's still a better than even chance that someone somewhere will set off a nuke before this all shakes out. And then all the models break down. No one can say who might start pushing buttons."

He faced Park, the forgotten thread still around his finger.

"People in despair, Haas, they don't curl up and die. They are foolish and dangerous. We've lost the fight against SLP. It had won before we knew what it was. Now we're fighting despair. Trying to convince people there's a reason to watch TV, go to work, clean up after the dog, pay the bills, obey traffic laws, not go next door and kill your neighbor's kid for playing his guitar too loud in the garage."

He noticed the thread and began to unwind it.

"Just let them believe for a little longer that there is hope and a reason to live."

He dangled the thread from between his fingers.

"Because some people *will* live. There's an immunity. Something to do with alterations in the prion gene. Whether you're heterozygotic plays into it. Some people are going to *live.*"

He pinched the ends of the thread and stretched it between his hands.

"And we have to make sure there's something left for them."

The thread broke.

Park finished taking the step he had started moments before.

"I'm going to arrest your son."

Senior dropped the pieces of string.

"Haas. No. What is going to happen is my people, those former Mossad and Shabak agents that work for *me*, they are going to escort you from the property. At the Bel Air gates you will be photographed by the Thousand Storks contractors that handle security up here. Then you will be driven to your car. And you will go home. And you will never come back here again, or come near my son, or you will be killed. Now, I don't expect you'll accept anything from me. Not as a bribe, I mean, but in the way of help. Nonetheless, I would like to help you and your family. All you have to do is ask, but you must ask now."

He stopped speaking, and nothing was said in the room for a moment, and he nodded and continued.

"As I expected. However, you had among your possessions when you were picked up, a bottle of Dreamer. It will still be with your possessions when they are returned to you at your car."

He tightened the belt of his bathrobe.

"In this house, the main house, I mean, are many members of my extended family. They are here because I can care for them. Most of them are sleepless. Some are in the suffering. They have almost unlimited access to Dreamer. They can take a cap or two whenever they feel disoriented or in pain, and sleep and dream. And wake feeling almost like themselves. Unlike most anyone else in the world, they can do that for as long as several months, until they die. Not just the last few weeks like they do in the hospitals. Or, if they choose, if they are tired and spent and sad with the world, they can swallow twelve to eighteen caps of Dreamer at once and go deeply to sleep. The sleep lasts for several minutes to several hours, it is characterized by a general relaxation of all muscles, brain waves fall into continuous deltas, profound REM dreaming, no indications of unsettled or unpleasant dreams, and as the muscles relax further, the lungs slowly stop expanding, and the heart stops beating. From everything I have seen, it is a peaceful and merciful death."

He stood at the door.

"As I say, that bottle of Dreamer will be with your possessions when you are sent home. It is yours. To do with what you will."

He twisted the knob.

"Odd to think, I'd not have met you if it wasn't for my son's unwilling-ness to use a proper security detail. I'm forced to have my boys spy on him from a distance. That's the only reason they caught wind of the man at your heels. If it had just been you, I don't imagine I'd have gotten in-volved. But I saw the file on that man. *Jasper*. No last name. Never a good sign, *no last name*. Not someone you want near your family. Some of my people had it in their heads the two of you were working together. But I can see pretty clearly they were mistaken. Any idea why he was following you?"

Park was at sea now, barely treading water, so he saved his breath.

Senior patted his hair.

"Well, I wouldn't say it was nothing to be concerned about, drawing the attention of such a man, but he won't be an issue for you or yours. Or for anybody. And the world will be a better place without him."

He opened the door.

"I'm grateful to him, in any case, for giving me an excuse to meet you. It was a pleasure, Officer Haas. I wish you peace of mind. Goodbye."

He stepped out of the room, leaving Park alone in the new world.

24

ROSE GARDEN HILLER, STAUNCHLY FEMINIST, LIKED HER OWN last name. So she kept it. But she thought hyphenated last names were stupid and was happy to give her daughter the name Haas.

She was born in 1982. Her parents were divorced but remained on friendly terms and shared the raising of their daughter, though she did live primarily with her mother in what was little more than a cabin in the Berkeley hills.

When forced by circumstances she could not thwart to fill out any official paperwork, Rose's mother would describe her profession as *Social Activist*. She and her ex had set divorce terms that did not include alimony. She'd refused any offer of "patriarchal patronage." She was, however, practical enough to have agreed to accept a stipend on Rose's behalf. There was no hypocrisy. Every penny of the checks she received was allocated to Rose's care. Any money left over at the end of the month went into Rose's college fund. She fudged only very slightly in that she occasionally used a small amount of Rose's money to help cover the utilities. Rationalizing to herself that water and power were both necessary to raising a healthy child, but always doing her best to eke the difference out of her own earnings so that she could pay back what she had taken out.

One of Rose's earliest memories, perhaps her single earliest, she couldn't be certain, was of riding on the back of her mother's Schwinn, holding her arms out straight from her shoulders, airfoiling her hands in the breeze as they careened down the steep potholed streets into town. Days spent at co-op vegetable gardens, on picket lines, going door-to-door with petitions, at the campaign offices of independent candidates for local office, watching her mother holding young women's hands at Planned Parenthood, and then sleeping in the same seat, as her mother pushed the bike back up the hills in the evening if no one from one of the causes had been able to put it in the back of her Volvo and drive them home.

Her father was a lawyer. Devoted to social change, but not so much that he was willing to work totally without recompense, he was a junior, eventually full, partner at a firm that specialized in environmental law. An early memory of days with her father involved, not coincidentally, standing unrestrained on the passenger seat with her face stuck above the windscreen of his 1973 Porsche 911 roadster as he drove them across the Golden Gate Bridge from his Marin home to his office in the city. Mornings spent in progressive pre-K, afternoons tagging along with him to inspect a stretch of wetlands where abuses were suspected, sitting on his office floor in a small corral of law books, being passed off to one of the women he dated monogamously for long periods of time before becoming distracted and gently showing them the way out of his life, women who almost invariably took her to the Exploratorium, then being bundled into the Porche for a sleepy ride back to the house for a spaghetti dinner and a bedtime song, Pink Floyd's "Wish You Were Here."

Parker Haas had been a surprise. In truth, he had been more of a tectonic shift in everything she had ever thought she wanted and desired from life. What she thought she'd wanted was unfettered freedom. A long string of lovers who were strikingly beautiful to look at but emotionally uncomplicated. Men and women who were, she would freely admit, not unlike her father in those qualities. Whether she chose to finish her fine arts degree or not, she wanted to pursue her interest in digital video manipulations. What she called, when pressed by a particularly cute grad student who taught one of her studio classes, "culturally ironic metatations." Said with utter seriousness and no pretense. She wanted children, or a child, but couldn't fathom marriage. She welcomed the idea of a coparent, but only if that person could be as respectful of her time with the child as her parents had always been of each other's.

When, during her sophomore year at Cal, her father died of a heart attack at forty-six, she found she wanted to stay close to her mother, who, it turned out, had been secretly and irreparably heartbroken the moment he had sat next to her on their bed three weeks after he had turned twenty-nine and told her that he thought their roots were too tangled and he needed new soil. The heartbreak was revealed at home after his memorial service, after the spilling of his ashes in the bay, when she collapsed in the middle of the kitchen floor and began wailing. A wail that continued intermittently for three days. Rose had had no idea of the depth of her mother's love for her father. She bestowed her own love freely and with abandon. She loved her parents, her surviving grandparents, her two aunts, three uncles, and five cousins, she loved her many friends, she loved her lovers. But she loved all of them lightly. As if the wide disbursement of her love had diluted it somewhat. What she saw from her mother in those three days, and not infrequently over the rest of her mother's life, was alien and terrifying. Passions in both her parents had been reserved for cases of social injustice, the idiocies of governments, wonder in nature, and certain works of art. She knew that emotion of that intensity focused on another person was binding. Contrary to the freedom she saw as her natural element. It shocked her. Yet, rather often, usually in the day or two after she had jettisoned an especially endearing lover, she sometimes caught herself reimagining that display of grief, substituting herself for her mother. Those imaginings were never very detailed, they took place not in her mother's kitchen but in a blank nonspace, the fate of her lost love was never specified, nor was his or her identity. She literally could not imagine who it was she might suffer for so. If she had forced herself to go deeper into this fantasy, to construct a vague ideal, that person would not in the least have resembled Park.

She couldn't remember the name of the boy she'd gone to The Game with. She couldn't remember why she'd agreed to go to The Game at all. The annual meeting between Cal and Stanford was a local holiday and call to arms, but her interest in sports faded the moment she walked from the soccer field where she played a bruising, slide-tackling style of defense in occasional pickup games. She *could* remember the boy's ridiculously handsome face. Vulnerable to beautiful things, it was that face that had blinded her to the fact that he was clearly a prick. As the day and the game had both ground along, his prickish nature had risen on the tide of beer he swilled. Hardly a teetotaler herself, Rose was nonetheless disgusted by anyone who couldn't hold his own. Uninterested in the game, rapidly finding her date's face less and less of interest, she began to people watch the crowd, and found as her eyes swept back and forth that the same young man in the Stanford section several rows away seemed to be just looking away from her every time her eyes fell upon him.

Her first thought regarding Park was *out of place*. Not just out of place in the stadium, not just out of place wearing a red sweatshirt in that blot of red fans in the middle of the blue and gold crowd, not just out of place sharing a high five with one of his schoolmates after the Cardinal sacked Cal's quarterback, but out of place in his skin. Under his hair, behind his eyes, on top of his feet, out of place in all his physical dimensions. She couldn't understand how anyone could be watching the game when there was such a unique spectacle to behold: a man entirely without ease. His discomfort was profound. She knew he would misinterpret her looks but couldn't keep from staring at him whenever he looked away from her. She wished for a camera. Why hadn't she brought a camera? She needed to shoot him, needed video evidence of his fabulous awkwardness. Someone started a wave, and it washed over them. She watched as he refused to lift his arms in the air, but did faintly shrug his shoulders and flap his hands. Later, in the jumble of bodies pouring out of Memorial Stadium down toward University Drive, she'd see him ahead, hanging at the end of a trail of fellow Stanford supporters. With little effort she'd steered her drunken date through campus, across Bancroft, and followed Park into a house party hosted by a Cardinal alum who'd washed up on Durant Avenue.

It wasn't long before Park noticed her. But he didn't approach until her date, realizing he'd been dragged into the den of the enemy, began acting up and hurling abuse about the room. Asked to leave by the host, he snapped his fingers at Rose, who showed him her middle finger, and then he walked out after calling her a cunt. She saw Park, standing nearby and straining to appear disengaged from the scene that had caught everyone else's attention. And she knew that he'd just barely held himself back from taking a swing at the prick.

He was clearly a difficult man. Awkward, judgmental, opinionated, guarded, uncomfortably intense, possibly violent, pensive, emotionally constrained. He possessed definite stalker potential. A list of traits any one of which could disqualify a potential lover, any two of which in combination most certainly would. Not that she had any intention at all of sleeping with him, but if she was going to somehow incorporate the idea of the man into her art, she had to at least speak with him.

The prick left, the unsettled moment settled, someone told her she should stay until it was clear the prick wasn't lurking outside, or at least not leave without company. A woman offered to call the campus escort service, Rose shook her head, said she'd stay awhile, walked to Park, and put out her hand. "I'm Rose. I was kind of fucking staring at you at the stadium." He took her hand. "Parker Haas. Yes, I noticed that. It was unnerving. I'm leaving. Would you come with me?"

She left the party with him and discovered that her assumptions about him had been more or less correct, except they left out his open honesty, thoughtfulness, generosity, remarkable manners, dry humor, eclectic and deep knowledge, challenging intelligence, and amber eyes that compensated more than evenly for his windburned angular features and narrow build. She took him home after they'd walked most of the night, slept with him, woke a few hours later to make love with him for the first time, and, lying next to him, his fingers drawing tiny circles around each bump of her spine one by one, had that vision of herself in the blank space, wailing as her mother had, all for the sake of Parker Haas, whom she had met just hours before. He asked her what was funny when she started laughing, and she said "nothing." Two weeks later they drove to Reno and got married.

There was more. She was complicated herself. Temperamental and judgmental and, raised by a lawyer and a social activist, rarely without opinions. Her mother died. She lost interest in her art, became more interested in pop culture and the technical components of video. He moved to Berkeley. She saw ghosts of her parents everywhere in the Bay Area and tired of inventing new routes to avoid the memories. He saw the daily progression of dark clouds on the front pages of newspapers, heard the voice of his father often, Cassandra in his head, and began to doubt the usefulness of philosophy. A doubt, oddly, that he had never before entertained. She was offered work in Los Angeles. Riding BART into San Francisco one Saturday, he saw an ad recruiting for the SFPD, and felt a sudden physical need to be useful. That evening he went online and researched the LAPD and LASD. And they moved south. Not long after he was hired and began at the academy, the strange outbreaks of FFI-related BSE and CJD that had been receiving greater coverage of late were redefined as a new disease: SLP. Park graduated from the academy. Rose alternately loved and hated her job. The world became more complicated, more daunting. Someone they knew well contracted SLP and died. They talked about leaving Los Angeles but didn't know where else to go. Rose became pregnant. And was soon after diagnosed.

There was more. But some of it was deeply personal and related to the secrets of a marriage that should not be shared. And some of it was incoherent, tangles of her life in the real world and of Cipher Blue and her life in Chasm Tide. What was relevant is what I have related. What she told me when I appeared unannounced at her home in the very wee hours of the morning and began to ask questions that one would not normally answer to a stranger, but which she did so willingly, once I explained why I was there.

█ █ █

7/11/10

I HAVE TO go inside. I have to go inside. I have to go inside.
I have to.
What do I do?
Have I been lied to? My father said the way to determine if you'd been told a lie was to first determine if the person you were dealing with could benefit in any way by telling the lie. If they could benefit by a lie, they were likely lying.

He said it was human nature. He said most people couldn't resist an opportunity to improve their position when it was offered them. I asked him if he ever lied. He told me that he sometimes did in the course of his duty, as a matter of statecraft. I asked him if he ever lied to me. He thought for a moment and nodded and said, "I confess to having told you that Santa Claus was real. Also, you once wrote a paper of which you were very proud and asked me to read it. I did. I found the argument spurious and unsound but told you I thought it was quite good. I'm not certain why I didn't tell you the truth and challenge you to defend your points. I may simply have been very tired."

Parsifal K. Afronzo Senior has told me several things. He has told me the details of A-ND sanctioned and controlled black market trade in DR33M3R. He has told me that the source of SLP is genetically modified corn. He has told me that far more people than the general public has been told of are infected. He has told me that infection rates are rising. He has told me that there will not be a cure. He has told me that most of the people in the world are going to die. He has told me that there is nothing left to aspire to but to see that something is left for the people who are immune. The people who will survive when the rest die.

And I ask myself, is there any benefit for him in lying about any of this? Was he lying?

I have to go inside.

My father said that the worst lies are the ones you tell yourself. I asked him if he ever lied to himself. He said, "I hope, Parker, that I do not. But, being an excellent liar when called upon by duty, I cannot be certain that it is so."

Was Afronzo Senior lying?

And if he was? And if he wasn't?

A lie changes nothing. Not what has happened. Not what will be. Not what you must do.

The truth changes what has happened. It changes what will be. It changes what you must do.

Whether he has lied or not, whether he is right or wrong, whether the frozen world can be saved or is already lost, it does not change what I have to do.

I can't do it. Without me. The baby. Without me. Rose. Who? Without me? Who?

The world, if it can be saved, it must be. If it is lost, something must be saved.

There is what I must do for my family. And what must be done.

Who can be told the truth? Bartolome won't believe. Or will be afraid. Hounds?

He's a criminal as much as he is a cop.

My father said there is a reason we have laws. He said, "There is a reason we have laws, Parker. We have them to measure a society's devotion to justice. And to show how far a society may have strayed from that devotion."

My father could not lie to himself. He used his favorite shotgun to keep from lying to himself.

I am afraid, Rose, that I am my father's son.

So late. So early.

I have to go inside. They are waiting for me. My family is waiting for me. Inside.

25

IT WAS STILL DARK WHEN PARK RETURNED TO CULVER CITY.
The horizon had not lightened; in fact, the sky had dimmed as many fires
had burned themselves out. Just one major blaze seemed to remain, what
looked like several blocks burning in Hollywood where the Guard
sergeant had said the NAJi church had been destroyed.

The drive from Bel Air had taken him through four checkpoints. At
one he'd had to get out of his car and lie facedown on the ground while
the Guardsmen ran his badge. They searched his car but did not find the
hiding place in the spare tire.

Sitting in front of his house, he wrote in his journal. There was no
order to his thoughts. He knew this but could do nothing but let himself
be tumbled about by what he had been told. He'd been raised to an ordered mind. His ideas, values, emotions, often felt fitted together like
brickwork. Or had until Rose had come into his life. But even then order
had been the rule rather than the exception. It just took more effort to
maintain that order. And the walls of his interior had become more eccen-
tric. Odd modifications had been made to what had previously been a
squared structure. Windows where one did not expect them, bits of orna-
ment, an extra door.

It was all a jumble now. Only the keystone was in his hands. The
thought that something could be done. That something could always be

done. That the world could always be made better. It required only that one act. Do the things one believed in.

He opened the car door and climbed out slowly. In the house were his dying wife and his baby. There was something he had to do. But he had no way of knowing what it was. It was hidden from him. Concealed by its perfect enormity.

Coming through the front door into the lighted house, he was absently pleased to hear nothing. Registering the silence as an indication that his daughter was sleeping or in some similar state that gave her peace. He stood just inside the door and looked at the hall that led past her nursery to the master bedroom at the back of the house. He thought for a moment about peeking in, but feared that he would wake her from whatever kind of rest she had. His mouth and throat were dry. He went through the living room, scattered with foam blocks, a stack of laundered burp cloths, a spilled basket of stuffed animals, through the adjoining dining room where a playpen sat in place of a table, and into the kitchen.

In the past the sink might have been filled with dirty plates and glasses, testaments to Rose's intense dislike for housework. Not that Park minded. He was a compulsive straightener of things. Until quite recently he had been accustomed to coming home from work and spending a peaceful thirty minutes picking up odds and ends of dirty laundry, cleaning the dishes, wiping a small spill from the floor, closing cabinet doors left open. The slight mess had been a trail of clues he had learned to read, indications of how his wife's day had been. Had she indulged her sweet tooth? If so, she was probably displeased with her work. Was there only one plate in the sink? She had probably been very happy in her work and forgotten to eat. Sweaty socks and sports bra on the couch? She'd been restless, needed to go for a run. CDs left out of their cases on top of the stereo? She'd been listening to old favorites, seeking inspiration. The photo album pulled from the bottom shelf of the bookcase? She'd been nostalgic, looking at pictures of their comically small wedding and Yosemite honeymoon.

These days any mess was left by the baby and Francine. Toys and blankies, bottles rinsed and drying in the rack, an unfamiliar black slipper at the mouth of the hallway, a rubber ducky tucked inside. Signs he could not read.

He took a clean glass from the dish rack and filled it from the filter screwed into the taps. The water was nearly flavorless; neither refreshingly clean nor carrying an urban tang, it seemed to pass through his mouth and down his throat without wetting. He refilled the glass and drank again, feeling some relief this time. Still, he filled the glass once more and drank again, eyes closed. He lowered the glass and opened his eyes. He was reflected in the window over the sink and did not like what he saw. Someone stretched thin with worry and exhaustion and indecision. He could see quite clearly why Cager had suspected he was sleepless.

He filled the glass a last time and took it with him, passing back through the dining and living rooms, into the hall, past the room where his daughter was silent if not asleep, pausing for a moment to consider again if he could peek in, moving on without doing so, and stopping when he reached the open doorway of the bedroom he shared with his wife.

The man sitting on the three-legged milking stool Rose kept next to her side of the bed as a nightstand seemed to have been waiting for him, looking at the door when Park appeared there.

He rose. Thinning silver hair brushed straight back from a forehead and face that were hardly young but could have been anywhere between a healthy forty and an excellently maintained sixty. His build was athletic, but not oppressively so. His movement, rising from the stool, suggested grace hobbled somehow. Dark slacks and a dark, collared shirt, thin black socks, silk no doubt, that showed a sheen of pale skin beneath. Seeing those stocking feet, Park finally registered that the slipper with the ducky inside had actually been a black leather loafer.

The man tilted his head forward.

"Officer Haas, your wife has been telling me about you."

Rose was on the bed, back cushioned by several pillows, knees drawn up, laptop at her side, the baby sitting up on her stomach, playing with a small flat rectangle that Park did not recognize but that caused a wave of nausea unsettling the water in his otherwise empty stomach.

Rose breathed in very deeply, inflating her belly, making the baby rise and bobble, then let the air out in a whoosh.

"Elevator going up, elevator coming down."

The baby cooed, put one end of the rectangle into her mouth, and bit down on it.

Park had a sudden wish for the gun he'd left in the spare tire in his car.

"Who are you?"

Rose made clucking sounds with her tongue, and the baby imitated her.

"Don't be an asshole, Park."

The man shook his head.

"No, Rose, your husband isn't being rude. I have caused some confusion."

Park tried to see an angle into the room that would put him between the man and his family.

"Who are you?"

Rose was smiling.

"Do you see how happy Omaha is? I haven't seen her like this in so long. Not since Berkeley."

Park took a step toward the bed.

"She wasn't in Berkeley, Rose."

She stopped bouncing the baby on her belly.

"What are you? Yes she was. We."

She turned to the man.

"What was I just telling you, Jasper?"

Park thought of the Hurtin' Man.

His family was in the room. He could not run. He could not attack.

The man nodded at Rose, never quite taking his eyes from Park.

"You told me very many things, Rose, all of which I am grateful for. You are a wonderfully truthful woman. But I'm afraid your husband is correct; you never had a baby in Berkeley. Not unless I missed some part of the story."

Her eyes stirred. Park saw that his old Rose had been in the room, that now she was being submerged again as her confused double surfaced.

"What? No. Of course not. We didn't have a baby."

She looked at Park.

"Where were you? Are you okay?"

A whine came from the baby's chest.

Park took another step, raising the hand without the water glass, palm out, warding the man from the side of the bed.

"Who are you?"

Rose shook her head.

"He's Jasper, Park."

The man did not move away from the bed, but something changed in his stance, a shift in balance that took him from his heels to the balls of his feet, bringing menace nearer.

"The confusion was caused, I'm afraid, by a lie I told. You see, Rose, I am not a detective, and Park did not send me to see that Francine went home early or, for that matter, for me to keep an eye on the house because of all the troubles this evening."

Park rapped the rim of the glass on the footboard of the bed that had belonged to Rose's grandmother. It shattered, leaving him with the jagged-edged base cupped in his hand.

"Take three steps directly back from the bed, keeping your hands where I can see them at all times."

The baby's whine rose in volume and pitch.

The man indicated her with two long white fingers.

"You're making the baby cry, Officer Haas."

Rose was pulling the baby to her chest.

"Park, I don't like it here. It's hot and fucking no one gives a shit about anything but the stupid fucking business and I miss the rain and my mom hasn't met the baby and I hate guns and I remember when it was better and I want it better again."

Park stepped closer, his arm raised, maneuvering to slip himself between his family and the man who refused to move.

"Back away and keep your hands visible."

The man displayed his hands.

"Keeping my hands visible will not make anyone in this room safer, I assure you."

Rose was squeezing the baby and starting to rock.

"I am going home. I have defeated the Clockwork Labyrinth, and I am going home."

The man nodded.

"It's true, you know. She did defeat the Labyrinth; I sat here and watched her do it as we spoke."

Park was clutching the broken glass; he knew that he needed to hold it lightly if it was to be any use as a weapon, but he could not help himself.

"Back up. Please back up."

The man's eyes flicked to the window.

"Officer."

The lights in the converted garage out back blinked quickly on and then off again.

"Officer, do you have houseguests?"

Park's brain stumbled over the question.

"Do we?"

The man reached for his daughter.

The glass cracked in Park's hand as he began to raise it.

The man plucked the small dark rectangle from the baby's mouth, flipping his thumb, causing a small sharp blade to appear at the end of the object.

He stepped back, slapping Park's hand as it passed in front of him, knocking the glass to the floor, turned his back, and walked toward the window.

"We are under attack, Officer. There will likely be three of them. I can handle that many. There may be six. In which case they will kill me. They will be well armed and trained. I assume you have a firearm. Please don't shoot me with it. Get it and stay in here with your family."

He pointed at the bedside lamp.

"Will you turn that off, please, Rose?"

Rose switched the light off. The man slipped the screen from the window frame and pulled himself up and through, a mongoose down a snake's hole.

Rose nodded her head.

"He's Jasper."

Omaha began to cry.

Park went to the safe for his other gun.

I FOUND THREE of them. One team.

An indicative number. Despite my hurried flight across town, my ID broadcasting my course, they apparently were unaware that I'd come to the Haas residence. If they had known, they most certainly would have sent more killers. That they expected a sleepless mother, a baby, a young and inexperienced cop, and perhaps a nanny, was heartening.

It heartened me to know they had no idea I was present. It heartened me to think they might not even know yet that I was alive and unfettered. Or, at least, that the information had not yet been disseminated through-out the Afronzo security apparatus. It heartened me to know they were the kind of mercenaries who rubbed against light switches, announcing their presence. It heartened me to think they were ill informed, appeared more than slightly careless, and were coming to kill a sick woman, her lost husband, and their baby girl. Not that I hadn't killed the helpless and meek in my own time. Most of all it heartened me to think that this must be their C team, the A and B teams having been dispatched already to my home. Quite honestly, I doubt I'd have been up to anything more.

Still, they were quite capable of capitalizing on my own carelessness.

The first was the light switch rubber. I watched him from the shadows of a moldering stack of firewood that Park must have bought in a fit of ro-mance when they moved into the house. Not quite accounting for the lack of opportunities the environment allowed for burning one's way through a full cord. Much of it had been chopped in advance to fit the modest fire-place inside. My hand found a wedge that suited my grip.

The man who'd flipped the lights was just inside the screen door of the converted garage, revealed by intermittent adjustments that caused the laser sight on his weapon to shiver over the steel mesh just in front of him. He was meant to be covering the rear. Making sure that no one fled the house as his teammates went in through other access points. Commotion within would draw him from cover as he moved to support. So I ignored him and backed away from the woodpile, down the side of the house where disused bicycles and a lawn mower were gathering ash from the assortment of wildfires, and found Omaha's bedroom window. I took down the screen, pocketed my knife, dropped the small log onto her crib mattress, and boosted myself inside, scraping my legs, biting the pain.

Rearmed with blade and log, I cracked the door slightly and watched as the second mercenary crept across the living room in perfect pistol-combat mode, presenting a minimum target silhouette, weapon raised, held in both hands, fingers overlapped, trigger finger parallel to the barrel to protect against accidental fire.

He began gesturing to someone out of my sight line, the third team member, for whom he appeared to be providing cover as they cleared the house room by room. He was making responsive hand signals, pointing at the hallway without turning his head, indicating that he would take point on the new course. I opened the door a bit more, passed through, and closed it behind me.

The hinges on that door had, until recently, squeaked badly. The squeak had been of little concern when Omaha was sleeping like any other baby, but as her sleep had become increasingly unsettled she had become more sensitive to small sounds. The squeak of those hinges could ruin any chance that she might find slumber. So Rose had given them a liberal squirt of WD-40. The door now swung open with no sound at all. One of the many sleep-related stories she'd told me. Her illness aside, she was in that regard quite like any new parent I'd ever met.

Hunkered in the dark corner where the hallway bent into the living room, I waited until the man with the perfect pistol form stubbed his toe on the stick of firewood I'd left in the middle of the floor. It didn't trip him, merely made him pause before moving on, relaxing his finger from around the trigger, where he'd placed it when surprised by the small obstacle. Thanks to that moment of relaxation he did not fire a round when he spasmed as I fit the blade into his neck just below the point of his left jawbone, cut a wide crescent across his throat, and left the knife there.

That was poor technique. Leaving the blade would suppress the flow of blood from the wound. Not to mention essentially putting a weapon in the hands of an enemy. But it was a calculated risk. He had more than enough wound from which to bleed, and I doubted his ability to be any further threat to me, no matter how well armed.

I stepped into the living room, quite surprising the cover man who'd just watched his partner round the corner into the hall. He'd not had time to take his proper cover position, for which he could thank the haste of the man bleeding from his neck on the floor. So ill prepared, how could he be expected to be ready to fend off attack? He could not. And he was not.

I'd taken the Tomcat from my ankle holster when I set down the piece of wood. Now I shot the man twice, once in the neck, once in the groin, targets left exposed by his body armor.

The other man was making a fair amount of noise now. Dying from blood loss is a wet and gasping affair. There is a great deal of struggling against the inevitable. A man bleeding to death looks very much like a fish drowning on dry land. And he beats out the same messages of distress. Combined with the two gunshots, more than ample commotion.

I bent to pluck the rubber ducky from where Omaha had placed it in in my loafer while she'd played with both earlier, took cover behind a rocking chair, and oriented myself toward the kitchen, waiting for the bootsteps that would tell me the rear support was entering by the back door.

I'd have an excellent shot, made superior if the man was the least bit distracted when I threw the rubber ducky and it bounced squeaking across the floor. I was poised and ready. If only the rear support had not seen me in the backyard, followed me around the side of the house, watched me enter through the window, pursued, and come after me through the well-oiled door.

Granted, he revealed his second-rate nature by not warning his partners by radio that someone had compromised their flank; but, I was still entirely surprised and the shot fired behind me jerked me upright and spun me around.

Hearing gunfire in his home, near at hand to his family, Park had ignored what he had been told and left the bedroom. Opening the door, he'd emerged just as a man at the opposite end of the hall came out of his daughter's room carrying a very short assault rifle with a trigger assembly mounted ahead of the clip. The man moved silently, the butt of his weapon pressed to his shoulder, tucked to his right earlobe, sighting down the stubby tube of an integral laser sight. Intent on what lay beyond the open doorway leading into the living room, the man was oblivious to Park.

Park's family was just behind him, lying on the floor of the bedroom closet where he'd left them. The door and a single wall would scarcely reduce the velocity of a round fired from a weapon like the one the man was carrying. And Park could not be certain the man wouldn't quickly turn and fire at the first sound. Once a bullet became a stray, it could find a home anywhere, in anyone. All the same, there was ample opportunity for Park to take some cover by pressing close to the wall, announce his presence as a law officer, and order the man to disarm.

But Park didn't think about any of this. It never occurred to him to attempt to disarm and arrest the man. It never occurred to him what risks might be involved in that procedure. He never had a chance to think or consider any of this. Action proceeded without thought.

Because Parker Haas came out of his room, and he saw a man coming out of his daughter's room, and that man was carrying a gun. So Parker Haas shot him. He fired a single round, the pad of his right index finger squeezing straight back, the man's face seemingly balanced atop the red dot that marked the front blade sight of Park's Warthog, framed perfectly by the rear sights. The gun went off, kicked, Park adjusted and re-aimed, but the man's face was no longer where it had been. Lowering his sights, Park advanced down the hall, close to the wall, lowering the sights farther with every step, until he was over the man, pointing the gun almost straight down, and he pulled the trigger twice more.

I'd not yet picked up the TAR from the man I'd shot in the neck, but I still had the Tomcat in my hand. When Park appeared in the hall doorway, shooting the dead man, I did what came most naturally and took aim.

Park had never killed before. He'd inflicted considerable injury on suspects in the course of an arrest, but he had never discharged his weapon at anything other than a paper target.

I knew this for a certainty. I knew it because he stood over the dead man and looked up and found me turned to the side in a duelist's pose, legs spread for stability, arm straight out from shoulder, small pistol aimed at his head, and he spoke.

"I never killed anyone."

To the best of my knowledge, I'd never had my life saved before. Yes, the anonymous bureaucrat who had halted my torture several years earlier had kept me from being killed, but believe me, that is not the same as someone shooting the man about to shoot you. Yet I had been handed *similar* moments in life. Instances when the suddenness of violence so shocked an adversary that an opening was created through which I could pass and take decisive action. Part of the genius of my self-preservation obsession. The ability to remain calm as those around me lost their heads. Literally. As I'd aged, this advantage had grown. Fed by experience. At sixty, just as I could not remember the last lover I'd had within ten years of my own age, I could not remember the last fight I'd had with anyone in the same range. My profession, however defined, did not foster longevity. I was inevitably the oldest gun in any given firefight. Those years more than compensating for any loss of physical ability.

This great age of mine, it had been earned with ruthlessness. Yes, I had a morality, but it was quite uniquely my own. There was no one I could kill or maim who would cost me a night's lost sleep. It was, in truth, less a morality than an aesthetic. Who, how, and when I killed were all elements in the composition of my life. Melody and harmonies. One great recurring theme being the seizing of the moment. Beauty all its own.

I was no longer concerned that Park might have passed the hard drive to the Afronzos. Their interrogation of me, and this assault, indicated that matters were different. The drive was nearby, I was certain. Finding it would not be difficult. That being the case, there was no reason not to kill the young man before he recovered from his shock and became an armed threat again.

Clarity in these things is without price.

My finger was on the trigger. Omaha was still crying. The moment filled with dissonance.

I lowered my gun and, at this extremity of life, allowed myself the indulgence of knowing things.

"Officer Haas, who do you work for?"

He looked at his own gun.

"LAPD."

He looked at me again.

"I'm a cop."

The truth of it, so simple and bare, unadorned with deceit, that I almost laughed.

"Yes, you are, aren't you."

He saw the other dead bodies.

"Why did you lead them here?"

I raised a hand in denial.

"No, these are not mine. I killed mine earlier. These were sent for you. And for your family as well."

He was shaking his head before I finished.

"They're Afronzo personal security."

"Yes, exactly."

"Your name is Jasper."

I nodded.

"It is."

He was looking at his gun, weighing it.

"He said you were dangerous. 'Someone you don't want near your family,' he said."

I nodded.

"I think he was correct in that. May I ask who?"

"Parsifal K. Afronzo Senior. He thought you were dead."

I cocked my ear for a moment. I could have been listening to Omaha but was in fact hearing the strange tune produced by the twining of this man's life with my own. Something I'd never heard before. Dissonance becoming assonance, perhaps.

I nodded again.

"I believe that the world may have become more mysterious these last few days."

Park had eyes only for his gun.

"More mysterious than a marriage."

I watched him watching the gun in his hand.

"I was married only very briefly, at a very young age, and still I know you exaggerate."

He may have smiled.

"Only a little."

"Yes, that I will agree with."

His finger had crept nearer the trigger.

"What's gone wrong? With the world? Why aren't people trying to fix it?"

My gun was still lowered, but my finger was curled on the trigger.

"I believe it is because they don't believe there is anything to fix. They have been raised to fatalism and slaughter. A feeling of powerlessness pervades the average person's interactions with the world at large. They want it comfortable and familiar. But they've stopped thinking about tomorrow in any tangible sense. They don't believe in it any longer. Because they don't want to think about it. How hard it will be. For the ones left."

He was still looking at his gun.

"I wouldn't have a chance, would I?"

I couldn't be certain what he meant, so I answered the question at hand.

"No. If you try to raise your weapon, I will shoot and kill you. And the long conversation we should have, the mysteries we should unravel, will be lost. Much to my regret."

He eased the hammer forward on the small pistol, thumbed the safety up, and dropped the gun next to the man he'd killed.

I still held my own pistol.

"I need the travel drive, Officer."

He turned away.

"You can't have it."

He took a step, presenting the back of his head to me.

"It's evidence in a crime."

I raised my gun.

"I need it."

He shook his head.

"No. I have to check on my family now."

He moved, beginning to pass out of my aim, down the hallway.

"We can talk after I see them."

Down the hallway, walking to his family, away from the dead, and I did not kill him.

Instead, I whispered a poem to myself, very brief and made up on the spot.

"Parker Haas, crying Omaha, and his sleepless Rose."

There are other things in this life than killing. I felt a chance to be near them. If only briefly.

2 6

OMAHA CRIED. AND ROSE WAS INCREASINGLY UNWELL.
The vibrancy she'd shown in the hours she and I had spent talking before Park came home had faded. She was no longer buoyed by the past but
wallowing again in the present. I watched from the bedroom door as Park
told her the truth about what had happened moments before. In her condition virtually any lie would have sufficed and perhaps been more merciful. Circumstances that made the honesty shine with greater brightness.

I left them then, for several minutes, long enough to drag the bodies
out the back door, across the lawn, and into the converted garage. Animated skeletons danced on three monitors. I watched them for a moment, then returned to my task. I found a bundled tarp and took it into
the house, draping it over the largest of the blood puddles in the living
room. Not much else could be done. An armful of towels from the bathroom scattered over the floor soaked through from underneath. By the
time I went back to the bedroom my burns were seeping similarly into the
legs of my slacks.

Park was holding his crying daughter, tucked into the crook of his left
arm, while placing a damp cloth on the back of Rose's neck. Rose was
facedown on the bed, muscles jumping in her jaw, the backs of her legs,
her upper lip. She made a claw of her right hand and dragged it down the
sheets in long strokes, her chewed nails rasping quietly on the weave.

She whispered.

"Up arrow, up arrow, shift, space, space, space, right arrow, tab, tab, up arrow, space."

Park looked at me.

"They're keystrokes."

I nodded.

"Yes. The Clockwork Labyrinth. She told me she'd memorized the sequence that got her through."

Her chant continued. A whispered incantation, the epic of her achievement.

I pointed at the floor.

"May I sit?"

Park didn't answer. I remained standing.

He was still now, crying baby in his arms, fading wife wide-eyed on the bed.

"I have to do something."

I pulled at my slacks where they continued to stick.

"Yes, as do I."

He looked at me.

"Why are you here?"

It was only when he asked the question that I realized how little I understood the answer. Why was I there? Surely I should have been gone long before. The travel drive in my possession, the dead in their places, all other concerns swept away as I discharged my contract with Lady Chizu.

I spoke without thought, letting my words inform me.

"I am here to complete something. Something I have been working on for many years. My whole life."

Omaha twisted suddenly and almost slipped from his arm onto the floor. He caught her, the movement disrupting Rose's recitation long enough for a moan to slip from her lips.

Park closed his eyes.

"I can't take care of both of them."

He opened his eyes.

"I need help."

I didn't move.

He came off the bed, walked to me, and put the baby in my arms.

I had realized long before that a gun is a kind of philosopher's stone. Only rather than transmuting all that it touches into gold, a gun transmutes the entire atmosphere around it. Hardening edges, sharpening the air, a glitter of clarity. Fear. Even an unloaded gun can turn the air in any room to pure fear. In the moment Park handed me his daughter, I discovered something else that could transmute everything in its vicinity. Creating an element that was also part fear but equally made of astonishment.

Omaha settled into my arms, stopped crying, closed her eyes, and slept.

WE TOLD EACH other our stories. The last few days of our paths looping and twisting over one another.

He would not give me the travel drive, but he did let me look at its contents.

I followed his directions, and found and opened the secret file. He explained to me the coordinate sequences. I thought about our dying city, seeded with secret Dreamer. I knew, of course, the great value of this information, but I did not see how it could relate to Lady Chizu. Certainly she might deal in Dreamer, but the idea of her buying and selling by the bottle was absurd. She was more likely to provide security and shipping for container loads of the drug being sent to Asia, or to finance a lab reverse engineering the drug.

I asked him what else was on the drive.

He looked at me with little expression.

"What else could matter?"

He tended his wife. I cradled his daughter in one arm and looked further.

There was Hydo Chang's photography, quite accomplished, I thought. Records relating to the buying and selling of Chasm Tide artifacts and gold. Bank account numbers and codes. Pornography. And a second partition.

The drive was divided in half. I opened the second partition, expecting to find it was a simple backup of the first, and found, instead, a wilderness preserve. A fragment of Chasm Tide, isolated on the drive, populated by three characters. ˙

In a glen, bordered by trees beyond which the evening blue sky became blank slate, three adventurers sat around a waning fire. A woman warrior, half her face disfigured by horrible burns, broadsword across her back, armored in opalescent black shells harvested from acid beetles. A young and slight ferrous mage, armed with an iron staff and gauntlets, his skin stained in mottled rust. And an aged nether troll, spindle-limbed, two fingers missing from his right hand, the other eight tipped with yellowed and cracked ivory nails, barefoot, wearing wine-stained white tuxedo trousers and a swallowtail coat over his wrinkled bare chest.

Deeper in the partition were the logs and files, the digital souls of the characters. Also a bill of sale.

I opened my mouth.

"Ah."

Park looked from the bed.

"What?"

I touched the screen.

"I have found what I was looking for."

He turned back to Rose.

"What now?"

Rose had been whispering all the while. Now her tone changed; she spoke with authority and excitement.

"Tab, tab, control-space, triple shift-jay-up arrow, space, space, space, backspace, down arrow, ex."

She buried her face in the mattress and screamed, rolled over sweating and grinning, reached up, grabbed Park, pulled him down, and kissed him.

"I did it! Fucking did it! No one thought it could be done. But I did it. Alone. I conquered the Clockwork Labyrinth."

Park smiled, pushed damp hair from her forehead, and kissed her.

"So I heard. That's great. I wish I could have seen it."

She scooted up in bed.

"It was so cool, Park. I just realized that I had to stop trying to run through that last gap before it closed. If I just waited, it swung back around. I used the Rod of Torquine, jammed it in there, slipped through, and I was in the center."

He put a hand on the side of her face.

"What was there?"

She shook her head.

"Nothing. Absolutely nothing. It was just quiet. It was just so perfectly fucking quiet."

Then she was gone again, repeating her adventure, starting with the first up arrow.

Park looked at the wall beyond which we had killed the three invaders.

"How much longer are we safe here?"

There was no calculation I could conjure to answer that question.

"We are not safe now. Every second we spend here increases our risk. But I cannot say for certain when the risk will outweigh the benefit of having a single position to defend rather than committing to travel."

He thought.

"Will they come back before dark?"

"Would your neighbors question the appearance of black-clad men with assault rifles storming your house in broad daylight?"

"Now? Today? I don't know."

I shrugged.

"Then there is a risk that they will come in daylight."

He took his wife's hand.

"I have to do something."

He looked at his daughter.

"And I have to know she's safe."

With great discomfort I stood and brought the baby to him.

"We are, none of us, ever safe."

He put his free hand on her head and looked up at me.

"I just need to know she's somewhere safe. Just until I come for her. Just until I do what I have to. Do you know a place?"

I felt the weight of the gun holstered on my ankle, the knife strapped against my crotch, the lines burned into my legs. And I thought about somewhere safe for a baby girl.

"Yes, of course. I know a place. Until you come for her."

Omaha grunted. We both wrinkled our noses.

Park squeezed Rose's hand and stood up.

"Come on, I'll show you how to change a diaper."

He did. A simplicity that I watched carefully, certain I could never master it.

And, knowing what course of action he was committed to, and the resolve that he required, I showed him something as well. A crime. A cold-blooded act. Irrefutable guilt. Armor in his cause.

27

WE'RE ALONE AGAIN. Rose. I've done things. Things I believe are right. Things I have to do.

I think you would agree with me. That there wasn't any choice.

You said I couldn't take care of her. And I can't. I can't take care of her. She can't be safe. Not as long as the world is this way.

Jasper says it's just changing. As if that is a small thing. Which I suppose it is.

Everything is always changing. Look at how you changed me. How we changed each other. How Omaha changed us both.

But it's still my world. The world where my father and mother met. Where she called him Peaches. Where I ran away from them to try to find a different way of understanding. Where I met you. This is the world where you wouldn't let me go. Not that I tried to run. This is the world where my mother died and my father killed himself because he couldn't live in it without her. This is the world where you got pregnant. Or is it? Or is that the world that was? Is this already the new world? The world where you got sick. And where Omaha was born. If it is, then it is her world. And she'll need to know how to live in it.

But only if it has time to breathe.

Afronzo Senior said they were "tapping the brakes." Trying to slow things down, give the new world a chance to be born.

My daughter's world. A world that should not have the crimes of the old world polluting its birth.

I have to do something. You understand, Rose. I know you understand. You said it when we met. I will die one day wandering into traffic. But I'm not wandering. I'm walking straight across all five lanes.

I have to do something. Someone has to do something. Otherwise, why?

I love you.

Good night.

28

WHEN I ARRIVED AT LADY CHIZU'S OFFICE, MY HANDS WERE not in my pockets, but they were full.

In one hand I carried the gift I had promised, a flower, a random lily, plucked from a withered bush in Rose's garden, fragrant. In the other I carried Omaha Garden Haas. Sleeping still. As she had been since I took her from the car seat Park had showed me how to install in my Cadillac.

Lady Chizu received the flower with all her long-accumulated graciousness. The child she received into her presence with a slight pursing of thin lips.

"This is unexpected."

I said nothing.

Chizu indicated the breakfast laid out on her low desk, set for two, noodle soup with spicy egg and salt cod.

"Is she old enough for milk?"

I tipped my head at one of the well-mannered, fabulously cheekboned young men who had escorted me in. A countermeasure in light of my hands not being pocketed. One carried the diaper bag I'd had draped over my shoulder when I came off the elevator.

"I have powdered formula. If someone would be so kind."

She nodded.

I looked at the man.

"Three scoops, six ounces filtered water. Room temperature, please."

Both bowed and left.

Chizu took a slight step back. I walked past her toward the table.

She observed my stride.

"Your wounds."

There was a small blue vase standing empty on the table. I slipped the stem of the lily into its mouth.

"Yes."

I placed the now-empty hand into my pocket.

She approached, small gliding steps.

"I am curious."

"Yes?"

She lowered herself to her cushion.

"When I invited you to breakfast, did it occur to you to think how you would eat with your hands in your pockets?"

I smiled.

"No, it did not."

She pointed at the second cushion.

"I would not have made the invitation if I had not intended for you to be comfortable."

I took the hand from my pocket and used it as I lowered myself, edging onto my bottom rather than sitting on my legs in her manner. Omaha burrowed more deeply into my armpit.

Chizu picked up a set of plain bamboo chopsticks.

"Were your legs injured in execution of my concerns?"

I was looking at the wall behind her. The typewriters were gone. In their places, filling only a handful of the cubbyholes, were a variety of objects: a lone thumb drive that seemed to have been crafted into the proximal phalanx of an actual thumb, its beaded thong draped over a framed screen grab image of a warty hag sitting astride a dragon. An iPhone running an animation of a bearded dwarf in plate armor, his long red hair wreathed in white roses. A framed and numbered piece of collage by Shadrach that I may or may not have seen at his show. And a hard drive, carefully disassembled, all the components laid out with schematic precision around a small card of linen stock on which someone had executed a beautiful copperplate script that spelled out a name with no vowels.

I looked from the displays to the lady.

"Yes. There were many unexpected turns of events."

"That is apparent."

One of the cheekboned men returned, placed a filled baby bottle on the table next to me, placed the diaper bag, now properly screened, at my side, bowed, and left.

Chizu's chopsticks were poised over her bowl.

"How is this best accomplished so that we might all eat?"

I considered the technical difficulties involved in eating hot soup one-handed while feeding a baby.

"It would be easiest, I think, if the ladies eat first. And then I may ask for your help."

She nodded, dipped her chopsticks into her bowl.

"It has been years since I held a baby. My little brothers. But I expect that one never forgets."

I didn't know if she was right or wrong in that. Before Park had handed me Omaha, I had never held a baby.

Chizu pinched a knot of noodles between her chopsticks.

"And perhaps you will tell me, while I eat, some of the turns of events you encountered."

"Yes, of course."

She bent her head and politely slurped her noodles. I picked up the bottle, shook it in the manner Park had instructed, tickled Omaha's lower lip with the nipple, and held it for her as she began to eat while still asleep.

What Park had called a dream feeding.

By the time the bottle was empty, and Lady Chizu's bowl as well, I had finished most of my story, and I handed the baby across the table. She woke when she felt new hands on her, and I expected she would cry, but she did not. Chizu played a game, first showing the baby her five-fingered hand and then hiding it and showing her the four-fingered hand. A game that made Omaha giggle.

"And my hard drive?"

I slurped my soup. It was slightly cold but still excellent.

"Lady Chizu, mistress of one thousand storks, I do not have it."

She flashed the four-fingered hand at the baby girl.

"It was destroyed before you could take possession?"

I used the tips of my chopsticks to pluck a sliver of egg white from the broth.

"No. I held it in my hand. And I returned it to the man who stole it."

She lifted Omaha from her lap and held her at eye level to herself.

"But you are here."

I could see the tension in her neck, the effort she was making to disguise it.

"I am."

She lowered her forehead, and Omaha reached out and ruffled her hair with both hands.

"To offer me what explanation?"

I put down my chopsticks and pointed at the diaper bag, and she nodded. From inside the bag I took Rose's MacBook. I woke it from sleep, opened the new partition I had created while at Park's home, placed it on the table, and turned it to face her.

She looked at the glen, the three adventurers huddled from the night's cold around the dying fire.

"Ah."

She said it with slight surprise and possibly a similar amount of delight. Though it could have been mild discomfort caused by Omaha yanking on her hair.

I laid a finger on the top of the screen.

"I do not have the drive, but I do have your property. I transferred the data from the travel drive, including the bill of sale and documents of provenance, and erased the partition where they had been previously stored. They are complete in every way that they were on that drive. And, to the best of my knowledge, as unique as the bill of sale states."

She turned Omaha, facing her toward the screen.

"Teessa Delane. Founder Pale. And the Vitiated Man. Together they plumbed the Chasm to a depth of thirteen leagues. None have gone deeper. Their creators, all sleepless, have since died."

She looked at me.

"The transference of these from one device to another impacts not only their value but their nature. I initially bid on these three in situ, as housed on the platforms from which the creators most usually played them. My broker failed to act quickly enough and could only ensure that the originals had been erased and his copies the only ones made. But he refused to renegotiate the price I had already paid. And further insulted me by insisting on a premium for the additional inconvenience he had suffered making the copies."

I was still.

"He is dead now."

She began her game of hands with the baby again.

"Yes, as you said. But killed in the course of his dealings with the Afronzo boy. Not for his offenses against me."

I held an open hand over the laptop.

"This belonged to Rose Garden Haas, the mother of the baby in your lap. Sleepless herself, and a player. I transferred your property in her home, as she was in the first grips of the suffering."

Omaha held tight to the thumb of the four-fingered hand as Chizu pulled lightly against her.

I continued.

"Does this addition to the provenance of your properties impact their nature and value in a manner that pleases you?"

She offered Omaha her five-fingered hand as well. The baby took each by a thumb and swung them together in a silent clap.

"It is a worthy addition, yes. I am pleased. Not that the woman should suffer, but it adds to the beauty of the item. Yes."

Omaha swung the giant hands.

I turned the laptop toward myself, clicked back to the original partition, opened another application, and showed Chizu.

"And this is Cipher Blue. Elemental mage. She walked the length of the Clockwork Labyrinth alone and found its silent center. Created by Rose Haas, as surely as she created the child."

Lady Chizu's empire was built on engines of destruction and the men and women who wielded them. She had armed militias and insurgencies, rebels and strongmen. She had fielded mercenary armies of her own, seized governments, and held them ransom. Her guns had killed thousands.

She leaned forward, her hands encircling the baby's torso, forgetting her discipline, letting the sickness inside twist her neck, and gazed at the young woman on the screen, sleeping in a perfectly silent catacomb.

"What do you want, Jasper?"

I pushed the laptop a few inches toward her.

"There is something I have to do."

I stood.

"I need help."

I bent and touched the top of Omaha's head.

"And I need for her to be someplace safe. Until I come back for her."

Chizu looked at my hand, so close to her person, and laid her four fingers over it.

"Yes."

Omaha reached up and slapped at our hands, laughing, somehow comfortable under the touch of killers.

Park needed to protect his daughter in a world changing. He could only try to save the one he knew. Or slow its demise. I knew he would pursue justice, but within the limits of the law, however irrelevant it might have become.

It would never occur to him to simply kill both Afronzos.

I was of another mind.

Afrono's security force had taken some recent losses. Eleven in all. Even allowing for extravagance, it was hard to imagine that Afronzo Senior employed more than fifteen to twenty former Israeli special forces. He might have many more sport-coated security guards, but they would be more suited to dealing with mail checks and property patrols than with covert terminations. Shooters, perhaps, but not killers. And any force that has recently had its numbers significantly whittled by a supposedly inferior opponent will suffer from a measurable loss of morale. Nonetheless, I'd need more than a great deal of luck.

My legs hurt. I'd have liked to have driven the STS up to the front door, but the Afronzos knew who I was. Even arriving in a hundred-thousand-dollar car I would not have been led into the patriarch's presence. Neither the team they had sent to my house nor the one sent to Park's had reported back. Whether or not additional men had been sent to investigate, they knew something was, at the very least, amiss. I'd crossed town twice on my adaptive ID. Once going south to Culver City and again heading north to Century City. Enough hours had passed for those journeys to have been logged any number of places. They must now know I lived.

Some camouflage was lent on my current journey by its being accomplished under the auspices of a Thousand Storks pass. It earned a sneer from the Guards, but to anyone looking for me via my NID, it would appear that I'd not left Century City since I arrived there in the morning. Still, a frontal approach would have required a vehicle more tanklike even than the Cadillac.

The Bel Air residents had been among the first to entrench their neighborhood, having fought a short but intense battle with the L.A. City Council over their right to do so. All streets entering off North Sepulveda and North Beverly Glen had been sealed by the Thousand Storks contractors that provided security for the entire community. Even along Sunset the access streets were closed; only the Bellagio entrance was still open. The decorative white stucco and black iron gates had been bolstered with more practical concrete barriers. A short maze of them meant to discourage any car bombers who might negotiate the thicket of spherical bollards that dotted the approach from the intersection. Patrolled by both Thousand Storks and dozens of private family security forces, there was at least one charity tennis tournament taking place there when I passed through the gate unhindered, as well as a wedding reception at the Hotel Bel Air, and a dog show at the country club.

I crossed a small property that I'd chosen because the Thousand Storks detail sheet reported it as being unoccupied, protected by only an alarm system and the TS patrols. From inside the tree line at the rear of the property I spent thirty minutes watching the Afronzo grounds beyond. I saw a single foot patrol. A man wearing a blue windbreaker rather than the expected blazer. He carried a flashlight that he played over the ground in front of him. I'd worried there might be dogs and was grateful there were not. Dogs are difficult. Small, fast targets; it can take up to three shots to hit one with small arms when they charge head on.

As soon as the man passed, I walked out of the trees, not at all steady on my legs, crossed the grass that looked no worse for the drought most people suffered the world over, went up to the lighted window of the guest cottage, peered through to see a man within a few years of my own age seated in an imitation Colonial chair, a bottle of overpriced cognac at hand, a book facedown in his lap, staring into the brown liquor in his snifter. I fired three shots. He was profile to me, so I concentrated fire on his head rather than his chest. Three bullets generally guarantee nothing flukish can happen. Odd deflections caused by a pane of glass, ricochets off the curve of the skull, bullets passing through areas of the brain that are used only for monitoring activity in the appendix, are all made allowable by the presence of the second and third bullets. Such things do not happen in threes. The gun was a silenced HK Mark 23 .45 from my travel kit. Three bullets in the head from that size weapon meant death. Satisfied, I headed for the main house.

It took only slight reflection to surmise where I might find Afronzo the younger. A conical tower was affixed to the back of the house, an architectural feature that suited his tastes as I had inferred them.

There was an exceptional mechanic's garage to service the fleet of luxury vehicles parked in the roundabout at the rear below the tower. One of the roll-up doors was raised three feet. Park's Subaru was inside, doors open, contents strewn, the hollow spare on the ground, empty. I wormed under and found the inner door that led to a laundry, thence to a kitchen, to a supplementary dining room, and a hall that ended at a curl of stairs.

Imelda and Magda were at the top. Sitting on a refinished church pew cushioned in gold velvet, outside a single door. Magda held a BlackBerry where they could both see the screen.

Imelda had a hand over her mouth.

"Oh, my God. You didn't tell me he was that nasty."

Magda clicked a button.

"Oh, yeah. Read this one."

"Oh. My. God. Is he?"

Magda was nodding.

"He totally backs it up. And he likes to send pics, too."

"Show me, show me."

Both had split the Velcro seams on their corset-style body armor, wearing it peeled open so they could bend to sit.

I shot Imelda in the heart. Magda flinched at the blood, causing her to move the BlackBerry, giving me an unobstructed shot at her heart. I took it. I closed distance and shot them each once more, head shots.

The door was unlocked.

The room on the other side covered 270 degrees of the tower's circumference, windows running the outer wall. Cager apparently had used the same designer as he had at Denizone. A postapocalypse medieval revival.

He was sitting in an imitation Eames lounge chair that had been made with oxidized copper rather than plywood. His right hand was fitted into the ergonomic contours of a glossy black gaming hub. His other hand held his phone, thumb flicking over the keys as he occasionally stole glances away from the wall-mounted LCD display to read the messages constantly announcing themselves with the opening note of the theme from *2001: A Space Odyssey.* On the LCD, an elegant figure in an absurdly long windblown black cape scampered and leaped on a plane of subtle geometrics, responding to the slight movements of his fingers and palm on the hub. It took me a moment to realize that his character was dancing, re-creating Cyd Charisse's dream ballet with the wind in *Singing in the Rain.*

On the floor next to his chair was a pile of several objects. The travel drive. A journal. The backup thumb drive Park had worn around his neck. The disk I'd given him with the recording of the mass murder at the gold farm. And his father's watch.

I closed the door firmly.

He didn't look up.

"What is it?"

I moved into his peripheral vision.

"I need to know what happened to Officer Parker Haas."

He looked up.

"You're that guy."

He removed his hand from the game hub and took out his comb and raked his hair.

"You look very angry. I think."

He put the comb away.

"That's odd."

I was not cruel. I had questions and I asked them. When he was slow to answer, unused to doing promptly what was required of him, I demonstrated the advantages of brevity. But I was not cruel. Not as I received the information I needed. Nor when I killed him. Three bullets. Like father, like son.

Confusion had begun to reign when I left several minutes after I had arrived. Something had been seen on a security screen somewhere deep within the house. Several blue windbreakers were gathered at the guest cottage. Their energy was focused on the grounds.

Still, as I came out of the garage, I was seen by one of the windbreakers. He called to me. I kept walking, cutting across the parking area through the cars that were already taking on the patina of relics from another age. Behind me I heard two sets of rapid footsteps. I measured the distance to the trees. Still moving, I glanced through the windows of the cars to see if they had been left with keys in the ignition. They had not. The HK was seated in its shoulder holster under the black sport coat I'd worn. I had two rounds still left in the gun and a twelve-round backup clip. But that was all I carried. My legs would not allow me to run. When my pursuers reached me, I would turn and use one bullet on each, swap to a full clip, and perhaps have time to strip them of their weapons. After that I would need to take cover before a full assault began. I was looking for the heaviest vehicle in the lot when two Thousand Storks fast attack vehicles pulled into the drive. I changed course and walked toward them. The four Storks in each vehicle jumped out and split into twos, ignoring me entirely as they ran past. And my pursuers, taking their cue from the specialists who clearly knew who I was and why I was there, pulled up and turned back, allowing me to walk unmolested down the length of Madrono, circling back to where I'd parked the STS. The car, myself, and all activity in my locale helpfully ignored by Thousand Storks for the one hour between 11 p.m. and midnight. As I'd requested, and as Lady Chizu had ordered, in exchange for the wonder that was Cipher Blue.

Park's journal and the other items in my possession, I now drove south to find the end of the story.

I did not linger in the nursery when I returned to the Culver City house. What I found there was not meant for me, or for anyone else. It was shameful to gawk at such a thing, since there were only two people who could understand its meaning. Perhaps a third person, some day. I left the room and searched for what I'd come for.

Park had left the safe open. From inside I took the certificates of marriage and birth, Omaha's medical records, the detective's badge Park had been given for his Dreamer assignment, and the broach that had been his mother's. In a nightstand cabinet I found a stack of black journals with red spines, Rose's diaries from high school to just a few days before. I took a case from a pillow on the bed and filled it with the black and red books. There was a photo album. A shoe box of letters. Park's academy diploma. A framed square of white cardboard with a smeared green imprint of a baby's foot. These all seemed relevant, and I took them.

The last item I took was the gun Park had used to kill. Everything else I had taken was alien to me. The gun was comforting in its familiarity.

There was nothing else of Park that I understood half as well as I did the lethal mechanics of such a weapon. I could follow the rationale in his choices and actions, but it was very much like a novice speaker of a foreign language translating everything he heard into his native tongue. The sense was there, but it was arrived at only after great labor, and with little nuance.

Fluency would take time. But I'd made a start, and learned this much.

2 9

PARK DID NOT WATCH JASPER LEAVE WITH OMAHA. HE COULDN'T. If he had stood at the door and watched them drive away up the street he would have broken in two. Instead he kissed her forehead and tapped the tip of her nose with his pinkie while standing at Rose's bedside, to remind himself that he could take care of only one of them.

It did not hollow him out to watch her sleeping in Jasper's arms, carried from the bedroom. He felt full, pressure at every seam, in danger of exploding.

He attended to business first.

He came back to Rose. Still reciting, she shivered from time to time or clenched her teeth as if a sudden pain gripped her.

From the bedside table he picked up the plastic-wrapped bottle. Rose's eyes were scanning back and forth across the far wall, as if monitoring the dangers of the game. He ripped open the plastic bag, and the bottle of pills dropped to the floor with a rattle. He picked it up, studied the instructions for opening the patented childproof cap, pressed down while pinching, twisted one way and then the other, and the cap popped off. He broke the foil seal, picked out the wadded cotton, and shook a light blue tablet into his palm.

"Rose."

She didn't answer.

"Rose."

She didn't answer.

"Rose. I love you more than life."

He put the tablet at her lips, pushed it past her teeth, placed a water glass against her mouth, and tilted it up. She coughed and then swallowed.

She wiped water from her chin and looked around.

"Park?"

He shook another pill into his palm.

"Yes."

Her eyes cleared.

"What the fuck, Park? Now I'm gonna have to start all over."

He shook his head.

"No, you don't, hon. You don't have to start over. You finished it. I wish I'd been here to see."

She smiled.

"It was so cool. So quiet. It was."

He put another tablet at her lips.

"Here, take this."

She took it between her fingers and looked at it.

"What is it?"

"It'll make you feel better."

She blew out her lips.

"Anything that can make me feel better. I mean, I feel like shit. What is this, cancer-flu or something? I've never been this sick. I mean, I never get sick at all."

She put the tablet in her mouth, and he gave her the water glass, and she swallowed.

"Hey. Have I been asleep for a long time?"

Park nodded.

"Yeah."

She rubbed her eyes.

"Because everything seems really weird. Like when you're a kid and you dream you missed Christmas and you wake up and it's August fifteenth, but you still feel like you missed it. I feel like that. And sick. Rub my neck, baby."

She rolled onto her side, and Park rubbed her neck.

The muscles in her back had stopped twitching.

She opened her mouth wide and yawned.

"Okay, whatever those are, they're great. Please tell me they're not illegal."

"Not illegal."

"Can I have another?"

"Sure."

He gave her another.

She smiled at him.

"I know it's not your thing, babe, but you should take one of those."

He shook his head.

She nodded.

"I know. Never lose control, Parker Haas, you never know who might be watching."

She touched his face.

"I love you. I love you more than life."

She closed her eyes.

He didn't say anything.

She sighed and opened her eyes and saw him.

"How am I going to be able to look after you?"

He shook his head and told her he didn't know, and she kind of sighed like she always did when she thought he wasn't getting something.

"No, I mean, really, how am I gonna look the fuck after you?"

He told her that she didn't have to look after him, that he was okay.

She was staring at the ceiling.

"You're such a, God, I hate the word, but you're such an innocent. I mean, how am I supposed to walk away from that?"

He didn't say anything.

She shook her head, wondering at something.

"I've known you how long? Already I can see it. You're destined to walk into traffic while reading a book. Or to get stabbed by a drunk asshole in a bar when you try to defend some tramp's honor. Or do something even stupider like join the Marines and go get killed for oil because you think it's the right thing to do."

He knew the rest, every word, by heart, but he let her say it all.

"And how am I supposed to keep you from doing something like that if you're up there and I'm down here? I mean, where did you come from? How did you drop into my life? You're, God, you're everything I don't want. Hold me."

He held her.

She yawned.

"I can only look after you all the time if we're together."

He held her.

She twisted partway around to see his face.

"Really together."

He nodded.

"So let's get married."

She blinked slowly, smiled, nodded.

"Yeah, let's get fucking married."

Her eyes closed. She slept. Just as she had years before when they'd first had the conversation the morning after the first night they spent together.

Park stood, scooped her in his arms, walked down the hall, didn't look at the blood-soaked towels on the floor, and carried her into the nursery.

Settling her into Omaha's crib, curled and slight; she opened her eyes once more.

"Park?"

"Yes."

"Where's Omaha?"

"She's with Jasper."

Rose nodded, closed her eyes again, nuzzled her chin against his palm.

"Oh. That's good. She'll be safe with him."

He spent five minutes slipping pills one by one into her mouth, offering her water, and making sure she did not choke in her sleep. Then he sat on the floor next to the crib and put his hand through the bars to hold hers.

Her eyes moved back and forth under her lids; she sighed once, breathing deeply all the while, until her breathing shallowed. Slowed. And stopped.

Leaving the room, he looked at the gun on the floor, next to puddled blood seeping. He was feeling what his father had demonstrated with his shotgun. But he was not tempted to pick up the pistol. He had something he had to do.

At the back of the closet he found his uniform wrapped in a dry cleaner's plastic. It had been over a year since he had worn it. In that time he'd become less disciplined in his workouts. The extra fifteen pounds he'd built up for the street through daily weight training and nonstop calorie cramming had fallen off. He had to snug his belt an extra notch, and his shirt hung loose at the shoulders and neck. He couldn't find his pepper spray. His baton was buried under a pile of shoes. His hat, on a top closet shelf, carried a thick layer of dust. He had only one pair of navy socks to wear, holes worn in both heels. The Walther did not fit the holster as well as his old nine-millimeter had, but it would serve the same task if needed.

Uniformed, Park drove north.

He was still stopped at checkpoints but was never asked to exit his vehicle. He'd thought about digging his red magnetic roof strobe from the garage and trying to use the emergency center lane on the 405, but feared getting pinned in traffic amid uncleared wreckage. As it turned out, the surface streets were nearly as barren as the night before.

He saw few people on the sidewalks, and those rarely farther than several steps from their own yards or the doors to the occasional businesses that were open. A knot of them congregated around a storefront that had been pushed in and looted. He saw a man with an unmounted hunting scope scanning the eastern horizon, apparently trying to find the source of a smoke plume rising from the cluster of downtown towers. A hot wind was breaking up that plume and the others that were newly sprouted in Hollywood and south of the Santa Monica, a Santa Ana smearing the smoke over the basin all the way to the sea.

At the Pico check he overheard two Guards talking about a siege at the Scientology compound on Sunset. Three Super Hornets streaked overhead in tight formation, and they paused to watch them scream eastward.

One of them pointed.

"Navy."

The other nodded.

"Looks like the *Reagan* just hit town."

The first slapped his sidearm.

"About fucking time we got some righteous air support. See what the NAJis think of car bombs with a fucking carrier group offshore."

The second shook his head.

"Fuck the NAJi. Those L. Ron Hubbard motherfuckers got more money than Jesus. Half the assholes in Hollywood are members. Don't even want to know what they've been spending it on. Hear they got an armory in there, all the stuff Saddam was supposed to have, they really got. Say fuck the NAJis, drop some ordnance on that crowd before they have a chance to go Dianetics on all our asses."

The Guard scanning Park's badge waved him through.

There was a protest on Olympic, hundreds of sleepless shuffling down the street, silent except for occasional moans or a scream. A single banner poking from the middle of the crowd: DREAM.

At the Bellagio gate he was politely asked if he had an appointment. The Thousand Storks man asking the question wore nearly seventy thousand dollars' worth of body armor, communications and computing equipment, and weaponry. Park told him his business was official. The Storks man looked at Park's ill-fitting uniform and beaten-up Subaru. He looked at the badge he'd already scanned. It was valid. He nodded and told Park he'd have to be escorted to his destination.

The Afronzo estate was tucked at the end of the curl of Madrono Lane. Surrounded by the grounds of thirteen other homes, it lacked any views to speak of but was almost perfectly sequestered. Anyone caring to approach could either take the road or risk crossing the property of one of the neighbors before trying the security on the Afronzo grounds itself.

Driving in on the road, followed by two Storks in an open fast attack vehicle, Park pulled into the cutout before the road circled to the back of the house. There, with the Storks waiting, he sat in the car and wrote in his journal. Finished, he left it on the passenger seat and got out of the car.

Going up the steps, he straightened his clip-on tie. Unlike some of his fellow cadets, he'd been smart enough when he bought his first uniform not to ask why a clip-on. Those who asked were never answered, receiving a grunt of disgust at most. Rose had giggled at the tie, clipped it to her T-shirt collar. He'd laughed with her. Never explaining that it was worn because a normal tie might be grabbed by a perp during a scuffle and used to choke the wearer.

The door was opened as he stepped in front of it, held aside for him by Parsifal K. Afronzo Junior.

"Park."

He waved to the Thousand Storks men, and they cut a tight U-turn and buzzed back down the road.

"Thousand Storks. I always get the feeling they're in a constant state of sexual arousal under those uniforms. They're nearly as fetishistic as Imelda and Magda."

He looked at Park.

"Your uniform doesn't fit."

Park placed a hand on his holstered weapon.

"Parsifal K. Afronzo Junior, you are under arrest."

Cager turned and walked into the dark interior of the house.

"Come inside, Park."

Park took a step inside, hand still on his weapon.

"You are under arrest for the murders of Hydo Chang and his associates."

Cager stopped walking and looked back at him.

"For what?"

Park pointed.

"Place your hands against the wall and spread your legs."

Cager stayed where he was.

"For the murder of Hydo Chang. That's. Not what I expected. My dad made it sound like you suspected much more. Much worse."

He began to comb his hair.

"It was kind of flattering. Being thought a mastermind."

Park walked to him, took him by the left wrist, swept it behind his back and pushed it up toward his neck while putting a knee in the back of his right leg. Cager went to the floor and Park finished the takedown, pushing his face flat against the marble while unclipping the cuffs from his belt.

Cager grunted.

"What are you doing, Park?"

Park snapped the first bracelet over his wrist.

"I'm arresting you."

"Why?"

Park snapped on the second bracelet.

"Get up."

Cager let himself be pulled to his feet.

"You don't understand even a little about me. You don't understand what I was trying to do. What Hydo did to ruin it."

Park stopped walking him toward the door.

"What? What did he do? What does a person do to get murdered? What does that take in this world?"

Cager wrenched free.

"It takes being greedy and stupid!"

He looked at the floor.

"I'd like to comb my hair."

Park didn't move.

Cager turned around.

"Will you comb my hair for me, please. It's out of place. I can feel it.

Park took the comb from Cager's back pocket and combed his hair back into place.

Cager relaxed slightly.

"Thank you. Can you put the comb back, please."

Park put the comb back.

Cager nodded.

"Thank you. I'm sorry I lost my temper. But thinking about Hydo upsets me. And I'm not used to being upset. That's probably why I reacted the way I did. But I gave him so much. I gave him the Dreamer. I'd tried so hard to make something physical with it. I thought it would be a way to push people into a quest mentality. Increase the investment in their lives. Get them thinking and feeling with the same level of commitment as they do in Chasm. But they didn't want to be that aware. They said, *Give me the Dreamer. Here's my money, give me the Dreamer.* Like you. I was trying to open eyes to the possibility that there was room left, time left for magic in this world, and they just want to score. If that's all people want, they can score off Hydo. I didn't even take anything up front. It was credits in my account at the farm. And he couldn't even get me the codex I needed. But I told him, one rule only. I told him, 'no selling to my gamers.' No selling to my sleepless. My sleepless, they are living at the absolute verge of human evolution, pushing barriers back. Not just living but creating. They're planting seeds. Because after we're all sleepless, Park, after we all die, something will persist. Information, energy coded as information, that will last when we are dust. When the last generator runs out of fuel, when the last windmill rusts and falls over, when the last solar panel cracks, the Web will stop, but the information will persist. After 9/11, they recovered hard drives in the ruins. They could still be read. Flesh turned to paste and mist, but data survived. When our society is excavated, our data will be our relics. And the characters, the personas the sleepless are creating, those will be the most unique, the most durable, the most diverse, the most cherished artifacts. They're what we're going to leave behind. And Hydo, he was killing that. Selling Dreamer to my sleepless, he was killing the future. Our future. So arrest me for murdering Hydo and the others. I did it."

Park was thinking again about the gun he'd used earlier to kill the man who'd come out of his daughter's room. The room where he'd left his wife. He thought of how it had looked, lying on the floor next to blood. He was glad it wasn't in his hand.

He took Cager by the arm and pulled him toward the door.

"You're under arrest."

"Officer Haas."

He stopped and looked back down the foyer.

Senior stood there, still in his pajamas and robe, Imelda and Magda just behind him.

"I'm sorry to see you again, Officer Haas."

Park nodded.

"I'm arresting your son for murder."

Imelda and Magda moved away from each other, creating firing lines.

Park put his hand back on his weapon.

"I'm arresting your son."

Senior's hands were buried in his pockets.

"It's not that I don't understand, Haas. I just can't allow it. You take those handcuffs off now, and you go home."

Park saw that Imelda and Magda had their weapons in hand already. Not the submachine guns that would spray indiscriminately, but high-accuracy SIG 1911s.

He shook his head.

"Your men already came to my home, sir. They're dead."

Cager shook his head.

"Dad."

"Be quiet, Junior."

"Dad, I can't believe you did that."

Senior took his hands from his pockets and plucked at a loose thread.

"That was something I had to do. I don't take any pride or enjoyment from it. And it's my own fault for talking at such length with you, Haas. But everything is at stake now. The whole world. Blood relations aside, arresting my son would cause too many questions to be asked. There'd be chaos. Too soon for that. Too much left to do."

Park opened his mouth, but he had no more to say. Instead he turned and pushed Cager toward the door. He'd never drawn his weapon. He never did.

Walking, he thought about what it had been like when he first felt himself made vulnerable by his love for Rose. The fear. How that had been compounded to terror when Omaha was born. How willingly he had embraced the horror that he might lose them one day, in exchange for their miraculous presence in his life.

He said something then, but it was lost in a sudden noise.

3 0

LADY CHIZU'S TOWER WAS SURELY SAFE FOR A DAY, BUT IT would not do over time. Nor, for that matter, was Chizu herself safe. She was sleepless, dying. And when she died, so too would Thousand Storks. And the maggots that would crawl out of that instrument of destruction would ravage anything she had touched. I saw her last when I returned from the Culver City house for Omaha. She was not disappointed to see me, but there was some regret, I think, when I took the baby girl from her arms and placed Park's father's watch in Omaha's hands. She stared at the light reflecting off it, and began to chew on the leather band.

Chizu thought for a moment.

"Her father was killed?"

I nodded.

She thought for another moment.

"And her mother committed suicide?"

Standing in the Culver City house, I had looked at Rose's body in Omaha's crib and thought of all the beautiful things that I had left behind in my house to be destroyed by either fire or water. My apocalypse collection, not one work among it casting a greater foreshadow than the dead body of a sleepless mother in her daughter's crib.

I shook my head, still awed by what I had seen.

"Her father killed her mother."

"Ah."

I watched her eyes, an act more brazen than I would have dared just a day before.

"Does that deepen the beauty of Cipher Blue?"

She looked at Rose's laptop, resting now in the center niche of the display wall.

"It intensifies what I feel when I look at it."

She touched Omaha's cheek.

"She is a quiet baby."

I watched her chewing the buckle of her grandfather's watchband.

"Her parents are dead. She's sad."

"No. Babies cry when they are sad, Jasper. She is watchful. Listening."

Both of us, childless, watched the silent baby.

We left Chizu in her tower, with her digital ghosts, the remains of the dead sleepless who made them.

In the lobby outside her office, I found that her ever-efficient greeters had packed certain mementos into a small box as I'd requested. They would see it delivered safely, just as soon as I told them to whom it should be addressed. I paused for a moment to consider, the greeter waiting, pen poised over the Thousand Storks label that adhered to the box.

Inside were the travel drive with Dreamer coordinates, the backup copy of Park's reports, scans of the last few days' entries from his journal, his phone with call log and the various relevant pictures he'd taken over the last few days, a voice recording I'd made on my own phone, our long conversation dubbed to a micro SD card, and a bloodstained left shoe with tread that matched the footprints from the gold farm, taken from the floor of Cager's closet. Although, considering the box contained as well the security disk showing Cager committing the murders, some of those items seemed redundant.

I could not guess what the addressee would do with the box. A person of a particular kind of intelligence and survival instinct would destroy it in the moment he became aware of its significance. The murders of the Afronzos would be sending massive shock waves through the world very soon. Revelations that suggested why they had been murdered would quite possibly tip the scale a final feather's weight into chaos's favor. That was the desirable course from my perspective. Nothing screens a retreat quite so efficiently as confusion and disarray. Which may explain why I sent the box to Hounds rather than Bartolome.

As described to me by Park, his captain sounded every inch a self-preservationist. I doubt he was aware of the true nature of the assignment he had placed on Park, but neither do I doubt that he was more than willing to do what was most expedient when pressure was applied. Obviously a man who valued social structure. And the following of orders. Hounds had rather the aura of an anarchist. I found it easy to imagine him as a boy, breaking things for no other reason than the pleasure of seeing them in pieces. I also recalled Bartolome's observation that Hounds had no love for "Washington suits."

And there was the gesture of the watch.

A grace note that spoke well of his humanity. Whatever meaning one may wish to ascribe to such a quality.

In all, I thought he might be damaged enough in his own person to be dangerous should he find out some of what was at the root of the world's ills. The very type to survey the gasoline poured about a powder keg in the basement and light the final match, so as to bring down the crooked house above before any more unfortunates could be injured within. The consequences to be dealt with later.

I also included the remains of the bottle of Dreamer. Whatever latent prints might be intact on its exterior, it was the contents that I thought would most interest him. As regarded his stepmother. A gift that seemed in keeping with Park's spirit. Something foremost on my mind at the time.

The box disposed of, Omaha and I rode the elevator to the roof. In addition to the air defense batteries, there was the helipad from which I had been carried to LAX just two days before. Chizu's gift to Omaha: transportation away from the city. I'd contrived several years before to have a final point of retreat. A house in the lower foothill of the Sierras several hours northeast. A few miles' walking distance of a small town, it sat on a property of several acres that included a length of freshwater stream. As the years had progressed, I'd thought to never use the house. It was out of balance with the times and my age. And then, suddenly, it made sense again. Was purposeful. As if I had known all along I would have something that needed protecting.

I reflected on this as we emerged to the rooftops, the Santa Ana whistling through the thatch of missiles. I looked up and saw a helicopter on approach, and carried the baby to the edge of the pad. My travel kit had been brought up already. In the duffel were Rose and Park's journals. His gun, her pictures and letters.

The helicopter dropped lower. It would carry us from the sleepless city. Was it too much to ask that it would be piloted by a mercenary legionnaire with a humanitarian past and a scar that pulled down the corner of his left eye, giving him a perpetually winking air?

Even in a sleepless world, a man could hope.

Even I, the Vitiated Man.

EPILOGUE

THIS STORY WAS DIFFICULT TO ASSEMBLE. I'VE WORKED FROM your mother and father's journals. His reports. The great and wandering conversation I had with your mother as she told me that night about "Rose and Park Falling in Love." Your father's memory allowed him to tell me in detail what he had experienced in the last days of his life. In some things I have been forced to use supposition concerning their states of mind. Your own readings of Rose and Park's journals will tell you whether I have overstepped my bounds. I think I have been accurate more often than not. Though in all my study I have never achieved fluency in their language, and the translation has no doubt suffered.

I have aspired to honesty, but, as Park's father said, we cannot always be certain what lies we tell ourselves. Park did not lie to himself when he put you in my care. Your mother was dying. He knew he could not protect you in the world that was emerging. Knew that he could not teach you how to live in that world. He could only try to save the old world. Bring crimes to light. Be who he would want you to want him to be. A man of justice. Doing what he believed was right, knowing what it would cost.

He tried to leave order in his wake. But there is no order.

How else to explain that I, more than twice his age, should be better adapted to the future than he? Why else should I, an unrepentant killer, share an immunity with you when your mother did not?

Or, perhaps, that is true order. Bringing what is needed into proximity with need. How else to explain the drift of my life into theirs? An aging creature whose nature was honed for an era of chaos to serve as protector to a child.

When I took you in hand, I wanted to leave only conflagration behind us. The higher the flames burned, the more cover they would give to our flight. As deeply as I needed to know what had happened to Park, going to the Afronzo estate and killing the father and his son were acts of purest reason and logic.

So I said to myself then.

However, it was not all logic.

As coolly as I proceeded, I can confess now that I acted in anger. Cager was correct in that perception. But it was far more shocking, what I felt when I pulled the trigger: justified. A disorienting sensation, when all I'd ever felt before at killing was the deep satisfaction and wellness of doing that of which I was most capable, most excellent.

A tremor of feeling that I have yet to resolve.

For though I can describe with anatomic detail the actions I took, what I saw and heard, the sequence of events, I know now that it is all warped.

My life was an accumulation of moments and objects. Actions and absences. A creation of my own. The dense kernel of obsession that had kept me alive in war was set in peace to the task of assembling a mosaic that could be completed only by my death. Putting the tiles in place had taken far longer than I had expected. I kept having to step back for perspective, to see if I was done or if one fragment more might make it complete. And finally, in a plague of sleeplessness, in a city at the edge of ocean and land, I'd been certain that death was at hand. Culmination imminent.

It is shocking to be so infinitely wrong. To discover that the point of your existence is not your death, but someone else's life. At the foot of your crib, your mother's body resting inside, I'd taken one more step back and seen that the wall on which I'd been creating my masterpiece did not stand alone; there was another that braced it, its pattern yet to be started.

Everything that I can remember of myself in this story about your mother and father is blurred by the gravity of that moment. Time bent around the mass of you when I realized that I would not leave you with Chizu, that I could not complete my work until I had ensured that you would be able to start your own. And I cannot say any longer if the person I have described here is me as I truly was, the killer of men and women and children, or a warped reflection of that man, his true brutality obscured by a lens of distortion.

A native speaker of your parents' language, and a deft student of my own, you will have to decide if I have bared all or, as warned against by your grandfather, exposed myself through lies.

For Omaha, the story you ask most often to hear,
written in my own hand,
Jasper
Grass Valley, November 13, 2022

ACKNOWLEDGMENTS

Some debts to source material are more profound than others.

To say that I would have been unable to write this book if I had not first read D. T. Max's *The Family That Couldn't Sleep* is considerably more than an understatement. A book of exhaustive research that plumbs the histories of both fatal familial insomnia and the prion itself, Max's book is everything that mine is not. Which is to say that it is a book of fact and science. Footnoted and well-referenced, it is a book that one can learn from. And the many mistakes, misunderstandings, and oversights regarding FFI and prions that can be found in *Sleepless* should be understood as a product of my own ignorance, laziness, and/or liberties taken with reality in the desire to tell an entertaining story.

This is also a book that I would not have written without virtually unlimited access to the Internet. My morning cruises through the Web; clipping, pasting, and archiving, provided a great deal of the primary and incidental details that helped flesh out the world of *Sleepless*. Some of the sites to which I am most indebted for making me aware, or setting me on the trail, of any number of oddities, technological trends, obscure current events, artworks, and ephemera are Dinosaurs and Robots, warrenellis.com, boingboing.net, beyond the beyond, NewScientist, nytimes.com, and many others.

Source material and references for many of the ideas, settings, and bits of technology found in this book can be found on my own website, www.pulpnoir.com, in the Sleepless category.

ABOUT THE AUTHOR

CHARLIE HUSTON is the author of the Henry Thompson trilogy, the Joe Pitt casebooks, and the bestsellers *The Shotgun Rule* and *The Mystic Arts of Erasing All Signs of Death*. He lives with his family in Los Angeles.

ABOUT THE TYPE

This book was set in Minion, a 1990 Adobe Originals typeface by Robert Slimbach. Minion is inspired by classical, old style typefaces of the late Renaissance, a period of elegant, beautiful, and highly readable type designs. Created primarily for text setting, Minion combines the aesthetic and functional qualities that make text type highly readable with the versatility of digital technology.